COAL CAMP JUSTICE

COAL CAMP JUSTICE

Two Wrongs Make a Right

Ricardo L García

UNIVERSITY OF NEW MEXICO PRESS | ALBUQUERQUE

10   09   08   07   06   05   1   2   3   4   5   6   7

Library of Congress Cataloging-in-Publication Data

Garcia, Ricardo L.
  Coal camp justice : two wrongs make a right / Ricardo L García.
    p. cm.
  ISBN 0-8263-3697-3 (alk. paper)
  1. African American coal miners—Fiction.   2. Coal mines and mining—
Fiction.   3. Distilling, Illicit—Fiction.   4. Missing persons—Fiction.
5. Mining camps—Fiction.   6. Depressions—Fiction.   7. Alcoholics—
Fiction.   8. New Mexico—Fiction.   I. Title.
  PS3607.A725C633 2005
  813'.6—dc22

                                        2005005925

Coal Camp Justice: Two Wrongs Make a Right is a work of fiction
and a prequel to *Coal Camp Days: A Boy's Remembrance* published by
the University of New Mexico Press, 2001. Its fictional coal camp,
Chicorico, and some of its characters appeared in *Coal Camp Days.*

For my sisters Becky and Carmen

PART I   SETTLING DOWN

ONE   GENTLE VOICES CALL

DURING THE GREAT DEPRESSION, the good men and women of the
Chicorico Company coal camp were grateful to have jobs to put food
on their tables and roofs over their heads. And they were willing to
wait for the promise of America—liberty and justice for all—but,
when the limits of Capitalism manifested in the excesses of men,
supplanting rule of law with the rule of chicanery, they hearkened to
what common sense and decency told them they must do. They
united in the name of simple dignity.

Swannie cursed the crows that clipped his nose. They swooshed
and squawked, gaw, gaw, gaw, gaw, swooping in greater numbers,
swirling and swarming. He spattered them with moonshine. They
scattered and returned, yapping and jabbering, gaw, gaw, gaw, gaw. He
shoved away from the barstool and wobbled out the Brass Rail Bar.
Relentlessly, the crows pursued, swooping and jabbering, swirling
and spinning around his head.

He staggered south on First Street and entered the Corner Bar,
fuggy with smoke and dank with whiskey. The Saturday night
frolickers mocked Prohibition, the grand and noble experiment.
Revenuers had reneged on the battle to keep Raton's First Street
dry. Railroaders, miners, merchants, clerks, secretaries, and other
good town folks swarmed to the saloons they called speakeasies to
chit, chat, and chatter over the clatter of the player piano.

3

For a spell, he didn't see or hear the crows. Pressure on his bladder impelled him to totter to the Stag room and sit on the toilet. The crows returned circling his head and pecking his nose, cheeks, and ears. Frantically, he flailed both arms, and they squawked, gaw, gaw, gaw, gaw. He squirmed on the toilet stool and relieved his bladder while grasping for the jabbering birds aligned on his shoulders. They slipped through his lumbering fingers. He stood from the stool, fastened his trousers, and wobbled out of the bathroom into the crowd. The crows pursued.

Nobody heard or saw the swooshing, squawking crows. They saw Raymond "Swannie" Swanson the drunk, arms flailing, slicing and cutting the air. He stumbled out of the Corner Bar, turned onto Rio Grande Avenue, twisted his ankle in a sidewalk crack, and crumpled into the gutter. He pushed to his knees and wretched . . . jerked . . . slumped, crumbling into a heap in his vomit.

When the sun rose over Johnson Mesa and flowed over Swannie's aching body, he awoke from a restless stupor to the sweet melody of gentle voices calling. They beckoned like heavenly angels at the Pearly Gates, yet he lay in the gutter, legs twitching. The pesky crows perched on his upturned shoulder, preening their breasts and fluttering their wings, waiting for Swannie to rise. He groped at the curb, brushed dried vomit from the lapels of his tattered blazer, knocked the dust and stone pits from the knees of his threadbare slacks, and tottered feebly on wobbly legs.

He staggered north up the sidewalk by the taxi stand, crossed Second Street and continued toward Third Street where he could hear the gentle voices calling in exultation,

Onward, Christian soldiers,
Marching as to war . . .

The crows swooshed and squawked, gaw, gaw, gaw, gaw, weaving and bobbing around his head, pecking his nose and ears, diving toward his eyes. He grappled with the birds and staggered toward the gentle voices exuding from a small church on the northwest corner of Third and Rio Grande,

With the cross of Jesus
Going on before . . .

The kiosk of the Church of Salvation Gospel read:

SERVICES—8 am
(Study Matthew 6: 7–13)

He crawled up the steps. The crows, pecking and picking his face
and neck, dived deliriously, jabbing at his eyes. He opened the door.
A gust of wind swept the crows away. The gentle voices soared like
a host of Heavenly Angels,

Christ, the royal Master,
Leads against the foe . . .

The heavy oak door slammed swiftly behind, propelling
Swannie onto the aisle floor. The crows skulked in the church
rafters. Engrossed in fervent rapture, nobody in the congregation
noticed Swannie crumpled in the aisle at the rear of the church.
The gentle voices faded, ending the hymn. Reverend Miller raised
both arms, standing before the congregation.

"Brothers and sisters, God is a great God today."

Voices pealed: "Um-hh—Amen—Hallelujah."

"Let us bow our heads and pray together as instructed in
Matthew, chapter six, verses seven through thirteen: Our Father
which art in heaven, Hallowed be Thy name. . . ."

Faith. Hope. Charity. The Lord's Prayer reverberated off the
church walls and sloshed onto the rafters, the skulking crows
jittering foot-to-foot.

Flashes flickered through Swannie's memories of a time, oh so
long ago, when he stood between both parents and his mother held
his hand. They gathered in the Methodist Church that once com-
muned on the second floor of a First Street mercantile and had
subsequently built a sturdy stone structure two blocks north of the
Church of Salvation Gospel. There was singing and preaching, and
more singing, then Sunday School Bible readings and discussions,

mostly the teacher telling what the Gospel meant. Peace surged throughout his aching body, as when he was a boy, oh so long ago, and the whole morning fled in talk and song about what should be in the here-and-now and paradise thereafter.

The old time religion was here-and-now in the Church of Salvation Gospel. Swannie lay amazed at the perky phrasing of the women and the hardy droning of the men. They harmonized in joyous rapture. Foggy incongruities swirled wildly through his head and melded into misty clouds and rose to the menacing crows perched in the church rafters. Through bleary eyes he glanced at so many shining faces, men, women, and children, all totally happy. They were truly ecstatic, enrapt in hymns, making magic in the air. None were drunk.

Another incongruity struck him harder. He rubbed his eyes as though he could rub away the image of the Negro family. Everybody else in the church was white and oblivious to the fact the Negroes were any different. The father, mother, and child were simply brethren of the congregation singing their hearts out, equally enrapt in the magic of the moment.

Reverend Miller spied Swannie, abruptly raised his voice, and jerked Swannie from the reverie: "Brothers and sisters, God is a great God today!"

"Hallelujah!"

"The Lord has delivered a miracle today! Look back to see Swannie Swanson, prostrate and repentant in the house of the Lord!"

Shuffles and gasps, folks strained to peek between and over each other to see Swannie stretched on the aisle floor. He gawked toward the astonished crowd. Through hazy, bleary eyes, he saw the contented faces of sober folks.

"Quit your gawking, brothers and sisters, sing! For the Lord hath delivered unto us a sinner in repentance!"

"Hallelujah!—Amen!—Praise the Lord!—Praise Jesus!" The congregation's cacophony churned into a zesty rendition of

What a friend we have in Jesus,
All our sins and griefs to bear!

"Ra-a-a-ise your voices, lift them high," Reverend Miller implored, "whilst this suppliant sinner comes to the Lord."

What a priv~i~lege to car~ry,
Ev~ 'ry ~ thing to God in prayer!

"Swannie, do you wish to be saved?" The parson beckoned him to come forward as the congregation sang.

Engulfed in the stirring hymn, he crawled down the aisle and raised to his knees before the pastor, who waited for the congregation to complete the hymn. Reverend Miller reached down and laid both hands on the tasseled tufts of Swannie's hair. When the hymn ended, the pastor raised his voice, thundering in baritone notes: "Swannie, you are a drun-n-ken sot! A sinn-ner! Have you come to the house of the Lord on your own accord?"

"You betcha!"

"Thou shalt not lie in the house of the Lord."

"Them crows is gone, leastwise."

"Have you found peace here?"

"You betcha."

"Praise Jesus!" members of the congregation yelped.

"Do you wish to repent?"

"You betcha."

"To cease in your debauchery?"

"You betcha."

"Praise the Lord!"

"Anything to keep them crows away."

"Praise Jesus!"

"Brother Swannie, you must forbear the bottle, never again to drink a drop. When you are weak and tempted, you must cast all thoughts of debauchery from your heart. How do you pledge?"

"Not even an itty-bitty nip, to fight a cold?"

"No! Total abstinence, sayeth the Lord."

The congregation murmured fervently: "Amen—Hallelujah—Praise the Lord—Praise Jesus."

The congregation anxiously awaited Swannie's reply while he hesitated and thought about the vow he was being asked to take.

"Hooch, my only solice . . . my way to forget . . . numbs the pain . . . forget for a bit." Then, Swannie blurted out his thoughts before he could think to check his words: "Hooch is my only savior."

"Not in the house of the Lord!" Reverend Miller accosted. "Surrender to the loving arms of His son Jesus."

"Amen—Praise the Lord—Praise Jesus."

Swannie glanced to the ceiling rafters and spied the crows, fluttering their wings and preening their breasts, waiting for him to falter. He sputtered, "I swear, I'll never drink a drop again, so long as I live. Nothin' stronger'n water."

"Praise the Lord! Praise Jesus!" the spirited congregation shouted.

"Nothing. I'll not imbibe! Just keep them blamed crows away!"

"Um, hum!—Praise the Lord—Oh, ye~ah!—Praise Jesus!" the congregation triumpantly shouted, and Reverend Miller regaled: "Praise Jesus! God is a good God, sayeth His Book. He will keep His word, if you do."

"You'll see me here every Sunday Reverend, dry as a bone."

"Brothers and sisters," Reverend Miller started the litany, "there is a tide of affairs—"

"Praise the Lord!" the congregation chanted in unison.

"—in the works of the Lord—"

"Praise Jesus!"

"—that sweeps us all—"

"Praise the Lord!"

"—to our dusty end!"

"Praise Jesus!"

Reverend Miller raised his hands from Swannie's head, and with open palms, waved the congregation to sing and escorted Swannie to the front pew.

Swannie sat in the front pew and fumbled through the hymnal. He joined the singing. His tenor voice soared above the sonorous jubilation. As Swannie sang, the incongruities returned in sudden snippets. Everybody sang . . . heartily . . . harmoniously . . . happily, and they weren't drunk, a queer notion long past—folks could be happy and sober.

And the Negro family, right there in a pew among the congregation was coal miner Julian Heard, his wife Dahlia, and son

Edward. Swannie vaguely remembered that Negroes were recruited to work in the coal camps in the early 1900s, but most had moved away. He went to school with Dahlia's younger brother Jimmy and remembered the Heard family as the last of the Negro coal miners. Dahlia and Julian's parents had come from West Virginia to Chicorico. Their fathers were recruited during labor shortages in 1906 and were guaranteed jobs. At ten, Julian was needed by his family to work as a breaker boy, separating slate from coal in the tipple. He advanced to underground work as a trapper, opening and closing ventilation doors in the Chicorico mine, driving mules, assisting miners, and finally, he advanced to the rank of miner.

Dahlia wasn't compelled to work and finished high school, the first in her family to receive a high school diploma. After her graduation, she and Julian married. Both loved to sing. Dahlia offered music lessons on an old family piano passed down three generations of her family. Now, here she was in church singing along with Julian and little Eddy. They were equal to everybody and nobody seemed to mind. The joyous jubilee lifted Swannie, baffled and bewildered as he was:

> Rock of Ages, cleft for me,
> Let me hide myself in thee. . . .

Enrapt in the congregation's warmth and jubilation, Swannie hardly noticed the service had ended and folks were slowly leaving the church. Reverend Miller and wife Emma greeted at the church door while folks milled about. The Heards were the last to leave.

"Reverend, Mrs. Miller, thank you for having us today."

"Julian and Dahlia, you're always welcome here, and you, too, Eddy." Reverend Miller winked at Eddy and brushed his closely cropped hair. Swannie approached Reverend Miller. He had been sitting in a pew waiting for everybody to leave. Again, the Heards thanked the pastor and lingered to view the notices on a small bulletin in the church's foyer.

The pastor turned his attention to Swannie. "I'm really pleased you came today. You proved to be a witness to salvation. We hope you can eschew the bottle and continue to come."

"Can I come, even if I can't?"

"Only you can answer that."

An awkward pause.

"Tell me, Swannie, if I may ask, what pulled you into the bottle?"

"Don't do no good to harp on it. B'sides, it's kinda long."

"Make it short without wallowing in self-pity."

Swannie's crooked grin shifted suddenly to a grimace. He stared at the ground.

The parson realized he'd been too harsh with Swannie and softened his tone. "Swannie, my boy, there's always hope a man can change his ways. I'd like to see you try. Start by coming to Sunday services."

"You sure got a lot'a faith in a lost soul." Swannie relaxed. "But, I'm a hobo, a no good bum. No job. No family. No home."

"Now, now, Swannie," Emma injected, "we're all good. We're all children of God."

"Yes, yes," the pastor assured Swannie, "we're made in His image. Sometimes we lose our way. You just have to find yours— in His tidal wave—sweeping all of us to our inevitable end."

Dahlia overheard the conversation and whispered to Julian, "That poor man's hard up and down on his luck. Doesn't have a job . . . or home. Can't you get him a job at the mine?"

Julian was concentrating on a handwritten note pinned on the bulletin board offering cords of pine for sale or exchange. He glimpsed toward Swannie and then responded in a whisper. "He's no miner. He's a wide-eyed, gullible yokel. Wouldn't surprise me if'n he's bought the Brooklyn Bridge more than once."

"No, he's not. He's just a boy, like Jimmy, once cleaned-shaved and dressed properly. . . . I believe he went to school with Jimmy."

"Schooling or no, a mule can't run the Kentucky Derby."

"Now Julian, even mules can work in the mines."

"Honey, be reasonable. We're only workin' two or three days a week, and Bower's not likely to give a job to a lazy, shiftless mule that'd rather drink than work."

"Maybe he could do odd jobs, or something besides mining."

"Still a yokel, far's I can tell."

"Julian Heard! I've never known you to be so little. The man needs our help. It's the Lord's wish, do unto others as—"

"Honey, where's he going to live?"

"With us. Now, tell Reverend Miller."

Julian wasn't pleased with Dahlia's charity. She was too much a Christian and believed the old saw about being a brother's keeper. "No good would come of it," he thought, "anyway, the lazy mule will tire of work and hunger for hooch, lose his job and take to drinking again, most likely. Then, I'll be done with him." Julian kept his counsel. Dahlia wanted to invite the man to their home and he respected her wishes.

"Beg pardon," Julian said to Reverend Miller, removing his hat and holding it by the brim. "I don't mean to be nosing in other people's business, but we couldn't help hear what this gentleman was saying, and it might be we can get him a job at Chicorico. They're always looking for a handyman that does most anything outside the mine. Don't pay much, but it's a job, leastwise."

"A job? A real job? I don't have a car or nothing. Don't have no way of getting to work. And—" interrupted Swannie.

"The Missus wants you to move in with us."

"Move in?" Swannie sunk. "With you?"

Julian was not surprised at Swannie's reaction, thinking, "He's going to decide to stay a sot rather than live with a Negro family." Julian politely addressed Reverend Miller, "Me, Dahlia, and my boy, we'll be out in the pickup. We'll wait ten–fifteen minutes. You and Mr. Swanson talk it over."

Swannie stood dumbfounded—a job . . . a home . . . a Negro family.

"Here, I'll come with you. Leave the gentlemen to talk." Emma took Julian's arm and left the church with him.

Swannie pulled a tiny knife from his pocket, opened the blade, and nervously picked at his dirty fingernails while he prattled, "Boy, phew! Heads aching, mouth dry, ain't had nothin' to drink for a spell. And, all the queer notions—attend church . . . work for a living . . . board with a Negro family."

"Spit on your queer notions!" Reverend Miller declaimed, annoyed. "You're adrift the Lord's river of salvation. The Lord delivered the Heards. Here! On the same tributary you're now afloat."

Swannie's attention diverted to the Reverend's agitated hand gestures rather than his theological treatise. Reverend Miller spied Swannie's diverted attention, placed his hands in his pockets, and spoke less excitedly. "Let me tell you something about the Heards. Back in 1918, when your folks, and your sweetheart—God rest their souls—when they passed with the influenza, they had Christian burials. Dahlia's brother passed at the same time. Jimmy wasn't a member of a congregation. There were no Negro churches in Raton, or the coal camps.

"Julian, Dahlia, and Eddy went from church to church in Raton seeking a Christian burial for Jimmy. They sojourned south on Third Street, and like the Holy Family in Bethlehem, they were sent away. No room at the inn. One pastor patronized them by offering to organize a church for Negroes-only, when there were enough Negroes to make a tithing congregation, and when a Negro pastor could be procured. They'd have to wait a month of Sundays under those conditions. They didn't have a prayer, and we were the church of last resort.

"Tired of the rejections, Julian stayed in the pickup. Dahlia came with Eddy to make a plea. She wanted a Christian burial for her brother. I offered one. The Lord was gently nudging me to do His work. Dahlia was pleased as punch. I insisted some of the brethren attend. They were leery, but they couldn't tell me no. Now, they're glad they attended the burial. Dahlia showed us the colored people's cemetery east of Chicorico. We were shocked! We never suspected Negroes were segregated in death. They are in Texas, we know, but not here. After the service, I invited the Heards to attend our church, and they've been coming regularly. The whole congregation loves and respects them. They're especially good singers, even their boy Eddy. We can't remember now what it was like when they're weren't brethern."

"That was mighty generous of you, Reverend."

"No, t'wasn't." He stroked the thick tufts of his silvery hair. "Gather the children to me, sayeth the Lord. He didn't say, keep the Negro children away. You've got to start thinking in different ways. You're lucky to be invited to stay with one of the most loving Christian families in the congregation—maybe in all of Colfax County. Don't think of living with a Negro family. Think of yourself as living testament to the salvation that God offers. You've drifted close to salvation's bushy shore. You best cling to that slim twig of hope. Or, drown in your vomit."

"I dunno." Swannie closed the knife and dropped it in his pocket, inspecting his nails.

"What's to know!" The Reverend gripped Swannie's hand testily and shook it vigorously. "Look around you. Where're the white folks who claim to be Christians? No white folks offering you shelter, a job."

"That ain't fair." Swannie pulled his hand from Reverend Miller's grasp.

"Fair! They're Christians, aren't they? Some white folks are all too willing to take your money for cheap whiskey. Yet, they don't take you in. If you don't take the offer, you condemn yourself to rot your liver and die in a gutter. Kiss a Christian burial goodbye. County would bury you in an unmarked grave."

Swannie glanced to the rafters. The demon crows glowered. "Reckon I got nothing to lose. Anyways, I kin leave after a good night's sleep and breakfast," Swannie muttered inaudibly.

They left the church.

"Swannie's coming with you," Reverend Miller gruffly announced to the waiting family. "Keep him dry, hear? No choke-cherry wine."

"You know we will!"

"Splendid!" Emma squeezed Dahlia's hand, patted Julian on the shoulder, and joined Reverend Miller. They strolled next door to their home.

"Well and good, Mr. Swanson." Dahlia took Swannie by the arm. "Julian and I are pleased you'll be staying with us for a spell."

"You kin call me 'Swannie.'"

"Well and good. We'll take you to your place and get your things."

"Ah, uh, don't bother. I been sleeping in a boxcar on Buena Vista. Don't have nothing, 'cept what I got on."

"Best we be on our way," Julian hastened. "Hop in back, Eddy. Mr. Swanson can ride up front with us."

"Oh, goodie!" Eddy started to clamber over the pickup's tailgate.

"Upsadaisy!" Swannie lifted Eddy by the armpits and hefted him into the pickup's bed.

"Thank you, Mr. Swanson." Little Eddy was pleased and enthralled by this vagabond able to move from home at a whim with nothing but threadbare clothing.

"Sit!" Dahlia scolded. "Up against the cab! Or, you're walking home!"

Eddy grinned ear-to-ear. He loved riding in the back of the Model A pickup. After positioning behind the cab, Eddy stared at Swannie.

"Now, Eddy, it's not nice to stare at people."

"Let the boy be, Mrs. Heard. He's probably never seen a hobo like me, up close, that is."

Julian stooped in front of the Model A to crank the engine.

Swannie gently shoved Julian aside to demonstrate what little he knew about cranking up an automobile. "Whoa, that kin break your arm. Git behind the wheel, hold the spark lever way high, the gas 'bout half down."

Julian grinned incredulously, thinking, "The yokel thinks he knows something about cranking up a Ford. Probably break his arm." Julian scoffed, "Suit yourself. Don't blame me if'n you break your arm."

"Soon's I start to crank, and the engine sputters and catches, let down on the spark and give her gas."

"Never turn down help." Julian winked at Dahlia, hopped into the pickup behind the steering wheel and adjusted the spark and gas levers. He laid a hand on the wheel and with one finger waved "okay." Swannie stooped over in front of the pickup and disappeared from view, yanking the crank. The motor caught, coughed, and sputtered while Julian adjusted the gas and spark levels. The motor settled into a steady clatter. Beaming, Swannie reappeared in front of the pickup and scooted onto the right-hand seat next to Dahlia.

TWO   TAKE ME HOME COUNTRY ROAD

LEAVING THE CHURCH, the pickup ground down the hill on Rio Grande Avenue, turned south on First Street, and ran out of town along the Santa Fé Railroad. The railway and highway ran parallel to the Old Santa Fé Trail by the Clifton House, once a lavish stage-coach inn, now in decay—a solitary stone fireplace and crumbling adobe walls on the swelling prairies. Out where the prairies swelled, Eddy could see far beyond Eagle Tail Mountain to the huge, volcanic loaves that had bubbled and cooled centuries ago on the grassy basin. The newly birthed blue grama and buffalo grasses gleamed in green, the yucca pods blossomed in pure white, and the piñon trees speckled the foothills and sandstone rimrocks. Purple sage and yellow ragweed flourished on overgrazed pastures.

Eddy admired a hawk hovering high in the upper wind currents of the turquoise sky preying upon an unwary critter crawling on open ground. "Little critter better keep an eye on the sky. It will fall." He laughed to himself, while the hawk nose-dived to the ground, extended its talons, smacked and broke the tiny critter's neck. With a powerful flutter of wings, the hawk flew away to breakfast, the unwary critter dangling dead in the sky.

For Eddy, riding backwards in the pickup's bed was a perfectly swell adventure with a panoramic view. He didn't have to fake civility like his father who wasn't happy about taking a stranger into his home and was scowling as he gripped the steering wheel tightly, grumbling to himself, "Jist another doughboy who come back from the War. Squanders time mooching drinks. Look'a them delicate hands, fingers. Shows he ain't worked much."

Julian made a game of concentrating on the highway, once a cattle trail, jostling the Model A over the dusty, rugged road to keep the skinny balloon tires from bursting on sharp rocks or an axle from breaking in deeply dug ruts. He stole a quick peek at Dahlia who was attempting fruitlessly to engage Swannie in conversation, who was pressed against the door, looking straight ahead, emmitting an occasional "yes'm" or "no ma'm."

Inside the confined cab, the sweet fragrance of Dahlia's perfume and the putrid puke on Swannie's blazer clashed repugnantly. "Hang it all," Julian again grumbled to himself. "Dahlia's done picked up a stinky, stray mule." Julian sidled the pickup to the shoulder and pointed to Swannie's blazer. "Eddy can hold it."

Swannie hopped out the cab and handed the rank blazer to Eddy, who handled it gingerly by the fingertips, folded it inside-out, and tucked it beneath him. While Swannie was outside the cab, Julian stole a glance at Dahlia who frowned and then smiled. Julian knew he was not angry with Dahlia. Just like when she insisted on hauling that dang piano. He wasn't happy about hauling it around, at first. Now, Julian knew he couldn't anymore live without the piano as he could without Dahlia. "She's got the Midas touch," Julian thought, "everything she touches, turns to gold."

Back on the road, Dahlia sat comfortably between the two men. Swannie now leaned to the right and jammed his head on the window-post to make a wide berth.

"Now, Mr. Swanson." Dahlia corrected herself. "Swannie, I don't mean to be indelicate, but how is it you've trapped yourself in the bottle?"

"I'm a bum."

"Nonsense, that's no explanation. I remember you in school. You and brother Jimmy were in the same class. He told me about you. You were quite the singer, Al Jolson's twin. The girls liked you, such a charming singer you were." A crop of curls crept from beneath Dahlia's small hat and poked her right eye. She shoved the winsome curls sideways. They whipped back.

"Here." Swannie tucked the ebony curls beneath her hat.

"Thank you."

"Think nothin' of it." A crooked smile etched Swannie's face. "Hate hair in my eyes."

"You're so kind."

Swannie blushed.

"Well, what happened?"

"It's a long story."

"Might as well get started." Julian broke concentration on the road. "Yer gonna tell it anyway."

"Hush, Julian. Be polite."

"You know I was drafted. Didn't really wanna go. Jist graduated high school. Next thing, I was in the trenches in France."

"In the trenches? In France?"

"Sure enough."

"Me, too, fighting for Ninety-third Division." Julian perked up, no longer feigning civility. He felt a special kinship with doughboys who'd fought in France. "We didn't have artillery backup. General Pershing turned us over to the French. I ended up fighting side-by-side French fellers."

"Met some of them fellers myself. Never fought with'em."

"Wasn't they a friendly bunch? They were smooth talkers. I was surprised how many spoke English. They tried to teach me French, but I'm afraid to use the words they taught me."

"Do tell."

"Mixed company, an all."

"Oho! Same goes with the other doughboys."

"What I figured, they didn't mind we was colored, so long as we fought on their side. When your life depends on another man, you don't care about his color. Color don't mean much in the trenches amongst lice, rats, dysentery, gangrene. No need to fight. We were bound to die. I hated it—puissant wounds, dead men rotting."

"It was terrible . . . jist terrible."

"Dear, let Swannie speak."

"Wasn't much fun, I own." Talk of war seemed to open up Swannie, also. "We stayed put in the trenches. Germans gassed us a lot. I try to forget." Swannie shifted to more pleasant concerns. "Howse come we never run across each other?"

"Because we were segregated from you white boys. I'd more likely run into a German, before you, the way we was kept apart."

"Heck of a note, but I do recall seeing Negroes fightin' with us."

"Well, you could'a seen some colored boys from the Ninety-second, the other Negro division, when the bullets was flying."

"Howse come I saw some of them Negro fellers?"

"Americans was segregated. But, didn't do much good. When German bullets and bombs was spewing, you fellers might've mushed together in the same trenches. Didn't matter much, huddled in the trenches. Germans didn't care 'bout a feller's color. We was all Americans to them."

Conversation lulled as both men briefly recalled their worst nightmares about trench warfare. It was futile, a war of attrition where the frontline never moved much in either direction. Backed by a huge barrage of artillery fire, Germans advanced, charging directly into the gunfire of the French and Americans, and piling up bodies on the barbwire stranded in front of the trenches. The Germans used their dead to build a defensive wall. Then more charged, overwhelming the Americans and French.

The Americans and French battled the Germans hand-to-hand with bayonets. But, more Germans came and the Americans and French retreated. Several days later, the Americans and French returned the barrage of artillery fire and advanced. This time, the Americans and French charged directly into the German gunfire and piled up the bodies. Then, the Americans and French hid behind their dead comrades before making a charge into the German trenches with the ensuing hand-to-hand combat. And the Germans retreated.

Back and forth, the warring armies fought over barren meadows and decimated woods no more than four miles wide. Like moles, the soldiers on both sides holed-in for weeks living in the ground, using each other's bomb craters depending on their positions.

"See this here scar?" Julian pointed to his cheek and glimpsed in the rearview mirror.

"Yep."

"A million dollar wound. Got part of my jaw and cheek blown off. And, I thanked God for taking me out'a the trenches. French medics toted me to an ambulance and took me to an old church where they'd set up a hospital. Half the roof was bombed out. It was a Catholic Church, first time I'd been in one, what was left of it. Must'a been pretty once, with all them statues of Jesus, Mother Mary, and the angels."

Julian leaned forward on the steering wheel and raised his voice as though Swannie couldn't hear. "Never saw so many seraphs, cherubs, and angels with swords and trumpets. We was snug, laid 'neath the roof wasn't blowed away. They patched me up right there by the altar 'cause I was expected to go back to the fighting. Then, the war ended. Got out the fighting before I got killed. I tell you, if'n I'd a stayed in the trenches, well, most of the fellers in that unit was killed. I'd be buried in France, someplace. I thank the Lord every day for keeping me alive."

Swannie took a long, deep breath and exhaled slowly, still gazing to his right through the open window. "What I can't figure is—why the Lord allowed us to fight at all? He could'a stopped the war."

"Can't blame the Lord for the deeds of men. No sir, He put us here and told us to take care of each other. It's generals and big shots that make a war. Us poor suckers, we get called to fight it for them."

"Julian," Dahlia accosted gently, "you're not giving Swannie a chance to talk."

"Got carried away yapping. You'll jist have to learn to interrupt."

Dahlia was pleased to see how comfortable Swannie seemed to be. He sort of wilted into his seat, slouched and casual, no longer crowding his head against the window-post. Yes, he was very much like her brother, fragile, frail, and affable except for the habit of casting aside his eyes as he spoke. At first, she assumed he was evasive and dishonest until she realized he was terribly shy.

"Don't like talking much about the War. Comin' home was no better." Swannie settled into his war story. "Jist one long train ride—except on the boat, which was mighty long, too—with some hoopla and hollerin' when I left France on the troopship and arrived portside in Houston, where I was herded with other soldiers onto the train bound for the Texas Panhandle, and other depots northwest."

"M'mm, do I remember the ship. We was packed tight. Got sicker an' a dog."

"Boat was a mite close, but didn't bother me much. Train ride wasn't much fun. Let me tell you, between Ft. Worth and Trinidad, the train crept along, stopping for doughboys to disembark at every dusty Texas town along the line. We stopped every ten minutes, it seems. Train was hot as the devil."

"Say, how 'bout them small town bands?"

"They was a hoot! After a while, I thought the band was travelin' with the train. Nope. Seems in them little Texas towns, every man and child plays in a band. Sure pretty to hear them bands as we pulled into the stations. . . . We moved along quicker, once in the Texas Panhandle up through Folsom, and then Trinidad where I transferred to the Santa Fé Railroad."

"I come a different way from Houston. Do remember them small Texas towns. I come up from El Paso on the Santa Fé most the way. All new country to me."

"Me, too, even the short ride from Trinidad to Raton. South from Trinidad, the train follows the Santa Fé Trail, yep, jist like this here road. We passed the Starkville coal camp where mules was still used for haulage."

"Some of them mules is stone-cold blind."

"Do tell."

"When they ain't workin', they're corraled underground. Fed there, too. In a few years, their eyes can't tolerate sunlight."

"Well, jist a few miles south was Morley coal camp. Didn't see no mules. The mine used all kinds of electrical machines, far as I could tell."

"You bet. More like Chicorico."

"Did see a pretty sight, the St. Aloysius Church. It's Catholic."

"That's what I hear. Been meaning to take a ride up there, see it for myself. See if'n it has all them statues, like the church in France."

"Can't say, but I recall hearing how miners built the church from scratch using local materials."

The church was an impressive visage considering it was built without a blueprint or artist's hand-drawn conception of what it might appear to be. Created from the imaginations of the miners, it was designed in the Spanish Mission style, an archway opened its entrance, and on top of it, another smaller arch sheltered the Angelus bell.

Just a few miles south of the coal camps at the Colorado–New Mexico border, the train passed through the tunnel at the crest of Raton Pass and descended gradually to Raton between steep canyon walls. Entering Raton, the train slowed to a stop at the spacious depot, roundhouse, and maintenance yard, bustling with mechanics maintaining and repairing steam engines. The depot, built in an admixture of Russian onion-shaped domes and Spanish Mission archways, opened to a brick promenade crowded with wellwishers waiting for family and friends.

Mothers and fathers held their children high so they could peer over the bonnets and stovepipe cowboy hats to see the doughboys as they waved from within the coaches. There was no band. The Raton City Band cermoniously greeted the first wave of soldiers two weeks before. Band members were volunteers and obligated to work on the day of Swannie's arrival.

"So your folks met you at the station?" Dahlia asked.

"Nope. They was dead, come to find out."

"Oh, dear, dear. Did anybody greet you?"

"Not a soul. Turned out, Rose Marie was dead, too."

"Oh, my Lord, nobody—"

"Leastwise, nobody stayed behind to say hello."

When Swannie didn't see his parents or sweetheart Rose Marie among the happy throng of wellwishers, he tugged his duffel bag from beneath the seat and hopped out of the coach car onto the brick promenade. Most of the throng had disbanded, walking hand-in-hand with the newly arrived passengers. He stood alone. The train wheeled away.

"Didn't know they was dead. I got to thinking maybe they didn't get my letter, saying I was coming home. I strutted toward home, happy as a lark. Be fun to surprise Ma and Pa, Rose Marie, too. Jist dropping in from France!"

He walked north on the depot's promenade onto First Street along the tracks that passed Ripley Park, crossed the tracks and continued walking north on First Street over the bridge at Raton Creek. Beneath, a tiny stream of early morning rain trickled from Raton Peak. He paused, gazing at the peak. Thin, wispy clouds cloistered at its crown.

As he approached home, he saw the house was abandoned and dilapidated, the paint cracking and peeling along the eaves and window ledges, shingles blown away. He couldn't go in the door—everything boarded—doors, windows, and even the glassed-in porch where his parents once sat on cool summer evenings. Weeds grew wildly where a lovely flowerbed and lawn had once flourished in the shade of the cottonwoods. Next door, he knocked at the Gallagers and waited for a while. Nobody answered. He walked south in the alley and turned left on Maxwell Avenue to Rose Marie's home. He knocked on the door.

"Swannie!" Mrs. Farrell flung the screen door open and embraced Swannie. "Come in! Come in! Herbie, look who's come home!"

"Swannie, my boy!" Mr. Farrell popped out of the basement door and bounded into the house. "So good to see you." He, too, hugged Swannie and slapped his shoulder in genuine adulation. "Oh, it's so good to see you."

"Rose Marie?"

Mr. and Mrs. Farrell stared dumbly.

"And, Ma? Pa?"

Mrs. Farrell hugged Swannie again and then led him by the hand to the living room sofa, sitting beside him, still holding his hand.

"Yes, please make yourself at home." Mr. Farrell pulled up a rocker. "Son, didn't you get our letter? We wrote when it happened."

"Letter? Happened?"

"You didn't get our letter, oh, Lord have mercy."

The last nine months in France had been chaotic for Swannie and most of the other soldiers. Troops were moved constantly. Letters trailed behind and were often lost.

"Your folks. . . . Our Rose Marie—they passed on—the influenza, months ago. We wrote you. The Red Cross told us they'd get the letter to you. We thought you knew and couldn't come for the funeral. We buried them in Fairmont Cemetery. Had your house boarded, till you could come home to care for it."

"Wrote Ma and Pa, told them to tell Rosie Marie I was comin' home."

"Oh, you poor boy. We never knew." Mrs. Farrell snuffled, daubing tears from her eyes.

Swannie was too stunned to weep or speak.

"Here, Swannie, have a shot of Jack Daniels. Gonna be illegal pretty soon." Mr. Farrell poured a shot for himself and Swannie, who gulped it down.

"Another, please."

"Sure, sure." Mr. Farrell poured two jiggers into the glass.

Swannie ended the flashback. "Mr. Farrell's whiskey numbed me up but good." He mimicked drinking from a bottle. "Been drowning my sorrows in the bottle ever since, and now with Prohibition, it's easier to get."

"That's cockamamie!"

"Mostly moonshine."

"Uh, what about your folk's house?"

"Should'a done something with it, all boarded up and all. Bank wanted me to start payments, now that I was back. I wasn't up to it. Didn't have a job. Told'em to sell it. They promised to give me what the folks had in it."

"Good. That's money in the bank."

"Ho! Don't I know! Bank never did sell it."

"Well, where have you been staying?"

"Speakeasies, gutters, in a boxcar mostly, over on the eastside by the cemetery close to where the folks are buried. Convenient to visit when the feeling comes on."

"My, my, but why not home?"

"Couldn't sleep in the old house. . . . Shoot! That was more'an ten years ago. Still a bum." Swannie held back the tears welling from his eyes.

Dahlia handed him a handkerchief.

THREE   SACRED AND TENDER ASSOCIATIONS

WHEN THEY ARRIVED IN CHICORICO, Dahlia busied herself preparing dinner while Julian took Swannie on a walking tour of the coal camp. Eddy tagged along, walking between the two men holding their hands.

"Most times, we walk the tracks. Road's either dusty or muddy. Tracks are clear most times. If'n they're not clear, best stay home. Nothing's moving." They walked the tracks west toward the mine. Julian pointed out the stuccoed Company store and clubhouse.

"The Santa Fé Railroad tracks splits the camp running west to the mine entry and tipple. Every man works the mine, or has something to do with it." Julian motioned towards the houses lined on both sides of the tracks arranged in square grids nestled against the hills on both sides of the canyon.

"Houses all look the same."

"Pretty much. Company owns 'em. Built in two waves. In 1895, the first houses was built of brown cinder brick. The Company store, clubhouse, doctor's office, and the general manager's house were constructed at that time. They all have electricity and running water indoors, except for the miner's homes."

"Why's that?"

"No indoor plumbing. Lucky to have houses, at all. The earliest miners and their families lived in tents until they could move into boxcars, which the Company emptied when the second wave of houses was built in the early 1920s. They was prefabricated."

"They was what?"

"Prefrabricated wood-frame structures, like them Sears and Roebuck houses in Raton. Made in advance, in a factory somewheres. Only the Company houses weren't made by Sears and Roebuck. Company purchased them from the American Portable House Company. In Seattle, the houses were assembled in sections, shipped by rail, and then erected in Chicorico at a cost of sixty-five dollars each."

"Sure know lots about the camp."

"Lived most of my life here. Saw it grow from the days of tents, and them houses are a God-send. Through rent, the houses pay for themselves within one year. Only trouble is, a man can't ever own a house. Maintenance and repair's the tenant's responsibility. For lots of folks, there's no incentive to keep the house up."

As they walked west on the tracks, Julian waved at his neighbor, Manuel Montaño, who was weeding his garden patch, and two doors further, he nodded at Onorio Chicarelli, who was raking his boccie lane. "Them two gentlemen care about their families and show it by caring for their houses."

The houses, cold in the winter and hot in the summer, were four-room, single family dwellings, except the much larger boardinghouse that held fifteen men and the keeper. Most houses had crawl spaces beneath them, although the Slavic and Italian miners had excavated the crawl spaces into cellars to make and store wine. Backyards contained outhouses, coal sheds, and water pumps. Many coal camp folks tended garden patches and raised chickens in their backyards.

At the tipple, Julian explained its purpose. "Think of the mine as a resevoir, the tipple as the spillway where coal's screened and funneled to ship away on trains over these very tracks where we're standing. By the way, here's where you come tomorrow, see Homer Bowers. Ask for a job. Can't miss his office atop the tipple. I'll tell him yer comin'."

They turned at the tipple and walked back down the tracks from where they'd come without saying much. Eddy broke the ice. "Can you spin hoops?"

"Uh, no, can't say so."

"Can you play kick-the-can?"

"No, can't say so."

"Hide-and-seek?"

"No."

"Wasn't you ever a kid?"

"Ho!" Julian chuckled. "Still is."

"Yeah, sure, I kin climb a tree better than any monkey. And shoot marbles."

"Goodie," Eddy swung Swannie's hand.

"And, if you ain't got a swing, I can make you one."

"Keen." Eddy's eyes glimmered. "Monkeys swing on trees, too!"

"Sure do. I'm a monkey in a man's disguise—keep my tail in my pants."

Julian was pleased to see how easily Swannie and Eddy talked. Ever since Jimmy had died, Eddy missed having an older boy for a pal to show him the ropes.

They completed the tour at the eastern edge of Chicorico by the row of schoolhouses and the colored people's cemetery where Julian showed him the family graves, including Dahlia's brother Jimmy's. "Like most cemeteries," Julian ruminated, "some graves are well tended, others plumb forgotten. Decoration Day, we clear out weeds, put up fresh flowers, even the folks that ain't family."

"What're them queer lookin' critters?" Swannie, starting to feel comfortable with Julian and Eddy, pointed to the brick beehive-shaped coke ovens directly across the way from the cemetery.

"Coke ovens. Come, have a look-see." They crossed to the coke ovens. "See how they're set in two parallel rows of ten to a lane. Between each row, mule-driven wagons haul in coal and haul out coke. They load the coal into one side of an oven and remove the coke from the other."

"How do they make coke?"

"Not sure, but the magic's in them ovens—kinda like pressure cooking the coal. Bet you didn't know coal is used for smelting iron and copper?"

"Never figured."

"Yep, that's what them ovens are for—to burn coal down to coke for smelting. When I was a kid, the ovens run day and night at temperatures hotter than a volcano. My pa worked the ovens till the heat got to him. 'Hell on earth,' he'd say, 'even in the dead of winter.' By the time he'd shoveled coal and fired up the last oven in a row, the coal in the first was pressured cooked and ready to empty. He'd open the oven door on both sides. Boy, when the air hit the oven chambers, swoosh! The oxygen-starved coke sucked up the air an' flared in gigantic flames. Then, he'd douse the flames with plenty of water."

"Job sounds hotter than hell."

"Ho! Hope to never find out. When I was a tad of a lad, I imagined the ovens was caves filled with cowering dragons, 'fraid to come out and face Pa. So they shot out flames. Pa said they'd likely fry a kid to a crisp, so best to keep away. And, I did."

"A smart kid!"

"Jist scared. Pa really made the ovens sound awful, but they were money-makers for the Company. Back before the War, all the ovens was going full blast. About a quarter of them is used nowadays."

"Demand down?"

"For a long time."

"Since Black Thursday?"

"Long before then we saw the Depression comin'. When you see Bowers, look'a the chart in his office. Demand for coal and coke got so low, he doesn't pay no mind to production anymore."

When they returned home, Julian immediately suggested dinner outside on the back porch, which surprised Dahlia.

"Honey, we never eat out there."

"Today's different. Nice day. Best way to have a picnic—moment's notice—b'fore the clouds come rumbling . . . ants come crawling."

"A picnic on the back porch?"

"We'll set on chairs, balance our plates on our knees, like high-tone folks." Standing behind Swannie, Julian winked at Dahlia.

"Oh." Dahlia caught the signal, obvious to everybody but Swannie, who had not bathed for a long time and smelled like it. "Quick now, chicken's getting cold. We'll serve on the table."

Julian, Swannie, and Eddy carried chairs to the back porch. Eddy selected the porchsteps for a seat. Then they carried glasses of water to the table where Dahlia had set the roasted chicken.

"Goodness gracious, St. Ignatius!"

"Oh my! What could be the matter?"

"Nothin', ma'am, nothin' a'tall." Swannie swiped his hand across his mouth and wiped a silly grin off his face. "Jist haven't seen such a handsome spread in a month of Sundays."

Modestly, Dahlia thanked Swannie, explaining, "It's our big meal of the week. You'll have to make several trips, perhaps one for the chicken, mash potatoes, and gravy. Another for the greens."

"What 'bout the sweet potatoes? An', what's the pie?"

"Crabapple. That's dessert. Have a piece after the main course."

"Don't know 'bout you, but I'm famished," Julian prompted. "Hurry, Swannie, you go first. And, seconds are okay."

"What about thirds?" Eddy chirped.

"Eat slow and you can take as many turns as you wish."

"Yum." Eddy smacked his lips and stood behind Swannie, forming a serving line.

Everyone served and sat on the back porch. Julian led the family in a blessing. They ate placidly, relishing the cool afternoon on the back porch and the tasty picnic dinner. Once Swannie interrupted the serene mood to commend Dahlia's roasted chicken. "Best roast chicken I've ever had." Eddy and Julian nodded in agreement without saying anything. Dahlia smiled contentedly. Swannie didn't add he couldn't remember when he'd sat down to a full course dinner with a family, but it was before he left to the Army in 1917.

After the picnic dinner, Swannie helped clear the table and wash and dry dishes. Dahlia treasured her chinaware. The amber colored, clear glass server, tureen, casserole dish, saucers, and cups were soaked and scrubbed in a pan of warm water. "I appreciate your help, drying dishes. Do be careful." Dahlia added, "No butterfingers."

"Yes, ma'm." Swannie politely nodded. "Ma tole me the same thing when I used to help her." With a towel made from a cotton flour sack, Swannie dried and stacked each piece near the cupboard for Dahlia to arrange on the proper shelf. Dahlia soaked the flatware spoons and forks while she washed the sharp knives. Finishing the flatware, she scrubbed the black cast iron pots, skillets, and pans, except those storing fat on the cookstove's upper shelf.

She showed Swannie where to place the flatware in the divided drawers. "Don't mix them. Tablespoons and teaspoons are separate, and so on. You'll see." She took Swannie's wet towel and hooked it to the cupboard. "Use this bucket. Bring in some water for the boiler," Dahlia said, handing Swannie a tin bucket, "and then fill the bucket for drinking."

Swannie hauled water from the outside pump and Dahlia showed how to pour it in the cookstove's boiler to warm for the next morning. After filling the boiler, he again pumped water into the bucket and replaced it on the washstand where a tin dipper was used for everyone to drink. Once finished with after-dinner chores, everyone gathered in the living room. Surrounded by the warm family, Swannie sank deeply into the soft sofa, profoundly tranquil, much like this morning when he stood and sang in church, only now he was at peace.

Swannie lounged . . . mired in tranquility . . . vaguely aware Julian was speaking but recurring notions prempted . . . sober . . . happy . . . okay . . . sober . . . happy . . . okay. Julian tugged lightly at Swannie's shirt sleeve while explaining the plan to partition the living room to provide Swannie a place to sleep and regress when he felt the need for solitude. Swannie lifted his focus from the foggy fens of contentment, "Cain't I get solitude walking in the hills behind the house?"

"Naturally, most of us do. I was thinking in the evenings, and weekends."

"Don't be changing for me. I'll fit in best I can."

"Well, don't get too comfortable," Julian jested. "Best we fix up your room. You'll sleep on the sofa. We'll partition the living room with some bedspreads and quilts."

"I'll bring some nails, and a hammer," Eddy volunteered.

"Good boy," Julian said, "and that string of cord in the basement."

Julian asked Swannie to help rearrange the furniture. Momentarily, Eddy returned with hammer, nails, and cord, handing them to Julian. "Good boy." Julian stood on a chair, pounded a nail on one wall, and then the other. Swannie steadied the chair while Julian hammered. They strung the cord between the two nails and tied it tautly. Dahlia handed Julian two quilts and a sheet, which Julian and Swannie draped over the cord, hanging the sheet between the two quilts for a folded entrance, like a tent. Placing an empty dynamite powder box next to the sofa, Julian apologized. "Best we got for an end table. It's washed. We use'em quite a bit, you'll see. You'll sleep on the sofa. You can rest here and get away from the family, as you please."

"Pretty swell to have my own room. Beats a boxcar all to heck."

"Best we can do. By dividing the living room in two parts, the easy chairs will be close to the stove, piano next to'em. Piano goes way back, part of the family. Dahlia gives lessons. Need it to where pupils can practice."

The piano was a "Chickering Upright–1855," four feet high, five feet long, and two feet wide. Constructed solidly of doubly cross-banded American oak to resist warping, it was an heirloom originating with Dahlia's grandmother, Lily Walker, who as a small girl listened to a music teacher give piano lessons to her plantation master's white children. Lily taught herself to play the piano, and as a house servant in the plantation home, Lily played Chopin and Mozart at holiday receptions and dinners. When Lily's master died in 1866, her mistress freed her and gave her the piano to use to earn a living as a piano teacher. Once freed, Lily's family moved to West Virginia where Dahlia's mother Daisy was born, later married, and given the piano by Lily. Dahlia was borne from that marriage, and when her family moved to Chicorico, they shipped the piano from West Virginia at high expense.

Swannie read a cardboard placard hanging on the wall over the piano:

The Piano
In many a humble home throughout our land
the piano has gathered about it the most sacred
and tender associations. With its music and with
simple song, and with its sacred hymn, the family
prayers are joined in chastened memory.
GROVER CLEVELAND
President of the United States of America

FOUR   JIM-JAMS AND JAVA

A RANK ODOR REEKED. Dahlia assumed it was drifting into the house from the direction of the outhouse until she spied Swannie's soiled shirt, armpits and back soaked with sweat, and remembered Julian's not too subtle signal about eating dinner in the open air of the back porch. Abruptly, Dahlia clapped and ordered, "Julian! Prepare a warm bath for Swannie! Edward, help your father! Swannie, come with me!"

Gratefully and immediately, Julian and Eddy shuffled to the kitchen to prepare warm water in a Number-4 tin tub. Dahlia tugged Swannie by the elbow toward the dresser in Eddy's bedroom and rifled through the dresser drawers, carefully lined with cotton flour sacks. Long johns, undershorts, and undershirts were in the top drawer. In the middle drawer, cotton and flannel shirts were ironed and starched, and in the bottom, bib overalls were folded neatly with balled-up socks placed on them.

"These were Jimmy's."

"Your brother's?"

"He shared this room with Eddy and would want you to have them. He was never one to waste. Quick, no dawdling. Get changed so I can measure the legs. You're pretty close to Jimmy's size. His legs were a tad longer, I believe."

"My left leg's a bit longer than my right."

31

"Don't fret. I'll measure each. For dress, you'll have to wear your old shoes. For work, Jimmy's shoeboots should fit fine with double-socks." She reached beneath Eddy's bed and retrieved a pair of steel-toed shoeboots commonly worn by miners. "I'll wash your clothing with Julian's." She paused to smooth over a pair of Jimmy's long johns. "You know, Jimmy always wore long johns. Worked in them, played in them, slept in them."

"Boy, howdy." A silly, simpering smile contoured Swannie's face. "Imagine he was powerful stinky—never a'changing long johns more an' me."

"Lord, no!" Dahlia didn't detect Swannie's playful tease. When she did, she smirked. "Oh, yo-u-u, you're corny."

"I can't take these. These ain't cast-off fripperies."

"You can't work in that wardrobe." Dahlia tugged at the blazer's frayed sleeve and frowned. "I wish we had better Sunday-Go-to-Meetin's for you. We don't have Jimmy's new suit, or dress shoes, but you're welcome to his white shirts. I'm sorry for the used wardrobe."

"No apology needed."

"I'll wash and sew your present trousers and blazer. When you've worked long enough, you can buy a dress shirt."

"Perhaps a tie?"

"You'll get one free, when you buy a suit."

"Me, in a suit?"

"Why not? You're a good-looking young man."

Swannie was flattered but didn't believe he deserved her kind words. He gazed toward the floor, avoiding direct eye contact. Then, rather than looking at her directly, he turned his face three-quarters and gazed across her left shoulder while he extended his hands to receive the neatly layered bundle of clothing. She turned her shoulder the opposite way, attempting to get a glimpse at his eyes. He evaded her gaze and timidly walked into the kitchen where Julian and Eddy had put up his bath.

"Try on the overalls, first."

He did as directed in his erstwhile bedroom and stepped from behind the quilts, prancing away from Dahlia like a model on the boardwalk, twirling, and returning. Dahlia knelt before him with pins in her mouth. She adjusted the length of the pant legs and stooped to pin the cuffs in place. A crop of curls picked at her right eye. She flicked her head and shifted the curls but they flipped back into her eye while she pinned.

"Ought to cut'em off," she mumbled with pins in her mouth.

"Wups-a-Daisy!" Swannie leaned over and held the curls away from Dahlia's eye. "Pins are rough in the belly."

"Can't pin when you're doubled-up!" she mumbled through the mouth full of pins. Her thick, slick hair glistened under the light. She flicked her head and the whimsical curls flopped. She took the pins from her mouth before ordering: "Stand straight! Attention!"

Swannie abruptly pulled his hand to the side and jerked to attention.

"That's better." She pinned the cuffs. "Believe your bath's ready. We'll leave you to your lonesome."

Swannie withdrew to his bedroom and waited. By and by, he peeped between the partition's sheets, tip-toed to the kitchen, and saw he was alone. Dahlia visited Clara Montaño where Eddy played with his best friend, Arturo. Julian had joined his friends Manuel Montaño and Onorio Chicarelli at boccie. He undressed hastily and slowly lowered into the Number-4 tin tub, the warm water lapping over his private parts and navel. Although cramped in the tub, he eagerly washed and rinsed his hair and enjoyed the warm water cascading down his face and over his sweaty, grimy back and chest, the water turning gray from dirt and grime.

Washing his private parts was a bit uncomfortable. Tiny, hard bits of feces had tangled in the hair of his scrotum and buttocks and required soaking before they could be removed. He did not like soaking in his own waste and rubbed the soap abrasively until his scrotum and buttocks were chaffed raw and stung like salt on a canker sore. Dahlia's bar of soap was homemade—lye mixed into boiling bacon grease and moulded in a cereal bowl. Soapy water trickled down his forehead into his eyes. He rubbed his eyes, ouch! He irrigated his eyes with bath water and again felt the sting of lye.

With eyes closed and bottom stinging, he stood quickly in the dirty water and daubed his eyes dry with a towel. Feeling better now that he could open his eyes, Swannie spotted a razor and lather brush, which Julian had placed on the table beside the towel. He prepared to shave in the nude to allow his buttocks and scrotum to air-dry without a painful towel rubbing. With water from the cookstove, he lathered a cup of soapy water and brushed it over his grizzled beard and moustache. Careful to keep the stinging lather away from his lips, he shaved in broad strokes, peering into a tiny tin mirror hung on the wall over the washbasin.

Dahlia kept a clean house, which inspired Swannie to tidy up the kitchen, wiping up splashed water from the floor, hanging the wet towels and wash cloth, and carefully disposing of the wastewater from the tub and wash basin. When done, he finished dressing in Jimmy's clothing—now altered for him—rinsed the tub, dried the floor where water had splashed, and piled his soiled clothing in a bushel basket Dahlia used for a hamper.

When Dahlia returned with Eddy, she found Swannie admiring her piano. "Shore is pretty. Nope, it's more'an pretty, it's beautiful." Swannie brushed his fingertips lightly over the piano top.

"I do baby it. Polish it once a week and dust the keyboard. We never move it."

"Do tell."

"To keep tuned. Moving it knocks it out of tune. Do you play?"

"No, ma'am, cain't play no musical instrument."

"I hear tell you used to be quite a singer."

"Long ago, ma'am, long ago."

"After supper, we'll get you started again." Dahlia called Eddy. "Run, get your Papa. Time for supper."

Dahlia prepared a light supper from leftovers. She sliced a loaf of bread, placed it on the kitchen table with the roasted chicken leftovers, and poured everyone a cup of coffee, milk for Eddy. Julian muttered an abbreviated blessing and then the family took turns fixing cold chicken sandwiches for themselves.

"Eat your fill," Dahlia encouraged Swannie, "chicken won't keep."

Swannie glanced about the kitchen. No icebox. He ate his fill. . . . Afterwards, Swannie assisted Dahlia, clearing the table, washing and drying the few dirty dishes. Then, Dahlia invited Swannie to join in song at the piano. Swannie was hesitant. He had noticed how well the Heards harmonized during church services.

"You folks are mighty good singers, I kin tell. I barely know how to read music. B'sides, been a long while since I—"

"Jist this morning," Julian encouraged, "I heard you yelping out a hymn."

"Je-e-pers, Mr. Swan-son," Eddy warbled, "you sounded re-e-al good to me."

"Oh, come now, don't be shy." Dahlia tugged at Swannie's elbow and nudged him toward the piano. "You're a regular Al Jolson." He didn't require much encouragement, although flattered she had compared him to Al Jolson twice. Julian and Eddy gathered around while Dahlia scooted the piano stool near the keyboard, adjusting for distance by spreading both hands over the keys. "Ready?—'Onward Christian Soldiers.'"

Julian cleared his throat and nodded. Dahlia sat erect at the piano, like a soldier at attention, yet not stiffly. She lay both hands gracefully over the keyboard and softly plinked at the keys as though the tone flowed from her ebony fingers. Her touch was soft yet direct, a mother lovingly caressing her newborn child. She played a bar for the melody and sang the lyrics. Julian, Eddy, and Swannie harmonized while Dahlia pressed the keys firmly and paced the tune's bold melody to the clip of a marching band.

Swannie sang transfixed in rapture lifting him above the numbness of an incessant hangover. His head was clear, and he was happy to be alive to sing with full lungs and sense the tug for high notes and the satisfaction of reaching them. Despair, hopelessness, futility evaporated as he sang the wonderous words, harmonizing with the Heards. Dahlia followed the upbeat Christian soldiers hymn with more mellow tunes, "What a Friend We have in Jesus," "Amazing Grace," "Rock of Ages," and "Revelation."

The hymns followed one another smoothly as though they'd sung them a hundred times before, their voices blending in a community of song. Whole and harmonious, individual identities merged, and for the moment, none were conscious of desires, wants, pains. By the end of the fifth hymn, Dahlia noticed stifled yawns and drooping eyes: "'Amazing Grace,' one more time," she insisted, "and we'll call it quits." She played the hymn lowly, lovingly. . . .

Dahlia lowered the keyboard cover and slid the bench back in place. The others closed their hymnals while Dahlia located a pillow, light blanket, and sheets and gave them to Swannie. She tucked Eddy in bed, said goodnight to Swannie, and closed her bedroom door where Julian was preparing for sleep. Swannie switched off the light, and in the dark, he laid one of the sheets over the sofa and covered himself with the other, tossing the folded blanket on the floor.

He snuggled his head into the pillow but couldn't sleep. The lyrics of the hymns jangled through his head and he couldn't turn them off. He rolled onto his back and mouthed the words repeatedly until his concentration faltered. His mind drifted to the nights he'd spent in the boxcar on Buena Vista Street in Raton where copious noises had crowded the quiet of the night: dogs barking, cars honking, passenger train whistles wailing, one long, two short, signalling entry into the depot—"Bo-o-op! Boop! Boop!" Freight trains coupling and uncoupling, clanging as the freight cars slammed into one another.

Too quiet—he'd grown accustomed to Raton's manifold night noises and couldn't sleep. The deep silence of the coal camp stuffed his head with anticipation, waiting for sounds to pierce the silence, but he heard nothing, not even the deep breathing of the Heards in the next rooms as they slept behind closed doors. Everything was closed, Company store, clubhouse, tipple, and mine. Not a single automobile rattled up or down the canyon road. No spooked dogs barked at phantom intruders.

Finally, in the distance, Swannie heard a faint "wh-o-o-o," a tree owl. "Wh-o-o-o," it hooted again, barely audible through the open window. Swannie's spirits lifted. He slid off the couch and crept quietly to the open window. Swoosh! Dervish demon crows dived through the open window, "gaw, gaw, gaw, gaw." They spun around his face and shoulders and pecked at his eyes and ears. Swannie flailed his arms, backpedaled to the sofa and tripped backwards onto it, and then slid to the floor. "Gaw, gaw, gaw, gaw," the crows pounced on him and pecked their beaks into his eyes, nose, ears.

"I-E-E-E-E-E!" Swannie wailed, "I-E-E-E-E-E!"

Julian switched on the light and popped into the makeshift bedroom followed by Dahlia and Eddy. They watched anxiously while Swannie flip-flopped on the floor, twisting and jerking in a spastic fit. His whole body writhed in convulsions, his legs twitching violently and his hands quaking.

"I-E-E-E-E-E! They're back, them demon crows! I-E-E-E-E-E!" Swannie's wail shrilled throughout the house. "Oh, Lord, get'em out'a here!"

"Swannie!" Julian admonished firmly.

"Oh, Lord, have mercy!"

"Swannie!" Julian grasped Swannie by the shoulders and pulled him to the couch. Wrapping his strong arms around Swannie, Julian sat beside him and kept him from shaking. "Swannie! There-ain't-no-crows-here!"

Scrunched in Julian's warm arms, Swannie hid his face in his hands. "I-E-E-E-E-E!"

Still grasping Swannie, Julian yelled, "It's the jim-jams! You got'em bad." He turned to Dahlia. "Run, fix some strong cowboy coffee. Eddy, git! Go to your room. Let this be a lesson 'bout drinking too much hooch." Julian turned his attention to Swannie. "I'm gonna bearhug you! Till you stop shaking! And, quit your yelling. Soon's Dahlia's back, yer drinking strong java—calm your nerves."

Julian persisted to grasp Swannie for about five minutes, though Swannie's screeches and blathers made the time seem longer.

"I'm nothin' but a lowdown bum. A drunk."

"Yer half right," Julian gently accosted Swannie. "Yer no bum, that's where yer wrong. Too much hooch, is all."

"Bum drunk more like it."

"Nothin' you can't change."

"God's punishing me. He don't like me."

"Why's that?"

"Something I must'a did."

"Naw. He didn't make you a drunk. You made the rut yer in."

"If'n they'd only go away, them crows."

"They're gone."

"You reckon?"

"They're gone."

"They'll be back."

"Never was here, far's I can see. Quit drinking bad hooch. Start eatin' better, an' you'll never imagine them crows again."

"Didn't imagine. Them crows is real."

"No crows. Jist jim-jams."

Dahlia carried a steaming coffeepot into the bedroom and poured a cup. She handed it to Julian, set the pot on the powderbox, and excused herself. Swannie stole a pathetic glance at her and saw a deep frown furrowing her brow. He was ashamed.

Julian slowly lifted the cup to Swannie's shaking lips while grasping his shoulders with the other arm. "Here, help pour down this java."

Swannie lifted his quaking hands to the cup and held it over Julian's hand. They cautiously placed the cup to Swannie's lips and he sipped reluctantly, waiting for it to cool. Before long, Julian grew impaitient and cajoled, "Com'on, chug it!"

After gulping successively, Swannie set the cup down.

"Now, try to relax on the sofa. Count sheep, or whatever fits your fancy. When I can't sleep, I say the alphabet backwards. Makes me sleepy. If'n the jim-jams come back, drink more java."

"Stay?"

"Beg pardon?"

"Please, stay, till I fall asleep." Swannie pleaded like a child afraid of what the dark might bring.

Julian scoffed to himself. "The yokel's a little kid—wants me to tuck him to sleep."

"Honey?" Dahlia called from the bedroom. "Everything okay now?"

"Yes, honey. You and Eddy get to sleep." Julian had no choice. Leave Swannie alone, and he'd soon be screaming and yelling and nobody would sleep. Julian relented and turned to Swannie. "Okay, for a while. We'll play blackjack whilst we wait for you to sleep."

Julian found a deck of cards in the kitchen and brought them back into the makeshift bedroom. He shuffled them. "Ever play?"

"With my Pa, when I was a kid."

"I play with no jokers. Aces are one or eleven." Julian dealt two cards down for Swannie, two for himself, and asked, "Want another?"

Swannie peeped at his cards and started to count on his fingers.

"In your head."

"Do tell."

"Count in your head. Not your fingers."

"Don't know how."

"Learn how! When you count on your fingers, you tell me what cards yer a'holding."

"Phew! Not sure I can."

"Do it. Counting in your head will tire you out. You'll soon be sleeping like a baby."

Swannie struggled to count in his head, which was difficult for him, and he tired after only a few hands. "Phew, I reckon I might sleep."

"Good." Julian switched off the light and heard Swannie mutter, "Thanks, pal."

FIVE   WHO CALLS THE SHOTS?

MONDAY MORNING CLATTER DIDN'T MATTER. Swannie slept soundly, gradually waking to sizzling bacon and perking coffee. He stretched his legs and splayed his toes, sea-sawing his ankles, stretching his back, and bursting with glory—stone-cold sober, body didn't ache, and no cobwebs to clear. He was a bit groggy but glad to be awake, wallowing in the soft sofa cushions. They didn't shove back like the bristled ridges of the boxcar floor or the gutter's cold concrete where he recently awoke, stiff and cold. Rolling off the sofa, he lounged lazily on the throw rug, whiffing the sizzling bacon and perking coffee when he realized it must be at least 8:00 a.m., the Heards busy and about.

Awkwardly, he struggled to slip into Jimmy's bib overalls. His legs jammed until he unsnapped the rivets at the waist. Then he grappled with the bib straps tangled behind his back, crisscrossed, and raveled into a knot. He hobbled into the kitchen, squirming to unravel the straps.

"How'd you sleep?" Dahlia giggled watching him grapple with the straps.

"Good, good."

"Scrunched on the sofa?"

"Beats a boxcar." He fumbled with the straps some more, turning his back to Dahlia. "Say, can you help me with these ornery straps?"

She set down the spatula, untied the knotted straps, and pointed to the washbasin filled with warm water and a towel beside it. She snapped ahold the spatula and resumed turning the bacon in the frying pan. "Swannie, when you're finished there, fetch a couple eggs from the hen house."

"A queer notion," Swannie thought. He knew hens laid eggs, but how were they gathered? He didn't know and didn't ask, already feeling the buffoon about the bib overalls. At the chicken coop, a rankled rooster blocked the door to the henhouse, strutting and squawking. Swannie scooped and spat on a handful of pebbles, tossing them to the backside of the coop. The rooster scooted after them, clearing Swannie's path. Inside, the hens sat in their nests, cocked their heads, and stared at him blankly. Swannie saw no eggs and walked back into the kitchen.

"No eggs."

"You're cuckoo. Hens won't hand you their eggs. Just reach-on under a hen and gently nudge her aside. You'll feel the eggs."

Swannie returned to the henhouse bent on fighting for access but the rooster still pecked at the shiny stones and wasn't interested in territorial disputes. Inside the henhouse, Swannie approached a nest and slowly slipped a hand beneath a hen's warm, feathered belly until he felt two eggs at his fingertips. He grabbed an egg and pocketed it carefully. He grabbed again. The hen cocked her head to the side, fully expecting Swannie to take the second egg. He did and returned to the kitchen, proudly handing the eggs to Dahlia, who cracked the warm shells on the edge of the frying pan and poured the eggs into the bacon grease. They sizzled, popped, and settled into a simmer.

Puffed up proudly over his victorious coup with the rooster and hens, he sat at the table and noticed everything in the kitchen served a practical purpose down to the nails in the wainscoting holding blackened pots, kettles, skillets, and Number-2 tin tubs. The cookstove and a powder box filled with coal sat in the northeast corner. Beside them, a tall, narrow washbasin and a bucket of drinking water shared a powder box. In the corner furthest from the cookstove, cupboard and pantry stood side by side.

Curtains Dahlia had made from cotton flour sacks were drawn to shut out the heat of day and keep out the insects. Last night, the drapes were opened to allow a crossbreeze. With Chicorico at 6,666 feet above sea level, insects rarely pestered at night. The kitchen was a clean, well-lighted place, bare and spare, the walls without framed pictures or shelved knick-knacks. Although Dahlia cooked with fat and lard, the kitchen's snow-white walls were not matted with the smoky effluence of fat and lard, nor did the kitchen smell stale like yesterday's grease.

"That white paint sure is bright. Do you paint the kitchen every year?"

"Every other year." Dahlia talked over her shoulder, still frying at the stove. "It's not paint. More like whitewash. Manuel Montaño brings it from down south in Ribera, where his folks live. He calls it 'yeso.' It's gypsum, common as weeds down that-a-way."

Dahlia carried the skillet to the table and served crispy slices of bacon and eggs simmering in bacon fat. "Here's the salt, pepper. Don't rush breakfast." Dahlia set the skillet on the stove, poured a cup of coffee, and sat at the table. "Julian left for work early so he could talk to Mr. Bowers about you. You'll be expected but no special time."

Swannie salted the eggs thoroughly. "Ma'am, er, Dahlia, got any chili powder?" he asked politely while breaking the bacon slices into bits and sprinkling them over the eggs. "Rather than pepper."

"Yes, certainly." Dahlia took a jar of chili powder from the cupboard and placed it on the table. "Where'd you learn to do that?"

"Mexican lady, Mrs. Jiron." Swannie spread the chili powder over the eggs. "She and her girls was my neighbors in the boxcar next to mine. Time to time, she invited me over for *huevos rancheros*. Shore good with warm tortillas."

"Sounds tasty, but stop wolfing your food. Eat slow."

"Sorry, ma'am, er Dahlia. Sure tastes good, me being sober and all."

"When you're done, should be time to go to the mine. Ask for Mr. Homer Bowers, the General Manager. If he isn't in, ask for Karl Linderman." Dahlia brought the coffeepot from the stove. "Some more coffee?"

"Please. Would'a thought I had enough last night." Swannie lifted his cup. "Julian mentioned Mr. Bowers. Who's Linderman?"

"You'll soon find out. He'll let you know. Too big for his breeches, like our rooster. He sure let you know who rules the roost, didn't he?"

Swannie stopped wolfing the huevos rancheros long enough to answer Dahlia's question with a crooked smile.

"Like you and Julian, Mr. Linderman served in France during the War. He was some kind of officer. Like our rooster, he struts around mighty pompous, full of himself. To his credit, his black leather belt, holster, and combat boots gleam with the luster that comes with persistent rubbing of polish and plenty of spit."

"Hmmm." Swannie nodded his head.

"He's a bit of a four-flusher. Likes to throw his weight around. Always carries a gun."

"Really, how come?"

"Say, more coffee?" Before Swannie could answer, she poured the last of the pot. "We might as well finish it. I don't get much a chance to chat with company. Mr. Linderman carries a gun 'cause he's head of security, a Baldwin-Felts guard contracted to the Company."

"Who calls the shots?"

"Mr. Bowers. Gets Mr. Linderman to do his dirty work."

Weighman James Osgood, a scrawny young man of about twenty-five belligerently directed Swannie to the lamphouse on the tipple, indicating the operation's office next door in a fading brown, wooden shed. Swannie found Bowers sitting at his desk and Linderman across the desk from him. Everything was dusty.

The cluttered office shelves contained ledgers of each miner's credits and debits. Dusty, unread copies of the *Engineering and Mining Journal* and the *Industrial Bulletin* sat on another shelf. Above the unread journals, a production chart was nailed to a joist. Swannie quickly noted the chart's line since Julian had mentioned it. The slumping line represented tonnage of coal produced at the mine by the year. It started at a high point in 1917, leveled off in 1918 and 1919. The line plummeted precipitously and dipped in 1928 to the bottom, left hand corner of the chart when coal production was so low record keeping didn't matter anymore.

"I'm looking for Mr. Homer Bowers."

"Speaking." Bowers remained sitting. He was a slight man with a thick crop of sandy gray hair contrasting with a jet-black stiletto mustache. His rimless, octagon eyeglasses amplified his mousy eyes. He wore wool dress slacks and a starched white shirt with garters strapped around its long sleeves.

"Mr. Julian Heard sent me." Swannie took a tiny knife from his pocket and nervously picked his fingernails.

Julian had mentioned Swannie to Bowers, but he remained nonplused, squinting, then smirking. "Don't say."

"Said you might have work for me."

"What can you do?" Best known for exceeding the niggardly standards established by Ebenezer Scrooge in Charles Dicken's *A Christmas Carol*, Bowers could recite any miner's indebtedness on any given day without looking in the ledgers.

"Most anything."

"He can't hold his hooch," Karl Linderman said scarcastically. He sulked in his chair while Homer interviewed Swannie. "He's a drunk!"

Swannie started at Linderman's blunt insult.

Linderman slunk like a tall drink of water, a bulging chest and tiny waist. As Dahlia said, he wore a wide, black leather cartridge belt, holster, and a .45-caliber pistol issued to U.S. Army officers. Minus the chevrons and insignias, his drab olive green Army uniform was wrinkled and soiled.

Swannie stopped picking his fingernails and pocketed his knife. He recognized Linderman from boot camp. "Say, wasn't you boot camp D.I. in San Antone?"

"For a spell. What's it to you?"

"Probably don't recognize me."

"Nope, you was a cipher. Lot'a boys come through on the way to France." Linderman pinched his lower lip, eyed Swannie carefully, and then turned to Bowers. "Like I said, he's nothing but a drunk. He's no miner. Can you shoot?"

"Thirty-ought-six. Good as any doughboy."

"Don't need soldiers. Can you shoot dynamite?"

"Do tell."

"Discharge dynamite. Fire in the hole."

"Guess if'n they was a call to."

"I'd lay odds you can't etch coal."

"Do tell."

"Dig coal with a pick."

"Reckon I'd learn."

"Ack, yer no miner. Can't shoot. Can't etch coal. Can you play ball?"

"Good as any boy."

"Boys play softball. Hardball players is needed to skunk Dawson." Linderman turned to Bowers. "He can't do much."

"But, he's a doughboy."

"So's the jig-a-boo."

"Karl, you gotta watch your manners. Learn to talk proper. That's Mr. Heard in my office."

"Well, you wouldn't give him an outside job."

"Go easy on this lad. He's white, an' he ain't no Dago or Greazer, neither. That ought'a count for something."

"Not much with the Super."

"Super won't know and don't care. Long's we make'a profit. I'll put the lad to work, outside—won't cost nothin'."

"Yer callin' the shots," Linderman grumbled, turning on Swannie. "See, here! I'm chief of security." Linderman poked a thumb against Swannie's chest. "Homer calls the shots. I back him. Get here on time. Don't leave early. No drinking on the job. One more thing, you see any women or their brats collecting coal along the tracks, you tell me or Homer."

"Yes, sir, you got my word."

"See to it." Linderman sauntered out the office and walked toward the mine.

"Didn't think he worked in the mine."

"He don't. Takes a walk into the hills this time a'day."

"What for?"

"Never you mind." Still sitting at the desk, Bowers cocked his head in the direction of the lamp house. "Lamp man's out. Tend the lamps for now. The miners'll keep you straight. Where you bunking?"

"With the Heards. They've been mighty good to me."

"Won't do. Might be room at the boardinghouse."

"No thanks."

"I can't allow you to live with them."

"Why not?"

"I won't quibble with you. You'll pay rent."

"Say, there is one more thing." Swannie lightly rubbed his hands. "Don't want to appear rude, but I've always wondered, well, uh—"

"Time's wasting, out with your question!"

"Well, why does a man like you wear garters around his arms?"

Abashed, Bowers's face flushed and he blathered, "What? Why . . . why, blast it! Them ain't women garters, they're, uh, they're bandeaus."

"Didn't mean nothin' by it." Swannie wiped off his habitual grin and defended himself, "It's jist I seen other savvy men wearing them."

"I use'em to pull up my sleeves and hold'em. Keeps the cuffs clean. Look'a the dust in here. The missus, why she'd be washing and ironing shirts all the time."

Swannie realized he'd overstepped his shaky start and quickly injected, "'Course, I seen professional gamblers wear them bandeaus. Keeps them honest—no dealing from the cuffs."

Bowers was somewhat placated, leering over the rims of his glasses. "I like you, boy, but Karl doesn't. Best you remember who butters your toast."

"Thanks for the job." Swannie offered a handshake. "You won't be sorry."

Bowers crossed his arms without shaking Swannie's hand, grumbling, "I already am."

The workday ended and the Jolly trolley motorcar whirred from the mine pulling coal cars full of big, black lumps of coal and men— young men, old men, stout men, thin men, bearded men, mustached men, scar-faced men, and baby-faced men, all sooty black, their garb, faces, and hands powdered with coal dust. They joked, jested, and jostled in Spanish, English, Italian, Serbian, and other Slavic dialects while scampering off the electric motor train. For the most part, they were glad to be alive and done with work for the day.

Swannie recognized Julian because he walked erect, shoulders thrown back, and the goggle rings around his eyes were brown rather than white. "Wait on me?" Swannie asked, checking Julian's carbide lamp.

"Catch up." Julian unlatched his lamp.

Swannie finished checking lamps and caught up with Julian and two other miners under the tipple where they walked onto the tracks heading east toward the coal camp.

"Swannie's boarding with us a spell." Julian swatted Swannie's shoulder. "Did'ja get an outside job."

"You betcha."

"Good. Swannie, this here's Manuel Montaño, and the other black man is Onorio Chicarelli."

"*Buono incontrare.*" (Good to meet you.) Onorio shook Swannie's hand and chortled, slapping Manuel's shoulder. "Hoo! Who's blackest?"

"Me—end of summer."

"Ha, Manuel, you'll never be black. Brown, yes, but not black."

"Goggle rings tell on you. They'll wash." Julian turned to Swannie. "Pay these fellers no mind. So Bowers put you on?"

"Yep. That feller Linderman didn't like it."

"*Guardare!*" (Watch out for those two!) Onorio warned cautiously, placing a hand on Swannie's shoulder. "They're bad eggs. They say play by the rules, but they change the rules." Onorio changed his tone. "Glad you got a job. *Lei giocca boccie?*"

Swannie grinned crookedly and then contorted his lips. He knew Onorio had asked a question but didn't understand Italian.

"Best speak English. He's from Raton," Julian said.

"Boccie, horseshoes, do you play?"

"Horseshoes."

Onorio slapped Swannie hardily on the back while stepping away from the tracks. "Pitch some shoes, play boccie with us sometime." Onorio left the tracks, walked to his gate, turned, and hollered at Swannie, "Well, what about it?"

Swannie stopped walking and shouted back, "Thought you was makin' small talk."

"Onorio doesn't ever make small talk." Julian nudged Swannie. "Not about boccie." Two doors down, Manuel left the tracks to his house but not before repeating the warning about Linderman and Bowers. Julian and Swannie continued down the tracks. At home,

Julian brushed off the coal dust and washed at the pump in the backyard. Swannie spotted Eddy shooing chickens into the coop.

"Chickens a bother?"

"They'll eat the marbles." Eddy took Swannie's hand and led him onto the meadow that sprawled back of the houses from the Heard's west to the Chiracelli's house. A cavvy of boys crouched in a circle on the ground.

"Been here all day?" Swannie had noticed the boys in the morning when he left the house to walk to the mine. They were almost in the same spot.

"Pretty near, except for chores and lunch."

"What's going on?"

"Tournament."

"Marbles?"

"Shh."

"Who's them boys?"

"Perkovich brothers, Nick, George, Roddy, and Max."

"They look serious."

"They're the best. Shhh, no talking. They wanna finish fast."

"What's the rush?"

"They gotta pick coal 'long the tracks, take it home."

After the game broke, Swannie and Eddy walked home for supper. Eddy grumbled, "Papa won't let me play till I practice more. He says other boys'll win all my marbles."

"He's right. Gotta practice or lose your marbles. "

"Mr. Swanson, will you play with me so's I can practice?"

"Sure," Swannie's answered perfunctorily, assuming Eddy would forget the promise.

SIX   GOT A SHOOTER?

EDDY DIDN'T FORGET. Early the following Saturday morning, Eddy and Arturo Montaño marched into the kitchen while Swannie finished breakfast. "Mr. Swanson, this is Arturo, my best friend. His Pa is Mr. Montaño. You know him. Arturo's got a little sister, Angela, too small to play with us big boys."

"Well, howdy there, Arturo." They shook hands.

"For Christmas, Pa gave me a bag'a marbles." Out of a Bull Durham tobacco bag, Eddy spilled the marbles onto the table. "Look'a the sparkling agates, rubies, and cloudys."

Swannie fingered through the marbles, asking, "Which is your taw?"

"Huh?"

"Your shooter. You gotta have one."

"Oh, sure. I knew that."

Swannie rolled a marble under his thumb across his palm and the ridges of his fingers. He leaned to the side of the chair and flicked his thumb. The marble shot across the slick oak floor.

"Whis-s-s-s-s," Eddy and Arturo whistled through their teeth.

"This'll do—my shooter." Again, Swannie rolled the marble in his palms.

"Out!" Dahlia ordered playfully. "Kitchen's my shop."

Outside, Swannie drew a small circle in the dusty, flat ground of the meadow where the older boys shot marbles on a regular basis.

"Pretty small circle," Arturo observed.

"We wanna play like other boys," Eddy chimed in.

"Okay, but yer gonna have a hard time again' me." Swannie scuffed out the small circle and drew a much larger one. "Here's the rules. Each player pitches a marble into the center of the circle. Your turn-to-play is decided by where your marble lands. The marble closest to the center goes first, second, and so on. Stand at the line and throw your shooter."

The boys stared blankly.

"Well, get your shooters, let's start."

"Be jist a minute," Eddy hedged.

"Yah, sure," Arturo stalled.

Neither boy had a shooter.

"Mostly, jist take any that feels good. Not too big or small." Swannie grinned as he deliberately tossed his marble to the edge of the circle while Eddy and Arturo fingered through Eddy's fine collection, seeking the perfect shooter. When they found one, they took turns tossing their shooters into the circle.

"I'm first."

"No, I'm first."

"Hold it boys. Might be a tie." Swannie dropped to his knees. Using hand spans, he measured the distances. "Arturo's first."

"Let's re-throw," Eddy whined.

"Naw, I wanna go first."

"Re-throw!"

"Go first!"

"I done called it." Swannie ended the tiff. "There's no advantage to going first. All's you do is splatter the marbles to kingdom come without knocking any out. The second shooter has an easy time of it."

"Okay, let's shoot." Eddy was mollified. "No keepers." Eddy spilled the bag of marbles into the center of the circle.

Swannie coached both boys about the proper way to hold their taw by making a fist with their thumbs inside the palms, placing it inside the index finger, and then flicking their thumbs. "Your thumb's like the hammer of a pistol—hits the marble, and blam!"

Arturo shot and splattered the marbles. None crossed the line. Eddy followed. He knocked two marbles out. Swannie deliberately missed at his first attempt.

Arturo skeptically eyed Swannie. "Not very good, are you?"

"Been a while." Swannie's crooked smile betrayed him.

"Naw, yer going easy 'cause we're kids."

"No good that way," Eddy shook his head.

Arturo kicked the ground and the dust layered over the toes that protruded from his shoes. "You probably weren't any good when you was a kid."

"Say, what's the foofarow?"

"We gotta play somebody better to get better."

"Shoot-a-mighty, I can wup the both of you."

"Prove it."

"Let's do her."

Arturo took his turn and knocked out two more marbles. Eddy followed with two. Swannie shot in earnest but was starting to tremble and missed, though Julian and he had been up again Friday night drinking coffee. Soon Eddy and Arturo emptied the ring.

Swannie grasped his hands, as if in prayer, and clenched them tightly to quell the jim-jams shakes. The boys' frisky exuberance eased Swannie's nerves, the quaking slowed, and the boy in Swannie swelled. "Let's go again. Pitch, see who's first."

Swannie won the pitch. Eddy and Arturo positioned the marbles in the ring. Splatt! Swannie's first shot scattered the marbles evenly. Arturo shot. His taw dribbled onto the ground, rolled erratically, and smacked out a marble. He repeated and failed. Eddy knocked out a marble. Game crept, finally ended with Swannie winning, quaking halted. Eddy gathered his marbles.

Swannie felt great and suggested a round of "follows." "I shoot. Arturo, you shoot an' try to hit me. Then, Eddy can shoot at either marble. When you hit a feller, then you go first. 'Follows' is a good way to hone your shooting for accuracy and distance." The boys listened intently as Swannie coached on the finer points of shooting. "Shoot with one knuckle touching the ground. Hold your spot till the taw's shot. No fudging, pinching, or throwing the taw. You must shoot by the flick of the thumb. If'n your taw slips out'a hand, holler 'slips,' and you get one more try. When yer shooting, it's common courtesy for other fellers to shut up, allowing you to concentrate on the shot."

Off they trailed curling their tongues to the sides of their mouths and shooting marbles in hot pursuit for a short while before they tired and scampered home, momentarily leaving Swannie alone. He sat in the grass, rubbed his nose in it, and whiffed the musty odor of the dew. Dainty gnats and nits nimbly swirled skyward, dodging his face. . . . Soon the boys returned with metal axle-ring hoops taken from the mule-drawn freight wagons that once hauled coal from the mines. The boys rolled the shiny hoops with a short, firm wire bent at one end into a U-shape, like a branding iron.

Rolling the hoops over tufts of grass and dodging stones, the boys sped through an obstacle course in the meadow—grassy tussocks, rusting cans, cactus spikes. They raced across the meadow toward the Heard's where they cruised the dusty path, rolling. Raced to the Montaño's, rolling, rolling. Pivoted and sped back west on the path passing the Heard house, rolling, rolling, rolling, and dashed speedily by Chicarelli's, rolling, rolling, rolling.

SEVEN

SLIVERS, SCALES, AND SCRIP

"HERE, TRY THIS ONE FOR SIZE." Bowers lifted a lamp by the wires. "Boys'll be using these new electric lamps. Safer than the carbide."

"What's that thing-a-ma-jig?" Swannie ran his fingers along the electric wires running from the headlamp to a leather casing hooked to his belt.

"Battery pack. Your job is to recharge the batteries. Plug'em in and let'em set all night."

"Shouldn't be hard."

"Piece of cake. Check'em out in the morning. Check'em in end of the day. Assign a battery to each man. Keep a record of the recharge."

"What for?"

"Dock a small fee for the recharge. Covers the cost of electricity."

"Hooey! Thought you generated your own electricity."

"Still costs. B'sides, it's a pittance."

"Boys won't like it, charging to use the lamps."

"Got no gripe about these lamps. They're much safer."

"Any complaints, I'll send them to you."

"You'll do no such thing! They, they got, they got no choice," Bowers stammered. "They're money mad, these foreign miners. Look'a here." Bowers opened *Mining Magazine* to the editorial page and read aloud: "'A large number of mine accidents were caused by the carelessness of those killed or injured.' Article goes on to say foreign miners are ignorant and greedy, willing to cut corners on safety jist to make a little more money."

"Lemme see somethin'." Swannie glanced at the magazine's cover. "March, 1906. Mighty old magazine."

"Doesn't matter, nothing's changed. Yer gonna hear lot'a gripes. They're stubborn about safety, these foreigners."

"Who's all these foreigners yer talkin' about?"

"Miners here—the Mexicans, Slavs, Eye-talians."

"That's most the miners. Some of them have Papas that was miners before them. They're no more foreigners than us."

"Küh! Yer as bullheaded as them. Don't forget—yer one of us. Don't forget who's buttering your bread. Go help Osgood. He's the weighman, a Company man. Doesn't take bull."

Swannie ambled to the west side of the tipple and recognized the surly young man who'd directed him to Bower's office. James Osgood ran the scale that weighed each coal car for tonnage. After digging coal from a seam, a miner loaded it into a coal car and hooked his brass "check" to the car. The coal car was pulled out of the mine to the west side of the tipple and weighed. Osgood's practice was to estimate the amount of slack, rock, and debris in the load and deduct that amount from the load's measure of coal. Osgood kept the check, a brass token stamped with the miner's number, to record the miner's output, which he reported to Bowers who calculated the miner's wages based on the tonnage excavated at seventy-five cents a ton.

"You Osgood?"

"Yeah, so what?"

"I'm here to help you."

"Don't need no help." Osgood rapped his knuckles on his forehead.

"Here 'cause Bowers sent me."

"Yeah, sure. 'Fore long, he'll fire me." Again, Osgood rapped his knuckles on his forehead. "An' give you my job at lower wages."

Swannie retrieved his pocketknife and picked at his fingernails. "Don't fret. Bowers don't think much of me."

"Humph! See to it you don't meddle when the boys argue, hear?" He glowered and Swannie glanced away. Osgood softened his tone. "That's some toad stabber."

Swannie handed the knife to Osgood. He inspected it and handed it back. "Put it to good use. Find some kindling. Whittle it down into itty-bitty slivers. About the width of an ant's butt. Bring'em to me."

Swannie scoured a lumber scrap heap and selected the stub of a two-by-four. He shaved four thin slivers into the width and length of tongue depressors and gave them to Osgood.

"Them's perfect." Osgood admired the slivers before wedging them between the scales' pressure plates.

"Scales need adjusting?"

"Might say compensating. Linderman ordered it. Make things even. Miners griped I scotched them by deducting too much for the slack."

"Do tell."

"Slack! Don't you know nuthin'? Them's the tailings, shale and such, comes when the coal's dug. Worthless as a Christmas tree in July. Company don't pay for slack, jist pure coal."

"How'd you measure slack?"

"Eyeball it, like when I worked the seams. Now we gotta weigh it. Bowers raised the per-ton amount by five cents 'cause the boys griped too much. Suits me fine. No more eye balling. Scales don't lie."

"These do."

"No fault of mine! Linderman saw to that with them slivers ratcheting the scale." Osgood glowered. Swannie turned his face aside, gazing over Osgood's shoulder and avoiding Osgood's hard eyes. "Get used to it. Yer a Company man. Linderman's the feller you gotta watch. He's mean and don't want us siding with the miners."

"Thought I was a team member."

"Company team." Osgood was confused by Swannie's evasive glance and crooked smile. Like Julian but much younger, Osgood started mining as a boy of ten and had learned the trade from the ground up. In the tipple, he worked as a breaker boy culling coal, and in the mine, he worked as trapper, opening and closing ventilation doors. When old enough, he advanced to underground mining from which he was quickly advanced to a relatively safe outside job. "I kin see yer new to mining. You'll see lot'a things don't look right. Well, keep your trap shut. Ignorance is bliss, mark my word." Osgood rapped his head with his knuckles.

"Say? Why do ya tap your head that-a-way?"

"Knocking on wood."

"Errrrrrrrrr," a Jolly trolley motorcar whirred toward the tipple pulling loaded coal cars. "Here come some cars. Push'em onto the scale. Read the check. Bark out the number. I'll record the weight."

The stubby, squatty coal cars were originally designed to haul ore from mines by mules. Now an electrically powered trolley motorcar pulled them on the tracks from the mine to the tipple's scale. The motorman drove over the scale, uncoupled the motorcar from the coal car train, and returned to the mine to wait for more loaded coal cars. Swannie uncoupled each coal car, shoved it onto the scale, and barked its check number to Osgood, who recorded the weight of the haul. Then, Swannie and Osgood shoved the car further along the tipple tracks to chutes where the coal was culled and cleaned.

At the end of the day, Swannie complained to Bowers. "Osgood rigged the scales."

"Did'ja flip your lid?"

"He made me whittle some slivers and slipped'em between the pressure plates. The scales underweigh that-a-way."

"That ain't none of your concern. Jist keep your trap shut. Remember yer a Company man." Bowers pitched an envelope to Swannie. "Here's your wages."

Swannie opened the envelope and found a spreadsheet itemizing his hours on the job by the week with deductions for the time Bowers had taken to teach the job and for rent at the Heards. "Where the cash?"

"It's there."

"These?" Swannie held forth paper coupons.

"Paying you in scrip."

"Company men, too?"

"Some."

"Meaning me. . . . Don't seem right."

"Scrip's good as money anywhere in Chicorico and the other Company camps."

"Prices are a lot higher than Raton."

"Company's having a hard time making a profit."

"What about charging rent? I ain't renting from the Company."

"Charging you the same rate as the boardinghouse. It's your choice, living with the Negroes. They don't think anything of packing a house chock-full and making money by it."

"They're not charging me."

"They're taking business from me, even they don't charge you. You plan to give'em some of your paycheck?"

"Well, yes, I suppose."

"Before you know it, the Slavs, Mexicans, and Eye-talians with try to pull a fast one. They're greedy, I tell you. They'll all be renting till the houses burst at the seams."

"Julian Heard's already paying rent on the house."

"Not that much, fifteen dollars a month."

"What's his wages?"

"Seventy-five cents a ton."

"Sounds good, till you do the arithmetic. Twenty tons to make the rent. Comes to forty thousands pounds of digging and shoveling coal a month jist to pay the rent."

"That's not much for Julian. B'sides, he can charge food at the Company store."

"Prices are inflated. Dahlia showed me an ad for groceries at Snodgrass Food Store in Raton. Seems the potatoes were, uh. . . . Look'a here." Swannie spotted a copy of the Raton Range setting in a pile of magazines. He opened it and recited:

"Potatoes, U.S. No. 1, 100 pounds $1.49
Pure Lard, Pike Peak, 8-pound pail 1.28
Flour, Major C, 48-pound bag.......................................1.85
Mexican beans, 4 pounds ....25 cents"

"That's not the whole ball of wax."

"Yer darn tootin' that ain't! Prices at the Company store twenty percent higher."

"We gotta make a profit. Twenty percent barely covers shipping and handling."

"On the Santa Fé?"

"Every day, pretty near."

"Don't get a deal for the coal business you give'em?"

"Maybe we do. Maybe we don't. What's it to you? Finances ain't your call." Nervously, Bowers pressed his lips, slipped out his tongue, and flicked it along his moustache. Brushing the saliva from his moustache, he wiped his hand on the leg of his trousers. "Swannie, my boy, I like you, but you ask too many questions—too smart for your own good." He leered at Swannie. "We're talking 'bout you. I told you the first day, best you see about bunking in the boardinghouse."

"Don't seem fair."

"You got a job, don't you?"

"Yeah, but—"

"The boys share jobs, each working one or two days a week. Keeps 'em employed, food on the table, a roof over their heads, and the mine keeps operating, producing coal."

"They never have cash to buy things in Raton."

"They're grateful to have jobs. They got all they need right here in the camp. B'sides, this isn't a prison. They can work wherever they want. It's a free country. Same with you—nobody holding you here."

That evening at dinner, Swannie gave Dahlia the scrip. "You're too generous." She thanked Swannie while quickly counting it.

"Think nothing of it. You treat me better than family, an' I wanna pull my weight."

"Let's wait till after dinner to talk business," Julian chided. "Dinner's for thankfulness. Let's enjoy it. Now pass the greens."

Swannie passed the greens and sat quietly eating. Eddy popped a question, "Mr. Swanson, are you a Company man?"

"Jist a flunky."

"Arturo said you weren't a miner."

"I'm no miner, that's certain."

"So it's true. Yer a Company man."

Julian looked at Swannie, and then Eddy. "More like he's an outside man. He works outside the mine."

"Boy howdy! It's real work, but none too hard."

"What'd you do today?"

"Mostly help Mr. Osgood with the scales."

"What's that?"

"Well, when your Pa loads a coal car, it's hauled out the mine, and weighed on a scale to see how much coal's in the car."

"Honey," Dahlia interrupted, "be polite. Let Mr. Swanson eat."

"No bother, an' I don't mind none." Swannie turned to Eddy. "Digging coal is how your Pa puts food on the table and pays the rent—by the tonnage he digs out the mine."

"Wow, that's important."

"You bet. So's the weighman's job. He weighs how much your Pa picks."

"What if he makes a mistake?"

"He shouldn't. The scales are right on the money. Checked by the State Mine Inspector." Swannie glimpsed at Julian. "'Course, might be some chicanery with the scales."

"Pardon?" Julian set his fork on his plate and stopped eating.

"Chic-cain-er-ree?" Eddy pronounced the word phonetically.

"A lie." Dahlia laid down her fork to answer Eddy's question.

"Like a fib?"

By the confused look on Eddy's face, Dahlia discerned he was grappling with the difference between deceptive speech and devious action. "It's no white lie. More like a bad deed. A lie is when you speak false words. When you do something wrong, that's a bad deed."

"Which is baddest?"

"They're both bad, but—"

"Enough questions! End of discussion." Julian abruptly blunted Eddy's curiosity. "Chicanery's a mighty powerful word. I'll be speaking with Mr. Swanson after supper."

"Is it a curse word, Papa?"

"No, son. Mr. Swanson didn't blaspheme. Jist too strong for dinner-talk."

"Beg pardon, I didn't mean to—"

"Now, Swannie," Dahlia mediated, "pay no mind. I got carried away, too."

After dinner, Julian ushered Swannie to the backporch. "Dahlia don't need help with the dishes tonight. Eddy's gonna help her." They sat on the porch steps out of earshot from the kitchen where Julian asked Swannie to explain the chicanery he'd seen. Then, Julian decided it was time to caucus. "Do me a favor, fetch Manuel and send him over to Onorio's."

While Swannie ambled to Manuel's, Julian stepped into the kitchen. "Going over to see Manuel and Onorio."

"Something wrong?"

"Jist man talk." Julian hesitated. "We're having wine. Ask Swannie to practice hymns."

"That'll be a joy."

At the Chicarelli's, Onorio, Julian, and Manuel descended into the cellar. Onorio ushered them to the dank, secluded room where he kept his best stock of wine. Onorio switched on the light, bolted the door from the inside, and poured each a small glass of wine. They sat on the cool earthen benches of the cellar.

"Swannie tells me Osgood's up to no good."

"What's he up to now?"

"Linderman and Osgood, they're in cahoots." Julian explained how Osgood had Swannie whittle two slivers and wedge them between the scales' pressure plates.

"Back to his old tricks," Onorio observed. "Now, we need a miner to check him."

"Linderman put Osgood up to it. The snotty-nose kid don't stand up to Linderman or Bowers. Used to be, the kid was a miner, like us. Now, he's a lap dog. Loyal to the Company, milking it for all he can get."

"We're part of the Company," Manuel added. "Without us, there's no coal. Time we had a union."

Julian and Onorio took a sip of wine and glanced at each other to avoid Manuel's eyes. Talk of union made them nervous.

"We gotta talk about it, among ourselves, at least," Manuel spoke guardedly. "It's not one thing, it's another. We gotta use battery lamps instead of carbide, and we gotta pay to charge the batteries. We complain about not getting paid for deadwork. Bowers pays us a nickel more per-ton to cover the timbering and digging we gotta do to get at the coal. Then, what happens? On the Q.T., Linderman orders Osgood to rig the scales and steals back the raise Bowers gave us by under-weighing our loads."

A hush fell. They were familiar with Linderman's chicanery in Ludlow, and with his presence in Chicorico, talk of union was imminently more dangerous.

Manuel took a sip of wine. "We don't have support. Most fellers are scared—afraid they'll get evicted and blacklisted."

"Or, killed, like Ludlow," Onorio added.

"We're alone," Julian lamented.

"That's the way it's always been," Onorio said. "Every man for himself."

"Doesn't have to be that way. We always lose against the Company. If'n we act alone, we hang alone." Manuel added, "That's why we gotta hang together. We need a way to get the fellers to understand—by hanging together, we can force the Company men to respect us."

"Bowers won't like it."

"Don't want him to like it. I want him to respect us—like he respects rattlesnakes."

Julian stared at the earthen floor while Onorio shifted his weight and shook his head. "In the old a'country," Onorio muttered, "we dreamed in America we would have jobs . . . own a house . . . be our own men."

"We won't be our own men until we have some push against the Company. We gotta make the Company respect us as men—not machines."

"Mules more like it."

"In the good old days before electric machines, mules got more respect than men."

"That's 'cause they was harder to replace. A good mule was hard to find. And, cost lots. Men? Well, there was plenty of us suckers needed jobs."

"This palaver won't get us anywhere," Julian inserted. "Union's too dangerous. You saw what happened in Ludlow. Linderman was there, too. Now, he's here, toting a .45."

"Maybe," Manuel cautiously crafted his words. "We should talk to Bowers—the three of us—without Linderman."

"Lot'a good that would do."

"Onorio! Julian! You know Company won't give us anything. We gotta take it. We got to make Bowers and Linderman listen to us, *mano a mano*. In numbers, there's strength. So we divide and conquer. We catch Bowers alone. Wait for Linderman to make himself scarce, like when he skips up the canyon into the hills. We corner Bowers."

Julian and Onorio listened intently as Manuel described a plan to confront Bowers. . . . In about a week, Swannie sneaked away from work to Julian's house and announced Linderman had pulled one of his disappearing acts. The three miners waited for Swannie to return to work. Early that afternoon, Onorio, Julian, and Manuel found Bowers alone in his office working at the books. "Howdy, Homer," Manuel opened the conversation.

"Come in boys. Grab a chair." Bowers was lounging. He kicked his legs off the desk. "What's going on with you boys?"

They remained standing. "Won't take much time," Manuel continued to speak. "We want you to know we're pleased the Company upped our per-ton wages for hauls."

"Yep," Julian injected obsequiously. "Sure glad to be paid for deadwork."

Onorio and Manuel shook their heads in agreement.

"Glad to hear that boys. Fair's fair, I always say."

"We knew you'd say that. That's why we're here."

A fly buzzed by the men and dived at a half-eaten cookie sitting on the desk. Bowers swept his hand across the desk and sent the cookie and fly whirling in the air. The cookie landed on the floor. Bowers didn't bother to pick it up. "Come'on boys, set a spell. Don't act like strangers."

"We're comfortable standing," Manuel persevered. "We hear John rigged the scales."

"What? Who's talking loco?"

"Heard it—miner's Western Union."

"Gossip, alls it is. Surprised you boys listen to the bull. You know some of these miners. They'd complain if 'n I hung them with a new rope." Bowers snorted loudly at his own joke. "You boys aren't like that."

"Thank you, Homer." Tactfully, Manuel persisted to drive home his point. "Yer a man of your word. That's why we're here. Do we have your word the scales aren't rigged?"

"You got it!" Homer stood stiffly at his desk and offered a rigid handshake. They took turns shaking, enveloping Homer's fleshy hand in their firm, muscular palms. "That's what I like about you boys. A nod and a handshake—all that's needed."

"We trust you, but Osgood, he's a rambunctious kid sometimes. Would you check the scales yourself?" Manuel lightly cuffed Bowers shoulder as the three left the office and headed home.

Bowers rushed across the tipple to the scales. Osgood was weighing coal cars with Swannie's assistance. "Take off, Swannie," Bowers ordered gruffly. "Yer done for today."

"What's up?" Swannie glanced at Osgood. "What'd I do?"

"Jist do what yer told." Osgood cocked his neck and signaled Swannie to leave.

"Okie-dokey." Swannie shrugged his shoulders.

After Swannie left the area, Bowers crowded over Osgood and scowled. "Did'ja rig the scales?"

Osgood crained his neck backwards to avoid Bower's face. "Linderman's orders. Said it was comin' from you."

"I ordered no such thing."

"Damn! I tole Swannie to whittle some slivers to rachet the scales."

"So Swannie finked! Brought Manuel, Onorio, and Julian down on me. Said it was a friendly visit and fed me cock-and-bull story a mile long—how I was a man of my word. They want me to check the scales, see if'n they're rigged. Best you pull the slivers. That'll keep Manuel and them other boys happy for a while. Don't wanna give them excuses to talk union. So play it up big when Swannie's back. Tell him you had a change of heart. Show it by pulling the slivers where he can see you. Play up how you used to be a miner."

EIGHT   BLUING KEEPS WHITES
FROM YELLOWING

SWANNIE WAS ELATED to have the day off and walked home leisurely without a care. At the clubhouse, the bartender was removing a poster from the marquee of El Carbon movie theater and replacing it with a poster that Swannie couldn't read clearly from where he stood, something about "Casey Jones." Passing by the Company store, Swannie overheard an argument between the manager, Tim Ruker, and gasoline customer Shorty García:

"Dang pump got stuck. Wouldn't stop pumping. Spilled extra gas on the ground."

"You cranked her too much. Should've waited for me to come out."

"You was pretty slow in comin'. My time's money."

"So's our gas."

"Not my fault it spilt over, dang pump."

"Yes, it is, and yer gonna pay for every drop you spilled."

"Say!" Shorty slapped Ruker on the back, "you Bowers' brother?"

"That ain't funny. Now, pay up."

"Ah, Tim, have a heart. Spilt gas don't do me no good." Unexpectedly, Shorty opened the door of his 1927 Chevrolet two-door coach, which looked much like a Model A Ford except for its two-tone blue coloring. Shorty poked about on the floorboard of the backseat. "How'd you like some trout?"

"Fresh?"

"This morning, Lake Maloya."

"Bribing me?"

"I'm no crook. Jist sharing my good fortune. Got more'an the family can eat. Run! Get some old newspapers. Soak'em."

"Got somethin' better," Ruker's voice trailed as he sauntered into the store. He returned with a large swathe of butcher paper. "Mind, this is no bribe."

"No bribe, honest to Pete, cross my heart and hope to die." Shorty removed two trout from the stringer and handed them to Ruker who wrapped them in the butcher paper. Then, Shorty returned the stringer of remaining fish to the bucket on the floorboard and closed the car door. Wrapping his arm over Ruker's shoulders, the two ambled into the store to settle the argument.

Swannie continued walking the tracks to the Heard's home, a short distance from the Company store. Dahlia was washing clothing in an exceedingly hot, steamy kitchen. Outside, the temperature was an arid eighty-five degrees. Inside, it was much hotter and steamier with three Number-2 tubs simmering water on the cookstove. Upon seeing Swannie, Dahlia lit up the room with a bright smile and twinkle in her eyes. With a red bandana pulled tightly over her forehead and hair, Dahlia appeared charming to Swannie. "Mighty fancy bandana."

"Nothing fashionable. One of Julian's kerchiefs."

"Keeps them pretty curls of yours tucked under covers."

Dahlia smiled coyly before leaning over the "Silver Duke," the corrugated tin washboard, to scrub Julian's overalls.

Right at that moment, Swannie adored her, feeling more than thinking, "She's so graceful. Makes hard work look easy. Even with the bandana soaked in sweat here in the steaming kitchen, she's as graceful as a doe."

Finished with the overalls, Dahlia turned to the whites that needed soaking. "Take that tub off the stove for me, Swannie."

He struggled to heft the heavy tub of water onto a powder box. "Hmm, what's that blue gunk yer a-pouring from the bottle?"

"Bluing."

"What's it for?"

"Bluing keeps the whites from yellowing."

"Howse come the whites don't turn blue?"

"I dunno. Be rich if I did." Dahlia stirred the whites into the tub and then removed her bandana and wiped the sweat from around her neck. She shook her head, hair flapping every which way, and the ebony curls poked into her right eye. She slicked back the curls and tied the bandana around her forehead. Swannie watched fondly, observing her every move.

"If you want to help, bring in some more water and heat it."

"Ma rinsed with cold water."

"I don't.

"There's plenty of warm water."

"Won't be for long. Don't be cutting corners. Toss the dirty water. Fill them tubs with cold water and heat'em up. Might need more coal in the fire."

Swannie hauled the dirty water from the kitchen and spilled it onto the garden patch. Pleased to be helping Dahlia, he rinsed the tub, and then filled and hauled it back into the kitchen. Sweating profusely, he hefted the three simmering tubs from the cookstove and replaced them with the one he'd just filled. "Reckon that's enough."

"Check the boiling pan."

"It's full." Swannie wiped his brow and exclaimed, "Phe-weee, sure is hot." He grabbed a towel and wiped his face and neck.

"You'll cool off presently. Now, stoke that fire."

"This is hard work," Swannie quipped as he tossed chunks of coal into the fire and relaxed at the table.

Swannie noticed that even while doing laundry, Dahlia was graceful and organized, keeping the white and colored clothing separated. She worked at several tasks simultaneously, soaking whites while emptying Eddy's overall pockets, removing dead toads, chipped marbles, and other forgotten booty. Dahlia inspected the shirts and bib overalls for dirt accumulated over time by Eddy as he frolicked in the dust, mud, and rocks of Chicorico. She dropped the dirty clothing into one of the tubs of warm water, soaking, and rubbing the spots. Some she scrubbed on the washboard and then dipped to soak. She returned to the whites, scrubbed them and dropped them in the rinse water. With the whites in the rinse water, Dahlia returned to Eddy's clothing.

"Now that you've rested," Dahlia said, her eyes twinkling, "take that pile of clothing and hang it on the lines. B'efore you hang any, swipe the lines clean with a wet rag." She handed Swannie a rag. "One more thing, be sure to prop up the lines with the poles."

Swannie snapped to attention. "Yes, ma'am. Where're the pins?"

"Bag's hanging on the line."

Grunting when he lifted the heavy tub of wet clothing, he struggled outside and dropped the tub on the back porch. He soaked the clean, white cotton rag under the water pump and swathed the galvanized clothesline wires until the white cloth was black as tar. He rinsed and hung it on the porch railing, and then lugged the heavy tub of clothing to the lines.

He found the pins in a bulging cotton bag hanging on the line. They were simple wooden pins, two-prongs and a round head. He tried to slide the bag along the wire as he pinned each article of clothing, but the heavy bag caused the line to sag. He loaded pins in his mouth and pockets. The pins-in-pocket-and-mouth method worked much better though he couldn't sing. He hummed. About midway along the line, it sagged toward the center and the clothing nearly touched the ground. He spied a long pole on the ground, remembered Dahlia's directions, and hoisted the pole beneath the sagging wire.

When done, Swannie trudged back into the kitchen, ladled a dipper of water, and gulped it down, wiping sweat from his brow and beneath his shirt collar. "Still have two lines."

"Good. Take that tub by the handle, we'll carry it outside, wring out Julian's overalls."

"No wringer?"

"Nope. You and me, now you're here."

Swannie took a handle with both hands and waited for Dahlia to grasp the other. She clasped it with both hands. Carefully, they heaved together, struggled to carry the heavy tub outside, and set it down. "Over by the garden." Dahlia pointed with her chin, and they dragged the heavy tub of overalls near the garden. She stepped between the rows of onions and radishes. "Toss the legs. We'll wring'em over the greens."

Holding the bib straps firmly, Swannie tossed the legs of the overalls. She caught them. They twisted and pulled the overalls in a wringing tug-of-war and the water dripped over the vegetables.

"Okay, let's get'em on the line." She tossed the legs back to Swannie.

Swannie tossed the overalls over an empty line, skipped back and tossed another pair to Dahlia. They played tug-of-war again, wringing excess water onto the garden greens. When they finished wringing the overalls, Dahlia returned to the kitchen and washed the last of the socks. Swannie pinned the overalls on a line and paused to admire his work—overalls hanging by their legs, shirts by their tails, and socks by the toes, flapping in an easy breeze.

Tiny twitches tingled down his back and leg muscles. They were not the spastic reflexes of jim-jams. He was sore—the result of working with muscles he didn't know existed. "This is the way it should be at the tipple," Swannie reflected, "the good feeling that comes from working together an' getting the job done."

"I'll hang these." Dahlia returned from the kitchen toting the last of the socks. "You toss the dirty water in the garden. Then you're done for now. Rest up. After supper, if you don't mind, you can help take the wash from the line."

Swannie carried the dirty water outside and poured it over the garden. He wiped the tin tubs clean, hooked them on the back porch railing, plodded into the living room, and plopped onto the sofa. . . .

Eddy woke him for dinner. Afterwards, Swannie helped Dahlia take down the clothing while Julian and Eddy washed and dried dishes. Back in the kitchen, Dahlia showed Swannie how to fold the towels and asked him to match and roll the socks into balls. Together, they folded the bed sheets. Dahlia put the clean laundry in their proper places and handed Swannie a neatly folded set of bed sheets, overalls, and shirts. When Swannie took the clothing, she poked his ribs, winked, and with a twinkle in her eyes, she chanted in falsetto, "Nighty-night, mind the bed bugs don't bite."

Swannie felt a blush that flushed from ear-to-ear.

"Say, want to sing some hymns?" Julian chuckled.

"Don't think poorly of me," a red-faced Swannie wearily explained. "I'm plumb tuckered from work."

"Thought you didn't work this afternoon. Bowers sent you home."

"Don't tease the poor boy." Dahlia grinned broadly. "He paid his keep today."

NINE   A LITTLE MONKEY BUSINESS

JULIAN AND SWANNIE DIDN'T WORK the first Monday after summer solstice. Julian fussed in the cellar repairing fishing gear and tying flies. Dahlia sorted pinto beans at the kitchen table, and Swannie chatted with her.

"Work's a curse."

"I'd say blessing."

"Man works livelong day, gits old, tired. They can you—fer a young feller. It's a curse."

"You're blessed. Want to trade folks in soup lines?"

"Didn't mean nothing. Wouldn't trade nobody."

"It's all accordin' to the way you look at it. I fault toward a blessing. Julian's always had work. We've never gone hungry. I make a little cash at piano lessons."

"Accordin' to the Good Book—"

"You're reading the Bible Reverend Miller gave you?"

"You betcha. Jist finished the part where Adam and Eve ate the apple, and the Lord canned them from the Garden of Eden. Made'em work the livelong day. If'n they hadn't been so weak, we'd be livin' in paradise. Here we're slaves to jobs."

"It's a curse you want, here! Toss these." Dahlia pointed to a pile of mud gobs and bantam pebbles culled from the beans. "This batch was particularly dirty."

"Boy, howdy, I told you. Even puny beans make work." He pocketed his knife and scooped the pile. "Work's a curse."

"Shush! Toss'em out." She waved off Swannie. "Then, how about pouring some water to soak the beans?"

Swannie did as directed and returned promptly. "Chicorico would be a swell place, if'n I didn't work." He opened his pocketknife and again picked at his fingernails.

"If'n you didn't work," Dahlia teased playfully, scooping the beans into the kettle, "you'd have the cleanest fingernails in all of Colfax County."

"Plumb rude of me." He chuckled nervously and pocketed the knife.

"Jitters more like it. Enjoy today—tomorrow will take care of itself." Dahlia was delighted to see the change in Swannie after one month of three meals a day and a pleasant place to stay. The resemblance to her brother Jimmy was even more striking with the return of a spring in his walk and tease in his talk.

Rap! Rap!

"Probably little Jean Bittner at the door. Here for a lesson. Let the child in, please."

Swannie ambled through the front room and saw what he thought was Lewis Carroll's Alice in Wonderland standing on the other side of the screendoor, a saucy, perky, pretty girl, beaming blue eyes, platinum blond hair, dangling curls tied with tiny rose ribbons. She wore a pink dress embroidered in forget-me-nots and daisies. Her white anklets were neatly cuffed over white, high top shoes.

"These are for Mrs. Heard." The confident, poised, eight-year old Jean scurried through the door and handed Swannie a bouquet of freshly picked cosmos. "Mama had me pick them."

Swannie took the cosmos and waved Jean toward the piano while he searched the kitchen for a vase. Jean followed Swannie. "Good morning, Mrs. Heard."

"My, what lovely flowers." Dahlia shifted to a sterner tone. "Have you been practicing?"

"No."

"We'll see about that. Set. Practice a spell. Swannie will watch you."

Jean scooted to the edge of the piano bench. Her feet dangled and almost touched the floor. Swannie placed a saucer on the piano top and then positioned the small jar of cosmos on the saucer.

"Mmm, they smell pretty."

"Do smell good," Swannie agreed bruskly. "Mrs. Heard says yer to start with a C-Major scale."

Jean giggled. Pretending to prepare for a grand recital in a palatial music hall, she wiggled her shoulders and daintily flared her pink, flowery dress over the bench. She sat erect, shoulders pulled back, and played two octaves of the C-Major scale with her right hand, tucking her thumb and lifting her fingers as she held her wrist at keyboard level. Her left hand rested in her lap. She repeated the octaves with her left hand and then again with both hands. She turned toward Swannie, smiled, and bowed deferentially.

"Pretty good, little girl." Swannie patted her on the head. "Mrs. Heard taught you good."

"Thank you, mon-sewer," Jean purred, mangling the French title *monsieur*. She wiggled again, fluttered her dress, and announced haughtily, "And, for the grand finale, I shall present—"

Dahlia walked into the room. "G-Major, my *little* prima donna. Show Mr. Swanson you've learned to use the black F-Sharp key."

Dutifully, she plinked the keys, G-A-B-C-D-E-F-sharp-G-F-sharp-E-D-C-B-A-G."

"You're getting sloppy, holding your hands like a spider descending on a bug." Dahlia showed Jean how to curve her fingers while keeping her wrists even with the keyboard.

Jean repeated the F-Sharp scale.

"Much better. Now, don't rush the keys. You're not running to a picnic. Repeat the scale ten times. Let's hear more music, less notes."

Jean drilled. Dahlia observed with discerning eyes and ears while Swannie mouthed the scale's hypnotic rhythm: "Bah-bah-bah-bah-bah-bah-bah, boom!" Keeping time by tapping his toes, Swannie closed his eyes, swayed his torso, and waved his arms like a conductor.

"Mrs. Heard! Mrs. Heard! They're here!" Arturo and Eddy burst through the back door.

"Tell your Papa, Eddy." He zipped out. She turned to Swannie. "Got change?"

"A little."

"Get it." While Swannie gathered lose change, she darted to the kitchen searching for knives and scissors, asking, "Arturo, where's your Papa?"

"Meeting Wobblies, I guess."

"Oh, well. Go with Eddy." She turned to Swannie. "You've got to see these folks."

"The Wobblies?"

"Heavens, no. Miss Scheherazade, the mysterious girl of the east and her monkey, Casey Jones."

"Honey, they're here." Julian emerged from the cellar, Eddy trailing behind.

"Take Swannie with you, Julian."

Julian searched his bedroom for small change and hurried out the bedroom. "Where's those knives and scissors?"

"Mrs. Heard, what about me?" Jean begged sweetly, "Can I go, ple-e-a-s-e."

"We should finish your lesson."

"Oh, pre-t-ty ple-e-as-e."

"Well, o-kay," Dahlia relented. "They're here once a year. Come back when it's over, or you mother will be unhappy."

"Yippee!" Jean squealed gleefully, crawled from the piano bench, and clutched Swannie's hand. Eddy and Arturo grasped hands and formed a train. Swannie led them out the house and onto the railway. Already Julian walked ahead amid a crowd of miners and children toward the clubhouse.

"Howdy, quite a crew."

"Yours, too," Swannie returned the greeting to the stocky miner pulling a train of four boys from the tallest to the shortest. He carried a girl astride his shoulders.

"Name's Judo, Judo Perkovich. Can't shake. Got my hands full. Hear yer boarding with the Heards."

"Yep, Swannie's the name."

"Yer with good people. I won't say nothing to Julian, but why'd you fink on me?"

"Beg pardon? I don't fink on nobody."

"Yeah, you did. You told Bowers my boys was collecting coal along the tracks."

"Jist doin' my job. Linderman ordered me."

"Jist taking orders don't cut it. Did you see my boys collecting coal?"

"Well, no. Eddy told me they was gonna."

"No worry. Water under the bridge. Damage done."

"Do tell."

"Bowers deducted an estimate from my wages."

"That was mighty little of him."

"Little to him. Lots to me." Judo planted both feet on a railroad tie, halting the train of kids. "Look, no hard feelings, you don't know better. Jist decide whose side yer on."

"Hurry, Pa!" Judo's boys cajoled. "Quit talking! We'll be late!"

The boys jerked Judo toward the crowd assembled around two weary mules hitched to a covered wagon. Pulling the train of kids, Swannie found Julian weaving through the crowd toward the back of the covered wagon where an elderly man sat in the bucket seat of a grindstone.

The old man was dressed to work in full-cut dark brown trousers, shins bound in puttees kept in place by leather bands. His wide-sleeved shirt and sash were embroidered in burgundy and his handlebar mustache matched his black sheepskin cap. Oblivious to the growing crowd, he pumped the pedals that turned the grindstone wheel. Next to the grindstone, sundry scissors, knives, hatchets, and axes were scattered on a table. Pennies, nickels, dimes, and quarters were tossed beside the cutting tools.

A shiver of anticipation rippled through the crowd when a tambourine clattered from within the covered wagon, then slipped through the wagon's back drape, clasped by creamy, white dimpled fingers of a young girl. Miss Scheherazade wiggled through the drape and hopped to the ground.

"Ah sha!"

Yeas, yahoos, and yippees! The crowd yelped and cheered.

Fresh as the first day of spring, she flitted about holding her skirt in one hand, slapping her thigh with the tambourine. Puffs of dust rose and matted the leather straps laced to her feet and around her ankles—a water sprite in the dusty, drab clubhouse courtyard. Her wavy, black hair, partially covered with a crimson *marama* headkerchief, flowed over her shoulders onto her back. She wore a wide-sleeved chemise with a falling ruffle under a bodice and full skirt. The multihued skirt flared in red, lavender, and orange vertical stripes while she fluttered about in half-circles. Sparkling glass tassels jingled gaily at her hems. Earrings dangled from her ears, bracelets bobbled on her wrists, and ruby rings spangled her fingers.

Swannie scanned the completely mesmerized faces of the children. Eddy caught Swannie's eye. "Isn't she good?" Swannie responded but Eddy didn't hear over the hardy hoots! Concurrent claps! Windy whistles! The crowd swayed to the rhythm of her dance. Skittering on her toes, she circled the crowd clattering the tambourine, returned to the back of the wagon, and curtsied. She stretched into the wagon, one foot extended in the air, turned and faced the crowd with a monkey on her left arm.

"Ah sha!" Thunderous applause and soaring hoots, Eddy, Jean, Arturo, and a cavvy of kids chanted in staccato, "Ca-sey Jones! Ca-sey Jones! Ca-sey Jones!" Dressed like a railroad engineer wearing a cap, cotton long johns, denim overalls, and a red bandana around his neck, he was a nimble steam-driving monkey. The capricious critter cringed and grinned, removed his dark brown railroader's cap, and waved it to the crowd. Then, he untied its strings, lowered the ear-flaps, and pulled the cap back over his ears and eyes, raising a howl among the crowd. "Ca-sey Jones! Ca-sey Jones! Ca-sey Jones!"

Eddy tugged on Swannie's hand. "I like Casey Jones. Re-e-eally, I do!"

Miss Scheherazade waved the clamorous crowd to follow while she swirled into the clubhouse foyer. Older boys threw open the doors to the El Carbon theater. Miners and children flocked behind, finding seats or standing on the sides. In the rear of the theater, an outhouse shanty served as a movie projection booth. In front, a low wooden platform served as stage. Directly above the stage, a rope dangled from a crossbeam and draped to the floor for the occasional gymnastic troupes that toured the camps.

Miss Scheherazade scooted the monkey up the rope and then ran with the rope back and forth across the stage. She flung the rope. The monkey swung himself like a pendulum, pumping his legs and jerking his hips, swinging higher and higher. She strapped a hand organ over her shoulder and cranked the handle. The melody of the "Scissors Grinder" ditty pealed in three-quarter time:

Round and round,
round and round
Goes the wheel
when scissors are ground.

As the organ pealed its mavis melody, the monkey wrapped his legs around the rope and dropped his hands, grabbing the cap as he lowered his head. He cavorted upside down and side-to-side, waving at the crowd with cap in hand. Miss Scheherazade continued to crank the hand organ:

The edge is sharp
that was flat!
Scissors
Grind~ers
tend to that.
Round and round, round and round . . .

The organ ground gaily. The enthralled crowd swayed in a pendular wave, clapping and shouting, "Monkey see, monkey do! Monkey see, monkey do!"

Abruptly, Miss Scheherazade stopped cranking the organ, released its straps, and laid it on the stage. Casey Jones hopped from the rope. She handed him a large can used to squirt oil into the axles and gears of steam engines. He jumped into the crowd and spurted water on the children. They squealed with joy, dodging the spurts and spews of water.

He stopped squirting, ending the show. Casey Jones allowed the kids to hold and pat his sleek hairy arms, legs, and tail. Miss Scheherazade weaved in and out of the crowd with Casey Jones's hat, pleading, "Pennies for my monkey."

Swannie drifted back to his school days, forgetting he was in a coal camp theater that used an outhouse shanty for a movie projection room. The graceful and captivating Miss Scheherazade reminded him of a book his fourth-grade teacher Muriel Gregory had read to the class, *Thousand and One Nights*, where another young Miss Scheherazade sat in King Shahryan's curtained bedroom telling tales to appease that brutal king—tales of genies, ebony horses, and flying carpets, of Ali Baba and the magical command, "Open Sesame," of Aladdin and his magic lamp.

"Might be another show." Julian managed to gently jounce Swannie back to the clubhouse. "If'n there's enough business for Danilo Petrovic."

"That the scissors grinder outside?"

"Yep. Never says a word. Nor the little lady—his granddaughter, I reckon. They been coming 'round here the past few years. Everybody hauls out their knives and scissors jist to see the show."

"I saw hunting knives, butcher knives, hatchets," Arturo commented excitedly.

"Even butter knives," Eddy chirped.

"No doubt." Julian chuckled. "It's worth the show."

"Papa, are they Gypsies?"

"Don't think so, maybe from Montenegro, like lot'a Slavs around here."

Usually after Easter, Danilo Petrovic and his granddaughter started the rounds of coal camps in Southern Colorado, traversed the pass to Raton and its coal camps, then moved south to Cimarron, west to Eagle Nest and the Moreno Valley, and over the mountains to Taos via another pass. This part of the trip was attempted in August when the mountain roads were passable. Then, they turned north to Alamosa, thence east back to Walsenburg and the southern Colorado coal camps. In the late fall, they camped in Trinidad through the winter months, then started south again in the spring making the rounds.

"Eddy, you and Arturo take Jean for her piano lesson," Julian ordered. "Then run tell her Ma she's with your mother."

"Yes sir!" Eddy and Arturo clutched Jean's hands and escorted her into the disbanding throng on the railway where miners and children carried home an assortment of knives, scissors, axes, and hatchets. Others were standing around chatting while they waited for Petrovic to sharpen their cutlery.

"That feller has a pick."

"Shorty." Julian chuckled. "Brings it every year. Loves the show."

"Good way to wear out a pick."

"Better'n etching coal with her." Julian rapped Swannie on the shoulder. "I'm going to another show. 'Fraid you can't come."

"A monkey show?"

"Might say a little more monkey business—winemaking."

"Onorio?"

"How'd you guess?"

"Italian, ain't he?"

"All the way! Say! Take the knives home?"

"Yah, sure, I'll while away time with Dahlia and the prima donna. Where'd folks get the cash? Pay the organ grinder?" Swannie asked while taking the knives from Julian.

Julian leaned close to Swannie and whispered. "Between me, you, and fence post?"

Swannie nodded.

"Lots a places—gambling with Company men. Wobblies pay cash for wine. Dahlia's lessons. But, I never told you, an' you don't know nothing about cash."

Swannie grinned, happy to be included on a coal camp secret.

Julian headed to Onorio's. In spite of Prohibition, vineyards raised grapes and Onorio made wine. Like so many generations of Chicarelli men, Onorio learned to make wine as a boy. California vineyards had a ready market with him and many others in the coal camps. Early each summer, the vineyards shipped a trainload of grapes on the Santa Fé in "reefers," heavily insulated boxcars refrigerated with blocks of ice. Miners converged on the train depot in Raton and bought crates of grapes directly off the reefers. Onorio was always among the swarm. Before leaving Raton north to the Southern Colorado coal camps, the reefers were replenished with ice excavated from Johnson Mesa caves.

"*Amico*, come down. Manuel's back." Julian entered Onorio's cellar. Hewed from the soil by Onorio with Julian and Manuel's help, the cellar maintained a cool temperature year round. The main workplace was near the entry where Onorio had placed a press and various sized wooden casks. Nearby, casks of wine lay on earthen benches.

"We pour the grapes into the press." Onorio pointed to the grapes in wooden crates on a table beside the press.

"Not stomping with the feet?"

"Used to, but I crush more with the press."

"And, you don't have to wash your feet."

"In the old a'country, wine tasted better, when you didn't wash your feet."

"This wine gonna taste good, like the old a'country?"

"Cleaner! Not better."

Julian and Manuel heaped grapes into the press while Onorio turned the crank, compressing the grapes and squeezing their juices into an open cask until it was practically full.

"Now, we wait for the must to rise and the gunk drops to the bottom."

"Must?"

"The first run-off, the pure grape juices off the top. It's the best."

"Like cream rising to the top?"

"More like gunk drops to the bottom. Now we drain the must into the cask. We do this till it fills with first run juices."

They toiled for a long while, gauging progress by the soft thud of grapes dropping into the press. Ambrosial whiffs of grapes permeated the dank air. Julian's head floated. Lightheaded, he stepped out the dimly lit cellar, blinked his eyes till his vision cleared, tossed the grape pits and skins into the garden, and rinsed the cask. When he returned to the work area, Onorio led them to his caucaus room where he stored prized stock.

He switched on the light, which he had wired by drilling a hole in the floor directly above and running an electric wire and socket from within the house. The caucaus room was musty and dank, much like a root cellar. Floor rafters provided a ceiling. Onorio had constructed a fourth wall for the cosy room with scrap lumber from the mine. Its slightly scorched oak door and frame were taken intact from rubbage after the Chicorico High School burned to the ground in 1923. Inside the room, the solid earthen walls were etched with banks where three small casks lay on their sides.

Onorio handed out glasses and pointed to the casks. "Help yourself. Right's dry, others are sweet." Julian drew from the dry cask, Manuel and Onorio from the sweet. They sat on the cool earthen benches and slowly savored the fine wine.

"How'd the meetin' go with the Wobblies?" Julian asked.

"Sold Onorio's wine. Got him plenty cash."

"Don'a worry. I'll trade scrip with you fellers—for poker. Did you tell about the scales? And, how Judo had'a pay for the coal his boys picked along the tracks?"

"Nobody saw them do it."

"Yah, but Swannie told Linderman he heard my boy Eddy say they were gonna pick coal on the way home."

"Wobblies said none of that mattered. Coal drops from coal cars all the time. If'n Company don't pick it up right away, it's fair game for anybody. Abandoned property, like losing a nickel. Finders keepers."

"And the rigged scales?"

"Illegal! Plain illegal. They was ready to call a strike! Or, take the Company to court. They got a radical lawyer in Denver. They make me nervous—too radical for my blood. They gave me a copy of a manifesto. Here, I'll read some, judge for yourself: 'The working class and the employing class have nothing in common. There can be no peace so long as hunger and want are found among millions of working people, and the few who make up the employing class have all the good things of life. Between these two classes a struggle must go on until all the toilers come together on the political, industrial field'—"

"Sounds good," Onorio interrupted Manuel.

"Does, indeed," Julian agreed. "Talking about a union of working people."

"Below their fancy words, they're pushing a revolution—to get rid of captialism."

"You mean like Russia where the poor people kicked out the Czar? Now, they're ruled by the communist?"

"And, they're still poor."

Julian injected, "Which would be tolerable. But, they're not free. Those poor suckers jist traded one dictator for another. I'm with you, Manuel." Julian quoted the *Gettysburg Address*, "'Government by the people, for the people, and of the people.'"

TEN   GAMES MINERS PLAY

AFTERNOON OF THE FOURTH OF JULY, Julian invited Swannie along to pitch boccie and horseshoes with Onorio and Manuel in Onorio's backyard. "Smooth running connection," Onorio muttered, tapping a two-by-four into the ground marking the end of the lane. His boccie lane was not fancy, hard-packed dirt about four feet wide and twenty feet long. Small pits bordered the far ends of the lane to catch rolling balls. "Same, same." Onorio pointed to the other end where Manuel was tapping another two-by-four into the ground. "You fellers, lend a hand." Onorio nodded toward a rake beside the lane.

"I'll rake the trash into mounds. Shovel it to the side," Julian directed Swannie. "Run, fetch the spade, over yonder by the coal bin."

As Julian raked and Swannie pitched debris to the side, Onorio paced back and fourth over the freshly raked lane, tamping the tiny clumps of dirt and pebbles that slipped between the rake's spikes.

"Flat as a pancake." Onorio finished the inspection and spilled a bag of balls onto the ground. "We play with these eight wood balls," Onorio explained to Swannie.

"What about the little one?" Swannie pointed to a smaller ball about two-and-a-half inches in diameter.

"Ah, the 'jackball.' We take turns throwing it. Now yer here, we can have two teams. You and I will be the best."

"You'll never win with Swannie," Manuel boasted.

80

"Dime on a dollar." Onorio winked at Swannie and pitched the jackball. It arched, landed, and rolled practically to the far end of the lane. "Now, we bowl." Onorio instructed Swannie, "We take turns throwing the balls toward the jackball. Don't hit it, and don't roll out the lane. Get close to jackball. Team with most balls closest to the jackball wins the round. Now, watch."

With both hands, Onorio lifted a ball to his face. He stood flat-footed at the boundary, bent both knees slightly, leaned forward, and aimed with his right eye as though he were firing a pistol. He dropped his left arm and pitched the ball underhanded. The ball appeared to glide in slow motion as it spun gracefully toward the end of the lane, landing and rolling beside the jackball.

"Boy, howdy!" Swannie was astounded. "That was some pitch."

"Now watch this," Manuel asserted. "I'll get even closer." He pitched the ball and it rolled to the other side of the jackball.

"Mine's closer," Onorio claimed.

"We'll see," Manuel answered. "Swannie's turn."

Swannie imitated Onorio, lifted the ball in front of his nose, aimed down the lane, dropped his left arm, and pitched the ball with his right. It rose into a high arch and fell about two feet short of the jackball.

"Good for first time. You'll get the hang of it."

Julian pitched. The ball glided in a flat trajectory, landed over Swannie's ball and rolled near the jackball. "Mine's closest."

"Wowie!" Swannie was amazed at Julian's accuracy. "You aimed and throwed th' ball with both eyes open?"

"Shoots that way, too."

"Sharp shooters in France taught me. Two eyes better than one."

"I can't do it," Manuel added.

"Me, either," Onorio conceded. "Let's finish. We have one more pitch for the round. Be hard to get any closer. Jackball's hemmed on three sides."

Onorio pitched. The ball sidled near Julian's ball. Manuel's pitch landed behind Onorio's second ball and drifted to the lane's end. Swannie's over-pitched off the lane's far end. Julian's ball landed near Manuel's.

"Way I see it," Onorio claimed, "my two balls are closer than any of the others, even with Swannie's bad pitches."

"My first one's closer than your second," Manuel insisted.

"So's mine," Julian added.

"Mine closest than both you," Onorio claimed.

"Let's measure," Swannie suggested.

"No need. My first one's the closest," Manuel asserted.

"And, mine's closer than Onorio's, too."

Swannie knelt on the lane. Using hand spans, he started to measure the spaces between the balls. Before he could finish, Julian tapped his shoulder to stop the measure. "Skip it. Onorio's right. His are closest."

"¡Hijo!" Manuel objected. "Whose side you on?"

While Manuel and Julian squabbled, Onorio coached Swannie on holding the ball, aiming, and tossing. "Follow through so the ball falls with a little arch, watch."

Manuel stopped quibbling with Julian long enough to interrupt Onorio. "Hey, no coaching."

"Got to. Swannie's on my side. His pitches don't count for much."

"Don't rub it in," Swannie complained.

"Don't worry, Swannie. Stick with me, I'll make you good."

"Howse come you don't measure, instead of jist eyeballing?"

They stared blankly at Swannie. . . . After a spell when nobody could think of a good answer to Swannie's question, Julian conceded defeat. "Your side won. No need to measure. Let's pitch some horseshoes."

Onorio set aside the boccie balls and brushed the dust from the horseshoes. Pitching horseshoes was less contentious than the boccie game. Clang! Julian pitched a ringer. "Ah, music to my ears."

"That's nothing," Onorio boasted. "Listen." He pitched a horseshoe, cla-ang! It reverberated over Julian's ringer. "Top that."

"¡Mira!" Manuel pitched. Cla-a-a-ng! His horseshoe landed over the others. "Don't feel bad, Swannie, if—"

Cla-a-a-a-ang! Swannie's horseshoe covered the others.

"Atta boy, Swannie!" Julian thumped Swannie's ribs. The game started in earnest and the rounds passed swiftly, although not as lucky as the first round. The thud of horseshoes falling short—the clang of ringers reverberating on the steel spikes—ended the summer games on that Fourth of July.

Early next morning, Julian and Swannie worked on the baseball diamond to prepare it for the Fourth of July match between Chicorico and Dawson, played annually on the Sunday after Independence Day. The Chicorico baseball diamond was laid out in a meadow just south of the Company store in what appeared to be an ancient lake when Chicorico Creek was much larger. Julian parked his pickup behind home plate. Manuel, Onorio, and Shorty García were already clearing the outfield. Every New Year's Eve, folks dragged their Christmas trees to the outfield, heaped and burned the dry spruce and pine trees in a huge bonfire, singing out the old and celebrating the new, "Auld Lang Syne," "Las Mañanitas," and Italian and Slavic carols inspired by the occasion.

"Good to see you," Osgood cheerily greeted Julian and Swannie.

"Same to you," Julian responded warmly. "Got the chain?"

"Yah, sure! You measure. I'll mix the lime." Osgood retrieved a survey chain from his pickup and handed it to Julian.

"Swannie, take the tail of the chain. Wrap the thongs around your wrist. Hold 'zcro' on the center of home plate. First, we measure distances for accuracy, then we draw white lines with the lime."

Julian walked the first base line. Swannie centered the chain over home plate.

"Ninety feet," Julian shouted and walked to second. Swannie followed.

"Right on the nose." Julian summarized as they finished measuring the distances between the plates. "Now, the pitcher's mound. Go back to home plate. Hold the chain over the center." Julian pulled the chain over the pitching mound's rubber plate. "Perfect, sixty feet, six inches."

"Now, if'n that don't get your goat!" Swannie stood, arms akimbo. "All this measurin' for a baseball game?"

Julian brushed off home plate. "No ordinary game. B'sides, plates might a'moved."

"Huh?"

"Earth turns three hundred sixty-five times a year. All that turnings bound to move the plates."

"Phooey! Plates ain't moved none."

"Pretty cold last winter," Osgood added. "Ground froze a lot. Julian's right. Might'a shifted the plates."

Swannie rubbed his neck in disbelief. "Yesterday, you wouldn't measure for boccie. Today, yer measurin' down to a gnat's ass."

"Bowling with Onorio?" Osgood chuckled. "No need to measure. He always wins."

"So does Dawson at baseball, I hear tell."

Julian and Osgood glared at Swannie, shuffled the dust beneath their feet, and reacted like a team of standup comedians.

"What's ugly and stands on eighteen legs?"

"Dawson team."

"What's uglier than the Dawson team and stands on two legs?"

"A Dawson fan!"

Swannie grinned.

"Jist pulling your leg." Osgood pointed toward the buckets. "Lime's ready." Osgood had mixed water into the white powder. "Use the cans." He handed Swannie and Julian tin cans and took one himself. They laid the chain in a square around home plate and poured the white, watery lime to mark the boundary for the batter's box. Then they laid the chain from plate-to-plate and poured the lime along the chain.

"Looks like a real baseball diamond."

"First class," Osgood boasted.

Julian confirmed Osgood's claim. "Yep. All accordin' to American League standards."

"Who foots the bill?"

"The Company," Osgood quickly replied. "Pays for the rubber plates, lime, even the boys' uniforms."

"Jist shirts and caps."

"Cleats, too."

"*Muncho* jack, huh?"

"Yep. Company men and miners agree—gotta have a good baseball diamond."

"And, a team to match," Julian added. "Good baseball players can always get a job at the mine, inside or out."

"Hey, Bowers did ask if'n I played ball."

"Well, are you good at it?"

"No."

"Too bad." Osgood slapped Swannie on the back. "'Cause you was right 'bout Dawson. We need more'an a little luck to beat them. See you this afternoon."

"You bet!" Julian cheerfully answered as he walked toward the tracks.

"Howse come we're walking?"

"We leave the pickup right behind home plate. You'll see this afternoon."

When Julian and Swannie returned home, Eddy was waiting them on the front porch and followed them into the kitchen where Dahlia was preparing a picnic lunch. Eddy complained, "Papa, I wish't you wouldn't umpire. Last year you almost took a licking."

"Somebody's gotta do it."

"Why don't you watch with us?"

"He likes calling the plays," Dahlia injected. "Makes him feel like a big shot."

Two hours before the game, throngs of folks from Chicorico and Dawson converged on the diamond. Those with cars parked around the diamond with fathers and sons on car fenders and roofs. Mothers and daughters sat inside the cars. Others spread picnic blankets on the ground to watch the game. A cavvy of boys climbed the Company store's fire escape and prepared to watch from the store's false front. Other folks seeking an eagle's view of the diamond sat on the store's high steps. Company store employees tended an ice cream and soda concession stand parked in a panel truck among the crowd beyond the right field.

The Chicarelli and Montaño families joined the Heards near the pickup behind home plate. They spread blankets, laid out dishes of Italian sausages, Mexican *chorizos*, loaves of bread, and salad greens. Onorio poured glasses of wine, soda pops for Arturo, Eddy, and Swannie. Everybody busily built and ate sandwiches, enjoying the greens.

"Your attention, please!" Homer Bowers blasted through a megaphone.

Julian wolfed his sandwich. "Time for the game to start."

"Everybody stand," Bowers directed, "for the national anthem played by the Dawson Town Band."

Everybody stood. Eddy, Arturo, and baby Angela jumped up, clutching small American flags Clara had packed in her picnic basket. Swannie scanned the electric crowd and was captivated by the pageantry of a Sunday afternoon game—women dressed gaily, some with bonnets or bows adorning carefully groomed hairdos, chatting comfortably among themselves; clean-shaved, casually dressed men bantering boisterously, awaiting the action of the game; boys and girls bustling about totally absorbed in everything other than the game's opening rituals.

The two teams stood as proud as doughboys queued for inspection. The Dawson team queued along the first base line, the Chicorico team the third base line. The Dawson team wore gray cotton shirts that displayed the cursive letter "D." The Chicorico team wore dull white cotton shirts with a circled "C" sewed over the heart. Their caps displayed a plain, capitalized "D" and "C" respectively. The players removed their caps as the Dawson Town Band played "The Star Spangled Banner." Children waved tiny flags, like tiny orchestra conductors. Folks sang robustly. When the anthem ended, Bowers announced, "Here to throw the first pitch is the Phelps-Dodge superintendent of mines for Dawson, Robert Nichols."

Nichols stood in his yellow 1930 convertible Chevrolet and blared in the megaphone, "Ladies and Gentlemen, I wish to acknowledge and welcome my good friend and Superintendent of the Chicorico Coal Company, Mr. Hank Van Cise!"

A smattering of polite applause.

Nichols waved across the diamond to where Van Cise stood surrounded by Bowers and other coal camp general managers. Van Cise waved both arms so everybody could see him, although most folks weren't paying attention. Nichols regaled boastfully into the megaphone: "It's just Jim Dandy! It's terrific! We gather again for this most auspicious occasion, the annual Fourth of July Dawson/Chicorico match-up. Last year, we skunked you in Dawson. This year, you have the edge here in Chicorico. Tables could turn! Doesn't matter! Every year we gather to play baseball. It's the American way! It jist shows that miners and operators can work together. It's proof-positive! We don't need unions to tell us how to get along!"

Pallid, anemic applause followed the speech.

"Boys! Visiting team bats first!"

Thunderous claps, whistles, hoots! The Chicorico team rushed to the field. Dawson players prepared to bat. Bob Durocavich sauntered to the pitcher's mound. Julian took his place behind the Chicorico catcher, Sonny Salvo.

"Play ball!" Nichols shouted, tossing the ball to Durocavich, who jogged from the mound to catch it. Durocavich returned to the mound and pitched to Larry Vukonich.

"Strike!" Julian shouted and folks settled-in for the game.

In six pitches, Durocavich blanked Larry Vukonich and Bill Pappas. Short and stocky, Durocavich pitched sidearm and overarm, depending on pitch and batter. He was unpredictable and very difficult to hit, except an occasional single. His clumsy sidearm pitch would never pass muster in the ballet, although that didn't matter to the Chicorico fans. He compensated for his lack of grace with accuracy across the plate.

Eddy and Arturo were glued to Durocavich's pitches. "You gotta whip'em," Eddy shouted, sucking nervously on a chorizo.

"Whip'em good!" Arturo shouted, greedily grabbing another chorizo from Clara's picnic basket and waggling it like a club.

"Boys, slow down," Clara cautioned playfully. "Yer making mincemeat out'a my chorizos."

Durocavich never threw a wild pitch without purpose. Though awkward and uncoordinated, his unorthodox windup and follow-through unsettled most batters. He struck out Mike Hernandez and retired Dawson's first time at bat. He raised his close-fisted arms above his head in victory and sauntered to the side.

The Chicorico crowded cheered wildly and the Dawson crowd clamored glumly until Tony Palomino took the mound for Dawson. The whole crowd simmered down. Guido Mangino batted. Zip, zip, zip, Mangino's out. Palomino was a classic overarm, fastball pitcher. Steve Segotta took the bat. Again, Palomino blanked him in three pitches. Sonny Salvo took the bat and faced the fearsome Palomino. In style, Palomino was the opposite of Durocavich. Tall and lanky at six foot two, Palomino wore his cap tightly over his brows. Before each pitch, he stood full-front behind the rubber, pocketed the baseball in his glove, beamed fiercely at catcher Bill Pappas, shook his head at the Pappas signals until he agreed, and then commenced the windup.

"You, you dirty dog!" Waggling their minced chorizos at Palomino, Eddy and Arturo shouted, their boyish chatter drowned by the boisterous clamor of the Dawson fans.

Clara noticed the boys were no longer paying attention to the game and were shouting because they had nothing better to do. She admonished them, "You boys settle down!"

"Yes, Eddy, settle down," Dahlia injected. "Here are some nickels. Get an ice cream, and bring some for Angela. When you're back, we want you to pipe down."

Gladly, Arturo and Eddy took the money and scrambled away to mingle in the crowd in search of adventure. She and Clara turned away from the boys to watch the game. The boys didn't return for a long time, which Dahlia assumed would happen. With left leg firmly planted on the rubber, Palomino cocked his right leg parallel to his arms and reached back with his right throwing arm. Gracefully shifting his weight and planting his right leg, his arm sliced forward like a wound spring, wumph! The ball thumped into Pappas's mitt. Three pitches, Salvo's out, Chicorico retired, and the first inning ended.

The first three innings passed swiftly with Dawson's Brillo Federicci and Ozzie Scarcelli hitting singles only to be stranded at the top of the third. At the bottom of the third, Chicorico batters were blanked out. Palomino's fastball was too fleet.

In the bottom of the fourth, a seesaw battle commenced. Given what appeared to be a long, slow game, Palomino relaxed his fastball. Chicorico's Zeke Tapia and Turk Zukie both singled. With men at first and second, Mary Chicarelli's brother Marco Antonucci took the bat.

"Bravo!" Manuel hollered.

"Show'em home, Marco!" Onorio waved excitedly and almost spilled his wine.

Antonucci stood outside the batter's box, slung the bat over his shoulder, and confidently scanned the outfield with the confidence of Babe Ruth, eyeing where he planned to smack the ball. Stately standing in the batter's box, taller and stockier than Palomino, he hardly crouched, poised to hit. Palomino threw a fastball. Aggressively, Antonucci positioned for a drag bunt. The ball beelined by Palomino and bounced toward right field. Nat MacDougal chased the ball, leaving first base open. Tapia, Zukie advanced, and Antonucci tagged first base.

The Chicorico crowd yelped, yowled, and howled.

Bases loaded, Palomino was in a pinch. The hoopla and catcalls simmered to a murmur. Everybody concentrated on Palomino who confronted "Shorty" Sam García. Stout at five foot one, García's shoulders bulged from beneath his cotton shirt. He bent his knees and squatted low in the batter's box. He knew what he was doing. By narrowing the strike zone, he forced Palomino to pitch sliders and curves.

"Atta, boy, Shorty! Show'em what a *paisano* can do!" Manuel cheered.

"He's no paisano!" Onorio countered, "he's Mexican."

"Maybe so, but he bats like the 'Bambino' hisself," Manuel boasted.

"Atta, boy, Shorty!" Onorio cheered.

Palomino threw three balls. The crowd's clamor cooled. Whoops weltered. Catcalls ceased. The next pitch was fatal, a slider that sliced into the center of García's strike zone. Whack! The ball arched high to an apogee over center field and landed in the crowd near the Company store.

"Babe Ruth, eat your heart out!" Manuel shouted as Tapia, Zukie, Antonucci, and García made the rounds and crossed home plate, 4–0 Chicorico.

The Chicorico crowd catalyzed into a clamorous cacophony of wahoos and yahoos, electrified and exhilarated. Last year's Fourth of July game, Palomino's pitching soundly defeated Chicorico. This year through gutsy tactics, Chicorico hitters had figured a way to use Palomino's fastball against him. Petrified and sullen, the Dawson's crowd wasn't accustomed to losing and didn't like the feeling of trailing behind. Yet, Palomino gave cause for hope. In three pitches, he struck out Freddy Cardarelli and retired Chicorico.

Durocavich was elated. He relished a shutout against Dawson, the leading coal camp team in northern New Mexico and southern Colorado. Dawson had a winning legacy beating most coal camp teams most of the time. Chicorico's fortune rose and fell like volatile shares in the stock market. Durocavich worked three scoreless innings. So did Palomino. Score remained Chicorico 4–0 at the top of the eighth with Dawson at bat.

Durocavich was careless and cocky, dreaming of a shutout. He allowed singles and loaded the bases with Mike Hernandez at third, Larry Vukonich at second, and Brillo Federicci at first. Palomino poised to bat, disheveled and defiant, an angered bull who saw red against Durocavich. He waved Palomino out of the batter's box, sauntered toward home plate, and smirked as he shouted to Julian, "Dust on the plate!"

Julian inspected the plate. "Clean, no dust."

"Something looks dirty on home plate!" Durocavich thumbed his nose at Palomino and turned to walk back to the mound.

Palomino's pocked-face flushed. He exploded expletives and blitzed at Durocavich, flailing the bat. Catcher Sonny Salvo leapt between Palomino and Durocavich. Palomino's bat smacked Salvo's shoulder blades and knocked him to the ground. Julian jumped into the sudden melee, wedging between the two pitchers. "Enough bull! No free-for-alls." Julian pulled Salvo from the ground. "You okay?"

Salvo winched, swinging his arms. "Let's play ball."

"Settle down, boys!" Onorio hollered. Manuel and others raised their voices in agreement, shouting, "Settle down! Cool off!"

Scowling, Palomino returned to the batter's box. Smirking, Durocavich returned to the mound, glimpsed at the three men on base, wound up and pitched sidearm—an inside curve that veered toward Palomino. He keeled backwards, "thud." Ball struck Palomino's left hand index finger.

Enraged, Palomino charged, swinging the bat. Durocavich back-pedaled, stumbled, and fell on his back. First baseman Antonucci and third baseman Mangino dashed to block the charging Palomino. Dawson's Hernandez, Vukonich, and Federicci darted from their bases to block the Chicorico players. Dawson and Chicorico players surrounded the fallen Durocavich. Antonucci hobbled Palomino in a headlock.

"Damn jackasses! Hell bent on stupidity!" Julian cursed vehemently from within the bombastic hubbub. Before anyone could argue, he pitched commands and shut-out the free-for-all. "Let go of Palomino! Help Durocavich to his feet!" He called the pitch: "Palomino, you got a home run, score's 4–4."

"Home run? Home run!" Durocavich protested.

"Not fair! Not fair!" Onorio snorted. Others in the Chicorico crowded joined in the raucous shouting, protesting Julian's call.

Julian ignored the angry Chicorico crowd by shouting above them to the two pitchers. "Shut up!—The two of you! Accidents happen."

"Sun-n-n! No accident!" Palomino protested.

"Bull! Did it on purpose! Boo!" The Dawson crowd booed and hissed.

"Wild throw!" Durocavich scowled.

Julian persisted to ignore the crowd and focused on the players. "Either you fellers cool-off, or game's over! A flat-out draw, and yer to blame for the disgrace in front of your folks." Julian turned to the crowd for their reaction.

Tempers flared in the crowd. Chicorico fans screamed, "It's a walk! American League standards!" Dawson fans wailed, "He did it on purpose! It's only fair!"

"Use American League Standards!" Onorio shouted encouragement and advice. "Don't matter, accident or no."

Manuel, too, saw that Julian had misspoken to the demands of hot tempers. He hollered, "Hold'em to the rules."

Julian heard his friends, listened to the unhappy crowd, and realized he had overreacted. According to American League rules, Palomino was entitled to a walk to first base. "Okay!" Julian relented. "It's a walk."

The crowd simmered down. Chagrined, the players returned to their prior positions while Dr. Monty, the Chicorico Company doctor examined Palomino's left index finger. Dr. Monty bandaged the finger, which was swollen but not broken. Palomino took his place at first. Mike Hernandez tagged home, Dawson 1, Chicorico 4.

Bases loaded, Durocavich was flustered. On the first pitch, Ozzie Scarcelli slammed a line drive immediately inside the right field line. The ball struck a rock and rolled erratically. Vukonich and Federicci tagged home, Palomino stopped at third, and Scarcelli at first, score 3–4. Durocavich was devastated and hastily pitched to Skip Mileta. Another line drive, Palomino crossed home plate, tying the score 4–4. Scarcelli made it to second, but Mileta was out at first.

Durocavich called catcher Salvo to the mound. At the mound, Durocavich whispered through his glove, "Gonna let Pug pop it. Look for a double-play." Salvo nodded and returned behind home plate. Pug Wilkinson stood in the batter's box. Durocavich pitched a fastball right down the middle. Wilkinson popped a fly ball to center field—out. Scarcelli dashed to third and was tagged, Dawson retired.

At the bottom of the eighth, Chicorico batters faced Palomino, who brimmed with bubbly rage. He blanked out Chicorico with sizzling pitches—one, two, three.

"Papa, can I have a dime?" Arturo badgered Manuel. "For ice cream, Eddy and me."

"You already had some."

"Ah, please, jist a dime."

Onorio handed the boys a dime while chastising, "Here, go away. Best part of the game."

"What about me?" Angela begged, clutching Manuel's pant leg. "I want some, too."

Manuel ignored the three-year-old, shaking Angela's loose grip free from his pant leg. Clara lifted Angela in her arms and then suggested to the other mothers, "Dahlia, Mary, let's take the children for ice cream." Clara scowled at the boys. "Give me the dime Mr. Chicarelli gave you." Reluctantly, Eddy surrendered the dime to Clara. The three mothers led the children away to the Company's panel truck that served concessions.

"Kids, I love'em, but—"

Onorio took the words out of Manuel's mouth. "But not at a ballgame."

"Maybe when the boys are older, they'll play ball."

"Be a lot different then."

"Hoo-ray! Bravo!" hardy yells interrupted. Here at the top of the ninth, Dawson's Yob and Pappas had singled. Hernandez popped a line drive down first base. He was sacrificed. Yob advanced to third and Pappas second. Vuckonich took the bat. More of a bear than a jackrabbit at six feet and 280 pounds, Vuckonich was best known to hit the ball hard and run slow. Durocavich pitched an outside slider. Vuckonich extended his massive arms as far as he could, "wang!" He connected. The ball buzzed between short stop and third base, struck a tuft of grass, and rolled toward center field. Yob darted home. The Dawson crowd roared as they took the lead, 5–4.

"Doesn't look good," Onorio lamented.

"Don't ever want Dawson in the lead," Manuel groused. "They'll keep it."

"Hope not."

Pappas at third and Vuckonich at second, Durocavich pitched fastballs to Federicci, who popped a fly ball to left field. Zukie caught it. One out remaining in the top of the ninth, Palomino stood in the batter's box. Durocavich eyed him carefully. Palomino had simmered down. Durocavich pitched an overarm fastball, whack!

The ball zipped off Palomino's bat and headed over García at shortstop. García backpedaled, but didn't call for the catch. Zukie darted from his left field post and collided with García. They tumbled along with the ball till García rolled onto it. From the ground, he tossed the ball wildly to third. Pappas crossed home plate before Vuckonich was tagged out, 7–4 Dawson.

At the bottom of the ninth inning, the Dawson crowd roared, Chicorico crowd fretted. Palomino took the mound. One, two, three, the dispirited Chicorico batters struck out. The Dawson legacy prevailed.

The Chicorico crowd milled in disbelief, so close and yet so far from victory. There would always be next year, a new game, the Chicorico crowd cautioned as they mingled with the Dawson crowd, visiting about friends and relatives. Dawson folks cheered and blew their automobile horns as they dispersed from the field. The players from both sides mingled, shook hands, and teased each other about the game. It was over, a part of coal camp history only to be replayed and disputed at poker games and weddings or wherever miners from the two camps happened to meet.

ELEVEN   TRIP-FOR-TRIP

SWANNIE TEETERED ON A HIGH CLOUD of sobriety and the gawking birds of his discontent flitted in the misty nimbus. His spirit strong, flesh weak, he craved alcohol. One night in mid-July, he awoke sweating with a bad case of the jim-jams, legs twitching spastically, fingertips quivering, hands quaking, and back muscles jiggling. He rolled the covers away, trembling head-to-toe.

A low muffled cough. Eddy coughed again . . . again. The overhead light bulb flashed. Eddy poked his head through the crack in the partition sheets and mumbled groggily, "Can you fetch me some cough syrup? In the cupboard."

His nerves steadied somewhat, Swannie rolled off the sofa, found the large bottle of "Elixir Cough Syrup," returned to Eddy's bedroom, and poured a tad in a teaspoon. Eddy sat up in bed, swallowed the syrup, licked the spoon, smacked his lips, and pulled the blankets over his head, muttering, "Thank you." Eddy slumbered soundly.

Swannie swiped a swig. Elixir contained two-parts molasses and corn syrup and one-part alcohol and claimed to cure most common maladies, including catarrh, coughs, doldrums, hysteria, lumbago, neuralgia, palpitations, and tremors.

Quaking ceased. Drenched in sweat, he lay limp until he slumped in exhausted slumber, dreaming of searching the Chicorico hills and dales for redolent Indian plums when he stumbled into a patch of wild strawberries flourishing in a bog beside a mere trickle of a stream. He gobbled the succulent strawberries and soared to a high more elevating than wine and less numbing than whiskey. The juices oozed from his lips, cascaded down the sides of his mouth, and soaked his shirt. He didn't care and persisted to devour the endless crop of strawberries until 6:00 a.m. when Dahlia nudged his shoulder to awake him to prepare for work. He awoke and wiped drool from his soiled nightshirt. His stomach rumbled from want of strawberries.

"A-choo!" Swannie faked a sneeze at breakfast.

"Here, take a teaspoon." Dahlia handed Swannie the elixir.

"Maybe I shouldn't."

"One teaspoon won't hurt."

"Reckon?"

"Might have miner's cough."

"Miner's cough?"

"Comes from breathing too much coal dust."

"Don't work underground," Swannie mentioned, but gladly complied.

The thick, soothing syrup oozed down his throat and he felt a soft glow, first in the chest, then the stomach, and by the time he sat for breakfast, he effervesced. At work, the glow wore thin, and by 10:00 a.m., it waned. The elixir's soft fire of the morning had burned its course, but while he worked, his body calmed. At day's end, he trudged home thoroughly drained. He'd clean, have supper, and then excuse himself to sleep. When he awoke the next morning, he secretively sipped a teaspoon of elixir to make it through the day.

Dahlia noticed the change in Swannie. He no longer lingered at supper swapping tall tales with Julian or stayed the evening singing hymns around the piano. And she noticed the elixir had practically vanished, although Eddy's summer cough had passed quickly. "Your cough's better." She asked Swannie, "Did the elixir help?"

"Yep. Kilt off the bugs."

"Did you have a lot of bugs?"

"No, not much."

"Hmmm, that's queer. Most the elixir's gone."

"Maybe Eddy or Julian needed some. That durn cough started with Eddy and is making the rounds."

Dahlia asked Eddy. He hadn't any, except the tad Swannie spooned him. She asked Julian and confirmed her fear.

"I don't drink that sweet goo," Julian answered. "You know I snuff to clear my catarrh. Swannie's probably nipping. Stuff's loaded with alcohol."

"Oh, goodness." Dahlia promptly drained the remaining elixir syrup and tossed the bottle in the outhouse pit. Disappointed and ambivalent, she confided in Julian.

"You did good, tossing the elixir and all. We can't be too careful with him. Don't want him back in the bottle." Then, Julian wryly divined a self-fulfilling prophecy, "Wait and see, he'll nip my chokecherry wine, next."

Soon as Swannie discovered the elixir's disappearance, he visited Dr. Monty and requested a new bottle.

"No bottle, no refill," Dr. Monty informed Swannie. "Each family gets a pint bottle." Dr. Monty waved to a cabinet filled with gallon jugs of elixir. "Refilled as needed, provided the bottle is brought."

More than one way to skin a cat, Swannie reasoned and rearranged his morning routine. Upon rising at 6:00 a.m., he took his morning constitutional at the outhouse, sneaked into the cellar, nipped a shot of chokecherry wine from a cask, and sedately returned to the kitchen, fixed to start the day.

At dusk one Saturday, Swannie studied the sunset over the hills of Chicorico. Resplendent in tones of azure gray, orange, yellow, and red, the sunrays flared from the horizon in vertical streaks, like spokes on a wheel, and struck the layered clouds, transforming the mellow tones into a vivid orange, blue sky. Then, the rays rolled off the clouds and cascaded toward the hills. Slumbering, gray shadows gave way to the dark. Diffident stars reappeared and gradually illuminated the sky from rim to rim of Chicorico Canyon.

Julian joined Manuel and Onorio at a clubhouse poker game. Dahlia bathed Eddy, took him to Mrs. Montaño's, and left him there to play with Arturo. She joined Mrs. Chicarelli. They walked to Dr. Monty's where they took turns soaking and bathing. The best known secret in Chicorico, the women rotated Saturday nights to soak and bathe in a real tub with hot and cold running water, a luxury encouraged by Etta, Dr. Monty's wife. "Rank has its privileges," she said to justify the luxury, "and women rank the highest."

Bathing at Etta's was pure pleasure. The tub was pretty much like others, indistinguishable from many in middle-class homes, except it was one of the few bathtubs—an oblong cast-iron basin coated with white porcelain standing on eagle claws clenching brass balls—in Chicorico with hot and cold running water. Long and deep enough for the women to recline covered to the shoulders in hot water, they could drain it and run fresh hot water without hauling buckets of water from the outside pump and heating it on the cookstove. And they shared store-bought soap.

On this serene July Saturday evening, with the Heards recreating elsewhere and the crickets chirruping in continual cadences, Swannie treated himself to a bath in a Number-4 tin tub. Afterwards, he sat on the sofa alone with the New Testament. . . . Dusk's light dimmed. Rather than squinting to read the Bible's tiny print, he flipped the tiny, square switch at the base of the light socket. A bare, bald bulb beamed brightly downward, casting a circle of crescent light that flowed outward and lapped against the walls, the tiny print easier to see.

His fingers twitched and toes trembled. Kicking off his shoes and socks, and scrunching his toes on the cool, wood floor, he attempted to ignore his hippity-hop heels and almost ripped a New Testament page with his jim-jamming, trembling fingers as he flipped it to continue chapter two of the Gospel according to John.

Gradually, the quaking quelled. He eased into a parable, attention riveted on why Jesus was invited to a wedding. When His mother Mary mentioned there was no wine for the wedding, Jesus requested, "Fill the pots with water." They were filled. Then Jesus requested, "Draw out now." Everybody was astonished. Jesus had changed water into wine. Chapter two, verse eleven explained: "This beginning of miracles did Jesus in Cana of Galilee, and manifested for His glory."

Enthralled by the Lord's splendid alchemy, Swannie recalled Julian's more mundane miracle of turning the acrid juices of wild chokecherries into a fine wine. Swannie thought, "If'n I drink some of the bottled wine, Julian will notice." He searched the kitchen for an empty jug, planning to take a little from Julian's wine cask to conceal the petty larceny. He found a jar under the wash basin, scrambled out the back door into the cellar, filled the jar from Julian's keg of chokecherry wine, and returned to the sofa, savoring the tart nectar.

His eyes blurred. Demon crows crowded the room, swooping, "gaw, gaw, gaw, gaw." Both hands clutching the Bible, he shielded his face. They pierced the Bible and picked at his nose and ears, "gaw, gaw, gaw, gaw." He tottered to his feet and wobbled out the house. He skittered forward, flung both arms frantically, and shooed the frantic crows away before stumbling limply down the porch steps. Remembering a quick cure used by doughboys to sober up, raw eggs mixed into black coffee, he hobbled up the steps into the kitchen and placed a pot of coffee on the stove.

He hobbled out the house to the hutch where the rooster and hens were sleeping. Clumsily, he shoved them aside, groping for eggs. Bedlam bristled! Squawking squeamishly, the hens flapped their wings and fluttered wildly about the crowded hutch. The rooster hopped to their defense and pecked at Swannie's shins. Swannie dashed out the hutch, the hens and rooster in hot pursuit. He tripped out the chicken coup and fell to his knees. Hiding his face in his hands, he lowered his head to the ground, prostrate as if in prayer. The crows circled, "gaw, gaw, gaw."

Later in the evening, Dahlia returned home with Eddy, cheery from the soothing bath. She put Eddy to bed and smelled burnt coffee on the stove. The coffee had boiled over. She wrapped a towel over the pot's hot handle and carried it to the back porch to cool off. Outside in the dark, she heard hens clucking in the backyard, shooed them back into the hen house, and stumbled over Swannie dozing on the ground.

Dahlia patted Swannie's face briskly. Groggy and limp, he awoke. She helped him to his feet and into the house and put him to bed on the sofa. He slumbered. Sadly, she slid a blanket over him and smelled the reek of vomit and chokecherry wine on his shirt.

"Thank-ee. Thank-ee," Swannie mumbled.

Dahlia started to leave Swannie in his misery, but couldn't without first asking, "You were doing so well. What happened?"

"Nothing."

"Nothing? Then why are you hitting the bottle?"

"Jist a bum, an'—"

"Nonsense! You make yourself to be a bum, but you are no such thing!"

"God's punishing me."

"The fault is not the Lord's. You know better."

"Then, must be the Devil."

"The Devil does your deeds—your will. The Lord gave you gifts, talents. You must choose to use them, for good or bad."

"Never had the chance to grow up—a boy in a man's body."

"You're no longer a boy! It's high time you face that fact. I pray you will." She whisked away from Swannie's makeshift bedroom. When Julian returned from the poker game, she confided in him.

"Humph!" Julian snorted. "First, our cough syrup, now my wine. Nothin' but a yokel. I have a mind to throw him out."

"He's got to grow up. Says he's a boy in a man's body."

"Lots of us fought in the Great War. Made us grow up fast. No place for boys in the trenches. Swannie's using that for an excuse to drown in self-pity."

"He suffered greatly, losing his parents and sweetheart—at the same time."

"Honey's there's lot'a doughboys like Swannie. The War turned them into drunks and drifters. Can't settle down to home and family. He's no different, but it's every man for himself. He's go to make the changes in his heart, his soul. He don't seem to give a care about himself. About others."

"We care for him. That should help him."

"Honey, I feel for him. . . . Come to like having him around. . . . World of good for Eddy. I'm at wit's end. We treat him like family, but he don't wanna change his ways. What more can we do?"

"I don't know. Try talking about that—we love him—and want him to change."

"Can't talk that way."

"Please talk to him, man-to-man.

The next morning, Swannie awoke home alone remembering little. He stuffed his reeking shirt into a bushel basket Dahlia used for a hamper and stoked a fire in the cookstove. He drew water from the outside pump and noticed the coffeepot on the porch railing, half-filled with thick coffee. He tossed the thick coffee in the garden. Back in the kitchen, he dolloped fresh coffee into the pot and placed it on the stove. Draining tepid water from the stove's boiler pan, he washed and shaved, replacing the tepid water in the boiler pan with some he'd fetched from the pump. He poured a cup of coffee, returned to the sofa, and studied the maps of the Holy Lands in his Bible. When the Heards returned from church services, Julian said nothing to Swannie about his prior evening binge but instead invited him on a fishing trip, asking Swannie to spade for grubs and earthworms while he gathered his fishing gear.

"Where should I dig?"

"About the garden. An' run, fetch Manuel and Onorio. They'll have worms, too."

Julian was fastidious about his fishing gear and stored it in an ammunition crate he used to ship his belongings home from France when he mustered out the Army. Designed to keep ammunition dry, the crate worked well for the gear. He treasured two bait casting rods and a bamboo fly rod. Spooled with a six pound–test cotton line, the reels were stored in their original cardboard boxes and sparkled when he removed and mounted them on the rod's handles. Before storing his hooks, he sun-dried them to prevent rusting. He also tied his own flies and stored them in a miniature Lane cedar chest his mother had used to store handkerchiefs.

The men converged on Julian's pickup and loaded their gear.

"Swannie," Julian asked, "crank the engine?"

"You bet."

"Then, if'n you don't mind, hop in back."

"Oh, sure, like Eddy."

"Manuel and Onorio'll ride up front. Maybe on the way home, one of them can switch with you."

The drive to Lake Maloya moved smoothly with only a few delays. After leaving Chicorico, the road followed a cattle trail that skirted the foothills and passed the coal camps of Van Houten and Swastika, where the road veered east to Raton. Paralleling the Santa Fé Railway through Raton on First Street, the road crossed the tracks north of the roundhouse, and turned onto State Highway 72. Julian parked in front of Ruiz's Café where Manuel and Onorio walked around the back of the café. Mrs. Ruiz observed the Sabbath. Manuel prevailed upon her to sell a batch of steamed *tamales*. "The best tamales in New Mexico!" Manuel claimed as he returned, handing the bag of tamales to Swannie to wedge between the tackle boxes.

They continued east from the café on Highway 72, ascended a slope onto a plateau, and passed Fairmount Cemetery where Swannie's parents and sweetheart were buried. Beyond the cemetery, Highway 72 intersected with Buena Vista Avenue at the highest spot of the plateau—a knoll overlooking the Raton area that served as a campsite for Santa Fé Trail traders and the U.S. Calvary in the early 1800s.

Spanish guides dubbed the knoll *"buena vista"*—a good view. At the Buena Vista intersection, a row of railroad boxcars had been arranged for temporary housing by Santa Fé Railroad maintenance workers and families when Raton was first settled. When they moved to newly constructed frame houses closer to the maintenance yard and roundhouse, other less fortunate people used the boxcars as regular housing.

Swannie spotted the boxcar he'd occupied for at least twelve years and fondly recalled the kindness of his Mexican neighbors. They were generous with their meager food supply and gave him enough to stave off hunger. *"Poco loco en la cabeza,"* touched in the head, they affectionately joked with him, giving food and company whenever he asked.

Mrs. Jiron's bread was the best. He recalled helping her bake bread in an adobe *horno*. Swannie's job was to stoke an extremely hot fire in her dome-shaped adobe kiln, and after the wood had burned itself out, clear away the embers and ashes. After Mrs. Jiron scooted rising loaves of bread dough into the horno, Swannie plugged the horno door and ventilation hole. In a few hours, the bread was baked with a slightly brown crust. For his help, she gave him a loaf of bread and a generous pot of beans. Lasted three days.

Outside Raton parallel to the Santa Fé spur railway, Highway 72 rolled over the undulating prairie leading to Yankee and Sugarite. Unpaved, deeply rutted in places, and ribbed in washboards, the roadbed was dusty and dangerous with jagged rocks and rutted gulches that could break an axle or puncture a tire. Julian held the Model A to twenty-miles-an-hour, negotiating among the rocks and ruts. At the Sugarite-Yankee junction, they exited Highway 72 and turned northwest to Sugarite Canyon.

The unpaved canyon road wound along Sugarite Creek with no guardrails or rip-rap on its banks to keep mud or rock slides from blocking the road. Recent thunder showers and flash floods had washed out parts of the road so Julian had to slow down considerably on some curves. Entering Sugarite, Swannie noted that without the blight of slack piles dotting the hillsides, Sugarite appeared to be a tranquil mountain resort rather than a coal camp, its stone-block houses neatly aligned in rows along both slopes of the canyon.

The Sugarite coal camp operated three mines, sported a Company store, an opera house, a Bell Telephone Company office, and a four-room, two-storied schoolhouse made of locally quarried sandstone. The second floor auditorium was used for school and community events, Saturday night dances, Wednesday and Sunday night movies, holiday pageants, school plays, sewing circles, fraternal lodges, city band practice, and all other community activities, except labor union meetings. The school grounds were always filled on weekends and holidays for picnics, soccer, and baseball games.

They passed by the Sugarite tipple, washhouse, and mule barns and then wound through the canyon to Lake Maloya. Julian parked on the lake's south side. Much of the south shore was lined with ponderosas, and while fishing was better on the north with plenty of deep pools, the men preferred the south—fewer anglers and shadier groves. They found a cool site under tall, stately ponderosas. Undergrowth grew beneath the ponderosas' majestic crowns where the sun seeped through the thick canopies, sprouting Colorado blue spruces in patches.

Talking ceased. Julian handed Swannie a fishing rod rigged with line, leader, hook, and sinker and pointed to a can of worms. "Bait up with two or three worms, Swannie," Julian advised, "jist in case you lose parts to nibbles."

Swannie had never fished and was too embarrassed to admit it. He copied the others as they wove earthworms on their hooks, pretending the squirming worm didn't bother him.

The men stood about ten feet apart along the shoreline. Swannie took a place to the left of Julian and cast. The line flung erratically before bundling into backlashes, jamming the reel. He unraveled the backlashes and reeled-in. He started, surprised by Julian standing beside him. Without speaking, Julian motioned Swannie to watch him hold the rod for casting. Thumb on the spool, Julian raised his rod to twelve o'clock high, arm slightly bent, and then flicked the rod, barely lifting thumb pressure from the spool.

Swannie imitated Julian and was pleased to see the line and sinker arch into the sky and kerplop into the water. Julian rapped Swannie's shoulder and returned to his fishing spot. Swannie waited eagerly for the big bites. None came. Nibbles . . . nibbles . . . more nibbles . . . itty-bitty nibbles. . . . A tentative tug on the taut line. . . . Line sagged. Swannie reeled the line taut. Water beads dribbled down the line. Another tug. He jerked the pole and reeled quickly—bait gone, hook barren.

Julian broke the silence, speaking softly from the side of his mouth. "Rainbows are nibblers. It's a jiggling act. Give a lot of play. Feel your line, like this." He placed the line between his thumb and index finger. "When you feel a Rainbow nibbling, set the hook in his mouth by giving a real easy tug on the line. He'll chase it, gobble the bait, and set the hook, catching himself."

"Then what?"

"Reel with jist the right amount of tension."

"How much tension?"

"So's not to snap the line."

Selecting a fat earthworm, Swannie laid it in his palm and watched it writhe before he jabbed its squirming belly onto the harpooned hook and threaded the worm onto it. He cast. The line arched much higher and sank much farther from the shore than his first cast. He felt good about the cast, relaxed his stiff stance, and gently crumpled to the ground.

He waited a long time without a nibble. . . . A tentative tug on the line. He stood, dug his feet into the ground, and stiffened his knees. The line sagged for a moment, then lightly jerked. "Bite it, bite it," he mumbled to himself, "bite it hard." He flicked his wrist ever so slightly and reeled slowly.

Pole bowed, line drew taut—"Gotcha!"

The fish swam back and forth parallel to the shore, then burst above the surface of the water in a graceful, arching leap, flaunting its resplendent rainbow hues before splashing into the depths and taking more and more line with it. Swannie couldn't hold onto the reel's spinning handle and released it, whiiiizzzzzzz! The reel spun speedily. The scrappy Rainbow pulled the line further from the shore and deeper into the water to the end of the line, pang! The line snapped and wiggled away into the water's slick, silvery surface.

"That dang trout!" Swannie hopped in a huff, lifting the pole to throw.

Julian gripped his wrist, "What'cha doing?"

"Stupid pole's no good."

"Don't blame the pole for your shortcomings. The pole's a tool you make work for you. You didn't make the catch."

"That durn Rainbow snapped the line!"

"Should'a give some play when you reeled, holding back a little to tire him. You let him run with the line till it snapped. Here, take my pole. I'll fix us some coffee." Julian released his wrist and took Swannie's pole.

Julian reeled in what was left of the snapped line, placed the pole in the bed of the pickup and rummaged through his gear for coffee and a charred pot. He cleared the ashes from an old campfire site and gathered some dry branches, twigs, and grass. Placing the grass and twigs in the center of the campfire stones, he lit a match to the dry grass. It wrinkled and turned black, the twigs shriveling into flames. He added the dry branches. A chipmunk bolted out of the fire from its nest in the stones. "Hu, hu," Julian chortled, watching the chipmunk scurry away. "Roasted chipmunk."

While waiting for the branches to burn down into hot coals, he poured fresh water and coffee into the pot and positioned it directly on the fire. On the open fire, he boiled the coffee up—and then cooked it down—until it was thick as syrup. While Julian tended the coffee, the others reeled in. Swannie looked on, not knowing what to do next. Onorio and Manuel had been fishing for two hours without uttering a word. They continued their silent ritual as they put away their gear, waving Swannie to reel in.

Onorio gave Swannie two cups and pointed toward the shoreline where Manuel knelt, rinsing two other tins cups. Swannie rinsed the cups in the cool water of the lake and joined the others around the campfire. With a pair of pliers, Julian lifted the steamy hot, charred pot and carefully poured thick coffee into each cup. They blew on the steaming coffee and sat sipping quietly. Manuel passed around Mrs. Ruiz's tamales. They peeled the cornhusks back and munched the moist cornmeal stuffed with strips of beef and chili, tossing the husks into the campfire.

After a long, quiet spell, Julian refilled everybody's cup and then pitched the surplus coffee and grounds over the campfire's embers. He scooped water from the lake and saturated the campfire. "Fellers, when we done here, let's walk over yonder." Julian pointed toward the spillway.

"Pretty deep. Water's running fast," Onorio observed.

"Won't be trout there," Manuel added.

"Maybe. Look to either side of the spillway. See the riffles. It's the backwash, grubs and bugs floating there. Might see some fish feeding on the surface. Let's have a look-see." Julian asked Swannie, "Whyn't you bring the stringer?"

"Stringer's okay here, ain't it?"

"Naw. Raccoons will get to it. Look'a them prints."

Swannie scanned the shoreline and saw the footprints of deer, raccoon, and turkey that had watered on the shore earlier in the day. "Okay, I'm no angler." Swannie lifted the stringer from the water. Four trout hung motionless. The other two writhed frantically.

He strolled casually along the shore savoring the cama raderie of the men, the clarity of the sky, and the bold profiles of Bartlett and Barela Mesa shouldering the canyon on both sides and converging into a bowl forming Lake Maloya. The others walked ahead. Julian swung his arms in rhythm with his strides. Onorio watched the ground and kept both hands in his pockets, listening intently. Engrossed in telling a *cuento*, Manuel held his head high and waved his arms wildly as though directing an orchestra.

Swannie caught up to them at the dam where they were clambering gingerly over mammoth basalt boulders. Swannie cautiously grabbled over the sharp-edged boulders, one hand firmly gripping the dangling stringer of trout above the boulders.

"Over here." Julian waved toward the riffles beside the spillway flowage. "Drop'em in the water."

Swannie wedged the stringer stick between two boulders and dipped the trout into the riffling current. The four dead trout floated and the other two wiggled in a futile effort to swim away from their dead comrades.

"Look'a here." Julian pointed to the waterline beside the spill-way. Swannie joined Manuel and Onorio on their knees, peering into the murky water.

"Over the years, the water's washed back on both sides the spillway, eroding a two foot bench below the water line. I've walked it in the fall when the water's down."

The water was translucent gray. Dead bugs, leaves, and twigs tumbled in the surly flow. Swannie spotted a school of suckers scavenging on the bench. "Hey, there's fish down there!"

"Join'em!" Julian shoved Swannie over the bank.

Swannie hit the turbid water, tumbled onto the bench, and plunged forward. Water flooded his eyes, nose, ears. His heavy shoeboots and soaked clothing pulled him further down. Water enveloped him. Eyes tightly shut, he held his breath, head bloating, felt like exploding. Onorio's and Manuel's muffled voices. Strong, powerful hands gripped his ankles and wrists and heaved him above the water line. Onorio and Manuel stood in the water and held him horizontally on the lake's surface.

"First, our cough syrup!" Voice surcharged with fury, Julian dunked Swannie's head under water and held it there.

Swannie's head pounded, his heart throbbed. He jerked his neck, but the hard strength of Julian's hands grasped him firmly. Julian lifted Swannie's face. Swannie gasped for air. Julian shouted again, "And, my wine!"

Again, Julian's hands covered Swannie's nose and mouth and shoved his head below the water line and held it there while Onorio and Manuel firmly grasped his legs and ankles. Swannie couldn't squirm, or breathe, or yell.

"Cold turkey!" Swannie heard Julian's muffled voice, a mouth full of marbles. "Keep away from the hooch! You can't control the hooch. It controls you. Don't drink it! Cold turkey! One more drink, I'll feed you to the fish!"

The cold of the water rushed through Swannie's hair and chilled him to the bone. Bubbles trickled from his mouth. He stopped resisting. Limp.

Julian jerked Swannie's head from the water. Swannie gasped for air. Manuel and Onorio dragged him to shore and laid him on the water's edge. He gasped, coughed, and squirmed. The putrid taste of Mrs. Ruiz's tamales soured his palate.

"Guess the suckers scrammed." Onorio gave a hand to Julian, lifting him from the water.

"Yep, after that accident."

"Wasn't no accident!" Swannie chattered through his teeth. "I could'a drownd." Swannie sputtered, coughed, and shook water from his hair.

"You lived," Onorio scoffed.

"You've been baptized in fire," Manuel added,

The men roared raucously at Manuel's mixed metaphor.

"Nothin' funny 'bout it!" Julian thwarted the levity. "Won't happen again. Next time you hit the bottle, you hit the road! You wallow in self-pity, like a spoilt boy. You gotta change. Break the mold you done made for yourself. Seems you don't care for nothin'. Dahlia and Eddy treat you like a brother. You ain't thinkin' 'bout them. All's you do is hit the bottle."

"What about you?" Swannie asked meekly.

"I can hold my hooch."

"Not talking about the hooch. Talking 'bout you. You want me to stick around?"

Julian pondered. Manuel appeared as puzzled as Julian, who turned his gaze away from Swannie toward the Barela Mesa rimrocks.

"Well?"

Without shifting his gaze from the rimrocks, Julian answered, "We ain't talking 'bout me. If'n you don't care none 'bout yourself, you best think 'bout Dahlia and Eddy. You wanna be 'round them, you best make the change now."

Conversation stopped. Julian glared at Swannie. Onorio and Manuel gazed numbly at the the rushing water clattering over the spillway. Lanky shadows of the tall ponderosas issued over the western shore of the lake onto its silvery surface. Swannie cast a cagey glance at Julian and then lowered his gaze, complaining, "Brrr, I'm cold."

"We're all soaked. Best we go home." Julian raised the trout stringer from the water. Dead. None wiggled and writhed. He offered his hand to Swannie, who was still squatting on the shore.

Swannie nonchalantly grasped Julian's hand and lifted himself to his feet. Still holding Julian's hand, Swannie jerked back his arm and thrust a foot forward. Julian tripped headfirst into the water. Swannie hollered, "Some of your own medicine!"

"Ha! Ha! Ha!" Again, Manuel and Onorio roared raucously. "Turn about is fair play!"

Julian thrashed about treading water before spotting the stringer of trout floating rapidly toward the spillway. Julian flailed his arms on the surface of the water, attempting to rescue the dead fish. They swirled into the rushing rapids and rolled over the spillway.

PART II   UNSETTLING AFFAIRS

TWELVE · HE GIVES AND HE TAKES

Been more'an a year, Julian reflected. *He's changed some. Lake Maloya baptism in fire scairt Devil out'a him. Some good come from the dunkin'. Tad more serious. Not terribly gullible, like he us'ta be. More like a kid coming to his own. Kinda late. Must be thirty ought years, 'bout Jimmy's age. He's managed to keep Linderman off his back. Bowers, too. Think Bowers kinda likes him. Leastwise, he tolerates a little guff from Swannie. 'Course, Bowers don't take him serious.*

"Honey—penny for your thoughts?"

"Uh, they ain't worth much."

"Oh?"

"Jist flying in the clouds."

"Well, light on a branch. I have good news. Anna's baby is due any time. Hope it's a girl."

"Man's better off with boys."

"Judo has five boys now. Only one girl."

"More boys the better. To care for you when yer old."

"By heck! How selfish."

"No more so'an you. Why d'ya want a girl?"

"Common sense. When she's little, she's a joy—dressing her in pretty attire. Curling her hair. When she's older, teaching her piano. Sharing her dreams, her hopes."

"Fret over her boyfriends, most likely. To marry her off, an' fret over her more. Husband may be a flash-in-the-pan—a yokel can't keep a job. He might beat her, which I'd have to stand up to. Or, get kilt, leaving your girl with a house full of kids and bills. O-yez! Once you have a girl, you have her forever."

"Why, Julian, you don't like girls."

"That's not my drift. I owe. Girls grow into ladies. They bring civilization to a man's world. Like you, your music. An' you take care of us right well. But, your Pa, he fretted about you till the day he died. 'Cause he loved you. If'n we ever had a girl, I'd love her till the day I die, an' that promises to be fretful."

"And Eddy will be on his own?"

"Once he's a man."

"You won't fret about him?"

"Not near the way I'd fret over a girl."

"Anna has enough boys. I wish a girl for her."

Within a few days, Dahlia's wish came true. Black leather bag in hand, Dr. Monty rushed to the home of Judo Perkovich where Anna was about to birth a child. Up to now, she had borne five boys and a girl. Dr. Monty sent Judo to fetch Dahlia who came promptly and prepared to assist with the delivery. She arranged for Nick and George to stay with the Montaños and Roddy, Max, and Sophia at the Chicarellis for the next few days. She warmed water, arranged towels and linens, and sterilized a pair of Anna's scissors in a pan of boiling water until Dr. Monty called for them to snip the baby's umbilical cord.

"She's a little angel." Dahlia wrapped the infant in a towel and handed her to Mrs. Perkovich. "Rosy cheeks. Auburn hair. Beaming eyes, only a few minutes old."

Anna took the baby girl in arms, uncovered her face, brushed aside the auburn hair, and examined the baby. "Jes, she is angel."

"What will you call her?"

"Joanna—'Jozef' after Judo's Papa, 'Anna' after Mama."

"Wasn't 'Jozef ' the first baby's name, the boy that died?"

"Jes."

"But, then—"

"Don' a-worry, she grow strong—a mama someday."

"Oh, yes, yes! And, she'll have the pick of the camp. She's so pretty."

"Good looking, like her Ma!"

"An' a free spirit, too."

Later that evening, Judo returned from the Montaños to find Mrs. Perkovich and baby fast asleep. Dahlia coached him on duties around the house for the ensuing days. "Come over at dinner. On workdays, come by for breakfast, if you want." She gathered her belongings and prepared to leave. "You're a lucky man, Judo. You have four strong boys, and now two beautiful girls."

Dahlia dropped by daily at mid-morning to tend to Mrs. Perkovich who was ordered by Dr. Monty to stay in bed for two weeks, a standard practice. Often Dahlia brought Mrs. Chicarelli or Mrs. Montaño to assist with housecleaning chores. Dahlia volunteered to do Anna's washing on a regular basis for the next few months. Swannie assisted Dahlia when he could. Daily, Dahlia kept Julian, Eddy, and Swannie informed of Mrs. Perkovich's progress.

"We're invited to Joanna's baptismal."

"Yahoo!" Swannie cheered. "Come to know Mrs. Perkovich, and the boys. Time to mend fences with Mr. Perkovich."

"Mend fences?"

"For finking on him."

"That's water under the bridge. He's ornery but has a heart of gold."

"Honey," Julian queried, "aren't the Perkovich's Orthodox?"

"Yes, why?"

"Who's gonna baptize the baby?"

"They're sending for an Orthodox priest from Pueblo."

On a Thursday afternoon in late September, Bowers took Swannie with him to the mine entry to assist with the repair of a gondola bucket. Normally, the tipple and surrounding work area bustled with men and machines. Motorcars pulled strings of coal cars from inside the mine to the tipple where the coal was weighed, sorted, and washed in the prep plant. Tailings—rocks, sand, shale—were hauled away by gondola buckets and dumped in growing piles of inert slack. When the broken gondola was detected, tipple operations ceased and outside workers gathered beneath the cable lines that suspended the broken gondola bucket.

Hanging overhead, the gondolas traveled to and from the slack piles to the tipple suspended on a steel cable that pulled them in a circle from a davit crane, which was attached to cement abutments and protruded from the entryway of the mine. The gondolas were shaped like water buckets with two pig-iron arms held together by an axle and wheel that rolled on the cable. The broken gondola's pig-iron axle had chipped and the gondola tipped to the side. A slight gust of wind, or a tug on the cable, could cause the gondola to fall to the ground and shatter into pieces.

As Swannie and Bowers arrived, Osgood was climbing a wooden power pole to take a closer look. He scrutinized the gondola's broken axle and then shouted to Bowers down on the ground: "Gotta move her! To where we can take her apart!"

"How do you figure?" Bowers shouted back.

"They don't make sky hooks! To hold her in the air! Change the axle," Osgood shouted testily. "Now get with it! Tell Martin to inch her slow-like—towards the slack pile. When she nudges again' the slack pile, we can tie her down—remove the broken axle."

"Kinda risky! Them buckets cost a lot!"

"Well, then, git some sky hooks!"

"Jist don't wanna break the bucket! Doesn't take much to shatter pig-iron!"

"She shouldn't fall—if'n we run the cable real slow."

"Let's try her, slow-like."

"Lemme get down! You boys git out'a the way!"

Osgood shimmied down the pole. The others edged a safe distance away. Bowers hustled to the crane's platform directly above the mine entry where Zack Martin operated the davit crane pulleys that moved the cables carrying the gondolas. Bowers instructed Martin to gradually sidle the broken gondola toward the slack until it nudged against the pile.

All eyes on the broken gondola, Martin started the cable's motor. The cable lurched! Jerked! The other gondolas waggled in succession, like puppets on a string.

"Squirrelly switch," Martin muttered, wiggling the motor's electric switch.

The cable crept, lurched, and stopped.

"Switch's shorting out!" Martin shouted while jiggling the switch. The motor started.

"Ram the switch!" Bowers shouted. "Hold it tight! Keep the juices flowing!"

Martin gripped the switch tightly to keep the electrical currents flowing and the cable moving slowly . . . The cable inched toward the slack pile. The broken gondola waddled against it.

Martin released the switch. Jammed—the motor continued running, the cable moving, the broken gondola slamming into the slack pile. Martin flipped the switch rapidly, attempting frantically to stop the motor. The gondola's cable line lurched and then humped into waves that rippled along the cable—fop!

The cable snapped. The gondolas plunged to the ground successively, like dominoes falling in a row, thud, thud, thud. Overhead, the end of the broken cable flung toward the entry, lashing like a huge whip.

Judo Perkovich—leaving the mine early to greet Father Grishan, the Orthodox priest due to arrive at the Raton depot from Pueblo, Colorado, to baptize his newborn daughter Joanna—strolled from the entry into the sunlight just beneath the davit crane. He didn't see the steel cable whipping down toward him at fifty miles an hour. It lashed around his neck, smacked him off his feet, threw him over a berm, and tumbled him into a shallow bar ditch. Unraveling, the cable continued to lash loosely, whipping wildly upon the railway. Judo lay facedown in the bar ditch in full mining gear, battery lamp beaming.

Swannie sprinted spider-swift toward Judo, jerked to a stop, and fell on his knees, lifting Judo's shoulders and cradling them. Eyes shut, Judo's head lulled and dangled to the side, like doughboys Swannie had cradled on the battlefields in France. Osgood, Bowers, Martin, and others congregated, crouching and glancing grimly at the dead man cradled in Swannie's arms. After a spell, Swannie felt the strain of Judo's dead weight. Delicately, he lowered Judo to the ground and disconnected the battery cable to Judo's headlamp. A subdued, befuddled Osgood asked: "Know this man?"

"Judo." Swannie sighed. "Judo Perkovich."

Anna's brother George Yaksich took charge of funeral arrangements. Because the Raton mortuary required full payment in cash from miners before preparing a body for burial, Judo's body lay in Dr. Monty's office for a few days, covered with a white sheet. George procured an itemized list of burial expenses from the mortician, who provided what he called a "bare-bones burial," preparation of the body, a pine casket and vault, a wake in the mortuary's chapel, and burial in the pauper's section of Raton's Mount Calvary Cemetery:

Burial Expenses ~ Judo Perkovich	
Casket (wood)	$30.00
Vault (wood)	5.00
Embalming, etc.	3.00
Cemetery plot	.50
Wake	1.00
Hearse	10.00
Suit	5.00
Dress underwear	2.00
Shoes & socks	3.00
Flowers (none)	0
Candles (none)	0
Headstone (wood)	1.00
Digging & Backfill Grave	0
(Judo's friends will do)	
TOTAL EX	*$60.50*

George quibbled with the ten-dollar charge for the hearse. "Got one to haul the stiff?" the mortician answered crassly. And, the one-dollar charge for the wake? "Rent" for use of the chapel, the mortician called it. Otherwise, George would have to pay for storage of the body in the mortuary's backroom or pay to have the body delivered to Judo's home for keeping until the funeral. "Six or one-half dozen, or the other," the mortician muttered, "makes no difference to me." George also objected to the exorbitant costs of clothing for Judo. "Get it from the family, or, bury him naked," the mortician smirked, "makes no difference. It'll rot either way."

George circulated among Chicorico neighbor and friends with itemized list in hand, asking for scrip and apologizing for the inflated expenses. They gave what they could. "A man deserves a good funeral," one said. And another, "When a man dies, the vultures and morticians move in fast to pick him clean." Others grumbled about the Company's share, "Company kills a man, wife pays to bury him." None embarrassed George, cheerfully noting "don't got much, but you can have it" and "give what I got."

George collected enough scrip to pay for the bare-bones burial and felt good about the warm generosity of Chicorico folks. Swannie donated his tattered but clean blazer and one of Jimmy's white shirts and silk ties. George decided Judo could be dressed in work clothing from the waist down. After he was laid in the pine casket, the lid could be nailed from the waist down, and none would be the wiser. Judo would be buried in style—blazer, white shirt, and silk tie.

When George took the scrip to Bowers to cash, Bowers made the exchange at seventy-five cents per dollar's worth of scrip. George knew better than to quibble over the scrip-for-cash ratio because Bowers could refuse to cash the scrip. Bowers also declared the Company would foot the bill for a pine vault for Judo's casket, leaving five dollars to pay for religious services. In addition, any miners or Company men could attend the funeral without pay for the day. Bowers delegated Swannie to represent the Company and oddly didn't dock his pay. Father Grishan, whom Judo had requested to baptize his daughter Joanna, remained for the wake and burial, his keep provided in the boardinghouse by the Company.

Along with Julian, Manuel, and Onorio, many of the miners and their families attended the wake in the evening. Fewer attended the burial, among those were Manuel, Julian, Onorio, and several other Serbian families related to Judo and Anna. Father Grishan conducted graveside services in the Serbian language.

While Judo's friends lowered the casket into the pine vault and covered it with dirt, coal camp families huddled around the grave offering condolences to Anna who clutched baby Joanna tightly, her four sons and daughter standing beside her. Swannie noticed two well-dressed gentlemen standing apart from the huddled crowd in the shade of a juniper tree. Both wore black suits and vests, high-collared, white shirts and ties, and derby hats. Swannie could tell by their formal attire they were not from the coal camps.

"Howdy," Swannie ambled toward the men. "I'm Swannie Swanson, representing the Chicorico Coal Company, here at Judo's funeral. Ya here to pay last respects?"

"Paah!" the tall, thin man snorted. "Respects better when you're alive."

"Thought I knew the big shots in the Chicorico Company." The shorter man extended his hand. "So yer a big shot?"

"Wouldn't say that." Swannie didn't extend a handshake.

"Any other Company men here?"

"Nope, jist me."

"Sorry, rube," the taller man offered an apology, "we forgot our manners. I'm Ed Doyle, secretary-treasurer, District 15, United Mine Workers of America. This is Frank Hayes, vice-president."

"Yer the big shots? From the Union!" Swannie gladly extended his hand.

"Yep." Doyle and then Hayes extended their hands. "And if you boys had a union, Judo might be alive today."

"Or, he'd be having a better funeral," Hayes noted. "His family would be cared for, too."

"Whyn't you talk to them gentlemen." Swannie pointed toward the crowd.

"You mean Moñtano, Chicarelli, and Heard?"

"Yep."

"We have. Onorio treated us to some wine. Nice cellar, good place for a meetin'. We understand it's the only place safe to talk union in Chicorico. We had a good talk."

"What'd they say?"

"Sorry, can't tell."

"Confidential," Hayes explained, "especially to a Company big shot." Hayes nudged Swannie on the shoulder.

"That's okay by me. Seems the more I know, the more dangerous things get."

Following Judo's burial, a somber baptism and reception were provided for all comers at the Perkovich home. Father Grishan asked everybody to witness the baptism of Joanna Perkovich, a blessing from Heaven. The Lord gives, and He takes.

Coal camp wives hosted the reception and provided plenty of roast beef, venison, and lamb, a favorite of Judo's. Also provided were brimming bowls of squash, peas, and beans from preserved garden stocks. White and red wine and coffee were plentiful. Swannie noticed folks tended to talk among themselves leaving the widow alone with her family.

"Com'on." Swannie nudged Julian and Dahlia. "Let's keep company with Mrs. Perkovich."

"Yes, let's." Dahlia smiled.

"May we sit with you?" Swannie asked graciously while Julian shoved chairs near Mrs. Perovich.

"In'a my house, you sit anywhere. You good man, the last to see my Judo alive."

Swannie blushed, his throat dried. "Was Judo in a big rush that day?" Swannie knew the answer to the question.

"Ah, jes, to get Father Grishan. Say, he look happy?"

"Yes, yes, absolutely. He was grinning from ear to ear."

"He have bad pain when he die?"

"No, I don't believe so. He didn't see the cable lashing down from the crane."

Tears flowed, Dahlia, Swannie, Julian, Eddy. Not the widow. She turned inward.

"Judo was a good man," Julian said, offering condolences. "Feel poorly for him."

"Ack, don'a be sad. He happy now. Working mine hell, mos' time."

"Sure sorry about your misfortune," Swannie sputtered kindly.

"Paah, don'a be sad for me. I strong. Can work like man."

"Won't let ladies work in the mine. They're bad luck."

"Ach, what more bad luck, Judo dead?"

"Will you go home to your folks?"

"Dey in prison. Or dead. Don'a know." Mrs. Perkovich shrugged her shoulders. "Before I come America, Papa no wan' fight in war. So put in prison. Mama, too. We kids stay on farm. We take care each other. We have bad farm, sand and rocks. School bombed, burn down. No learn to read, write. Judo's sister, dat's Zita, she marry my brother George. De come'a here to Chicorico, run boardinghouse full of Serbians.

"Judo come to America. To Chicorico to work in mine. Stay in boardinghouse. George tell Judo 'bout me. He send for me to marry

Judo. I come myself, on boat to New York. Den come all way in train. No speak'a English, nothin'. I first see Negroes on train by Chicago." She gazed toward Julian and Dahlia. "To tell trut', dey scare me. I no see color people till dat day on train. They talk real nice to me. After while, I like dem."

"I'm not surprised," Dahlia exclaimed, "you've got a good heart."

"Me and Judo, we marry before Christmas come. Ah, Christmas so much fun, dose days." The widow's eyes softened. She reminisced. "Christmas we have big celebration. We follow de old calendar in our church. On January fifth Serbian men buy pig, sometimes lamb, from farmers at Maxwell an' Eagle Nest. My Judo bring home big pig and slaughter in backyard. He no cut de head. Next day, men go hills, roast pig. Boys help, my Nickie and George. Boys chop wood, make chips for fire. Judo use big branch for spit. He run spit in pig's head all way through hole in rump and put over fire an' roast. He turn pig long time, boys help, t'row more sticks on fire. All day, he roast, den bring home and put pig on table.

"Good eatin'. Best roast pig in the coal camp." Julian added, "Say, tell us about his Christmas pistol."

"Ack, he crazy. Like to shoot *pistola*. No hurt nobody. Morning January seven, Christmas with old calendar, men go to Serbian houses. My Judo knock strong on door. Sometimes shoot a pistola." She pointed her index finger toward the ceiling, and with her thumb, mimicked a pistol shot in the air. "In'a house, dey hear big bang! Den he go in house and eat some pig. He kiss everybody on cheek. Some Serbians come here. Same t'ing. When Judo come home, we go to boardinghouse. Everybody bring food. We have feast. We dance, take turn singing. I remember one Serbian song. Some boys in corner sing to de girls, 'Whose girlfriend are you?' From udder corner, de girls point and sing, 'Dat one! Dat one!' Den de boys and girls dance."

"We've been to some of those celebrations," Dahlia noted. "I recall an elderly gentlemen. He played a concertina."

"Oh, jes, old man Sepich play concertina. He can no-see. One Christmas, he play for feast. Two young boys fight. Dey bad rascals, sock old man Sepich, knock down. Vot for dey sock de old man? Wagh! Dey crazy over same girl. Dey drink too much wine. Dey sock each other hard, an' one boy sock old man Sepich. Pow! On jaw. Poor old man, he drop concertina and fall down! Music stop. Everybody stop dancing and singing—no concertina. We get mad at boys and give'em hell! Terrible bad to hit old man! Judo want to whip dem hard. 'No! No!' old man Sepich holler. 'Don'a whip boys.' Everybody say—whip dem rascals! Whip de rascals! Teach dem lesson for socking old man! 'No whip! No whip!' old man Sepich holler from'a floor. Den he get up, and say, 'Look, jaw okay. Concertina okay.' He squeeze concertina. It work. Den, he laugh happy. He say, 'I t'ank the boy dat hit me. I see stars. Long time, I no see stars, Christmas, dat's good.' Haa! Everybody laugh. Old man Sepich, all time, he can no-see, but he look at bright side. Everybody like him. A good man. . . . Ah, me, we no have much. . . . We happy den, ah, me."

THIRTEEN   A REGULAR FREAK ACCIDENT

"WRONG, WRONG, JIST PLAIN WRONG," Swannie groused. "Company don't care. Judo gets killed. Throwed away, like a bad spark plug. Wife and kids, too. Can't pay the rent. Make room for new spark plugs."

Swannie confronted Bowers. "Howse come the coroner jury wasn't called? To conduct an autopsy?"

"Not needed," Bowers explained guardedly. "Coroner's called to inquire into the cause of a violent death. Judo was killed by dumb luck—a freak accident brought on by himself. I wrote it up in my report to the Super."

"Dumb luck?" Swannie scoffed.

"Yep. A regular, freak accident," Bowers replied smugly.

"My foot! Bad equipment caused this accident, plain and simple. Faulty switch jerked the cable, broke it."

"Never knew a cable to go bad."

"Both plenty old, cable an' switch."

"I swear, I didn't know they were on the fritz."

"When's the last time you inspected them?"

"Haven't ever."

"Figures. You hang them buckets over our heads and don't give a care they might fall. Should'a shut down the cable system. No, you allowed Martin to run it with a bad switch."

"Go easy on Martin," Bowers warned testily. "He's down-and-out and none too happy.We was watching the bucket, figuring it might fall. We didn't figure on the cable popping."

"Don't ruffle your feathers!" Up to this point, Linderman had remained aloof. "Freak accidents happen. Don't nobody know why. Cable broke, nothin' we could do. Dumb luck. If'n Judo had left the mine when he was supposed to—when his shift ended—nothin' would'a happened."

"So Judo brought the accident on hisself?"

"Quit splittin' hairs. Yer insinuating we kilt him. It was his time to go, cut and dry. Accidents happen around mines. They come with the job. You wouldn't know. Yer no miner."

"Accidents don't need to happen."

"Yer tryin' to change the world—the way things is!" Linderman raised his hands in disbelief, his voice strained and strident. "You ought'a be a preacher!"

"Don't blame God for the doings of men. Should'a figured the cable'd break—all that lurching."

"Lurching was the fault of the switch. Don't be so bullheaded about it."

"Gotta be a dimwit to run the cable with the broken switch."

"Damn it!" Linderman slammed his fist on Bowers' desk, startling both Bowers and Swannie. He glared angrily at Swannie and shrieked, "Git out'a here! Git to work!"

Swannie glanced at Bowers, who nodded and lowered his gaze. Swannie huffed out of Bower's office.

In the lamphouse, Swannie stewed. "Callous, capricious, lackadaisical. They don't care. Should'a shut down the buckets, replaced the switch. Easier, cheaper to replace Judo. Anyways, his fault for being in the wrong place at the wrong time. Tell that to Anna Perkovich. They won't. Can't admit responsibility. Bowers offers to buy the vault for Judo's coffin one day, and the next, he kicks the widow out'a the house jist after she had a baby. And, what about her others? The whole lot of them can't work and got nowhere to go."

At home after work, Swannie found Julian and Dahlia sitting at the kitchen table. Their coffee cold, he asked, "Wanna warm your coffee?" They shook their heads no. He poured himself a cup and sat at the table. Imperceptible sounds soared—sounds that bounce about most homes and aren't normally heard—children squealing at play across the meadow, beams creaking in the living room, embers in the cookstove crumbling into ashes.

The windup alarm clock in the bedroom stopped ticking. Dahlia glanced at Julian and dropped her gaze. Julian scooted his chair back, glad for some activity, went to the bedroom and wound the clock, "ding." He returned. Dahlia handed over her cold cup of coffee. Taking both cups to the back porch, he pitched the cold coffee over the railing onto the dry, hard dirt. When he returned, Dahlia filled both cups with warm coffee.

"Poor, poor Anna, we're no real help to her. All we can do is her washing. When she's gone from here, I can't even help with the washing. Oh, what will she do—four boys, three-year-old Sophia, and baby Joanna?"

"Boys too young to work in the tipple. Or, outside the mine. Don't matter much. Company don't hire breaker boys anymore, like when I was a kid."

They dropped into doldrums. Forgot to drink the coffee. The bedroom clock ticked . . . embers popped in the cookstove . . . a door slammed next door. Gloom hung over the clean, well-lighted kitchen. . . . Accidentially, Swannie noticed markings on the wall over the doorway—screw holes evenly measured and slightly dimpled with yeso.

"Gunrack," Julian spied Swannie's wandering eyes and tersely explained the marks. "Built a rack for the rifle."

"He took it down. Bothered him, that gun hanging in the kitchen."

"Seemed like a dang trophy, but it's a killing machine."

"Your Army rifle?"

"Use it for deer hunting now."

"Only time he has it out—deer hunting."

"I wouldn't have nothin' to do with mine. Left it in France."

"Smart man."

They continued to sit in gloom. Dahlia sighed. "What will Anna Perkovich do?"

"Not much she can do."

"It's not what she will do." Swannie picked his nails with the blade of his pocketknife. "What will we do?"

"What can I do?" Julian felt guilty for what he couldn't change. "Most anything will get me fired and evicted."

"Jist for speaking up for the widow?"

"Yep. Dahlia, Eddy, even you, we'd be out in the cold. Standing in soup lines. Sleeping under rusted hoods of wrecked cars, or abandoned boxcars, like you used to."

"Jim-in-nee! Why did I—you—why'd we fight in France? 'To make the world safe for democracy,' President Wilson said. What good's democracy, if'n you can't speak your mind?"

Julian and Dahlia had no answer. They cast their eyes to the floor—fear, naked and numbing. Swannie shuddered. Julian, afraid? Never saw Julian afraid of anything. Maybe sweet Dahlia, but not Julian. They sat solemn and dejected without looking at each other. The bedroom clock ticked louder. Julian peeked in the bedroom, noted the time, and returned to the kitchen. "Glad Eddy's still over the Montaño's, playing with Arturo. Not good for him to see us hunkering."

"Hey, maybe Onorio or Manuel will have some ideas?"

"Not likely, but it's a free country," Julian scoffed. "Talk to them."

"Honey, surely something could be done to help Mrs. Perkovich."

"Maybe speak to Bowers," Swannie suggested.

"She'll do nothing of the sort!"

"Referring to you, not Dahlia."

"Are you loco! Wasn't long ago Manuel's brother-in-law, Baltazar, and his missus was evicted. Baltazar got blacklisted. Can't even get a job on the Santa Fé section gang."

"I didn't know—"

"There's a lot we haven't told you," Dahlia interrupted. "At election time, two years ago, Mr. Bowers and Mr. Linderman went about the camp showing the foreign women how to vote—now that women could."

"That was right nice of them."

"Dear, you don't understand. They were telling us *who* to vote for."

"You mean to say—"

"Yes, a straight Republican ticket. Julian told me to agree with whatever they said. Anyway, voting's private. Mr. Bowers came by with a ballot. Julian was at work. Mr. Bowers showed me how to vote a straight Republican ticket. I said 'okay,' and thanked him. Then, he went over to the Ribera's—that's Baltazar and Feliz. Baltazar was away at work, too. Mr. Bowers showed Feliz how to vote a straight Republican ticket. Feliz told Mr. Bowers she was proud to vote and would vote as she pleased. When Baltazar came home, their things were throwed out of the house. Strewed all over the front yard. Feliz was at the Montaño's. Baltazar had been fired and evicted, all on the same day."

"Why that's wrong," Swannie sputtered.

"Disgusting!" Julian injected. "They got no right—"

"Why put up with it?" Swannie interrupted. "What kind of man would put up with such chicanery?"

Julian bolted! His chair slid backwards, screeched, slammed against the wall, and wiggled to the floor. "Gull durn your hide!" Julian reached across the table, grabbed Swannie's bib overalls, and shook him violently. "Gull durn your hide!"

"Yeow!" Swannie's head wobbled, like a falling spinning top. He clutched the table's edge to steady himself, his little pocket knife falling on the table.

"Don't question my manhood!"

"Honey, don't!" Dahlia screeched.

"Yeow! I didn't—"

"Ya did! You asked what kind—"

"Didn't mean nuthin'—"

"Stop! Swannie's family!"

"Gull durn you! You'd peeve a priest!" Julian's voice trembled full of rage. He persisted, tugging Swannie's straps and flopping his shoulders and head. "Don't-you-dare-question-my-manhood."

"All's I was—" Swannie sputtered inarticulately.

"I'm the kind of man puts food on the table! A roof over my family's head! That's the kind of man I am—a peon, but I got a job!"

"Stop it! Quit shaking him!" Dahlia clutched Julian's tight grip and jerked at his hands. She squealed stridently, "Swannie's family. Apologize!"

Julian paused. Stared at his hands, loosened his grip, and wrung them. Shuddered. Hid his face in his hands, ashamed he'd lost his temper. Still standing, he reached over the table to Swannie. "Sorry." Julian smoothed over the wrinkled straps of Swannie's bib overalls. "Hope yer not hurting."

Swannie's faced was etched with his silly grin, more startled than afraid. "No worse for the wear." He rubbed the back of his neck. "Jist scairt the Devil out'a me." He spotted the open knife and closed and pocketed it while Julian lifted the fallen chair and sat down, clasping his hands.

Julian leaned his arms on the table and spoke despairingly: "It's jist we're better off than those poor souls in soup lines. Even so, my Gran'pa had it better. When he got too old to work, his master allowed him to pass his waning days in a shanty behind the plantation. Fed and took care of him, for all the work he'd done. Loyalty paid off for him. Not for us. We're one step away from Judo and Anna."

"Thought your Gran'pa was never a free man."

"Always a slave . . . but put food on the table for his family . . . and a roof over their heads. He never had to beg for scraps of food. He died with dignity."

Swannie was thoroughly confused. He cleared his throat to give himself time to think. "But, your Gran'pa was a slave? Never a free man?"

"I owe that. He was luckier than others. Some were sent away when they were too old to work. On pretense of being freed. They were free to starve in their old age."

Embarrassed by his lack of profundity, Swannie continued grinning apologetically. He simply did not understand Julian. Worse, Julian was exasperated at his own confusion and inability to resolve the paradox satisfactorily—old, tired questions he couldn't answer. Was security possible with freedom? Was dignity possible without freedom? Or, was security the wages of bondage? And, insecurity the price of freedom?

"Hang it all, Swannie! You questioned my manhood. My honor. A man's got to have honor, or he's got no self-respect . . . no pride. He's defeated and can't protect himself. Or, family. The Company takes away a man's self-respect, his honor. 'We're free to leave the coal camp and work elsewhere,' Bowers says, 'but there ain't no jobs elsewhere.' So we're free to work till we die. Or, get killed in an accident—our women and young'uns starve to death—nothing to show for all the years we worked for the Company."

Gloom returned to the kitchen. The clock ticked in the bedroom, the hens clucked outside, and children yelped playfully from the meadow.

"Believe I understand. Living here's the lesser of evils. You put up with the rowdies 'cause that's better than begging for a living."

"Not forever," Julian cautioned. "Things will change. We'll change them."

"God willing," Dahlia added.

Swannie muttered, "'Know the truth, and it shall make you free,' the Bible says, but it ain't helping us none."

"'Truth beareth away the victory,'" Dahlia retorted. "Do something with the truth."

"Yeah, sure." Julian reached in his pocket for a key and pitched it to Swannie. "Take the pickup. Pay Reverend Miller a visit. Maybe he's got a notion or two."

Immediately after Swannie left to Raton, Julian called for a caucus with Onorio and Manuel in the wine cellar. Onorio poured them a glass of wine.

"Swannie wants me to do something about the Widow Perkovich."

Onorio and Manuel frowned furtively, waiting for Julian to continue.

"Nothing doing, I said. He wanted to see you fellers. I told him it's a free country."

"Didn't call on me."

"Nor me."

"He did get my goat. Almost punched him."

"What'd he do?" Manuel asked with concern.

"Not what he did. What he asked."

"Asked you to take on Bowers. That's enough to peeve a priest. Takes some gall. He was gonna ask us to do the same."

"Maybe we should," Julian injected.

"Then, why'd he peeve you?"

"He questioned my honor—asking what kind of man I was to put up with Bowers' chicanery."

"The road to hell is paved with good intentions, " Onorio sarcastically observed. "Our hands are tied. Nobody can win a fight with Bowers, much less the Company."

"For all Swannie gets my goat," Julian mused, "he's taken to high principles of right and wrong, good and bad."

Manuel crossed his legs nervously, and then uncrossed them, all the while speaking. "He called it 'chicanery.' That's the way it works around here—fuzzy rules between right and wrong."

"Say what we will, Swannie's no saint. But, he's right about the widow."

"He thinks the Company gives a damn," Onorio scoffed. "Swannie needs to mind his own business."

After a while, Julian spoke softly. "It is our business. What happened to Judo could happen to us, our families. 'You gotta change the mold you made,' I told Swannie. Maybe, I better practice what I preach. Maybe, we gotta break the mold we're in."

"We didn't make the mold. We're jist got stuck in it."

"Don't matter much who made it. We're in it. We gotta get out of it. Like we did with Bowers and the scales. We acted together—a united front—whipping Bowers and Linderman."

For a long time, they sat pensively sipping wine. A delicate bouquet from the casks permeated the cellar.

"Been talkin' to Don MacGregor," Manuel broke the quiet spell.

"Pah! The Wobblie?"

"Wait, wait, he's a good man. Took our side in Ludlow. Lost his job for it."

"Job?"

"He was a reporter, sent by a Denver paper to report on the Ludlow strike. When he saw how bad it was, how the Militia took the side of the Company, he took the union's side. Newspaper fired him. Too radical for'em. He's a bit touched. Joined the strikers. Took to drinkin' too much. Says we got to organize."

"I believe he's right, but nobody would back us. They're afraid." Julian added, "Like us."

"Like the folks in Ludlow now. Don't have a real union. They're afraid," Onorio said.

Before speaking, Manuel gazed solemnly at Onorio for a while and then Julian. "Nothing good ever came by doing nothin'. Company won't give up respect. We've got to take it. Make the Company respect us. And, it's smart to be scared. Only thing is, we gotta break the back of folks' thinking—it's every man for himself. We gotta act together."

"After Ludlow, fellers not scared, they're, they're crazy."

"We're not in Ludlow," Manuel tried to offer encouragement. "Maybe folks here would back us."

Onorio sat forward. "Who?"

FOURTEEN   DIVINE INTERVENTION

AFTER HEARING SWANNIE'S ACCOUNT of the widow's dilemma, Reverend Miller made an appointment with Henry Van Cise, the Chicorico Coal Company superintendent whose office was in the brick two-story building that covered half of the one hundred block of North First Street in Raton. When Reverend Miller arrived at Van Cise's office, he was greeted officiously by the secretary, Miss Marlene.

"Have a chair, Reverend Miller. Mr. Van Cise is expecting you, but is running late. Be with you in a minute." What Miss Marlene didn't say is that Van Cise tended to keep all visitors waiting, except corporate board members who rarely visited him, to create the impression he was a very busy man.

While Reverend Miller waited, Miss Marlene sat behind her desk, filing her long, red fingernails. Splaying her fingers, she inspected the nails meticulously, delicately shaving ragged edges. Satisfied the nails were precisely sanded, she tucked the file into the desk drawer. A few moments later, she opened the glass-paneled door to Van Cise's inner-office and invited Reverend Miller to proceed.

Van Cise stood abruptly, walked around his desk, and extended a hand. "I'm Hank Van Cise. Please be seated." Van Cise addressed Miss Marlene, "We're not to be disturbed." Van Cise turned to the Reverend. "I'd offer you coffee, or a cigar, but I presume a man of the cloth would not indulge." Van Cise knew the Reverend would decline. Besides, Van Cise wanted to speed up the meeting, assuming the Reverend would drop a long spiel before asking for contributions. I'll give him a twenty dollar check, Van Cise had decided, and send him on his way quickly. That'll make the Company look good, too.

"Much obliged for the courtesy." Reverend Miller sat at the seat positioned in front of the bulky mahogany desk that matched the bulky chairs and filing cabinets. "Your family?" Reverend Miller pointed to a framed photograph on the desk.

"Why, yes." Van Cise lifted the photograph and gazed at it wistfully, wiping the dust from the glass cover. He set it down and reclined in his soft, leather-bound chair. He snuggled back into the chair, clenched his hands, and propped them beneath his cleanly shaved chin.

"And, your children?" Reverend Miller sought to make small talk before addressing his mission.

"They're in college, back east."

"Back east?"

"Well, daughter is—Vassar."

"I hope all's well with Laura. Emma missed her at the meeting last week."

"The WCTU ladies, oh, yes. Laura must have forgotten. She intended to call Mrs. Miller. She was called to Denver to arrange a marriage."

"An arranged marriage?"

"Ho! Not like the old days, when the fathers decided the arrangement. My boy, he's to marry a Gates girl."

"Of *the* Gates family?"

"None other. Lucky man, that Gates. Didn't lose his shirt Black Thursday. Are you acquainted with the Gates family?"

"Only through the seminary. They were generous donors."

"My boy attends—"

"The seminary?"

"Not him! He's a free spirit. In the business school at the University of Denver."

"When's the happy occasion?"

"Reverend, if you don't mind," Van Cise cupped his lips, "we'd like to keep it hush-hush, if you get my implication."

"Certainly. I'm not here to pry on your family. I'm here on Company issues."

Taken aback, Van Cise frowned. "I think of the Company as my family. What brings a man of the cloth to a mining office?"

"I'm here to speak for the Widow Perkovich."

"I don't believe I know the lady."

"She was Judo Perkovich's wife."

"Don't think me rude, but I'm not acquainted with these people."

"Judo Perkovich was the miner recently killed at the Chicorico Mine."

"Oh, yes, dreadful affair. Mr. Bowers mentioned something about it," Van Cise vaguely recalled, adding, "in his report. . . . Some kind of freak accident, I believe."

"The way I heard it, the gondola operator at the tipple was using frayed cables pulled by a faulty electric motor. It jammed and jerked the frayed cable so hard, the cable snapped. The cable lashed down and struck Judo Perkovich and killed him instantly."

"A costly accident, I might add. While the gondolas were down, Mr. Bowers couldn't mine coal. Good thing Pueblo's nearby. The CF&I Steel mill shipped good cables and buckets quickly. Lost time is lost money, you know."

"What about the loss of life? Mr. Perkovich's accident could have been prevented."

"That's not how I heard it. He brought it on himself. Understand he shouldn't have been there. He was leaving early." Van Cise smirked snidely. "I didn't know you studied mine safety at the seminary."

Reverend Miller ignored the snide comment. "I understand Judo had permission to leave early. He was taking a cut in pay to arrange for his baby's baptism. Apparently, had the frayed cable and faulty motor been replaced, the accident would not have occurred."

"I'm sure Mr. Bowers would never use faulty equipment. Safety is in our best interest."

"That's not what the miners think. They think Mr. Bowers is niggardly, cuts corners on cost to save money."

"The miners exaggerate. They're not safety conscious. Mr. Bowers tells me they refused to use the new electric lamps, even though they're safer than the carbide lamps."

"Mr. Bowers deducts from their earnings to recharge the batteries for the lamps."

"Hogwash, Reverend, surely you don't believe that? Those foreigner miners are unmitigated gossips and malcontents. They complain all the time."

"You have a problem on your hands. Were you aware Mr. Bowers has evicted Mrs. Perkovich from her house in Chicorico?"

"No I am not, but I don't know many things about Chicorico. I have five camps to worry about. Each is a stand-free operation that must pay for itself. It would not do for me to meddle in the trivial affairs of each camp."

"Trivial? Her man's dead. She has six children, the last recently born."

"Mr. Bowers must have a good reason. He's not Ebeneezer Scrooge."

"She can't pay the rent. Has no means of livelihood. Mr. Bowers told her he needed the house for another family man who would work in the mine."

"There must be more to it. I have the utmost confidence in Mr. Bowers' management of the camp. Many of the men don't like his finicky bookkeeping methods. He certainly would not evict a widow before she'd made arrangements to move in with her family. Possibly, you've been listening to gossip."

"I don't believe Mr. Ray Swanson is a gossip."

"Who?"

"We call him Swannie. He's one of our brethren in the church. He works for Mr. Bowers at the tipple office. He heard it directly from the horse's mouth. Mr. Bowers told him. Swannie is concerned for the widow. He also fears a communist lawyer would hear of the situation and sue the Company for the widow."

Briskly, Van Cise sat forward in his chair. Hard and rigid, he gripped its leather-bound arms. "Where did you hear that?"

"There's considerable agitation going on by the Wobblies. Surely you know that."

"Here in the Raton area?" Van Cise feigned disinterest but his puffy knuckles paled as he clutched the dark leather arms of his chair.

"Here. Up in Ludlow—all over the coal fields. You need to visit with Mr. Bowers. Perhaps he can shed light on these political affairs. My concern is the widow. She has no place to go. She can't afford to return to Serbia."

"Reverend Miller." Mr. Van Cise abruptly stood at his desk, signaling the end of the meeting. "I allow Mr. Bowers full autonomy in the daily operations of the mine. He's an efficient operator and manages to keep in the black most of the time. I will have a talk with him. Does this widow have sons? I'm sure we can use one of them in the mine. Take his father's place."

Reverend Miller shook his head. "Whole family, boys and girls, too young to work."

Van Cise guffawed a bit. "Much ado about nothing. I'm sure Mr. Bowers has offered Mrs. Perkovich some sort of work. We . . . uh . . . take care of our own." He called for his secretary and briskly extended a hand without stepping from behind his desk.

The day after Reverend Miller visited with Van Cise, Bowers called on Mrs. Perkovich. He offered a job as janitor of the school and assured she could continue to rent the Company house.

The elementary school was actually nine Company houses in a row located beside the railway on the east end of Chicorico. The principal lived in the first house, and the inside walls of the others were gutted to provide a classroom for one grade, sometimes two depending on enrollments. As janitor, Mrs. Perkovich would tend to each house during the school year, building fires in stoves, cleaning the chalkboards, shoveling snow, and tending to sundry other maintenance duties. During the summer, she would sand and varnish the wooden desks and floors, paint the walls, and clean the outhouses.

"That's no hard job. I can do."

Bowers handed Anna a pen to sign the contract.

"Judo never sign paper."

"Mrs. Perkovich, you'll be a Company man, er, woman, but we need your iron clad promise you'll live up to the agreement in the contract."

"My word is good."

"I'm sure, but I need more than an oral promise."

"Promise?"

"You must promise, in writing, you will not sue the Company."

"Sue?"

"A lawsuit in a court of law for Mr. Perkovich's accident. Furthermore, all Company workers register Republican."

"Paah! Accident! Maybe I sue. Get more money. No work."

"Don't be too hasty, Mrs. Perkovich. Think of your children. They need a roof over their heads. Food on the table. You'll have to hire a lawyer. Take a long time to get to court."

"Ach, need to feed babies, not pay lawyers. Where I sign?"

Bowers pointed to the contract's bottom line, commenting, "In the long haul, you'll be glad you agreed to sign."

"Pay in cash?"

"Nope, scrip—like everybody else."

"Company men get pay in cash."

"They're different."

"How?"

"Why, uh, they're, uh, they're men. They got families to feed."

"Me, too."

"Don't fret. The contract provides enough scrip to buy food at the Company store, and rent's deducted. Doctor's free, being as yer a Company gal."

"Don't call me 'gal.' In the old a'country, I called 'ma'am.'"

"No offense meant. American ladies call themselves 'gal.'"

"I am American now, and I no like 'gal.'"

"Suit yourself. Be sure to register Republican. Easy to do at the school."

FIFTEEN   PECULIAR PLACES FOR MOONSHINE

BOWERS FILED ANNA'S signed contract with Van Cise and promptly called Swannie into his office. "Bad news for you. The Super forced me to hire the Widow Perkovich as janitor over at the schoolhouses. Letting you go. Can't afford the two of you. The way I figure, by the time your rent's deducted, you come out owing the Company. But, we'll call it even. I expect you out of Chicorico by tomorrow."

"Huh, how do you figure?" Alarmed by the sudden news, Swannie prattled, "School's been there. You paid the janitor. No new expenses. You have that money to pay Widow Perkovich."

"No such thing. Teachers, and the older boys, took care of the schools."

"You got no call to fire me."

"I'm not. Jist a lay-off. Had to hire Mrs. Perkovich. Don't have the cash flow to pay you anymore."

"Yer letting me go 'cause I stood up for the widow. You think I'm a fool. I'd lay odds yer paying the widow in scrip."

"That's none of your—"

"Tell him, yet?" Linderman sauntered into the office.

"Yah, but he's giving me a hard time."

"See here Swannie," Linderman bellowed, "take your things and get out!"

"So, you are firing me."

"Fer Chris' sake!" Linderman glared at Bowers. "Didn't you tell him?"

"Well, ah—uh—"

"Bull!" Linderman grasped Swannie's collar and pulled his face close, eyeball to eyeball. Linderman's nostrils flared, his breath reeked of moonshine. "Boy, you soiled your own nest by finking to the preacher. Made us look like we was beating up on the widow."

Swannie narrowed his eyes and gazed directly into Linderman's, speaking distinctly with uncharacteristic severity, "You were."

Linderman flinched at Swannie's audacity, loosened his grip, and glanced away from Swannie's penetrating glare. Linderman sputtered, "Yer a disgrace to the Company, bitin' the hand that feeds you."

"Let go." Swannie shook loose from Linderman. "This ain't over, yet. Chickens come home to roost. You won't always bend the rules and get away with it."

"Yah, says you!" Linderman yelled as Swannie marched out the office.

Swannie strode down the tracks stinging at the thought of being fired. "Knew I could be fired for drinking or sleeping on the job. Never thought I'd be fired for defending a widow." At the Heard's, he shared the bad news. Dahlia motioned for everyone to sit at the kitchen table, but Swannie excused himself to his makeshift bedroom. Julian and Dahlia followed.

"I was afraid of this." Julian watched Swannie sort the few items he had accumulated. "I'll fix us some coffee. We'll talk about this. You don't have to leave right away." Julian scurried to the kitchen and rattled about the cupboard finding the coffee and casting away old grounds. The turn of events had rocked him. Frustrated. Impotent. Baffled. Julian hated helplessness, the gut wrenching grip on his stomach when he could do nothing to fix *it*. Elusive and slippery, *it* squeezed his stomach and tugged at his throat.

When the coffee perked, Julian offered Swannie a cup—who showed no interest in coffee or conversation—and Julian wrenched at the tug on his stomach. He groped for ideas. "If'n I was you, I'd go see Reverend Miller. He know lot'a folks. Maybe he's got pull with somebody in Raton."

Swannie continued to pack his few belongings.

"Well, you got your mind made up to leave without coffee. Wish I could help." Julian retreated to the kitchen. "When yer ready, I'll take you."

Dahlia watched Swannie stuff a cotton flour sack with his belongings. He packed grudgingly like stuffing dirty laundry in a pillowcase. Tears welled in Dahlia's eyes. "Take Jimmy's clothing, and the Bible Reverend Miller gave you."

Swannie noticed for the first time Dahlia's eyes were turquoise green, a dimple in her left cheek. Although her hands were rough and ruddy from too much washing and scrubbing with lye, the touch of her fingers was delicate and sure. Tears welled in his eyes. He wanted to hug Dahlia but didn't.

She did not suddenly catch his eye. The radiance of her smile and delicate touch of her hands captivated him but he never saw the beauty in her all at once. She had grown on him by incremental portions, starting the morning he first saw her through bleary eyes singing in church standing with Julian and Eddy. Then, she was a Negro. Now, she was a dear, lovely lady.

Swannie had never given much thought about Negro men or women, much less falling in love with Dahlia. Negroes were just that—black people cursed by God to be spurned by others. "How could anybody spurn Dahlia, Julian, and little Eddy? Come to think of it, I almost did. Yet, this wonderful family never spurned anybody. They took me in when I was down and out. And, Dahlia, was nicer than any women I've every known." Swannie did not covet her lewdly nor lust for her. His feelings ran deeper and he was not ashamed.

He took one last, lingering gaze around the makeshift bedroom and spotted his pocketknife on the powder box beside the sofa. He pocketed it, tied a knot at the sack's open end, and slung it over his shoulder. Leaning over the smooth top of the Chickering piano, he ran his fingers across the keyboard, and lowered the cover. His heart crowded into his throat. He managed to eke out an insincere "A-dios, Mrs. Heard," extending a limp hand as though he were saying goodbye to a landlady he saw once a month to pay the rent.

Dahlia did not fake her feelings. She grasped his limp hand, threw an arm around his shoulder and pulled him so close he could feel the buttons of her blouse against his chest. She kissed him on the cheek—her lips warm, supple, soft.

Outside the Heard's home, everything was calm as Julian drove Swannie by the Company store. Attempting to make conversation, Swannie told Julian of the time back in June when Shorty attempted to bribe Ruker with a fresh catch of trout over spilt gasoline. Julian nodded vaguely. Beyond the Company store, there was no activity. The baseball field lay fallow, its diamond's powdery, white lines fading. There were no children at play among the row of schoolhouses and nobody puttered among the graves at the colored people's cemetery. Across from the cemetery, a few coke ovens glowed and spewed spiral columns of cinders and soot. Swannie's eyes misted from the sulfuric stench of unburned gases, cinders, and smog polluting the air. He tried to make a joke. "Guess I'll be breathin' better air."

No response from Julian.

For both, this ride was much more disconcerting than their first ride from Raton when Swannie consented to stay with the Heards. Now, they were like men at a friend's funeral. The void was too vast, the abyss too deep, and silence seemed the most appropriate invocation, muted prayers jammed with unspoken clarity.

At Reverend Miller's home, Julian accompanied Swannie into an austere but cozy parlor with bare walls, except for an ink drawing of what appeared to be three men. A tiny bookshelf contained Bibles and various other black leather-bound books. Across from the bookshelf sat an upright piano that appeared unused, its cabinet and keyboard cover cluttered with doilies.

Reverend Miller sat in a dark oak rocker next to the tiny bookshelf and invited Swannie and Julian to sit in the matching parlor bench. He asked Emma to join them. She carried a chair from the dining room into the parlor and placed it next to the Reverend's, folded her hands in her lap, and prepared to listen while the men conferred. As Swannie explained the chain of events leading to his dismissal, Emma grew increasingly incensed until she couldn't hold back: "Those scoundrels! Knaves! You're better off."

"Emma, dear, judge not."

"Can't be helped! Swannie's being punished for doing right by the Widow Perkovich."

"Darling, it's partly my responsibility." Reverend Miller attempted to calm Emma. "When I met with Mr. Van Cise, I should've kept my wits about me. Instead, when he asked how I came to know of Mrs. Perkovich's plight, I blabbered with pride that our newly joined brethren—Swannie Swanson—had brought it to my attention. I let the cat out the bag, a slip in good judgement, because, well, Van Cise was so high almighty pompous . . . so patronizing."

"Don't see how it's your doing," Julian injected reprovingly. "Mr. Bowers fired Swannie."

"Don't you gentlemen see what's happened?" Emma impatiently intruded again. "Mr. Van Cise gives free rein to his lieutenants, and allows Mr. Bowers to do as he desires so long as the mine makes a profit."

"And, Linderman, I reckon," Swannie muttered to the carpet on the parlor floor.

"Mr. Miller, you must do something!"

"Well, Emma, dear, we can put up Swannie for a while."

"Naturally, but we've got to help him find a job."

"A job? Here in Raton?" Julian asked dubiously.

"I hear tell they're looking to put on another revenuer," Emma hinted.

Julian asked incredulously, "Where'd you hear that?"

"Depression's everywhere," Swannie chimed in.

"My Union," Emma said proudly.

"Union!—Union!" Julian and Swannie exclaimed concurrently.

"Our WCTU. I'm Evangelistic Superintendent."

Reverend Miller gazed lovingly at Emma. She was cut from a different cloth. That's why he fell in love with her. She could be calm and demur one minute and righteous in another, without being rude or abrasive.

As evangelistic superintendent of the local chapter of the Woman's Christian Temperance Union, she had reinvigorated its membership, asking every woman in the congregation to join the Union. She also requested that each bring along a friend. WCTU meetings were conducted in a climate of urgency without social frivolities. At one of the first meetings, she invited the two dry agents housed in Raton. She reminded them of the duty to enforce the Volstead Act and that the WCTU was poised and ready to assist them.

The agents expressed gratitude for the assistance, then maneuvered to gloss over their failure by painting a lurid picture of Colfax County as Sodom and Gomorrah, amuck with rogues who had no respect for the law and blatantly made, sold, and drank alcohol. The agents likened themselves to John the Baptist, voices in the desert crying in the wind. They claimed even some of the high-muck-a-muck in the county imbibed and called themselves "sports." When asked for names of some of the sports, they said, "You don't want to know. It could be dangerous."

The agents also claimed to be understaffed and couldn't possibly do a thorough job in all of Colfax County, especially when so many people were tight-lipped about moonshiners and the whereabouts of their stills. Given their broad jurisdiction, Emma insisted they request another revenuer. They complied to get her off their backs, and to their surprise, they were authorized to hire another revenuer.

"You'd be perfect, Mr. Swanson. You know all the speakeasies. No doubt you know the sources providing the moonshine."

"But, but," Swannie awkwardly protested and groped for his tiny pocketknife to pick at his fingernails. "That's a civil service job. I'm a ignoramus—never pass the test."

"Oh, put that silly knife away! And, listen!"

Instantly, Swannie closed the knife and fumbled with his pant's pocket to insert it.

"To be a hard-boiled revenue raider, you needn't be an intellectual giant. For revenuers, the standard on the civil service exam has been lowered—to accommodate the many men in Alabama who couldn't pass it."

"Too dangerous!" Julian blurted out bluntly. He was highly agitated and implored with great fervor, his concern for Swannie's safety apparent. "I owe Swannie will do fine on the exam. After all, he is a high school graduate, but—" Julian clenched his right hand, punched his left palm, and shook his hands—"but, a hard-boiled revenuer! He's not!"

Reverend Miller and Swannie acquiesced meekly to Julian's forceful assertions. Emma did not. Equally obdurate, she held her ground. "Nonsense! He's perfect for it."

"Mrs. Miller, you jist don't know how vile some men are 'bout moonshine and money. They'd soon kill a revenuer to protect their moonshine money. Happens all the time."

"Oh, my heck, Mr. Heard." Emma stiffened her back. "That's only hearsay, spiteful gossip to intimidate God-fearing men."

"No, ma'am, it's not." Julian relented and leaned back in his chair, retreating from his assertive posture realizing it was his suggestion Swannie seek assistance from the Millers, and Mrs. Miller was offering a solution. Yet, Julian felt compelled to explain his abrupt outburst, although he stammered for words to express his feelings for Swannie. "Jist that I, er, we—Dahlia, Eddy and me—we come to think of Swannie as family, like Dahlia's kid brother Jimmy. So I, er, we, we are protective of him." Julian turned his gaze to Swannie. "You gotta promise me to watch your back. . . . Always watch your back."

"Shucks, don't worry 'bout me. Made it through the war, nary a scratch."

Julian cringed, thinking, "Swannie doesn't know how lucky he is. Some say the Lord watches over children and drunks. He's no yokel, jist too trusting, like a kid. May the Lord look over him." Julian prayed to himself and then repeated his request: "Jist promise to watch your back."

"'Course, I promise."

"Tut-tut, nothing to worry about Julian." Emma patted Julian's shoulder as she rose from her chair, addressing Swannie, "You've the best qualifications, a sober, God-fearing man." Emma decisively terminated the discussion and excused herself into the kitchen where she could be heard cranking the telephone and then speaking.

The men sat agog in the parlor while she spoke. They heard her hang up the receiver and shout from the kitchen, "Tomorrow morning, Mr. Miller and I shall speak to the two revenuers." She entered the parlor. "Their office is behind the Shuler Opera House next to where Sheriff Boots Najar runs the jail. I'm going to ask Boots to join us."

Bewildered and dazed, the men gaped as Emma took the bull by the horns and wrestled it to the ground. "You'll stay with us for a while. We have a pleasant apartment in the basement. Now, I have

143

a dinner to prepare." Emma returned her chair to the dining room table and removed an apron from back of the kitchen door. "You may stay for dinner if you'd like, Mr. Heard."

The next day, the Millers asked Sheriff Boots Najar to join them in a meeting with the two revenuers. The revenuers and Boots were incredulous. The town drunk turned Christian with only a year of sobriety? Hardly plausible he would walk the line—once exposed to moonshine. Emma wasn't deterred. She quickly pointed to the many sudden conversions of men who had lived lives of bacchanal, drunken revelry. "There was, of course, St. Augustine, who found peace in Christian temperance and then led an exemplary life."

"And, in our time, the Reverend Billy Sunday, a drunken baseball player, who is currently the leader of a nationwide church," Reverend Miller added. "Furthermore, Swannie will be living with us. We shall keep a vigilant eye on him."

"Naturally," Emma added, "although I'm sure he will do well without our supervision. Boots, you've been quiet, what do you think?"

Nobody knew David "Boots" Najar by baptismal name. He acquired the nickname by way of the flamboyant cowboy boots he wore, which he had custom-made by the boot maker, Tony Lama, when he vacationed annually in his wife's hometown, Juarez, Mexico. "Does sound unlikely. Swannie was on the bottle a long time. I used to let him dry out in the jail. Wasn't long, he was back on the bottle. I tired and didn't think taxpayers ought to pay his room and board. Told him to sleep elsewhere."

"Surely, you believe a man can change his ways?"

"Well, yes, I've seen some men change for the better." Boots nervously rubbed the sharp, silver plated tips of his black leather boots against the back of his pant legs. The seams of the black boots were lined with delicate threads of silver filigree. To exhibit his boots, he tucked his baggy but pressed trousers into them. A bit of a dandy, he dressed in flashy western garb Hollywood cowboys would come to imitate fifteen years later. "Mrs. Miller, I'm not one to hold a good man down. In fact, I too, will keep my eyes on him. Help when I can."

The two revenuers had little to lose. They knew few conscientious men cared for their dangerous and thankless work.

Within two weeks, Swannie was sworn-in as a revenuer with broad authority to seek and destroy places where alcohol was made or sold. "Perhaps," Swannie thought, "there is a smidgen of truth in the parson's proclamation—about the tide of affairs in the Lord's Great Plan—that sweeps us all to a dusty end." Only days after the dismissal, Swannie had been swept by Reverend Miller's tide of events onto the swelling waves of Kingdom Come, and Mrs. Miller had tossed him a Mae West life preserver, keeping him afloat. He had a government job with health benefits, a pension plan, a pickup truck, and a holy crusade with the sanction of law.

Convinced of the righteousness of his cause, Swannie pursued the holy crusade with a vengeance, shutting down the speakeasies in Raton that had sprouted in former saloons. He started with the Brass Rail Bar on the one hundred block of North First Street near the corporate office of the Chicorico Coal Company.

"Whaddya say Swannie?" bartender Bardo Griffis greeted in a phony, treble pitch. "Long time no see, amigo. Been giving the ladies a hard time?"

"Last time you saw me, I was a drunk. Now, I'm dry. You better be."

"Dry as a bone."

"Bones ain't dry."

"Dead bones are. And, soda pop's wet."

"I ain't funnin' Bardo."

"Hey, I ain't either. I got no hooch—not like the good old days."

"Old days weren't so hot."

"Hoy, boy! Now ain't you hoity-toity. Not like the ol' Swannie. Lemme tell you, when I heard you was a dry agent," Bardo pointed to the sink behind the bar, "I dumped all my hooch down the drain, every drop."

"I'll look around."

"Go ahead, pick it dry." Bardo laughed at his own pun.

Swannie checked the coolers in the back room. They were filled with soda pop and cold cuts. "What's the meat for?"

"Sell soda pop and sandwiches now. Can't sell hooch, you know."

"Folks still dance?"

"Hell, yah—a regular juke joint! Saturday nights, player piano gets hot . . . but no drinkin' allowed. We're dry. Sometimes, the boys drop in Saturday afternoons, listen to a ball game."

"They bet on the games?"

"Naw, never," he lied.

Swannie walked behind the bar counter and inspected the shelves, finding soft drinks, crackers, and candies. "The bottle openers?"

"Soda pops."

He stooped to open a closed cabinet beneath the counter and caught the toe of his shoe on a throw rug. He knelt to flatten the rug and spotted an iron ring on the floor beneath the rug. He hooked the ring and pulled. A trapdoor creaked on its hinges and propped open. A gust of pent-up whiskey fumes whooshed in his face. "Phew! That moonshine down below?"

"Naw, smell's from the old days." Bardo slammed the door shut. "When hooch was legal."

"I'm looking for myself." Swannie opened the door, switched on the light, and clambered down the ladder. The rays of a single bulb filled the room and revealed kegs of moonshine whiskey. "Dry as a bone, huh?" Swannie yelled from the crawl space. "I'm impounding them kegs. Take'em out."

"Ain't you uppity? Used to drink here yourself, in the good old days."

"Them was the bad old days." Swannie climbed from the crawl space. "Out! Take'em out!"

"No! You want'em, you take'em. You'll get drunk on'em, or turn'em over to the Wobblies, knowing you."

"You don't know me. Now, move'em."

"Make me."

"You sure?"

"That's what I said."

"Easy as pie." Swannie walked out of the bar. The lock on the door clicked shut behind him. At his pickup, he found an axe, returned to the bar door, and knocked.

"Git!" Bardo yelled from behind the locked door. "You got no call to raid me."

"In the name of the law, open the door!"

"Let's deal. I give you one keg for every ten I got."

"You provoke a man's demons to save yours!"

Whack! Swannie furiously axed the door. Bardo keeled backwards from the brutal paroxysm, the violent, staccato explosions from Swannie's axe hacking at the door. Bardo tumbled back to the bar, shielding his face and eyes as slivers of broken glass splattered into the barroom followed by splintered slats of wood. Swannie stomped through the shattered door, scurried behind the counter, opened the trapdoor, and shimmied down the ladder where the wooden kegs sat in orderly rows.

"Onward Christian soldiers . . ." Swannie tried to swing and sing in rhythm, but the crawl space was only five feet high and the moonshine kegs were stacked on planks. He couldn't stand straight to swing broadly and dropped to his knees, hacking each keg individually. Singing joyously again and hacking the kegs, "Onward Christian soldiers. . . ." He spilled the moonshine onto the cellar's dirt floor.

Satisfied he had destroyed every keg, he made a cross from the wooden rubble, climbed the ladder steps, slung the axe over his left shoulder, and sauntered toward the shattered door. Before leaving, he handed the wood cross to a stupefied Bardo.

"The cross is free! You'll get a citation in the mail. You can pay the fine an' be done with it. Or, tell the judge—why you wouldn't surrender contraband whiskey. Cain't say I didn't warn you."

Thus, Swannie attacked the speakeasies of his former binges when he had staggered from bar to bar during the wasted days before the gentle voices had called him. Now proud and self-confident, he stalked from speakeasy to speakeasy wielding an axe to the stock of moonshine in the speakeasy's proper and then its storeroom, wherever that may be, attic, crawl space, or basement. When bribes wouldn't work, bartenders cursed and threatened retaliation. With the law and Lord on his side, Swannie wasn't intimidated. Fearless and fervent, he axed and hacked the speakeasy stocks. The word spread among bartenders, dry up or the crazy drunk will shut you down.

At Sunday services, Swannie continued to sit with the Heards. They were delighted and proud to have Swannie share their pew, but he no longer belonged to them. He belonged to the congregation.

During services young ladies glanced at him with approving eyes, and after services, their mothers introduced them properly. Only months before, brethren at the Church of Salvation Gospel had glimpsed at him in pity, lowering their gazes when he tried to make eye contact. Then they saw a lost wretch, living off the charity of the Heards. Now, the brethren envisioned a holy knight wielding an axe on a crusade to dry up Colfax Country. After Sunday services, the brethren made a point to greet him, shaking his hand, slapping his back, and listening attentively to sallies of his noble quest.

Swannie's basked in the adulation, although he wasn't sure what to make of his sudden jump to fame. In the evenings and weekends when he was alone in his basement apartment, the euphoria of knighthood paled. The apartment was cozy and clean—an iron-frame bed with cotton mattress, sheets and blankets, an end table, a portable closet, a pine chest of drawers, and a chair. A braided, oval throw rug covered the cement floor beside the bed. A ground level window and a solitary light bulb strung from the basement ceiling illuminated the apartment. Unlike the Heard's cellar, there were no shelves of preserved vegetables, jams, and jellies. Tucked in the corner were a few dusty, dilapidated cardboard boxes containing yellowed newspapers, old church bulletins, and receipts.

After dinners, he was free to while away the evenings in the basement apartment. Mrs. Miller discouraged Swannie from helping with the dishes. The kitchen was hers, she said, and she didn't want any man working in it and putting everything in the wrong place. Also she explained, he need not concern himself about laundry. His dirty laundry would be sent out, along with theirs, to a sister of the congregation who did laundry to make ends meet. In the wintertime, he would be expected to stoke the furnace mornings and prepare it for the day, tossing out ashes and keeping water in the furnace's humidity pan. Normally, this was Reverend Miller's chore.

"Do you sing hymns around the piano?"

"No, it's a pity," she informed him, "but, for Mr. Miller, singing hymns in the evenings is too much like work."

Living with the Millers just wasn't exciting. "Good people, kind, compassionate, virtuous, generous," Swannie thought, "jist no fun." For a few evenings, Swannie concentrated on reading the Bible on his bed in the basement. Wasn't long he grew restless and sought to while away time with Reverend Miller, who preferred a quiet evening reading alone in the parlor.

"You're welcome to read any of the books." Reverend Miller halfheartedly waved over the bookshelf. "Don't dog-ear the pages."

"Do tell."

"Some folks, say they don't have a bookmark . . ." Reverend Miller held open the book he was reading. "They crimp the top, outside corner of the page, such to mark the page when they set the book aside. Ruins the page."

"I'll be careful."

"I figured as such." Reverend Miller turned to his book and Swannie lapsed into silence. . . . Eventually, Reverend Miller noticed Swannie wasn't browsing through the books and sighed wearily. "Don't mean to be boorish, but you didn't come here to talk about books."

"You got that right. I'm lookin' for something to pass the time."

"What did you do at the Heard's?"

"Helped Mrs. Heard in the kitchen. Played with Eddy. And, practiced hymns with the whole family."

"Why don't you try that. You can sing in the church. Keys are in the kitchen. Be sure to dim the lights when you're done."

Swannie took the keys and walked next door. He entered the empty church and groped about using moonbeams to find his way to the light switch. When he turned on the lights, the church felt emptier than when he had entered in the dark. Alone among empty pews, he took his place at the Heard's pew and fingered through the hymnal, locating the hymns for the next Sunday service. He stood, cupping the hymnal in both hands, feet squarely on the floor, took a deep breath, and struggled to sing. . . .

Nothing came. He looked around, hoping to see others preparing to sing. He tried again, this time humming the first few bars, but nobody was there to pick up the words and share the jubilation. Disappointed, Swannie set the hymnal on the pew and switched out the lights.

Moonbeams flitted through the clear parts of the stained-glass windows and threw stirring shadows of tree branches onto the pews and floor. "Now, that's moonshine worth keeping," he thought and then chuckled. In the shadowy church partially brightened by the moonbeams, Swannie imagined hearing the hushed hummings of Chicorico, like putting a seashell to your ear and listening to the ocean wash the beach. After reveling in the calm of the dark for a long spell, he locked the church doors and returned to the parlor where Reverend Miller was reading comfortably.

Rather than disturb Reverend Miller, Swannie studied the ink drawing hanging over the bookshelf. He had thought it was a drawing of three men. A closer look at *Knight, Death, and Devil 1513* by Albrecht Dürer revealed only one of the images to be a man. In the background, a castle and a church tower loomed atop a hill. In the foreground, a fully armored knight rode on a sinewy, muscular horse. Beside the knight, death-personified wore a crown of snakes and rode astride a sickly horse. Death carried an hourglass with its sand falling rapidly, depicting the perennial passing of time with death lurking nearby. Behind the knight and death, the devil walked. The devil was depicted as a hybrid between horse and goat with a stupid, befuddled gaze on its face.

"Shore a strange picture, Reverend."

"A common reaction." Reverend Miller glanced longingly at the ink drawing. "Given to me by Mother upon ordination."

"I reckon it has religious meaning."

"You reckon correctly. It's a Christian allegory drawn in the Dark Ages. The three persona are on the road . . . on the journey of life itself. The knight represents the guardian of the good. He stands ready to protect the castle and church. Death reminds us of the finite time we all have for our earthly journey. If you look closely, you'll see the sand of time spilling rapidly to the bottom of the hourglass. The devil, well, he's along for the ride to entice the fallen."

"Looks to me he don't play cards with a full deck."

"I noticed that, too. I inferred you can't be very smart, if you've chosen the road to perdition. You don't have to be a sage to pick off the poor critters that fall by the wayside. I'm surprised you've never seen him." Reverend Miller turned back to his book and continued to read.

"Jist pesky crows," Swannie muttered as he leaned closer to study details of the drawing. He noticed a skull on the ground beneath the knight's horse, and a small, scrappy dog trailing behind the knight. The scrappy dog appeared to be leery of the devil. "I don't mean to sound ungrateful, Reverend," Swannie tactfully broached, "but I can't practice alone in the church. It's nothing like practicing with the Heards."

Reverend Miller sighed and then laid the book on his lap. "You've got ants in your pants—learn to relax, my boy. You've been getting a lot of public admiration. That's likely to make you restless."

"It's swell, for a change, to be something other than a drunk."

"This is true. You've proved a man can change for the better. But be wary, like walking on ice—'pride goeth before destruction, and a haughty spirit before a fall.'"

"A man needs a little pride."

Reverend Miller responded forcefully, "No, he doesn't!"

"Do tell."

"A prideful man puts himself above the laws of God . . . and of man. That's prideful. Downright wrong and dangerous. The history of the world is replete with tales of death and destruction of the innocent by the hands of prideful men."

"Don't fret, Reverend, I ain't cocky. That's what yer a'calling pride, ain't it?"

"'Arrogance' is more like it, but 'cocky' will do."

Swannie noticed that Reverend Miller's silvery hair was really gray, and without his parson's collar and black suit, he appeared haggard and weary.

"Now that you have almost completed the Bible, perhaps you should take a library card. Read other books. Learn new knowledge."

"Hmm." Swannie pondered the suggestion and jested, "Live and learn, I say!"

"I fear it's mostly live for you," Reverend Miller retorted. "A library card will open the world of adventure. You can hack through the Cuban jungle with a machete, ride a train through the snowy plains of Siberia, climb the Himalayas, bathe in the River Jordan, ride a camel in the shadows of the Great Pyramids, drive a dogsled through the Yukon's blustery blizzards, and never leave home."

"All that?"

"And, much more. A library card opens a window to new knowledge. Every day in every way, scientists are making manifest the miracles of our Lord, feeding the hungry and curing the ill. Every day, it seems, we hear of new machines. When I was a boy,

I marveled at the telegram zinging messages across the continent in skinny wires. Then came the telephone, and I could hear my grandfather's voice across the continent. Now we have radios that beam our voices across the miles, even across the oceans. It's marvelous, the world we live in, and a library card will put you in tune with that world."

"Ignorance is bliss," Swannie responded flippantly.

"Only where 'tis folly to be wise.'" Reverend Miller completed Thomas Gray's epigram. "Knowledge is sure defense against arrogance. You can never know enough. You should read Alexander Pope: 'A little learning is a dangerous thing. Drink deep,' he said. He wrote of knowledge and the power it gives."

Swannie's eyes glazed over.

"Skip the poets. Read some novels, like Mark Twain's books."

"Them's kid books."

"Not all of them."

"They're jist stories."

"Just stories! What do you think history is? Just stories. The Latin word for history is *historia*, which also means story in English. History's a story about the past."

"Past is dead and gone. Don't mean nothin' now."

"Does so. Yer standing on the shoulders of history."

A thoroughly befuddled Swannie peered toward the floor, searching for the supposed shoulders of history upon which he stood. A frustrated Reverend Miller found his place in *Paradise Lost* and tactfully suggested, "Read some histories at the Ripley Park library."

SIXTEEN   LOVE'S SWEET MELODY

MONASTIC LIFE DID NOT SUIT SWANNIE WELL, though it promised to keep him from hell. At the Heard's, there was a time to work and a time to play. At the Miller's, there was only work, even reading the Bible in the quiet of the night. Swannie needed a way to play. On a Saturday afternoon in mid-October, he thought to tour the park and library. He strolled down Rio Grande Avenue to South First Street, grinning his crooked smile while meandering by the speakeasies he had recently raided. Where winos once mooched drinks, women shopped briskly in the revitalized stores and food markets now that many of the speakeasies had been closed with a song and an axe.

The large windows of Marchiondo's Golden Rule Mercantile Store displayed current women's fashion, mostly mannequins dressed in flapper styles with boxy dresses cut above the knees. Next door, Swannie dallied at the screen door of La Rocca Meat Market to inhale the odors of freshly stuffed sausages. A slightly stooped, elderly woman wearing a shawl over her head and shoulders tottered toward the door. Swannie stepped away and opened the door. *"Grazie, grazie,"* she thanked him in Italian.

On the next block, the Brass Rail Bar was permanently closed. Its heavy doors were boarded shut and the false-front Brass Rail sign was painted over in black with the scrawled message "Closed by the Drunk." Swannie's wooden cross was nailed to the sign. He grinned pompously, his face flushed with pride. He passed the large, brick business offices of the Chicorico Coal Company and continued the pleasant stroll on the last block before Ripley Park where the homes were well kept and tiny as a postage stamp on a business envelope.

Other than size, the tiny homes had much in common with Chicorico's houses. Every piece of their material was prefabricated in a factory with the correct number of shingles, nails, laths, and a hundred other items, including kitchen and bathroom plumbing, electrical wiring and sockets, and sufficient paint for the sides, trims, and windows. They were ordered from Sears and Roebuck catalogues, shipped in bundled pieces via rail, and sturdily erected from scratch by local carpenters. Though they were miniscule Sears and Roebuck vintage, and though the yards were landscaped with sandstone and basalt rocks, wild flowers, and lilac and chokecherry bushes, they were splendid homes, miniature country manors in their own right.

Ripley Park radiated in the fading flamboyance of Indian summer. Partially barren cottonwoods and elms lined a network of cinder paths within a carefully manicured lawn. Fallen leaves cluttered in clumps along the edges of cinder paths and beneath the many wooden benches scattered among the trees.

A mother and child relaxed at one of the benches. She knelt about five feet from the child and held out her arms, encouraging him to walk away from the security of the bench. "Come, come to Mommy," she eagerly enticed the toddler whose short, spindly legs wobbled as he clutched the bench, half-trusting his mother, half-fearing a fall. Hesitantly, gingerly, he wobbled from the bench and flailed his arms, waddling toward his mother. "Weeeeeeee!" She hefted him high in the sky. He kicked joyfully and she set him down to walk again.

In the center of the park, a hedgerow circled a rose garden planted around a lava stone memorial to the Battleship Maine of the Spanish American War. One of its sirens was embedded in the memorial commemorating the Rough Riders Theodore Roosevelt had recruited from the Raton area to fight in Cuba. At the north and south ends of the park, two inert Civil War cannons guarded the park. New Mexicans had fought on the side of the North when the Civil War was brought to New Mexico by Texas Confederates via the Rio Grande Valley as far north as Santa Fé and Glorieta Canyon.

Swannie examined the ornate style of the Carnegie library building, a rococo Spanish Revival edifice with concave, crimson ceramic tiles for roofing. "Raton Public Library" was engraved on a granite slab over the doorway. He climbed the concrete steps and opened the library's dark oak doors. The moldy odor of archived books gushed from within as he scanned the great-room's dark oak interior paneling, bulky tables, oak chairs, and an imposing front desk.

"Can I help you?" A perky voice coming from a young lady whose beaming smile matched a sparkling voice caught Swannie's ear. The young lady whisked from behind the desk. Although her dress covered most of her body and flowed over the lovely curves of an hour glass figure, the lines of her knees and the upper part of her legs were distinctly apparent beneath her dress as she approached Swannie assuredly.

"Uh, jist looking. Never been in a library before."

"I'm Mildred, Mildred Ammons." She extended her hand. "With whom do I have the pleasure?"

"Oh, uh . . ." Swannie was not accustomed to courteous, cheerful, and assertive young ladies. "I'm Ray Swanson." He awkwardly extended a limp hand. "Folks call me Swannie."

"Gosh! I've heard of you." Animated and effusive, she sprinkled Swannie with praises. "You're that gallant revenuer, shutting down the speakeasies on a crusade like St. George, the dragon slayer. Mother says it's a relief. Ladies can now shop on First Street without drunken wretches begging for a dime."

Swannie relaxed and felt less awkward. His fame had spread far and wide. Even the town librarian had heard of him as something other than a drunk. He prattled eagerly, "It's trying. The past week, I pulled in front of Thunderbird Saloon aiming for a surprise raid. Spotted Squeeze Ruiz—double-parked in his taxi—blocking the parking place near the front door. I hollered: 'Move it!' He shook his fist and cussed like a sailor. I jumped out the pickup, run over, and told him to move it or get arrested. Claimed he was waiting for a passenger. During the ruckus, all the folks in the Thunderbird lit out, includin' the bartender. The Thunderbird was empty, an' there wasn't a drop of hooch in it. Stunk like a speakeasy, though."

"What's to be done?"

"Nothing, for now. Did tell the sheriff—you know Boots? Well, told him how Squeeze Ruiz blocked me from raiding the speakeasy."

"What did he do?"

"Nothing. Instead, he said, 'Shoot! Most any place a taxi parks on First Street is blocking a speakeasy.'"

Mildred giggled, holding a hand to her lips.

"Didn't see the humor, but Boots shore did."

"I'm sorry. Couldn't help myself." Instantly, she clapped her hands lightly, suggesting, "Let's do a dry run, look up a book. How about *The Adventures of Tom Sawyer* by Mark Twain?"

"Reverend Miller mentioned Mark Twain."

"He was a popular writer."

"Reverend Miller doesn't write books."

"No, silly, Mark Twain."

Mildred thumbed through the card catalog. Swannie gazed over her shoulder. She smelled good, like lilacs in a spring rain.

"See here, up in the corner. That's the call number. Get a slip of paper, write it down." Swannie wrote while Mildred recited the call number, "817.44 T."

"Follow me." Mildred escorted him by the reference tables of neatly arranged magazines and newspapers from Boston, New York City, Chicago, and San Francisco and by a shelf of newly arrived books. He paused.

"What are these?"

"New acquisitions, just arrived and catalogued."

"Can we come back, look at 'em?"

"Absolutely, you may browse at will. This is a public library. It belongs to the taxpayers. Before you browse, I want you to get the hang of finding your books using the Dewey decimal system. As we approach each row of shelves, look for the range of call numbers." She located Twain's book by call number and showed it to Swannie.

"Read it in grade school," Swannie murmured, "it's a fiction book for boys."

She returned the book to the shelf and suggested he seek another book from a call number to assure he understood the procedure for locating a book. "Helps to know the author's name. If you don't, you can look under the category of subject. That will show you what books we have under that category."

"How about Negro history?"

"We have *Uncle Tom's Cabin* by Harriet Beecher Stowe."

"That's a fiction book. I want the truth."

"It's very close to the truth. That's what made it so popular. Good fiction is based on truth."

"So's the Easter Bunny and Santa Claus. That don't make them true."

"Those are myths people believe to be true. What you believe to be true is a matter of faith, don't you think?"

"No, it ain't," Swannie snapped sharply. "Truth is a matter of fact."

"Do you believe we descended from monkeys and apes, just because the facts imply that?"

"Imply what?"

"That mankind descended from apes."

"Bible's clear on that. Lord made Adam from dirt, and Eve from the rib of Adam."

"There, you see. You believe the tales of the Bible to be true."

"They are true. They're not fish stories, even Jonah and the whale ain't a fishing story."

"Don't you think it's an allegory?"

"I suppose." Swannie had no idea what an allegory might be and realized Emma was bright and thoughtful. Yet, he enjoyed bantering with the pretty librarian.

"Goodness, we've digressed. What *ever* were we talking about?"

"How man came from monkeys, so some folks claim. Going by the way some folks deport themselves, I'd say they had monkeys for kin."

Mildred giggled again.

"Pardon me, Miss. I don't mean to be rude. The Heards—the Negro family in Chicorico—they took me in and treated me kindly when I was down. Other than Reverend and Mrs. Miller, white folks never lifted a hand to help. I want to know more factual history about Negro folks."

"It was I who misunderstood," Mildred insisted. "I presumed you would rather read fiction."

"There's been many days I wallowed away feelin' sorry for myself. Done it too much. Nowadays, I don't have time to squander. Living with the Heards, I learned I don't know squat about Negro folks. I'd like to read a book or two that is factual about them. If'n you don't mind, I'd like to browse through the new books."

"Please do. You might just find the right books. Bring them to the front desk. I'll check them out to you."

"I don't have a card."

"That's not a problem, silly."

Mildred returned to the front desk and continued processing recently returned books. Swannie browsed through the new books and settled on two of them. He carried them to the front desk where Mildred took his information, issued a card, and checked out the books. "They're due in two weeks. I'll give you an extension, if needs be. Let me know."

Swannie thanked Mildred and left the library. Outside at the bottom of the steps, Swannie crumpled comfortably on a wooden bench and started to read the first volume of the two-volume set of books he had checked out with his new library card. . . .

Mildred greeted Swannie as she locked the front door to the library and walked down the steps. "Have you been here all the while?"

"Uh, huh." Swannie raised his befuddled head from foggy concentration, idea-sodden enough to barely understand two hours had passed, and Mildred was locking up the library for the day.

"I'm sorry to intrude. The library closes at five." She adjusted a hat over her curly red hair and canted the brim to the right. "You may stay outside as long as you like. The electric street lamps will soon illuminate."

"That's okay." Swannie blinked to clear his fog and marveled how Mildred's slightly canted hat made her appear mysterious and flirty. "Time for me to go home, too. May I walk you home?"

"Yes, I'd like that. I live close by—literally *up* Savage Avenue."

"Ho!" Swannie laughed at her quick wit. Savage Avenue rose gradually west from Second Street and then abruptly ascended at a forty-five–degree angle.

She walked in short, brisk steps. Swannie held a book in each hand as they strolled along the cinder lane shaded somewhat by cottonwood and elm trees. Swannie's blood coursed under his skin with exciting, inexplicable expectations as ancient as Adam and Eve, Antony and Cleopatra, Romeo and Juliet.

A slight breeze clattered the drying leaves in the trees. The two newfound friends crossed the street onto the walkway and strolled along Savage Avenue.

"Oh, my!" A tiny *tornillo*, a sand devil whirling dust, swirled and swiped Mildred's hat from her hair. The tornillo swirled skyward and pitched the hat forward before wedging it on a bare branch of a tall cottonwood.

"Hold these!" Swannie handed her the books, skipped ahead, bear-hugged the gnarly bark of the tree, and scooted up the trunk until he reached the branch that held the hat. He stretched to grab the hat. Too far out. He couldn't shake the branch—too thick at the trunk. On hands and knees, he crawled toward the elusive hat. It slid further away and fell. Then, the branch cracked at its base. Swannie slid, fell to the branch below, and clutched it. He swung and caught the falling hat.

"Be careful! It's just a hat!"

Exhilarated by Mildred's anxious pleas for his well being, Swannie thought to impress her with his agility and dauntless courage, like St. George the dragon slayer. He kicked his legs and swung with one arm, and then switched to the other, waving the hat.

She shrieked. "Do be careful! Careful! Careful!"

The more frantic Mildred squealed, the more exhilarated Swannie became. He flipped a leg over the branch and hung from it, both arms dangling toward Mildred. Monkey see, monkey do, the mocking phrase fluttered through his head as he dangled upside down—the very words the coal camp kids squealed to the monkey Casey Jones. Blood rushed to his brain and may have facilitated fast thinking. He didn't know the meaning of the word *faux pas*, but he recognized he was about to commit an irredeemable social blunder.

"Wups!" Swannie feigned falling very much unlike a monkey, clumsily bending at the knees as he landed on his feet and fell onto the walkway.

"Are you harmed? Did you hurt yourself?"

"Naw, piece of cake." Swannie's knees stung, but he swelled his chest in bravado, awkwardly rising to his feet. He lifted the hat to her head. "Here, I'll pin it on."

Standing close enough to see the tiny freckles flecked on her cheeks and the crumbly mascara dabbled on the lashes of her blue eyes, Swannie noted a small scar below her left eye partially covered by powder. He fumbled clumsily for the bobby pins in her finely stranded red hair, which smelled clean like fresh flowers, as did her lightly powdered cheeks. His toes tingled. "There, believe it'll stay put." Swannie dropped his hands and reached for the books.

"I'll carry one." Mildred handed him a book, grasped his right hand, and meshed her fingers into his.

"Zippitty-do-daw, zippitty-yea, me oh my, what a wonderful day!" Swannie rhapsodized. Frenetic flashes and fuzzy feelings coursed throughout his body. Her warm hand . . . fragrant hair . . . cute freckles. Leisurely and literally, they strolled up Savage Avenue, swinging their arms and disregarding the abrupt ascent leading to Mildred's home, which sat in the shadow of Goat Hill, so called for the wild mountain goats once dwelling in its crags. The long-gone goats were killed off and eaten by early settlers.

Swannie felt great. The stiffness . . . the awkwardness . . . the caution dwindled. He warbled the lyrics from "Star Dust," "Sometimes I won-der why I spend. . . ." While Swannie warbled the beguiling tune, Mildred pressed his hand to her heart. He could feel her heart beating and imagined his heart throbbing loudly above the notes he warbled. He thought to steal a kiss but suppressed the urge. Holding hands was brazen enough.

"Beau-ti-ful," Mildred said and dropped Swannie's hand from her heart. They continued walking, hand in hand. "Your voice is so . . . so . . . tender."

"My favorite." Swannie explained lucidly, "Hoagy Carmichael wrote the melody, Mitchell Parish the lyrics. Came out in 1929."

They arrived at Mildred's. From the front gate, they could clearly see Raton's grid plan with streets running north and south and avenues east and west. The Santa Fé railway ran north to south and served as the town's dividing line with streets running parallel to the west and east of the tracks where Mexican and Lebanese folks lived. The Santa Fé roundhouse, maintenance yard, and depot served as the town's hub, and First Street was the main thorough-fare, although the new Hotel Swastika and International State Bank Building on Second Street were fast becoming the town's commercial center.

At the gate, Mildred coyly turned and patted Swannie's hand. "You're sweet, not like so many boys around here." Mildred saw in Swannie the same qualities Dahlia had sensed, fragile, delicate, and naïve in an ungainly sort of way. "Mother speaks of you, now that you've shut down the First Street speakeasies, and the wretches are gone. Her friends in 'Circle' all speak of you so highly."

"That makes me proud. What's 'Circle,' a club?"

"A Christian women's circle at church."

"What do they do?"

"Have meetings and stuff."

"Stuff?"

"Oh, you know, talk and have tea, I guess. I really don't know."

"Gossip?"

"I have no idea."

They lapsed into affable silence . . . enamored . . . neither wanted to say goodnight. "Come, meet Mother and Father. They're in the parlor, I see."

"Why, I . . . sure, if'n it's no inconvenience." Swannie glanced through the transparent, organdy curtains hanging in the front window and spied her parents sitting comfortably in soft chairs beside floor lamps.

"Inconvenience! Don't be silly. Mother and Father want to know my friends. Come." She tugged his hand.

Swannie opened the gate. Mildred lead the way, tugging Swannie by the hand until they entered the parlor where she dropped his hand. "Mother! Father! This is a new friend. You've heard of the Grand Knight of Prohibition, Swannie Swanson. This is he!"

Mrs. Ammons rose abruptly from her chair, clasping the hooked needle and crochet work in her hands. Mr. Ammons buried his face inside the day's issue of the *Raton Range*.

"Gracious!" Mrs. Ammons exclaimed in an agitated, appre-hensive tone of imminent crisis. Her nose was long and narrow, and her cheeks puffed like a squirrel's carrying acorns to store for the winter. She gasped and took in a deep breath. Her chest expanded and breasts swelled beneath a tight fitting, black satin blouse, stretching its buttonholes and revealing the white fringes of a brassiere. She chastised Mr. Ammons, a rasp of irritation in her throat, "Thomas, mind your manners!"

Swannie watched Mrs. Ammons cajole her husband and detected where Mildred acquired her good looks and hourglass figure, but not her perky disposition.

"Milly's brought home a . . . a . . . a friend!"

Mr. Ammons slowly lowered the newspaper. A spent pipe drooped from the side of his mouth. He gazed boorishly over the top of his eyeglasses and scrutinized Swannie head-to-toe. "How-dee-do." He tactlessly raised the newspaper and continued to read without giving Swannie the opportunity to reciprocate.

The discord between Mildred's parents bewildered Swannie. Her mother was nervous, edgy, and father dull and insipid. Mildred was neither.

"He's a man of few words," Mrs. Ammons said, conjuring an excuse for Ammons's rude reception. "But, I am not. You may visit our Milly on the porch—when she invites you."

"Of course, ma'am."

"Mind. You're too old for her. I want her to finish college."

"Mighty good idea. She's a smart little chicken."

"Naturally, I don't want her to marry any of the ne'er-do-wells here in Raton."

"Why, Mother, you never—"

"It was only a matter of time we had this talk, Milly."

"I meant to say—you never talked this way with other boys."

"Dear! Mr. Swanson is *not* just another boy."

A thick silence infused the parlor. Mr. Ammons persisted to bury his head in the newspaper without showing his face. Outside, the faint whistle of a train caused a dog to bay eerily as though it felt the coldness of the Ammons's reception.

Swannie heard the dog's wail and felt the chill in the parlor. "Nice meetin' the two of you." Deferentially, he backed out of the parlor, opened the front door, and stepped onto the porch. Mildred followed.

"Thought she approved of me?"

"Oh, that's Mother. She doesn't warm up to boys I bring home." She lowered her voice, speaking in a loud whisper, "Hope to see you soon, at the library, that is." She handed Swannie's book back to him.

"Ho!" Swannie chortled, taking the book. "Back in two weeks, I reckon." He offered a hand. She shook it, giggled, and slipped into the house.

Cold reception or no, Swannie could care less as he made egress. He clicked his heels and walked through the gate, heading home at a heady rate. He skittered gaily down the sidewalk with a hop and a skip, shuffling at a manly, Manhattan clip, kicking his feet through the lagging leaves. In the afterglow of the lover's stroll, he composed lyrics to a song and sang as he skipped along.

SEVENTEEN   LOVE'S LABOR LOST

IN THE WEEKS TO COME, Swannie spent his spare time at the library. He devoured information, hungrily perusing newspapers and magazines from cover-to-cover, absorbing everything he read. Politics, economics, and race relations galvanized his attention. He craved knowledge of the world as he once craved alcohol, voraciously and totally, immersing himself in news articles and editorials of the *New York Times*, *Christian Science Monitor*, and *Wall Street Journal*. He found them surprisingly easy to read.

Whenever the opportunity arose, he made small talk with Mildred. Between library patrons, Mildred fostered the small talk and he regaled in her quick wit and flirty eyes. Mysterious and exotic, she was a sprite—sighing, laughing, pouting. On Saturdays, he timed the visits to walk Mildred home after she closed the library.

"You've walked me home several times. You might sit for a spell." Mildred pointed to the swing on the porch.

"Okay with your mother?"

"We'll stay on the porch where she can watch."

Swannie released the gate latch and allowed Mildred to lead the way. The porch faced the north and was shady and cool.

"You seem to enjoy the newspapers." Mildred rocked the swing lightly.

"Yep. Mostly, they're factual."

"I suppose you read the sports. Most boys do."

"Sometimes. Always good news, 'less you like the losers. I like the news articles, editorials, they're most factual."

"They're supposed to be, except the editorial may distort facts."

"Been reading too many editorials. Seems the politicians can't get together."

"Most must agree the country's in a deep economic depression."

"That's nothin' common folks don't know. Some editors support President Hoover and the Republicans in Congress. They believe the economy will bottom-out and then begin a slow recovery toward progress. Depression's a natural business cycle, they say. Democrats think the government ought to step in, prime the pump, stimulate the economy, get us out of the muck. Makes horse sense to me. I'm with the Democrats."

"The Republican's hands-off policy worked for a long while, starting with President Coolidge ten years ago."

"It sure ain't worked for common folks."

"Someday, it will. Wait and see."

"Folks been waiting a long time."

"They've got to be patient. President Hoover shouldn't tinker willy-nilly with the economy."

"Willy-nilly, my foot. Folks need jobs."

"They're just lazy."

"Why? 'Cause they can't find work?"

"Mr. Henry Ford said there's plenty of work in America."

"He might be a big shot, but he makes mistakes, too. I read where his engineers put a flat six-cylinder in the Model K truck. The truck's chassis wasn't worth a candle in a tornado, but the engine really pulled a load. Mr. Ford stopped makin' the truck. Said he didn't like an engine that had more cylinders than a cow has teats."

"Uhh, how vulgar!"

"Chevy and Dodge, they started building six-cylinder trucks and left Ford in the dust. Ford could'a been the leader on trucks, like he was on the Model T."

"Well, I was saying, Mr. Ford was correct to say people need to get busy, look for work, instead of expecting welfare."

"Mr. Ford's for the birds. He ought to know better. Government needs to step in and fix things."

"Heavens, that's communism."

"Shucks, communism, socialism, do-goodism, call it what you want. Folks need jobs."

"I suppose you support the Wobblies and their anarchistic ideology."

"Them's big words, but I tell you, the miners in Chicorico don't support the Wobblies, 'cause they *are* communists."

"The miners?"

Swannie laughed at Mildred's humor. He knew she understood him but liked to tease. "The Wobblies. They wanna overthrow capitalism and the government that supports it. Miners don't want that. They support a union."

"I've been led to believe that a union is the first step toward communism."

"It's all accordin' to the way you look at it. If'n you lived in Chicorico, you'd think different. Miners get skunked out'a their tonnage at the scales." Swannie described Osgood's caper where he slid the wood slivers between the scales' pressure plates to under-weigh the miner's coal. Then, he described the use of scrip rather than money for wages: "They get paid in scrip so's they have to buy at the Company store. Prices are high, and folks can't get out'a debt. The mine's dangerous, accidents happen, Company don't care. Folks are afraid to speak their minds—for fear of eviction and blacklisting."

"Blacklisting?"

"That's where the Company fires a man and puts his name on a list as a troublemaker, maybe 'cause he complained about working conditions, or 'cause his missus blabbed how she was gonna vote any way she wanted."

"That's wrong! In America, individuals have rights."

"'Course, it's wrong. Company don't care."

"This is all so hard to believe." Mildred was appalled. "Surely, you're telling tall tales? Making it all up?"

"I'd swear on a stack of Bibles, it's the truth. Mr. Montaño's brother-in-law got fired that-a-way. His Missus didn't want to vote a straight Republican ticket, and told the Company man so. They was evicted that same day, their belongings thrown out the door. And, he can't get a job in the mines now, even with Phelps-Dodge.

His name's on the list. Santa Fé won't hire him to work on a section gang."

"Why not?"

"'Cause they're in cahoots, the Company, the railroad. They jist care about making money for themselves. They treat workers like dirt. I saw so myself. So, if'n a union makes me a communist, I'm a communist."

"My heavens!" Mildred stopped the swing. "You're radical."

"I am, if'n hard-cash wages is radical, if'n accurate scales is radical, and if'n safe mines is radical—"

"That's not communism."

Mildred lightly shoved the swing. "What other bad news have you read?" She was surprised and pleased but not sure what to make of the fact Swannie had become such an avid reader, learning so much since she'd met him.

"Drought's getting worse in places like Oklahoma and Kansas. A Dust Bowl, they're callin' it."

"That's a concern here in Colfax County. Many farmers are moving away for want of rain. They can't dryland farm. There's not enough moisture to cultivate, and the lakes are down."

"Except Lake Maloya. It's pretty wet."

"Silly, water's always wet?"

"Jist joshing. Went fishing last summer with Julian Heard and two of his neighbors, and I got dunked." Swannie chuckled nervously without explaining the reason for the dunking, diverting the conversation away from himself. "I am troubled by the news about Negroes. Did'ja know in Texas alone, there's been three lynchings in the past three months, the latest in Thomasville?"

"No, I didn't. Such news makes me sad. I try not to read about it."

"A nineteen-year-old white girl screamed a Negro attacked her. She identified the villain as Willie Kirby a'working on a chain gang near the town. The sheriff provided Willie an alibi. Said Willie hadn't left jail the day she said he attacked her. Anyways, a mob broke him out'a jail, strung a rope over a branch of a tall oak tree, and hung him. They shot into his dead body whilst he was still swinging. Then, they tied him to a truck and dragged him up and down the main street of town, five or six times, for folks to gawk, like he was a dead mountain lion."

"That's terribly gruesome. I don't think that could happen here."

"It was the sixteenth lynching in America, and the Texas Governor didn't do nothin' about them mean-spirited folks."

"What could he do? It's a matter of conscience. People can believe what they want."

"But they mustn't hurt each other."

"Do you want the government to tell you what to think?" Mildred liked Swannie's concern for people and smiled, but she continued the bantering.

"Government should make folks obey the law."

"There's no law to stop you from being mean-spirited."

"There is in the Good Book. There should be such a law to stop all them mean-spirited people from lynching Negroes."

"That's communistic."

"Call it what you want. It's wrong to lynch a man without a trial, jist 'cause he's a Negro."

"Just politics. The governor's kowtowing to the Ku Klux Klan. They're very influential in Texas, can get a governor elected. Or, defeated."

"Mean-spirited folks, ain't they?"

"We can't change people. Some are just plain bad."

"I suppose, but we can try." Swannie smiled his lopsided grin that endeared him to Mildred and Dahlia.

"Won't do much good. You'll go crazy trying to change the world."

"Jist 'cause things are the way they are, don't mean they have to be that-a-way."

"You *are* a radical." Mildred couldn't imagine having this conversation with any of her dates. Most mainly boasted of their exploits and tried to steal kisses.

"For a dying cause. Accordin' to the papers, there's a push to eliminate Prohibition, and I don't like it."

Mildred teased, "You don't like Prohibition?"

"The push to legalize the sale of alcohol. It's a curse that makes men weak. Greedy men take advantage of the weak. I won't give up on Prohibition, if'n it kills me."

"Don't talk like that. The Wets won't have their way. Prohibition's in the Constitution."

"You know, Mildred, ignorance was bliss, once upon a time. I was happier before I started visiting the library and reading the papers. I reckon I'll read books at home . . . alone in my basement apartment."

"You can always read them here in our parlor, if you choose."

"Why, thank you."

"Call. Let me know. I'll arrange it with mother."

Four days later, Swannie called Mildred and arranged to visit. He dressed in a pressed, starched white shirt and the Sunday trousers and socks Dahlia had given him. He shined his shoe boots because his old dress shoes had holes in the soles, and the heels were practically worn to the last. Book in hand, he walked briskly across town without stopping to gawk in shop windows. When he approached Mildred's house, he spotted her waving from a second floor gable window. The nearer Swannie walked, the more frantically she waved.

Below on the steps of the front porch, her three brothers stood in a defensive line. Two stood with arms crossed; the third held a baseball bat over his shoulder.

"Howdy." Swannie stood at the gate. Mildred clasped her hands to her face and covered her eyes. The three brothers blitzed— stopped to fumble with the gate latch. Swannie whirled and fled, dashing down Savage Avenue. Bad memories of boys and a baseball bat flashed through Swannie's mind: *Jack-o-Lantern. Some boys bashed it. Bat. Temple mushed, candle wax oozed out mouth. Me, Ma, husked it, stringy and seedy. Cut triangle eyes. Round hole-nose, jagged werewolf mouth. Some boys bashed it. We gave'em treats. After. They come. Porch steps. Bashed it. Temple mashed. Jack-o-Lantern. Mushed, why? We gave them treats.*

He practically leapt over Second Street onto the cinder lane bisecting Ripley Park, the beastly brothers blitzing in hot pursuit. Swannie sprinted across the park, hopped onto the railroad tracks at the First Street crossing, dashed south to the roundhouse, and darted through its wide front door.

An engineer was revolving a steam engine toward the south. Swannie hopped into the engine's cab. Instantly, the engineer tried to shove him out, but then recognized him, and pulled Swannie into the cab. The three brothers scrambled into the roundhouse, frenetically searching for Swannie.

"We'll get you!" one brother yelled and waggled the baseball bat. Fists doubled, the others yelled simultaneously, "Dirty commie! Drunk! Red fink! Trash!"

Engineer Angelo Ferranti whispered to Swannie, "Stay down." He motioned to Swannie to stay on his knees beside the engine's hot firebox. Angelo leaned out the cabin, sneered, and ordered: "You boys git out! Roundhouse ain't no place for boys! They ain't nobody in here, but us workers!"

The brothers looked askance, angrily grumbling among themselves.

"Stoke her up," Angelo quietly ordered Swannie, pointing to the coal bin and shovel. "They cain't see you."

Gladly, Swannie opened the door to the firebox and ducked the blazing hot air by hefting wide-brimmed shovels of coal into the open firebox. The fire roared. Beads of sweat trickled down Swannie's temples.

Angelo chugged the engine out of the roundhouse while the gang of brothers searched inside the roundhouse and couldn't find Swannie, who was steaming slowly south on the tracks and energetically shoveling brimming shovels of coal into the firebox. Down the line south of the railroad station, Angelo released the throttle and slowed the engine. "End of the line, for you." Angelo waggled the "okay" sign with his index finger and thumb. "Keep up the good work, Swannie."

"You know me?"

"Who don't?"

Two weeks after Mildred's brothers chased Swannie with a baseball bat, he sneaked to Ripley Park and hid behind the lava stone memorial to the Battleship Maine ensconced in the rose garden. From behind the memorial, he had a clear view of the westerly side of the park and Savage Avenue where he feared Mildred's beastly brothers might appear in search of prey. . . . About 4:45 p.m. Swannie sneaked from behind the memorial and crossed the park by crouching stealthily behind the trees as he stalked toward the library. Before reaching the front of the library, he glanced in every direction, searching for Mildred's brothers. Coast clear. He slipped around the lilac bushes that grew behind the wooden benches at the foot of the library steps.

Mildred stepped out the library, fumbled with a key ring, and turned to lock the front doors. Swannie slipped onto the park bench, slumped back, and crossed his legs, assuming a comfortable posture as though he had lounged on the bench for a long time.

"Swannie, I didn't see you."

"Been here all the while. Your brothers coming for you?"

"No. . . . But, you mustn't walk me home."

"Why not?" Swannie asked gently.

"Dear, dear, dear—I wish you hadn't come."

"Don't want to see me?"

"No! Yes! I want to see you, but I can't."

"Why?"

"Dear, dear, dear. Father says you're on the blacklist."

"How's he know?"

"Oh, dear, you don't know. He's a bookkeeper for the Company."

Swannie frowned, contorted his lips, asking, "Did he show you the books tellin' I got fired for helping a widow?"

"He never said anything about that."

A thick silence ensued, each unsure of the other. Finally, Mildred sighed grievously. "I don't know what to think."

"I know I want to see you."

A little snuffle escaped from Mildred. "It's not that. It's Mother, too."

"What's she got to do with it?"

"There's talk, oh dear, at Mother's Circle Society."

"Jist gabby women gossiping."

"Mother's had a change of heart."

"About me?"

"You're such a gallant, young man, but you used to be—"

"A drunk?"

"Mother doesn't believe a leopard changes his spots."

"Once a drunk, always?"

"Once a wretch, always. She thinks the moonshine you confiscate, you drink. Or, give it to Wobblies, and they sell it to make money to support their violent affairs."

"Do you believe that?"

"Mother does."

"Don't you have your own mind? Can't you think for yourself?"

"I have to live with Mother, Father. You don't know what they're like."

"Maybe if'n they got to know me."

"Oh, dear. You'd show your true colors. They're sure to believe—"

"I'm not good enough for you."

"You can always visit at the library."

"Sneak behind your folk's back?"

"That's spiteful."

"It's my pride—sneaking is sneaking."

"Many famous lovers have had to be secretive about their love, like Romeo and Juliet." Mildred didn't mention Romeo and Juliet died of broken hearts.

"Can't be sneaky about my feelings. It's my pride, what little I got. Lost it after the war. Been workin' at getting it back. I'm good as any boy—when it comes to courtin'."

"You are, Swannie, better than most. You're too sensitive. Making too much of my mother's opinion. Swallow your silly pride."

Another chasm of thick silence fell between them. They darted glances at each other. . . . After a lengthy, awkward spell, Swannie spoke sententiously, "You're makin' too much of your Ma and Pa's opinion. An' what little pride I got, ain't silly." Swannie turned briskly and walked across the lawn onto Second Street toward home.

"It's not that—oh, dear, dear. " Mildred held her hands to her eyes, tears leaking.

EIGHTEEN   CROSSES IN THE COAL CAMPS

WHACK! WHACK! WHACK! Swannie axed Onorio's cellar door—*Onward Christian soldiers.* Whack! Whack! Whack! He mangled the door into splinters—*marching as to war.* Crushed it beneath his shoe boots—*with the cross of Jesus going on before.* He stomped into the cellar—*Christ, the royal master, leads against the foe*—he axed the jugs of wine and splattered the press. Wine flowed freely, trickled over the earthen benches, and lapped lightly against the soles of his shoe boots. Fragrant whiffs of perfume wafted, like thickets of blooming honeysuckle roses. Swannie hesitated, inhaled lustily but did not waiver. He tied two staves into a cross and wedged it on the doorknob of the oak school door leading to the prized stock, Onorio's best wines undetected. Swannie pranced proudly out the cellar, singing "Onward Christian soldiers marching as to war. . . ."

Bitter since his break up with Mildred, Swannie vented his anger at work. As a one-man invading horde wielding an axe, the law, and Christian zeal, Swannie's onslaught ruined the coal camp wine cellars. First, Onorio's wine cellar demolished, then Bruno Bergamo's in Dawson, Joe Sonchar's in Sugarite, Mike Arcangelli in Swastika, Saul Ferkovich in Gardiner, and Francesco Cherubini in Van Houten. After each righteous, rampaging raid, he erected a plain cross wrought from the staves and slats of the ruined racks, casks, and wine presses. Within a month, he had wrecked every known coal camp wine cellar.

"You can't be destroying folk's private property!" Boots chastised Swannie. "Home brew's allowed for personal consumption."

"Common knowledge. They're selling that hooch."

"How d'ya know?"

"Julian told me. They sell for cash."

"They can cash their scrip."

"Not much in that. Seventy-five cents on a dollar of scrip. B'sides, they get a high price on the wine. Not rot gut—the Italian and Serbian wine—like the moonshine brewed in these parts."

"Shouldn't be axing the cellars doors."

"You wanna come with me—politely ask them to let me in?"

"With a search warrant."

"They wouldn't allow no search, claiming they wasn't selling their wine."

"I'm warning you. Don't get carried away with folk's private property."

Swannie took Boots's warning to heart, but lost all caution as he pondered over Julian's cellar. "Not real wine," he rationalized, "made from chokecherries. Nobody would buy it, even if he sold it, which he don't. Ah, no use kiddin' myself. I can count my friends on one hand. Julian and Dahlia are the best. Folks might make it hard on them, saying I favor'em, which I do, mostly Dahlia. I'll pretend to raid their cellar. I'll flash a search warrant. Dahlia will come out. I'll make her promise to never sell the hooch, jist dump it, I'll say. Giving friends a warning, I'll say. Then, I'll tell her my real purpose for the raid—that I come to say I love her and ain't had too much luck finding a girl in Raton to take her place. So, I'm leavin', I'll say."

At dawn one workday morning he crouched behind the large, concrete steps of Chicorico's Company store where he could watch the Heard's house without being detected. He waited till Julian walked to the mine and Eddy skipped to school with Arturo. Now was his chance to see Dahlia. He strode boldly along the lane circling around the Heard's backyard, spotting Dahlia through the kitchen window standing at the table. "Probably preparing supper," Swannie thought. "She starts early." His mouth watered with remembrance of her hardy meals. This would not be as easy as he thought. "Jist go about your business, pretendin' a raid," he muttered half-heartedly.

He proceeded to the cellar door, humming loudly "Onward Christian Soldiers."

"Why, Swannie, why didn't you knock?" Dahlia poked her head out of the kitchen door.

Swannie reeled back from the cellar door. "Er, I got a search warrant." Swannie flashed a folded sheet of paper. It fell open. "Gonna search your cellar for wine."

"Whatever for? You know Julian doesn't sell his chokecherry wine."

"Well, 'cause—" He glimpsed at Dahlia but couldn't make eye contact. Instead, he banged the cellar door open-and-shut repeatedly and strode into the cellar. A shadow fell over the cellar door. "It's Dahlia. She's outside, waiting," Swannie realized but couldn't face her. He sang limply, hoping Dahlia would come into the cellar. "Onward Christian soldiers. . . ." She didn't show. He axed Julian's wine rack and bottles of wine. After erecting a cross, he turned abruptly, and Dahlia's elusive shadow vanished from the door. He briskly broke a trail through the shattered bottles and rack and hopped the cellar steps, two at a time.

Outside, he was apprehensive and didn't glance about. He focused directly ahead, huffed hurriedly to the backyard gate, unlatched it, and stepped through. He turned to re-latch it and glimpsed toward the house. Dahlia stood behind the kitchen window, her hands to her mouth, her crop of ebony curls unfurled over her right eye.

When Julian arrived home from work, Dahlia took him to the cellar and showed the destruction wrought by Swannie. "Happened so fast, I didn't hear—till it was too late. I went to the kitchen door and greeted him. Said he had a search warrant. He banged open the cellar door and fell into a frenzy, singing and chopping."

"Gall durn his hide!"

"It really wasn't our Swannie, but a stranger."

Disappointed, Julian shook his head, the damage not yet apparent. "No stranger. It was our boy Swannie. Look'a his cross."

"Oh, my, my." Dahlia placed her hands over her eyes to avoid seeing the cross, muttering in undertones, "He walked out the cellar with his axe and out the backyard. Looked at me, like he didn't see me."

Julian kicked the broken bottles and slats into a pile, noting the trickles of wine spilled in puddles on the dirt floor. Swannie had been careful in his wrath. Julian's fishing gear was untouched, as were Dahlia's jars of preserved garden patch vegetables and chokecherry jelly.

"He was only doing his job." Dahlia tried to cool Julian's swelling rage.

"Humph! Chokecherry wine!"

"It's against the law."

"Home brew's allowed."

"Honey, please don't do anything. Swannie has the law on his side."

Julian glared at Dahlia. They stared past each other in consternation, standing that way for a long time. Finally, he yanked Swannie's makeshift cross and charged out the cellar. At the coal shed, he axed the flimsy cross into tinder.

"Honey," Dahlia pleaded. "Ple-ease. Don't do anything you'll regret later."

Without confirming Dahlia's plea, Julian slung the axe over his shoulder, crossed the meadow, and disappeared into the brush, yelling, "I'll be back!"

"When?"

"When I get back!"

Julian hiked a steep slope until he found a charred grove where lightning had struck and shattered a ponderosa. The burning tree had fallen on smaller piñons and singed them. With the destructive fury of a tornado, Julian walloped the axe into the trunk of the ponderosa, rived it into small logs, and split them into firewood sizes. Furiously, he hacked into the dead-standing piñons, trimmed their drying branches, split them into segments, and cleaved them into stove logs. Sweat poured down his brow and back as he stacked the cord-high pile of firewood. He girded it with broken branches and then searched for another fire to cool his anger.

Swannie's crusade against homemade brew became the center of talk in the coal camps, especially at poker games at the Chicorico clubhouse Saturday evenings. The poker game was a rare time when Company men and miners mingled. With Prohibition, alcohol was not served in the main saloon and serious poker players retreated to a spare, dimly lit room in the back of the main saloon where wine and moonshine were sold for cash. Like the alcohol, all poker antes were in cash. The cost of both was high but the serious players drank slowly and played deliberately, sometimes treating themselves to stogies, cheroots, and other five-cent cigars. The games were played in almost complete silence, except for the dealer, who used grunts and hand and facial gestures to conduct the games. After the dealing was done, the winner for the evening was obligated to buy a round of moonshine.

One Saturday evening after the game ended and cards were folded, Julian testily complained about Swannie's crusade against homemade wine. Onorio joined him, complaining, "*Mannàggia*, homemade wine and beer are allowed under the law."

"Any kind of home brew, chokecherry, dandelion."

"Big shots can't agree. Some say it is. Some say it isn't."

"Swannie's become his own law."

Linderman and Bowers sniggered in apparent pleasure, relishing Onorio and Julian's anger. Manuel was silent. He did not enjoy watching friends vent their anger in the presence of Company men.

"Devil must'a got into Swannie. We put him up, and all, and here he goes and wrecks my wine. Broke every bottle."

"Chokecherry wine to boot!" Onorio scoffed.

"Some good come from Swannie's hubbub." Julian eased up and smirked. "To vent my anger, I chopped a bunch of cords. Sold the wood in Raton. Made some cash. An' the chokecherries will come again. Make me some more wine. Didn't really drink much. Marinated venison, mostly."

"H-uh, what's that?" Linderman narrowed his eyes.

"Marinate," Julian quipped. "That's when you dunk meat in a sauce. I soak my venison in it."

"Use onions, too?" Bowers queried, smacking his lips.

"Oh, ye-ss, when fryin' it."

"You do all that," Linderman said, sniggering, "jist to eat deer meat?"

"One of life's pleasures."

"Sometime, I'd like to try it." Bowers smacked his lips again.

"Shhh." Linderman sneered. "I eat real meat."

"I would too, if'n we had cash to buy it," Julian countered. "Company store beef's rotten most the time."

Bowers removed his rimless octagon glasses and rubbed the skin behind his ears. "Be fresher if'n more of you folks bought it at the store." Bowers replaced the glasses.

"Costs too much, fresh or rotten. For meat, we eat venison, rabbit, chicken. Don't matter much. Won't be marinating for a spell. Swannie's raid spilt all my chokecherry wine." Julian paused momentarily and added, laughing, "Somebody's got to knock some sense into him."

"Ha!" Linderman chortled, swaying his arms above his head as though he were wielding an axe. "He's got the sense God gave a grasshopper, a drunk turned Holy Roller. They're the worst."

The gripe session ended. They gulped the last of the moonshine and disposed of their spent cigars in a brass spittoon.

Following Thanksgiving, Osgood surprised Swannie by calling on him in a lighthearted, talkative mood. "So you gotta government job, desk and all."

"Office ain't much." Swannie stood from his desk and approached the counter. "Pretty spare. Got a telephone and typewriter I learned to use. Type citations, mostly."

"How's a boy get an office job like yours?"

"Take a civil service test. Gotta read and write. But, this ain't no office job. It's plain, hard work raiding speakeasies."

"Well, you did good. You closed down all my old haunts."

"Did it for your sake—in His name." Swannie was surprised but pleased that he responded like Reverend Miller, invoking the Lord. Yet, he thought to deal cautiously with Osgood. At times, Osgood was a crotchety Company man, at others, an affable, good old boy.

"Ho! Yer in like Flynn with the Lord. He's only one knows where there's hooch in Raton."

"It's the law. This ain't Chicorico—where you boys make up the rules to suit yourself."

"Don't I know. How'd you ever get the old man's ear?"

"The Lord's? You can't push your weight with the Lord."

Osgood blinked, puzzled. "Naw, I ain't talkin' about the Lord. What I'm asking, when you was pulling for the Widow Perkovich, how'd you get the Super's ear?"

"Oh-h-h, Van Cise." Swannie was still skeptical. "What's it to you?"

"Set 'side what you think of me. I know we ain't best of friends. I got no friends, even Bowers don't take kindly to me." Osgood paused with a hang dog expression, anticipating a response. When Swannie kept his counsel and responded like a dead fish, Osgood continued, complaining, "Appears I ain't invited to the Super's Christmas gala. La-tea-da! Too rowdy at the last one, Bowers says. So I wanna talk to the Super 'bout the matter."

"Shoot a'mighty, I never talked to him myself. Reverend Miller did. I reckon you could traipse right over to his office. Ask to see him on important business. Don't say what the business is."

"Reckon he'd see me?"

"Sure, why not? Yer a Company man. He'll think it's 'bout the mine. Be real po-o-lite with the secretary. If'n she asks your business, say it's confidential."

"Right good advice. Yer square."

Embarrassed with the compliment, Swannie waved off Osgood, like throwing a baseball from center field. "The Company building's right around the block."

Osgood walked around the block to the Chicorico Coal Company office and requested humbly to see Van Cise. "My name's James Osgood." He politely removed his cap and nervously folded it in his hands. "I work for Homer Bowers at the Chicorico mine. I'm here on business to see Mr. Van Cise."

Van Cise's haughty secretary, Miss Marlene, eyed Osgood disdainfully, scrutinizing his faded bib overalls and scuffed shoe boots.

Osgood felt like a boy under the critical eye of his mother. Quickly, he added, "Them's sure pretty fingernails, polished red and all."

Miss Marlene's faced beamed vainly, but without acknowledging the compliment, she held both hands forward for Osgood to observe. Then, she scrutinized Van Cise's calendar, noting blandly, "Hmm, you don't have an appointment, I see."

"No ma'am, but I'd be obliged if'n you'd be so kind to allow me to talk with the gentlemen."

"Mr. Osgood, you say?" The secretary wrote his name on a pad. "Work for Mr. Bowers at the Chicorico mine, do you?" She wrote Bowers name.

"Yes, ma'am, I'm a Company man."

"One moment, please." She took the pad and knocked at Van Cise's office door. She entered. Osgood could hardly hear her muffled voice as she spoke to Van Cise. She returned. "Have a seat, Mr. Osgood. He'll be with you—when he can."

Osgood sank into the leather-bound cushion of the dark oak chair. He was a bit awed by the aura of efficiency pervading the cavernous room. Secretaries and clerks bustled about their divers dealings, speaking in undertones scarcely discernible over the clatter of typewriters and jangling of telephones. Van Cise's office was the only private enclosure in the sepulchral space. His office was enclosed in walls of frosted-glass panes depicting an elk harem pasturing in meadows of pines in high country. There were no other private cubicles or partitions separating the office workers. The chief accountant's desk faced a host of others lined up like rows of school desks.

Osgood rather enjoyed the comfort of the soft leather cushion for the first ten minutes of his wait. Fifteen minutes . . . twenty minutes . . . thirty minutes. . . . "Um-uh, um-uh." Van Cise cleared his throat from within his frosted-glass paneled office. Miss Marlene caught the signal. "You may see Mr. Van Cise now." Miss Marlene waved limply from her desk and did not escort him as she did Reverend Miller and other important people.

Osgood opened the door and spotted Van Cise writing at his desk. Van Cise gazed obliquely at Osgood, laid aside the pen, and glanced at the secretary's notepad with Osgood's name on it. "Mr. Osgood, what can I do for you?" Van Cise did not stand to greet Osgood nor did he offer Osgood a seat.

"I work with Homer Bowers over at the Chicorico mine."

"Yes, yes. My secretary told me. Now get on with your business."

"About your Christmas gala?"

"My Christmas gala?"

"The party you hold for Company workers."

"Oh, that! It's marvelous fun, don't you think?"

"I was wonderin' why I never got an in-vite to it." Osgood tried not to stammer nervously.

"What! Why ask me? It's the Missus, her flap. I've nothing to do with it. She solicits the guest list from the mine managers." Van Cise couldn't believe this fawning manual laborer would have the gall to ask about party invitations.

"Ever since I been a Company man, I got an in-vite. This year, nothing."

"My good man, talk to Homer Bowers. I'm sure it's a little mix-up. Now, I must return to my labors, taa, taa." Van Cise waved Osgood off.

"Thank you kindly, Mr. Van Cise." Osgood backed away from the office and thanked Miss Marlene on the way out. He walked around the block and returned to Swannie's office near the Shuler Opera House.

"How'd it go?"

"Didn't."

"Oh?"

"Made me wait thirty minutes an' give me three minutes of his precious time. He don't know me from Adam."

"And, he don't care to know you."

"Told me to see Bowers. Well, hell, Bowers told me I wasn't going this year, jist 'cause I had a few too many drinks last year."

"Drinks?"

"Bowers had more. And, you should'a seen Linderman, drunk as a skunk."

"Drunk as a skunk?"

"Super sets up a cash bar near the punch."

An awkward pause.

"Oh, Christ A'mighty." A sheepish smiled flickered across Osgood's face. "I forgot you was a dry agent."

Another awkward pause.

"Ah, what the hell. Suit them right to get busted."

"Super sells alcohol at the gala?"

"Yep, he's too cheap to give it away to Company workers." Osgood grinned widely. "He's cheaper than Bowers."

"Probably meaner than Linderman." Swannie smirked. "That's why he's rich."

"Swannie, I ain't telling you out'a friendship. It's pure revenge I want. I saw the way they treated Judo and his widow, and, you, too. I didn't say nothing 'cause of my job. So what I get? Bowers tells me I can't go to the gala. He got drunker than me last year. So did Linderman. The way I see it, Bowers don't like common folks."

"Yer a Company man."

"I was a miner first. That's what galls them. I been loyal to the Company, busting my butt. That don't matter. If'n I don't get kilt like Judo, they'll figure a way to get rid of me when they're ready."

Again, an awkward pause.

"It's Friday night, the twelfth."

"What?"

"The Super's gala. Show up a little after eight. Most the Company men will be there with their women. That's a sight to see, too!"

That evening Swannie discussed Osgood 's conversation at home. Reverend Miller was skeptical. "That Osgood feller may be setting you up for something."

"Whatever for?" Emma was less skeptical. "Apparently, he's not happy with the Company."

"So he just conveniently runs into Swannie and tells about the cash for moonshine whiskey. Something's fishy in Denmark."

"I'm with Mrs. Miller." Swannie winked at her. She smiled, pleased Swannie agreed. He continued, "At first, Osgood didn't say outright about the hooch. He come over to gripe, a'cussing I shut down his haunts in Raton. He tole how he wasn't invited to the Super's gala. I tole him to see Van Cise. He did. And, he come back down-in-the- mouth. Van Cise gave him the brush off. Then, it jist slipped out about the gala, and, yes, he does want revenge. I don't think we're at odds."

"Maybe," Reverend Miller said, laughing quietly, "Osgood was more interested in an invitation to the gala than a raid."

"The law of the land applies to everybody—not jist working folks."

"I agree, Swannie. I do think it would be more than whimsical," Emma murmured, "to drop by the gala—discover how the other side lives."

NINETEEN

HOW THE OTHER
                                  SIDE LIVES

FRIDAY EVENING AT EIGHT O'CLOCK Swannie donned his Sunday
Go-to-Meetin' outfit and walked north on Third Street, passing the
printing offices of the *Raton Range* where he turned the corner and
walked west on Cook Avenue to Fourth Street to the home of
Henry Van Cise. The Victorian house sat like a fortress atop a knoll
on the northwest corner of Fourth and Cook. Designed in the late
1890s by the same architectural firm that planned mansions in
Denver for railroad and mining barons, it was much smaller than
the Denver mansions yet presented a solid stone façade fitted with
a turret at the entrance and three gables on a peaked roof.

Swannie crossed the street and passed the rows of well kept automobiles parked diagonally along the curbs of Cook and Third—
Chryslers, Essexs, Locomobiles, Pierce-Arrows, Studebakers, and
Stutzs with blackened tires that rarely rolled over dirt roads
and waxed chassis that occasionally left their garages. The gala
swayed to the jagged rhythm of the ragtime music blaring from
within, which Swannie recognized emanating from Squeeze Ruiz's
combo, "Hot Soup." Swannie climbed the wide steps to the covered,
wraparound porch, and reached for the door's iron knocker wrought
in the shape of a lion's head gritting its teeth. Before rapping the lion's
jaw, he peered through the foggy panes of the bulky doors. Revelers
dressed in formal attire stuffed the air with lively chatter and chortles scarcely above the jagged beat of the band.

He entered the vestibule without knocking. Mingling odors of perfume, cologne, and cigarette and cigar smoke whooshed into his face and assaulted his sinuses. He pinched the septum of his nose. While rubbing across his eyebrows and feeling his sinuses pop, he glanced upward following the rising sweep of the ceiling inside the turret, much like gazing at the vaulting arches of a cathedral's ceiling. The turret's walls were paneled in dark oak and vaulted three floors to a center point where a glimmering, crystal chandelier suspended from the apex. Of older vintage, the chandelier once was lighted by gas burners, although the Van Cise's did not burn gas. For the gala, they had draped various colored, electric Christmas bulbs over the chandelier. The bulbs beamed softly and the chandelier's crystal tassels glistened.

Swannie toured the first floor unobtrusively, an easy stroll since nobody paid attention to him. Having lived most of his adult life in trenches, boxcars, and makeshift apartments, Swannie was captivated by the mansion, which felt more like a hotel than a home, including an improvised ballroom. He popped into a large reading room. Soft cushioned chairs and sofas were shoved along the walls lined with built-in shelves containing leather-bound books with gold lettered titles. He pulled *Essays* by Ralph Waldo Emerson from the shelf and thumbed through the stiff, yellowed pages, crackling from disuse.

The band played in a corner near an extended dining room table decorated with pine wreaths and green candle centerpieces. Covered with white linen tablecloths, the table tops offered tiny tidbits of tasty hors d'oeuvres and savory canapés on delicate chinaware beside a crystal punch bowl, quartered oranges floating atop the punch. Swannie scooped a teaspoonful and sampled the punch, a tangy, cheery flavor with no apparent alcohol.

Women with lightly powdered faces and rouged cheeks chatted punctiliously; others danced with Company men—the Lindy, the Charleston—to the ragged beat of Hot Soup's repertoire of ragtime tunes. Others were enwrapped among themselves like balls of water snakes on riverbanks. Shaded lamps pleasantly lighted the room. The sitting women wore figure-hugging coats, tapering toward the hems, topped with broad shawl collars of fox or mink, which they took off while dancing. Although they shifted in their seats uncomfortably warm, they rested punch cups and saucers on their laps. Some dangled cigarettes adroitly on their lips, and as they chatted, the cigarettes bounced in rhythm to their chatter.

Swannie scooted closer to the corner where Hot Soup was performing and spotted Mildred, her small hat tilted at an angle, face half-shadowed by the brim, mysterious and enticing. Her bouncy red curls bobbed from beneath the hat.

"What'cha doing here?" Swannie blurted rudely as though Mildred were the intruder.

"And, you?" Mildred responded loudly over the blare of Hot Soup, delighted by the prospects of spending an evening with Swannie.

"I asked first."

"Daddy's a bookkeeper for the Company. Don't you remember? And, you?"

"See how the other side lives."

"What's your appraisal?"

"No Depression here."

"Isn't the music a hoot?"

"Yep, Squeeze puts together quite a combo. That's 'Lucid Larry' Wilson at the piano, 'Stan the Man' Lark at the bass, 'Georgie Orgy' Tomsco at the banjo."

"You know them?"

"From the bad old days."

Music ceased. "Hey, Swannie. Jam with us?"

"Don't know rags."

"Too bad!" Squeeze sidled closely and spoke secretively, "Sorry I busted your Thunderbird raid."

"Water under the bridge."

"Lemme make it up wid'a tip. Yer in a high-class bordello. Later they'll drag out the hooch. I won't snitch your cover. Nobody know ya, man."

"Except Mildred."

"Who?"

"Gal over there—the librarian—she won't fink."

"Good! Good! Check out the scene. Company sports will drift out'a the room. Take the little ladies for some hootchie-coochie hoo-haa. Others'll drift back—after the hoo-haa's done! In the bedrooms.

Upstairs." He pointed with his head toward the staircase outside the room. "What'cha wanna hear?"

"'Star Dust.'"

"'Star Dust,' it is!" Squeeze turned to the combo and announced "Star Dust" to Lucid Larry, who plinked out a bar on the piano with Georgie Porgy at the banjo and Stan the Man at the bass chiming in. Squeeze started singing.

"Would you dance with me?"

Swannie grinned, pleased Mildred would ask, but suddenly feared her brothers. "Sorry. Don't need trouble with your brothers. Excuse me. Got work to do." The minute he rejected Mildred, he hated himself, but he couldn't turn back—a matter of honor. Or, was it silly pride? he wondered while ducking into the parlor, crowded with men who lounged on brown, leather-bound cushions of bulky, dark oak chairs and sofas. Fuggy clouds of heavy tobacco smoke muffled their voices as they muttered in small conversational groupings, puffing on rotund cigars and sipping on what Swannie assumed to be punch for the time being. The men, lawyers and Raton businessmen currying favors with Van Cise, sat stiffly as though they wore tight corsets, stuffed in woolen suits and harnessed by ties and vests.

Swannie casually climbed the stairs to the second floor loft where sitting areas were arranged beneath the three gables. The gable windows were gaily trimmed with pine boughs and wreaths, and the fresh smell of pine needles permeated the loft. There were no men in the loft. The loft ladies were some of the help, mostly secretaries, typists, and filing girls, who weren't dancing with the Company men. They chatted at divans and parlor chairs arranged for the occasion, smoking skinny cigarettes and sipping punch. None wore wedding rings. They were single and varied in age. Some wore evening dresses with deep décolletés, both front and back, held by narrow shoulder straps and belts that drooped at hip level. Others wore bare, flimsy dresses trimmed with flounces that exposed the knees. The short-skirted women appeared boyish, their hair cut close.

The raspy, cropped voice of one woman distracted Swannie. Her fingernails were long, curvy, and painted red, like Miss Scheherazade's. Unlike the robust, cherubic Miss Scheherazade, the woman was flat-chested and her pale cheeks were gaudily daubed with red rouge. She wore flesh colored stockings rolled down over her ankles, highlighting her tight, pointed shoes. Sitting at the edge of the divan, she puffed rapidly at a cigarette, speaking secretively to an equally ashen Company secretary sitting beside her. Swannie didn't know she was Henry Van Cise's secretary, Miss Marlene, until he overheard the two secretaries chatting covertly, but loud enough for Swannie to comprehend.

"Trudy's in trouble."

"Super's son?"

"She did it—hoping to marry."

"Fat chance. We're pleasure toys to that boy."

"I wouldn't know." Indignantly, Miss Marlene drew deeply on the cigarette and exhaled slowly, shooting rings of smoke in the air. "Do know them bedrooms upstairs are busy. When the old man throws a party, they're busy as a train station. Company men play around with gals that allow it. Trudy did, too."

"With Company men?"

Miss Marlene shrugged. "More'an one, I suspect."

"Goodness."

"He's to marry, hush-hush, in January."

"Not Trudy?"

"Forget Trudy. Some rich gal. Big shot's daughter, in Denver."

"That's jist gossip."

"Heard old man Van Cise tell Reverend Miller. That's when I put queer things together."

"Oh?"

"Bizzare, really. Old man had me buy a one-way ticket for Trudy to Albuquerque. On the Santa Fé. Shipping her to live with her aunt."

"To have the baby?"

"To disappear from Raton."

"He ordered me to lie. 'To subtly tell Trudy,' he put it, 'she was being let go, cost-cutting measure,' get what I mean? The ticket's so she can look for work in Albuquerque. 'No fuss, no stink about it,' I was to tell her."

"She ought to sue the Super's son."

"Find a willing lawyer in Raton. Easier to smell a fart in a tornado. They're in the parlor, kissin' butt while their ladies are dancing and getting poked by Company men. Haven't you noticed?"

Swannie had. The stream of couples coming and going from the third floor was obvious once Squeeze Ruiz drew his attention to the prurient parade, reminding Swannie of the elk mating ritual Julian told about, having observed it in Vermejo country. In the late fall, the urge to mate surges through the bull elk's body and blood. They become irascible and are fitfully eager to mate any cow elk they see or smell. The cows are particular and will mate only with the most dominant bulls. Thus, they cloister in harems, loyal to a dominant kingpin bull. Other bulls challenge the kingpin for dominance and battle rack to rack over the dominion of the harem.

While the mighty bulls battle, younger bulls bugle lovesick calls desperately attempting to draw a cow away from the harem to mate. Some do. Others remain in the harem. The unsuccessful buglers slip into the crowded harem and attempt to mount a cow, with or without permission.

So goes the propagation of the species. New harems are formed by force or friendly persuasion. The gala was a variation on the ritual. The big bosses sat in the parlor while lawyers and businessmen licked their boots. In the reading room, lesser bosses danced and frolicked with the Company women, coaxing them to one of the two third-floor bedrooms for hoo-haa.

Swannie slipped away before the secretaries discovered him eavesdropping and clambered up the stairs to the third floor and found a half-bath situated between two bedrooms that could be entered through either room. One bedroom door was open. He walked through it to the bathroom and realized he needed to use the toilet. He hung his blazer on a hook behind the door, loosened his belt, lowered his pants and undershorts, and sat at the toilet. The door to the other bedroom was slightly ajar. Swannie reached to shut it.

"He-he-he-he-he," the gleeful giggle of a woman emanated from the bedroom.

"Shh. Not too loud." The cautionary warning of a man.

"You can kiss me, but don't touch me—there."

"I didn't," the man insisted.

"Yes, you did," the woman complained.

"Didn't."

"Ouch, you did it again."

"On a stack of Bibles, I swear—"

"Oh, hush. Give me your hand. Now kiss me. . . . Ouch!"

"That's not my hand. It's my pistol," the man explained.

"Take it off."

"No."

"I can't kiss a man with a gun poking my ribs."

Swannie recognized Mrs. Ammons's agitated, apprehensive tone of voice. His stomach gurgled and he almost burst into bubbling laughter but constrained himself, sitting absolutely still on the toilet while the impetuous paramours quarreled over the gun and kiss—she insisting he remove the gun and holster, he refusing. Through the crack of the door, Swannie saw only a blur of a woman preparing to leave the room, her blouse pulled tightly and her breasts protruding. "It's gotta be her," Swannie surmised, the crack in the door too small to see her face clearly, but the apprehensive, agitated voice, the tight blouse, and protruding breasts matched the Mrs. Ammons he had encountered in her parlor.

Swannie started to feel the heat of the third floor in the small, confined half-bath. Heat rises, and in Swannie's case, his head was heating hotly, although the third floor was cool in the winters. The Van Cise house was heated by hot water from the basement boiler, and steam didn't always reach the third floor radiators. Yet, he was in a hot predicament with his pants down around his ankles and an *hombre* in the next room who preferred his gun to a kiss. He leaned forward to lift his pants when the hombre slipped by the bathroom door along with his holster and .45 pistol.

"Close call." Swannie chuckled softly while speaking to himself, "Had to be Linderman, his .45 a dead giveaway." He quickly pulled up his trousers and left the half-bath, fretting as he descended the stairs among the gala crowd, "Good thing I wore my Sunday Go-to-Meetin's or I'd stick out like a sore thumb. These people aren't having a Depression, going by the furs the ladies are a-wearin' and the fancy duds and rings the men are touting. Them ain't five-cent cigars they're smoking, either."

Back downstairs, Swannie examined the brightly beaming Christmas tree decorated with what appeared to be hand-painted ornaments. One ball with a Currier and Ives winter scene, caught his eye. Another larger glass ball was hand-painted in Austria, according to a tiny label printed at the ball's neck. Near the tree, Swannie leaned on the staircase railing, which was garnished with pine boughs.

"Well, if'n it ain't the holy crusader hisself!" Linderman thwacked Swannie on the back. Bowers followed behind. "Lemme buy you a drink, old sport!" Linderman was drunker than usual.

"Linderman? Bowers?" Linderman's hardy thwack crudely reminded Swannie of his task. So engrossed in the festive Christmas decorations, and the intrigue of the Company's high society, he'd forgotten his mission.

"Karl, it's Swannie," Bowers whispered fretfully.

Linderman slurred his words, bellowing, "Swannie, Bonnie, Connie who cares? Com'on." Linderman dragged Swannie by the arm toward the canapé and punch table into the reading room. Hot Soup's ragtime still swayed, couples sashayed. Swannie spotted four partially filled narrow-throated carafes now placed beside the crystal punch bowl. Also, a serving plate covered with fifty-cent pieces, quarters, dimes, nickels, and a few silver dollars had been added to the table. A placard propped behind the plate was bold-printed with:

$ On your Honor
No Gratuities

Linderman tossed a quarter in the plate, clutched a cup in his gnarly hand, and ladled punch into it. Then, he poured from the carafe. He handed the cocktail to Swannie and picked up his cocktail. "Here's to, here's to—Ah, come on Bowers, toast to the crusader."

In total panic, Bowers's face flushed and crow's feet prickled up both temples. He stroked his stiletto mustache and blurted contemptuously, "Yer drunker than a skunk!"

"Maybe I am. Only difference is—when I get drunk, I'm a 'sport.' When Swannie gets drunk, he's a 'drunk, wretch, wino.'" Linderman sniggered stridently.

Swannie sniffed his cocktail—moonshine whiskey made from mash for sale at the Christmas gala.

Clink-clink-clink-clink, Swannie tapped his cocktail cup with a teaspoon, yelling toward Squeeze, "Stop the music!"

Squeeze grinned broadly and abruptly stopped the music, shouting, "Give the law an ear!"

"In the name of the law, I demand to see the man of the house!"

The clamor and merriment subsided. Swannie persisted to clink the cup and shout for the man of the house in the name of the law.

"I'm Henry Van Cise," Mr. Van Cise said as he plowed through the crowded room. "This is my home."

"Mr. Van Cise," Swannie authoritatively droned, "under the provisions of the Volstead Act, it is illegal to sell alcoholic beverages. You are in violation of that law."

Now subdued, the crowd emptied the living room and parlor. In curious anticipation, they jammed into the reading room and clustered around Swannie, Van Cise, Linderfield, and Bowers. The women on the second floor loft peered over the railing.

"Don't be ridiculous!" Van Rise scowled.

Mrs. Van Cise strode into the center of the crowd. She planted both feet firmly on the hardwood floor and filled her lungs and held her shoulders and head erect, as though she were about to yelp an operatic aria. She whooped, "Dearest, what's all the commotion?"

"This crazy man says I'm selling alcohol."

"I'm no crazy man. I'm Ray Swanson, agent for the Internal Revenue."

"Haa! Nothing but a drunk!" Linderman blurted rudely. "I'll throw him out."

"Boo-hoo-hoo-hoo." Mrs. Van Cise fell to one knee. While copious, crocodile tears streamed from her eyes, she wailed, "Ye-e-e-e gods, withhold your wrath." Like a bad method-actress, she leapt to both feet and shoved a stiff arm toward Swannie in rejection. "You have ruined my gay party. Ann-ually, every year, oh, boo-hoo-hoo, I host a grand festival for our employees, oh, boo-hoo-hoo. We would nev-var purvey in alcohol. Don't you know, I am a member of the Women's Christian Temperance Union?" She withdrew her stiff arm and covered her forehead with her hand. "Ah, a thoughtless, wicked deed, stinging sharper than a serpent's tooth, oh-boo-hoo-hoo."

"But, it's the law. You can't sell alcohol!"

"Sir, if it were my last breath . . ." She sliced the air with her hands as though she were cutting tall grass. "I would deny these infamous charges. Show me! Or, desist from your charges!" She pointed to the punch and canapé table.

Swannie glanced toward the table. The carafes, zip. The money plate, *nada*. The little sign, *nullo*. "They're gone? Somebody ditched them. Karl? Homer? Am I the only one who saw them? They were right there." Attempting to justify his charges, Swannie held out the cup Linderman had given him. "Smell this cup! Reeks with moonshine! No amount of fruit juices can cover that up."

Mrs. Van Cise thrust forth her hefty breasts. "Mr. Swanson, how dare you plant alcohol at my party, and then attempt to crash it—just for a little publicity!" She flailed her arms as though she were declaiming from atop a castle wall to the multitudes. "I speak the truth. I dare to speak it. Now, leave my house!" Mrs. Van Cise pointed to the door, her left hand over her heart.

"Git! Git!" Linderman shoved Swannie to the door. He stumbled but kept from falling. As the amused crowd opened a path to the front door, Swannie overheard someone say, "I told you a leopard never changes his spots."

"And, stay out!" Linderman shoved Swannie off the porch.

Swannie walked home, hands in pockets, face to the walkway, the night air cold and nippy, his foggy breath misting his eyes. An ambivalent war waged in his mind—a numb, hollow feeling of rejection and a fuzzy, giddy feeling of redemption. This war wasn't a succession of brutal, bloody battles between men who were strangers, and in other circumstances might be friends, like the trenches in France. It was an ethereal, spiritual war, more like the armies of Michael and Lucifer, clashing for dominion over the souls of men.

"Mildred's a part of that world—even if'n she doesn't wanna. As for me, I can't be, even if'n I wanna. Mildred's brothers did me a favor, I reckon. Now I got an answer to Judo's chastisement—'you gotta decide whose side yer on.'"

Lost in thought, Swannie found himself undressing in his basement apartment. He flopped onto the bed. His mind spun dizzily as he recalled the evening. "Hooch was there. Smelled it. Bowers and Linderman drunk. Saw the sign: pay for hooch on your honor, no tips necessary." Fleeting images of Mrs. Van Cise's melodramatic posturing, and Linderman's tomfoolery, preferring his pistol rather than Mrs. Ammons's kiss—the ludicrous images brought on a smile—and he slumbered satisfied, grinning to himself.

That Saturday morning after the gala, Osgood telephoned Swannie at the Miller's residence. "What the hell you tell'em at the gala?"

"Nothing, 'cept they was breaking the law."

"You must'a said something 'bout me," Osgood spoke rapidly and excitedly.

"Didn't have much a chance to say anything. One minute I was gawking at the big shots and their women. Another minute, turned around, there was Mrs. Van Cise playing the prima donna."

"The what?"

"Prima donna, the, uh, well, boy, howdy! All's I know, there she was sobbing, swinging her arms, and making a spectacle, acting like a stuck jackass braying in a opera."

"Ha-ha-ha-ha!" Osgood burst into laughter, momentarily relieved.

"You would'a got a kick out'a the melodrama."

"Ha-ha-ha-ha!" Osgood continued laughing. "Wish't I could'a seen."

"Didn't miss nothin', except grown boys licking Van Cise's boots, and women flaunting their fur coats, an' doing the hoo-haa."

"Was Linderman there?"

"Drunk."

"Tain't right. I been fired and blacklisted. Bowers evicted me from the boardinghouse. Sure you didn't tell anybody what I told you about the hooch?"

"I told Reverend and Mrs. Miller. They didn't tell nobody."

"Bowers must'a put two-and-two together." Osgood 's voice dropped.

Click!

"Somebody's on the line. Where you callin' from?"

"Clubhouse."

"Clubhouse! If'n Bowers didn't know before, he knows now. Better get out'a there fast."

"Not till I give Bowers a piece of my mind."

"Don't bother. He don't care."

"I been with the Company for a long time. I been loyal, worked hard."

"Don't matter. Yer odd man out. Best you git! 'Fore he sics Linderman on you."

"A man's gotta stand up for what's right. Like you did for the Widow Perkovich."

"Got me fired, is all."

"Me, too—so what have I got to lose?"

"Be careful."

"Say! Got a better idea. Come out. Meet me at the Company store. Show you a still—the mother lode."

Swannie hopped in his pickup and drove to Chicorico recalling his first trip there with the Heards. Feeling warm all over, he remembered the good times at the Heards and sang some of the hymns learned around the Chickering piano in their living room. Recalling his first and only Christmas at the Heards, he wished he could drop by to visit his family. His family? That's what he called them. They were his family ever since they took him in—the one place in the world where he belonged without question or doubt. Then, the warmth receded, an empty, sinking feeling replaced it, remembering how he had betrayed them, had failed to be loyal to the one family who saved him from the gutter and boxcar and a pernicious death by rot-gut hooch.

Swannie spotted Osgood sitting on the steps of the Company store, who stood as Swannie stopped his pickup and hopped out. "Gonna show you the biggest still in Colfax County," Osgood claimed in hushed tones. "Follow me." They crossed the railway and walked south along the little path between the Company houses and then hiked up the side of the hills to what appeared to be a deer path. "Best to use this here back route. There's a shorter path, straight up the hills from the tipple. Linderman uses it all the time." They sloshed through the snow, four inches deep in places on the slanted, rocky path.

"Almost there. Look'a the rimrock. Still's hidden in them trees 'neath the outcropping." They walked through the grove of trees and found an established still complete with copper pots and pipes, the ground matted where many feet had trod. Osgood spotted

Linderman huffing up the path that leads directly from the tipple, blurting, "Linderman's comin'! Hightail it—other path! I'll ward off Linderman." His voice trailed as Osgood skipped forward to greet Linderman before he arrived at the still.

Swannie swirled about and darted away full-tilt, in leaps and bounds reserved for evading hungry mountain lions, until his lungs burned and heart jammed into his throat. Stopping to catch his breath, he scooted behind a thicket of mountain mahogany bushes on the path's upper side, grousing, "Bull crap! Why am I a-runnin'? Mildred's brother, an' Linderman, they're the thugs. I'm on the side of the law. Why have I worked so hard to walk the line—to take the straight and narrow path? Linderman ought'a be runnin'." Swannie grabbed a basalt rock the size of a shot put. "Don't gotta take no bull from him! I'll wait him out. Get him b'fore he gets me."

Eventually Swannie's wind returned. He hardly noticed, his gaze turned inward, his eyes piercing the fading daylight but not focusing on the brush or the path. "Lord, forgive me. Linderman's like a bull in a china shop. He don't care what he breaks. If'n he comes by, snorting like a bull and totin' his gun, I can't take no bull off him. . . . Lord, I been cold turkey for many moons. Read most your Book. 'Tend church. Been upholding the law. Linderman has a grudge again' me. Shoves me 'round—'cause I'm punier than Julian and all them other miners."

Swannie became so absorbed in his prayer, which was more of a harangue than a plea, that the time passed swiftly and the daylight faded quickly as it always does near winter solstice. Before darkness descended entirely, Swannie decided to return to the site of the still by taking a circuitous route away from the path, which took him to a rockslide that provided a bird's eye view of the still. He sidled to the slide's brink, peered over and spotted the still nestled in ponderosas and piñons. No signs of Linderman or Osgood. The hills were ghostly silent without scratching mice, chiggering squirrels, or chirping birds.

On his way home, Swannie debated with himself about what to tell the Millers of the preceding events and decided, in Reverend Miller's poetic words, 'ignorance is bliss where 'tis folly to be wise.' He would tell only of the operatic melodrama of the Christmas gala without mention of Osgood and the still. If confronted by Linderman, they could in good conscience deny any knowledge of it. When Swannie arrived at the Millers, he found them in the parlor anxious to hear about how the other half lived. They listened gravely as he told about the Christmas gala until he finished.

"Hypocrites!" Emma was livid. "The whole coven of them with their tailor-cut suits and mink coats! As for Mrs. Laura Van Cise, she's the apotheosis of duplicity. Comes occasionally to our meetings around Thanksgiving, to offer tidbits of food for the children of drunks. Noblesse oblige, she calls it. A woman of her high rank—she makes claim to be a Daughter of the Texas Revolution—and, she's *so* concerned for the children of drunken wretches. Fudge! Fudge! Fudge!"

"They mock all of us, don't they?" Reverend Miller was perturbed and visibly spent. Brows wrinkled and cheeks sagged, he appeared to be an old soldier who had fought too many losing battles, his senses stunned. He turned to Swannie. "The dishonor is on us. We asked you to do what we could not—perform miracles in the land of Sodom and Gomorrah. You may blame us for the degradation."

Although the Millers were visibly perturbed by the spectacle, Swannie appeared amused and unaffected by the fiasco. "There's been no dishonor, Reverend. Folks like the Van Cises don't degrade me none."

"Even so, Prohibition is a losing battle." Reverend Miller's voice quivered as he reported, "The *New York Times* states that our nation's capitol is inundated with speakeasies, even government buildings that are supposed to be dry. It printed a map showing nine hundred and thirty-four speakeasies in Washington, D.C., many grouped around the Capitol, White House, the Department of Justice building, your headquarters in Washington."

"Don't be too downhearted. It's the Lord's plan. We got no choice." Determined to keep his optimistic mood, Swannie hardly listened to the Reverend's gloomy news. "Maybe we shouldn't be too glum."

"They should! You caught them, and they feared you," Emma said.

"Yes," Reverend Miller agreed with Emma. "They feared you."

"You saw too much. You saw firsthand: they live high off the hog on the sweat and labor of their workers—who they keep in serfdom—terrified to exercise their rights as Americans. It's a bigger war you've stumbled into—a war of classes, like the French Revolution. They're eating cake while the poor have no bread."

"Don't think me rash, Mrs. Miller, you sound like a Wobbly."

"Wobbly it is! Anarchist, too! Those are only words that conceal the harsher truth."

Swannie and Reverend Miller stared open-eyed and fearsome as though Emma had uttered a horrific blasphemy. She glared back at them before noting their alarmed expressions. Concerned they misunderstood, she placed a hand on each of their shoulders, stood from her chair, and spoke softly and deliberately, fashioning each word carefully: "Swannie, they tried to make you look like a fool. When you tell folks about their extravagance, some folks will write you off as a fool. But, you're no fool. You threatened them, and their way of life, like never before. Someday, the guillotine will fall and their heads will tumble into baskets, I fear."

"There is one man a'bothering me." Swannie's tone implied simple curiosity rather than trenchant concern, but the Millers were too grave to perceive that Swannie was in a good mood and unscathed by the Christmas gala fiasco.

"Who might that be?" Emma asked earnestly, sitting back in her chair.

"Yes, son, tell us." Reverend Miller was similarly sober.

"That Linderman feller—the security guard at Chicorico?"

"The one tossed you out the Van Cise's?"

"That's the feller. He's a mean-spirited man." For an instant, Swannie thought to tell about the still Osgood had revealed, but kept his counsel. "He also kicked me out'a my job at the tipple— jist when I had Bowers about convinced to keep me on. Both at the tipple, and the Van Cise's, he grabbed and shoved me, rough and rowdy."

"He's a bully. You must push him back, or he'll take advantage of you," Emma advised doggedly.

"Emma dear." Reverend Miller was taken aback. "One must forgive his enemy. The Lord sayeth, 'whosoever shall smite thee on thy right cheek, turn to him the other also.'"

"Dearest, that's hardly practical—with men like Mr. Linderman!" Emma was resolute and wouldn't retreat from her contention. "It's not wise to allow men like Mr. Linderman to have his way. He'll push and shove to get his way—using violent means."

Reverend Miller was profoundly perplexed by Emma's passionate argument and wasn't sure how to respond. Thinking as he spoke, he attempted to rationalize his tenet. "Emma, dear, it's a paradox, one I've wrangled over for a long time: what happens when forgiveness doesn't work? When the evil perpetrator perceives forgiveness as a weakness?"

"I kin tell you what I'd do," Swannie sniggered.

"Yes, sure, Swannie my boy. How would you resolve the paradox?"

"Yer askin' if'n a man slaps my cheek, and I turn the other cheek, and he slaps the other cheek—what would I do?"

"Yes, but remember, you are a Christian, and the Lord sayeth—turn the other cheek."

"Well, I done what the Lord wanted, and that feller—he went ahead and slapped the other cheek!"

"Yes, yes, but how would you—"

"I'd slap his cheek!"

"That's hardly Christian."

"Yes, 'tis! I'm a'givin' him a chance to be a good Christian."

"Huh? What?" Both were confounded by Swannie's convoluted thinking.

"Now, he gets a chance to forgive me!"

The Millers burst into boisterous laughter. Both exploded in mirth, grabbing their sides as though their laughter would burst through their ribs and spill onto the parlor floor. "Oh, dear, dear," Emma sputtered ebulliently as she bubbled, and Reverend Miller laughed uncharacteristically robust and loud, unable to sputter over his effervescent chortles.

Swannie joined them in laughter, delighted to bring levity to his overly grave hosts who rarely laughed and only sang in church. "Let's cheer up." The glint in Swannie's eyes returned, and he flashed his habitual grin. "When Eddy had the doldrums, Mr. Heard used to say: when the going gets tough, the tough get going."

"That's wisdom," Emma said, still giggling. "Let's get going."

"I intend to," Swannie smugly averred. "I got one more big job. Sometime after Christmas. That'll rattle the big shots. Now, let's leave the Reverend alone to plan his sermon for tomorrow."

Sunday morning, Reverend Miller eschewed his sermon about the Lord's plan of sweeping tides that carries fateful consequences. Instead, he had composed a special Christmas message and taken up a collection to have it printed. After the opening prayers, hymns, and announcements, he distributed copies of the card to the brethren. The card revealed an ingenious combination of phrasing. Quoting Scripture, he arranged a free verse poem. Each line of the scriptural phrases began with a letter from the word "gospel." Proud of his creativity, he stood regally before the brethren and invited them to read aloud while he recited the good news, a Christmas sermon short and sweet—hark, the herald angels sing:

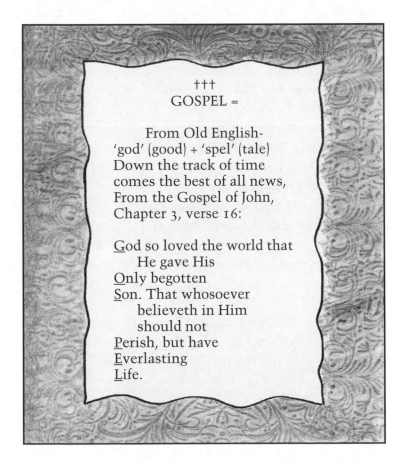

> †††
> GOSPEL =
>
> From Old English-
> 'god' (good) + 'spel' (tale)
> Down the track of time
> comes the best of all news,
> From the Gospel of John,
> Chapter 3, verse 16:
>
> God so loved the world that
>   He gave His
> Only begotten
> Son. That whosoever
>   believeth in Him
>   should not
> Perish, but have
> Everlasting
> Life.

TWENTY   HABEAS CORPUS

ON A BRIGHT AFTERNOON IN FEBRUARY Swannie drove his government pickup to Chicorico and parked in front of the Company
store. Dahlia spotted the pickup from her living room and darted
outside, shouting from the front porch, "Yoo-hoo!" Swannie rummaged in the bed of the pickup, searching for an axe and gasoline
can. She waved and shouted again, "Yoo-hoo!"

He jerked about, spied Dahlia, stiffened, and gazed askance at
her for a long spell. Then with a gasoline can in one hand and axe
in the other, he strutted across the front lot of the Company store,
crossed the tracks, slipped between the Chicarelli and Montaño
houses and into the hills. Hiking was slow through snow drifted
high on shaded slopes. Sloshing about the thickets, he found the
slippery, slushy path leading him higher into the hills to an outcropping of sandstone and basalt, a stand of ponderosa and piñon
trees clustered at its base where the still was concealed in boulders and trees.

Setting down the gasoline can, Swannie splayed his fingers,
pulled on his gloves, and sang lustily, slashing and gashing the
still's copper kettles and tubing into smithereens,

> "Onward, Christian soldiers,
> Marching as to war . . ."

Warbling lustily, he set down the axe, opened the can, poured gasoline over the still's remnants and tossed a match,

> "With the cross of Jesus
> Going on before . . ."

Flames erupted and rapidly climbed nearby tree trunks. Orange tongues of flames licked high and spirals of black smoke billowed into the sky. Swannie warbled fervently, flames whipping over the pine-needled forest floor,

> "Christ, the royal Master,
> Leads against the foe . . ."

As quickly as the fire erupted, popping and crackling, it simmered and died. Most of the trees and the pine-needled floor were laden with snow, and there was no wind to blow the fire along the treetops.

Swannie's pickup sat empty for the rest of the day in front of the Company store. That evening coal camp folks saw what appeared to be two men leaving Chicorico in Swannie's pickup. The pickup was driven north from Chicorico past the Stockton ranch and parked near a section of Highway 85 under construction. The next day, the pickup was noticed at the construction site and reported to Swannie's co-workers in Raton who knew he had planned to go to Chicorico the day before. His co-workers inquired at the Miller's. They hadn't seen him since the day before. They called Boots Najar, Sheriff of Colfax County.

Boots and the two revenuers drove to the construction sight where Swannie's pickup was parked. Everything inside the cab was in place. Nearby, Boots noticed a culvert had been recently backfilled. He ordered the foreman to excavate the soil. The foreman balked. Boots reminded the foreman an investigation was under way and a refusal was tantamount to obstruction of justice because a man was missing and might be buried in the backfill. Grumbling, the foreman ordered the excavation.

With picks and shovels, workers excavated the soil from both sides of the culvert. As the workers dug, Boots noticed the soil was loosely tamped. Sometimes road contractors will quickly backfill culvert trenches to save time and money. Later, when the ground settles and the highway surface collapses, the builder is again contracted and paid to repair the damage. Boots persisted. Somebody other than the contractor may have excavated some of the backfill to bury Swannie. Boots carefully examined the soil and saw no signs of a body or any other foreign matter. "I've seen enough!" he shouted to the foreman. "You can fill her up. Tamp her better!"

"Jist a ploy to throw me off the trail," Boots told the revenuers. "You boys, take Swannie's pickup back to the office. I'll meet you there. Take you with me to Chicorico." The revenuers drove away. Boots followed.

Rumors ran rampant by the time the three of them arrived in Chicorico. They pulled up to the Company store and a stampeding cavvy of boys, including Arturo, Eddy, and the Perkovich brothers, clamored around the pickup and on the running boards, constricting Boots and the two men as they struggled to open the doors.

"Git along little dogies!" Boots shooed the boys crowded around the pickup. The boys hopped from the running boards and permitted the men to open the doors. When Boots stepped out, the kids stampeded, pummeling him with a barrage of questions. Lips shut tightly, his bearing intense and serious, he grinned nervously as he plowed through the kids. He climbed the stairs and entered the Company store. Sheepishly, the two revenuers followed.

The adults congested in the store opened a path for them. Men, women, and children mixed and muttered in discordant accents of English, Italian, Spanish, and Serbian. The Heards, Chicarellis, Montaños, Perkovichs, Shorty García and Bob Durocavich from the baseball team, and many others congregated as though Miss Scheherazade had returned with the inimitable Casey Jones.

Boots inquired about Swannie's possible whereabouts. The adults were reticent. "Did'ja think to look up yonder?" He scanned the crowd enquiringly. "To see what may have happened to Swannie?"

No responses—only mutterings.

"For Heaven's sake, what can you say?" Boots asked scornfully, a tone he used to cut to the chase. Yet, he won re-elections regularly. Folks joked among themselves but never to his face: "Looks like a stuffed sausage, tied at the waist." And, "Naw! Two fat, stubby sausages." In fact, his barrel chest sloped into a slight case of middle age obesity, and he wore his black leather cartridge belt with his .38 Smith and Wesson snapped in place girding his waist.

"Well? What can you say?" Boots repeated his question, less scornfully.

Folks were ambivalent. Swannie was a traitor. He worked for the Company and had betrayed his friends and didn't deserve much sympathy. They wouldn't say much, except that they heard rumors two men had driven Swannie's pickup from town. Nobody said they actually saw two men drive Swannie's pickup away from the Company store. Manager Tim Rucker told what he knew. He saw Swannie hiking into the hills with a gasoline can and axe. Dahlia confirmed Rucker's observations. She had not seen Swannie return.

Boots and the revenuers plowed a path through the crowd, stepped out of the store, and stood on the stoop, leaving the doors open so everybody in and out the store could hear what he had to say: "These two gentlemen are revenuers. They work with Swannie in Raton. I'm taking them with me back into the hills, in the name of the law. I don't want anybody tailing. Did'ja hear clear? Nobody goes! You, too, kids! Something's wrong here. I don't like it, and I don't need any of you snooping around for me. Let me do my job. I'm the sheriff of Colfax County and need your cooperation. So, stay put. I expect you parents to keep these curious varmints away. You love your kids and don't want them in danger. Or, in jail."

"Swannie was like kin." Julian broke from the crowd. "I'm going with you."

Boots glowered at Julian and shouted so everybody could hear. "I'm the sheriff of Colfax County, duly elected by you folks. I don't want a vigilante posse, is all. Or, evidence trampled over."

Manuel and Onorio stepped from the crowd and stood beside Julian. "You won't," Manuel assured Boots, "you have our word, but Julian goes."

Boots scanned the crowd and realized they were supporting Manuel and Onorio. He relented. "Okay, nobody else."

Manuel reminded the disbanding crowd of the promise to Boots—no vigilante posse. Parents gathered their children and dispersed. Eddy, Arturo, and the Perkovich boys were confined to the house until the search crew returned.

Julian had a good idea where Swannie had gone and led the crew into the hills. The going was slippery and muddy. The path slanted most of the way and trickled with melting snow until they found the location of the fire in what had become a charred meadow. The still had been destroyed and burned, its copper tubes and pots melted and mangled. The fire was confined mainly to the areas where gasoline was poured and ignited. The fire had climbed the branches of ponderosa and piñon trees that weren't laden with snow and crawled along the ground where the snow had melted.

No signs of Swannie except a charred gasoline can and the head of an axe, its wooden handle burned. They searched for evidence of foul play, signs of a struggle or fight but found no broken branches, trampled weeds, scuff marks, or dried splotches of blood. There were footprints in the snow around the fire's perimeter, but they led toward the fire.

Julian discovered footprints in the snow leading directly to the outcropping that shouldered the still to the west. The prints appeared to be Swannie's, judging by the way the right footprint etched a drag mark behind it. Swannie's right leg was slightly longer than the left, and he dragged the right heel when taking long strides.

At the base of the outcropping, the prints appeared to trample the snow down to the pine needle matting as though Swannie may have climbed the well-nicked boulders. Julian clambered up the boulders to the top of the outcropping. What appeared to be an outcropping of the bedrock was actually a rock glacier, a wide tongue of broken rocks lubricated by rain and snow, that flowed incredibly slow.

Julian called the others. They clambered up the rocks and saw thousands of small and mid-size rocks piled chaotically upon each other. The crew was standing on the end of a river of rocks that ascended toward the mountain's treeline. The river of rocks flowed down a ravine, widening as it descended. Besides lichen and moss, there was no vegetation on the glacier and no snow in cracks and rocks. Barren of vegetation and snow, there were no signs of any man or animal trekking across the rocks, not even the ubiquitous droppings of deer and other critters.

The men trekked across the river of rocks. Long and wide, it was difficult to walk. Had Swannie hiked this way, he could have exited the glacier at many different places on either side without leaving footprints. Hope faded. They returned to Chicorico. At the Company store steps, Boots announced to a much smaller crowd: "Not much up there. A burnt still, mostly. No sign of Swannie. Say, whose still did Swannie raid?"

Folks muttered among each other in an indistinct clatter of chatter: "Who knows?"—"Company men, I hear."—"Wasn't no Serbians."—"No paisanos, neither."

"Well, what did you see? Or hear?"

Within the crowd, the chatter swelled into debate. "Heard gunshots up yonder!"—"Wasn't gunshots."—"Trees popping."—"Gunshots!"—"Trees popping!" Over the roar of the chaotic debate, someone asked loudly, "Was there a cross?"

"A cross?"

"Swannie's trademark!"

"Nah, no cross!" Boots scoffed and scowled. "Gunshots! Trees popping! Murderous insinuations! No doubt, Swannie made plenty enemies!" Boots quelled the raucous debate. Folks stood subdued. In a more conciliatory tone, he explained, "All we know is—Swannie's not here. He might've run off. Tracks appear to show that. He might've died in his own fire. Might've been shot. Jist speculation and hearsay is all we got."

"When will you know more?" Julian asked.

"Not sure. I'll report what I found to the district attorney." Briskly, Boots and the two revenuers shuffled through the crowd, entered the pickup, and drove away.

Hesitantly, Julian walked home to tell Dahlia the little he knew about Swannie. Normally, Julian did not dally home, but he needed time to reflect: "What to tell Dahlia? Lucky she stayed away. She didn't hear Boots' abrasive remarks. The crowd's callous comments about Swannie. 'Traitor,' somebody called him." Unwilling to cause Dahlia further pain over Swannie, he walked slowly, reluctantly.

Anna Perkovich caught up to him, sensed he was bothered, and tried to console him. "Eh, Julian, t'ink on'a bright side, like old man Sepich, 'member him?"

Julian chuckled, remembering Anna's tale about old man Sepich, the blind Pollyanna, who was socked at the dance and considered himself fortunate to see stars. Before Julian could respond, Anna quipped as she hurriedly passed him by on the way home: "Swannie get out'a coal camps for good!"

Julian waved at Anna, thinking, "That's it. I'll take the bright side, or at least, try to."

At home, he broke the news. "Honey, the news isn't all bad."

"O-o-o-o-o," Dahlia keened shrilly.

"No sign of Swannie." Julian embraced her. Eddy embraced her at the knees. "There was one good sign."

Dahlia stopped keening.

"Footprints that led away from the fire."

"Footprints?"

"Believe they were Swannie's."

"How can you tell?"

"Markings on his right heel."

"Markings?"

"Honey, didn't you ever notice? Swannie dragged his right leg sometimes."

"My, yes, now you mention it. I thought it was a baby hop."

"Ho!" Eddy nervously chortled. "That's Mr. Swanson."

"Shh, honey. Let's hear what your Papa has to say."

"Prints led up a rock slide and disappeared."

"Is that good?"

"Maybe. Prints vanished on the rockslide. No snow there. Sun melts it fast. Swannie may have run off over the rockslide."

They lapsed into silence for a long while. Finally, Dahlia asked, "Swannie's gone, isn't he?"

Julian considered Dahlia's question carefully and then answered softly, "Yes, he's gone. Doesn't mean he's dead. No tellin' if'n he's alive. He was a doughboy, trained about fires. He knew better than trap himself in his own flames."

Eddy declared in an accusatory tone, "Maybe some mean man throwed him in the fire."

"No sign of a burned body."

Dahlia hugged Julian tightly. Her voice muffled, she spoke into his warm chest, "Nothing?"

"Nothing. No bones, not even a rivet from his overalls, or the steel toes of his shoes."

Again, the Heard's home was dismally quiet as it had been when Swannie announced the bad news of his dismissal. Julian and Dahlia stood a long while and didn't dare look into each other's eyes. Eventually, they sat on the sofa.

"Honey, please don't raise my hopes. If you know he's gone, please tell me. Don't spare my feelings."

"I'm not sure, is all. 'Habeas corpus,' Boots said. That means the body of the crime. No body, no crime. Swannie may be gone, and he may be alive. He may have run off."

"Why would he? He had a government job. A place to stay. No, he'd never run off without telling us . . . or the Millers."

"You know Swannie, honey. Hard to read. Thinks with his heart." Julian was consciously evasive, attempting to spare Dahlia's feelings. He didn't tell her the whole truth, according to Boots. "Buzzard bait," Boots had speculated at the site of the burnt still. "Somebody might have chased him over the rocks, thumped Swannie on the head, and dragged him off to where mountain lions an' bears make short order of him. Buzzards and coyotes would pick his bones clean. Even if'n he ran off without being chased, he wouldn't last long in the Vermejo high country. Either way, the buzzards, coyotes, and other scavengers would feast, too."

After returning to Raton, Boots reported his findings to Fred Loshbahl, the district attorney. Loshbahl doubted the speculation Swannie simply left to other places, although footprints seemed to indicate that somebody took flight. Swannie was like most other folks in Chicorico, Loshbahl reasoned. With the Depression widening, he had no place to go. Yet, Loshbahl kept all options open. The possibility of foul play was not ruled out. Someone may have struck and then shoved Swannie into the fire. The mysterious footprints may have been those of a man who shoved Swannie into the fire. Without a body, and without concrete proof of foul play, Loshbahl directed Boots to treat Swannie's disappearance as a missing person's case. Boots terminated the active investigation.

TWENTY-ONE   GONE

FOR JULIAN, DAHLIA, AND EDDY, Swannie was more than merely missing until further evidence proved otherwise. Swannie was gone, vanished like a fallen leaf in the wind. For the first few weeks, Dahlia sat intermittently on the living room sofa where Swannie once slept. She weltered in tears remembering how Swannie took to singing like her brother Jimmy, mockingbirds who warbled wonderfully, their music now muted. She remembered how Swannie took to Eddy and played with him like a big brother. How he worked with her, drying dishes, doing wash, and likewise, helping Mrs. Perkovich.

Anxiously, she sent Julian to inquire. Weeks passed and Boots knew nothing more about Swannie. Boots would only wait for new evidence and wouldn't probe to seek evidence of Swannie's whereabouts. Dahlia was inconsolable. Her grief cast a pall over the household and trickled into the neighborhood. She canceled music lessons. Gone were the merry melodies for neighbors and friends to hear at the jangle of piano practice. Gone were the repetitive notes of the chromatic scale, and the mangled measures of études, as her pupils struggled with a particular point of technique. Gone were the evening songfests when her family practiced hymns praising the Lord and gracing the neighborhood. Gone. Gone. Gone.

She wept. "Swannie was too good for this world. He called himself a bum, but he proved himself wrong." She wept every time something or somebody reminded her of Swannie's absence.

Julian was similarly distraught though he didn't weep openly. Swannie had grown on him. Despite original misgivings, Julian had taken a liking to Swannie. With the begrudging affection of a big brother, Julian had extended his help to the fragile, lost soul and grew to appreciate Swannie's sensitivity for music and naïve questions about the realpolitik of the coal camp. "I was rough on him," Julian confided. "Should've lectured him on drinking. No, I went and dunked him. Got Manuel and Onorio to help."

"That time you took him fishing?"

Julian nodded yes.

"You did him a world of good. He never nipped again, never."

"Swannie proved to be a real sport. Onorio and Manuel had come to like him."

"Oh, Julian." Dahlia sobbed, an empty, despairing wail. "Do you think we'll ever see him?"

"Dunno."

Eddy was saddened. He was too young to understand the depth of his parent's remorse, and yet old enough to surmise he may never again play marbles with Swannie. He complained plaintively, "At least, with Uncle Jimmy, we knew he was gone."

Eddy's complaint prompted Dahlia to ask Julian to take her to Raton to visit with the Millers. She had an idea to reconcile their loss and soothe their grief—hold a memorial service in Swannie's honor. After taking Eddy to the Montaño's to play with best friend Arturo, Julian and Dahlia drove to Raton and called on the Millers who were similarly grief stricken by Swannie's mysterious disappearance.

"Feel like somebody knocked the wind out'a me," Reverend Miller lamented. "Never had a son, but I know what it feels to lose one." Emma didn't speak, expressing her despondency stoically. . . . Dahlia proposed a memorial service to honor Swannie. The Millers instantly liked the idea.

"Let's do it. I'll invite the brethern," Reverend Miller suggested.

"Best you do. Not many camp folks would come."

"Why not?"

"Some folks consider him a traitor. Wouldn't take sides."

"We thought he did that quite well." Reverend Miller jumped to Swannie's defense, then remembered Swannie's indiscriminate raids on the coal camp wine cellars. "But, I understand how

Chicorico folks might feel. I believe things happen for a reason. We don't often understand the Lord's plan. Maybe someday." His voice trailed off, and the four of them sat in the parlor in a solemn wake, bereft of words. The clock on the small fireplace mantle chimed the four o'clock hour.

"The afternoon's nearly spent with work to be done." Emma politely asked Dahlia, "Would you please help me sort Swannie's things? I can't do it alone."

"Certainly, yes." Dahlia replaced a handkerchief in her purse and followed Emma to the basement. Swannie's apartment was arranged tidily with no litter and the bed neatly made. "My, my," Dahlia exclaimed. "Did you clean up after Swannie?"

"Never. He was meticulous. Insisted on keeping a tidy place. Learned at your place."

"The poor dear. Didn't have much, but he took care of it."

Emma gathered Swannie's clothing from a small chest-of-drawers—formerly, Jimmy's flannel shirts, denim overalls, cotton long johns—folded and stored them in a box. "Look at these." Emma handed Dahlia a pair of long johns.

"Oh, my." Dahlia wistfully stroked the long johns' flaps. "He never asked me to sew the button back in place." She explained a prank played on Swannie that was meant for Jimmy. She had sewed shut the bottom flaps of one of Jimmy's long johns, which she'd forgotten when she gave Swannie Jimmy's underclothing, and which Swannie discovered when he couldn't open the flaps to sit on the outhouse toilet. "I meant the prank for Jimmy. I forgot about it till Swannie called for Julian's help. We had a good laugh. And, Swannie, he took it well—a good sport."

Dahlia collected his few personal items from the bedstand, a bag of marbles, a library card, and pocketknife. Running her fingers over the smooth, black handle of the pocketknife, Dahlia recalled Swannie's nervous habit of cleaning his fingernails to let off steam. He didn't smoke or curse. He just picked at his fingernails with the pocketknife's tiny blade. The nightstand was crowded with books. Dahlia thumbed through them.

"Here's his Bible. Why he practically finished it." Dahlia lifted the Bible's purple ribbon marker to "The First Epistle General of Peter."

"Why don't you take it with you?"

"No, no, Emma. We've always had one. Best to leave it in Reverend Miller's parlor. Give it to some other lost soul."

Dahlia carried the Bible to the parlor and caught Reverend Miller and Julian smoking cheroots. Hearing her approach, they snuffed out the cigars hastily, although the heady odor and heavy smoke of the cigars exposed their futile efforts. They hunkered like boys caught with hands in the cookie jar. Reverend Miller rose to his feet briskly, and like a bodyguard, stood between Dahlia and Julian, sputtering sheepishly, "Now, Mrs. Heard, please don't chastise Julian."

Dahlia looked around Reverend Miller and spoke to Julian. "Honey, you're a bad influence on Reverend Miller."

Too embarrassed to reply, Julian lowered his gaze toward the floor while Reverend Miller lightly tapped Dahlia's shoulder attempting to deflect attention away from Julian. "Please, don't fault him. I'm the mentor here." Reverend Miller grinned, slightly embarrassed. "Tryin' times, an' I was bound to give in, sooner or later."

She smirked, and then scolded playfully, "Not takin' to drink, are you?"

"I haven't fallen that far. You won't tell Emma, will you?"

"Doesn't take a hound dog to sniff out cigar smoke. She'll know. You're good as caught."

"That's a relief." Reverend Miller chuckled as he sat, then handed Julian a match.

"We might as well finish the cigars."

Slightly embarrassed, Julian glanced at Dahlia.

"Don't allow it in my house, but then—" She hesitated, then smiled. "Better here than the clubhouse."

Julian struck the match on the sole of his shoe and offered a light to the Reverend.

"Anyway, both of you will have to answer to Emma, not me." She handed Swannie's Bible to Reverend Miller. "Please keep Swannie's Bible. Give it to somebody else. It was a consolation for dear Swannie."

Dahlia returned to the basement and found Emma sitting on the bed with a vacant stare fixed on a sheet of paper in her right hand, a book in the left. Lost in thought, Emma hardly noticed

Dahlia's reappearance until she sat beside her and teased mirth-fully: "Schoolgirl daydreams?"

"Wondering, hmmm—" Without finishing, Emma glanced woodenly at Dahlia while handing her the slightly crumpled sheet of paper. "Found it in this book. Swannie's bookmark."

Dahlia read the beginnings of an unfinished letter:

Dear Mildred,
Someday, I will be gone. Don't ask where I have gone. I'll not return, like a bird in the spring full of promises and hope, unless you want ~~~

"Hmm, sounds as though he was trying to say goodbye."

"At least to Miss Ammons."

"Oh?"

"Mildred Ammons, the librarian. I believe she was sweet on Swannie. He was a constant visitor at the library."

"Was romance involved?"

"Oh, yes, but Swannie didn't think of it that way. He really enjoyed being with her, and I believe her feelings were mutual."

"Why would he be saying goodbye—unless he intended to run off?"

"Maybe he intended to run off, but didn't find the opportunity. . . . I'm sure he wouldn't run off into the wilderness." After a long, thoughtful pause, Emma continued, "I regret insisting Swannie take the job."

"He *was* good at it."

"Even your Julian protested when I insisted Swannie take the job. Revenuers disappear all the time. Most are believed dead, killed at the hands of moonshiners. I never considered it would happen here. I thought we were more civilized."

"I, too, fear the worst. . . . But, let's hope for the best." Dahlia handed the letter to Emma. "Now, this note? Maybe Swannie did run off?"

"There wasn't much to keep him here." Emma folded the let-ter and placed it back exactly at the page she'd found it. She brushed the light coat of dust off the book's cover. "Look'a what he was reading." Emma handed the book to Dahlia.

Dahlia opened the book to the cover page and smiled as she read the book's title aloud, *"The Story of the Negro: The Rise of the Race from Slavery* by Booker T. Washington." She flipped the page. "Look, here, a photograph of Mr. Washington." Dahlia handed the book to Emma and pointed to a photograph in the book's front, inside page. Dressed in formal attire, a dark suit and vest, a white shirt and tie, Booker T. Washington was posed sitting at a table with a leather-bound writing tablet in his hands.

"He was a handsome man," Emma observed. "Very dignified."

"There's a second volume." Dahlia opened the second book. "Same title, volume two. I should read these books. I don't know a thing about my people."

"A good idea. Go see Miss Ammons. She'll check them out to you."

"I couldn't do that."

"Why not?"

"Negroes can't get library cards."

"We'll get you one."

"Really?"

"Certainly. We're not in Texas."

The next day the Millers drove to Chicorico for Dahlia. Together they rode to Raton to acquire library cards for the Heards and return Swannie's overdue books. At Ripley Park, Reverend Miller announced he'd wait outside. "I'll browse around, revisit the Civil War cannons and the Battleship Maine monument."

"You mean to say," Emma teased playfully, "loiter on a bench."

"That, too. Don't rush on my part."

In the library, Mildred greeted the two women affably but a bit subdued. "May I be of assistance?" Mildred asked, a slight tremor in her voice.

Emma sensed Mildred's apprehension and spoke to the point. "We're here for library cards. For the Heard family. I trust that isn't a problem?"

"Of course not. This is a public library." Mildred opened a small oak box and withdrew a stack of blank library cards. "How many will be needed?"

"Goodness, where are my manners? You don't know the Heards, do you?"

Mildred smiled and a slight sparkle returned to her eyes. "Well, yes, so to speak. My friend Swannie told me so much about the family." She gazed admiringly at Dahlia. "Are you Mrs. Heard?"

"Yes, please call me Dahlia." Surprised and pleased at the ease Mildred assumed regarding the issue of library cards, Dahlia promptly requested, "We'll need two cards, one for me, the other for Julian."

Strictly business, Mildred slipped two blank cards and a fountain pen toward Dahlia. "Please fill out the lines. Sign at the bottom. Sign for your husband, too. That'll save you a trip."

The ink in the fountain pen eked out slowly causing Dahlia to write even more slowly. While Dahlia filled in the cards' blank lines with requested information, Emma retrieved Swannie's books from a cloth sack and placed them on the main desk. "I'm afraid they're overdue. I'll pay the fines."

"Don't be silly!" Mildred protested, revealing more of her perky temperament. "It couldn't be helped."

"Why, thank you, Miss Ammons."

"Please call me Mildred. I feel we have much in common. Swannie and I were friends, you know? And, I know both of you were his very best friends."

"Thank you. You were a good friend of his, I gather. In this Booker T. Washington book, there's a note addressed to you." Emma withdrew the unfinished note and handed it to Mildred, apologizing profusely, "I read it and realized it was not meant for my eyes. You have my word—I'll not reveal its content to anyone."

"And, you have my deepest apologies. I, too, read the note." Dahlia extended her hand. Mildred took Dahlia's hand and then folded her left hand over it. Dahlia smiled and suggested, "If you wish to read the note now, we can browse in the library for a while."

"Oh, my, my." Mildred gleefully glanced at the note and then placed it over her heart. Pleased to see the note, her eyes glistened. "Let's tend to our business, and when finished, I shall succor the note." Promptly, she placed Swannie's overdue books on a shelving cart and reviewed Dahlia's completed cards. "Everything's in order."

"Good, I'd like to check out the Booker T. Washington books."

Mildred retrieved the books and stamped due dates on a slip of paper on the inside-back cover. She recorded Dahlia's library card number and then handed the books to Dahlia. "They're due in two weeks. Call, or bring the books by, I can grant extensions."

Dahlia was pleased with Mildred's courtesy. "You're a lovely young lady. I thank you for being a friend to Swannie." She flashed her disarming smile. "We're holding a memorial service for Swannie. Next Sunday. You're welcome to come."

"I do hope you can come," Emma added. "Church services are at eight in the morning. Then, we'll form a caravan to Chicorico and hold a memorial there, also. You may come with us."

"I'd love to."

The following Sunday, Reverend Miller devoted the regular service to a memorial for Swannie in the little Church of Salvation Gospel on the corner of Third and Rio Grande Avenue in Raton where Swannie had harkened to the gentle voices calling him to redemption. Mildred sat with the Heards.

Absent Swannie's vigorous voice, the congregation sang without spirit. He was sorely missed, and his loss was felt all the more because the congregation had become accustomed to his exuberance. His voice had added splendor to their joy, and the joy and splendor were gone.

"Brothers and sisters," Reverend Miller waited for a response. None.

"We grieve the loss of a brother, who had fallen and risen again, only to perish in the flames of righteousness."

A few responses barely audible.

"Amen, I say to you, brothers and sisters, Swannie came to us in sin. With your prayers, he lifted his voice to the Lord and sought salvation." The Reverend paused for the last time. The congregation was too dispirited to respond. He set aside his prepared text sprinkled with quotations from Scripture, and extemporized a brief testimonial: "The Lord delivered Swannie to us for a purpose. The Lord's purpose was made manifest in Swannie who found himself by renouncing debauchery and succumbing to a higher cause. Amen."

With no response from the congregation, Reverend Miller terminated services. "I'll meet you outside. Julian will take the lead."

The brethren formed a cortège of Chevrolets, Dodges, Flints, and Fords. Led by the Heards in the Model A pickup, the cortège moved slowly out of Raton. Mildred accompanied the Millers, who took up the rear. At Chicorico, the brethren parked their cars and trucks in front of the Company store where the Chicarelli, Montaño, and Perkovich families waited.

Everyone was formally attired. They hiked in solemn procession to the burnt still where Swannie had committed his last deed in the name of the Lord. Although they had no body to inter, they constructed a memorial grave for Swannie by heaping rocks into a mound and neatly arranging them into a six-by-three oblong plot. They propped a white, wooden cross at the head of the mound, facing east. When the mound was completed, Reverend Miller asked for testimonials. Julian stepped forward, removed his hat, and cleared his throat:

> "Swannie was like the Saints. They must'a been hard to live with. He sure was. Saints want folks to do more than jist be good. They push us to do what's right. Swannie did. When the Widow Perkovich was in need, and the Company was evicting her, Swannie pushed us to do right by her. When we acted cowardly, and wouldn't stand and be counted, he sought help elsewhere. He found Reverend Miller, who shamed the Company into doing right by the Widow Perkovich."

Some brethren nodded, a few uttered "amen" and "praise Jesus." Julian paused and fumbled with the hat he held, rubbing his fingers along its brim.

> "I confess. At times, my heart was filled with rancor toward Swannie, may God forgive me. Mexican folks in Raton, Swannie's neighbors, said he was touched, called him '*poco loco en la cabeza.*' Swannie was touched—by the desire to do what's right."

Julian paused again, his thoughts disrupted by the spirited jabber of crows gathering overhead in the charred branches of a ponderosa whose barren crown had been seared by Swannie's fire. Julian pointed toward them.

"Look up yonder to them crows, perched a'top the tree seared by Swannie's fire. Swannie believed his demons were them pesky crows. Not so. His demons . . . our demons . . . are not them crows. Our demons are in us. They can make cowards of us, and they can stop us from doing the right thing, if'n we allow."

Julian noted a shift in mood among the small crowd. Some nodded, others smiled meekly. Spontaneously, Dahlia started singing, slowly, lowly. Everyone harmonized,

"Onward, Christian soldiers
Marching as to war . . ."

Softly . . . sadly . . . sweetly, the gentle voices varied, wavered, and lifted into the turquoise sky from the outcropping of sandstone and basalt boulders, burnt piñon and ponderosa trees. Squirrels scurried about gathering acorns. Deer mice scratched for seeds. The crows fluttered in flight, and in the distant sky, they cawed over newly found carrion, gaw, gaw, gaw, gaw.

PART III   SETTLING UP

TWENTY-TWO   REVIVAL

THROUGHOUT THE SUMMER Julian tended Swannie's memorial site. Occasionally in July and August, Dahlia and Eddy accompanied him. The meadow flourished—dead standing timber and thick underbrush burnt to a crisp. Insect infestations and blights incinerated. Swannie's fire burned enough to destroy the still, char the grass and pine needle floor, and singe the branches of some of the piñon and ponderosa trees. The fire, confined mainly to the forest floor, sparked an opulent garden of flowers, seedlings, and bushes.

"My, my, it's utterly beautiful." Dahlia was awestruck by the verdant meadow. The heat of the surface burn had catalyzed pinecones to pop, spouting batches of ponderosa seedlings that now sprouted five and six inches above the burnt ground. She couldn't comprehend the wondrous transformation. "Eddy, Julian, do be careful. Don't trample the tiny trees and flowers, so pretty . . . pink . . . blue, and look'a the red and yellow one."

Eddy asked enthusiastically, "May I pick some, Mama? To take home."

"No, honey. They belong here, for everybody to admire. They'd die soon—in a vase." Tiny flowers and ferns had invaded the burned-over surface and quickly spread. Blue, silky lupines and golden peas speckled the ground around the newly sprouted mountain mahogany, four feet tall only in a few months. Some scrub oak and a few Indian plum bushes were taking hold.

Swannie's memorial was partially buried under the opulence of new life. Julian noticed old, scratchy tracks of birds in the hardened mud on the fringes of the memorial. In the early spring when the ground was wet with melting snow, the white wooden cross and newly piled rocks attracted birds. They pecked about on the wet ground, found little to eat, and flew away. Julian also noticed fresh deer tracks and droppings. Deer came to browse on the tender undergrowth, entering the meadow from the northeast, grazing in the center, and then ranging west toward the canyon ridge.

As summer faded into fall, Julian baited the newly germinating meadow. The deer weren't particular. They ate almost anything Julian brought from the produce garbage cans of the Company store and Dahlia's cast-offs of crab apples full of worms and pocked with bird peckings. He added a deer blind to the meadow, gathering brush from the surrounding woods to erect a wall of sticks. Situated on the south side of the meadow, it provided an unobstructed view across the clearing to the northeast where the deer entered.

Prior to the opening of deer hunting season in late October, Julian broke precedence. He interrupted a poker game in progress in the backroom of the clubhouse to invite Onorio and Manuel to plan a deer hunt. They folded their cards and joined him in the clubhouse bar where soda pop was sold.

"Been baiting them deer on the meadow, the one Swannie fired up. Crab apples, mostly. Deer took to them like flies to honey."

"*Buono, buono!*" Onorio complimented Julian and turned to Manuel. "Coming?"

"*O, sí. ¿Como no?*" (Sure, why not?) Manuel responded. "Venison comes in handy. Can't eat all the chickens."

"Bucks, some does come to the meadow, going by the prints."

"Or, they're mighty big does."

"We'll soon see, real early Saturday morning."

"*Chi dorme non piglia pesci,*" Onorio recited an Italian proverb. Perplexed, Julian and Manuel stared at Onorio.

"*Su, avanti,* fellers, *non fare così.*" Onorio grinned at their puzzled look and switched to English. "Come on, fellers, don'a be that way. Mexicans don'a have a monopoly on proverbs. I jist said 'he who sleeps late catches no fish.'"

"Five o'clock." Julian chuckled. "I'll brew coffee."

Friday afternoon before the hunt, Julian took his rifle from the bedroom closet where he stored it in a wool Army blanket. On Dahlia's request, the rifle was never loaded or cleaned in the house and was off-limits to Eddy. Julian took a box of bullets from his sock drawer and called for Eddy. They left the house, crossed the meadow, and entered the piñon forest where he returned every fall to a moraine piled centuries ago by a glacier. The moraine had formed into a bowl with a stone floor. He laid the blanket on the stone floor and rolled out the rifle. There it was, exactly as he had wrapped it last year, his bolt action Springfield 1903 A3, the rifle issued to him for battle in France that he purchased when he mustered out of the Army.

"Papa, can I touch it?"

"Run your fingers along the walnut stock." Julian skimmed his fingertips over the rifle. "Feel the smoothness of the barrel."

Eddy knelt on the blanket and rubbed his fingertips along the side of the stock, feeling the smooth flow of the walnut grain and the blue steel of the barrel.

"Don't get to liking the gun too much. It's no toy."

"Don't you like it?"

Julian rubbed his scarred jaw, took Eddy's hand and brushed it over the scar on his cheek. "That wound was caused by a gun. Some German feller pulled the trigger."

"He was mean."

"No meaner'an me. We was shooting at each other—both of us was pointing the rifle and pulling the trigger. Jist a tool, like an axe, 'cept gun's a killin' tool. Use for good or bad."

"Did you ever shoot somebody?"

"Don't know. Might have. Like the feller shot me. He doesn't know, and don't matter. Listen good. Don't so much as touch this rifle without askin'."

"You told me that last year."

"Can't be too careful. It can kill a man, or a boy like you, faster than killing a deer."

Julian's rifle was the envy of Chicorico miners. None had Springfields. Like Onorio and Manuel, some had side-breech .30-30 Winchester level action saddle models, a reliable rifle used by ranchers to shoot coyote and other small game. The .30-30 could down a deer at close range. The Springfield was perfect for high country hunting where brush was sparse. It was designed for long-range shooting with a muzzle velocity of 2,700 feet-per-second, a ladder style rear sight that could be adjusted for distance, and a very fine, front blade sight. A careful shooter could hit a deer from quite a distance.

Julian inspected the rifle meticulously before giving it a dry run. Eddy watched in wonderment. Using the wool blanket, Julian rubbed the full-length walnut stock and its blue barrel, delicately wetting the tip of the front blade to remove lint. Pulling the bolt from the chamber, he lifted the rifle backwards into the sun, peeped into the barrel's bore, and saw clear daylight. He inspected the bore's riflings, seeking specks of dust or gunpowder. None. He replaced the bolt-action and pointed the rifle to the sky.

Placing the butt squarely on his shoulder, he jerked the bolt-action back and forth in a dry run, loading, clicking, and loading. He slid the magazine cut-off to the "up" position, which prevents bullets from firing. He pressed the trigger. The firing pin was locked, as designed. Then he slid the magazine cut-off to the "down" position, pointed the rifle toward the tip of a ponderosa further up the slope, adjusted the ladder sight for distance, aimed, and pressed the trigger, click. Everything was in order.

He didn't test the bullets. Once fired, they were spent. He no longer practiced with live ammunition. In France, he had plenty of shooting practice at Germans using the many hints French sharp-shooters provided. Before he returned home from France, he vowed to never again fire his rifle at another man.

Deer hunting was different. It put meat on the table. He took pride in felling a deer with one shot. Since 1919, the first year he hunted with the Springfield, he had fired it exactly eleven times, downed eleven deer, and put many meals of venison on the table. The hunt tomorrow would be his twelfth. He wiped each bullet before inserting them in the magazine but did not bolt a bullet into the chamber. Running his fingers along the rifle's soft, well-oiled leather straps, he wrapped the wool blanket around it.

Saturday morning, 4:45 a.m., Julian rustled quietly from bed, kissed Dahlia's cheek, dressed, pulled the blanket-wrapped rifle from beneath the bed, and went into the kitchen where he stoked a fire in the cookstove and brewed coffee. He removed the blanket, folded and laid it on the living room sofa, and propped the rifle in an empty corner. Outside, stars pierced the pitch dark of the pre-dawn. Julian heard Manuel and Onorio walking in the backyard. They rapped lightly on the kitchen door and entered with their .30-30s, also without chambered bullets, and propped their rifles alongside Julian's.

Julian poured each a cup of coffee and returned the pot to the stove, shoving it to the back of the hot plates to stay warm without perking. "Fellers, let's set a spell." Julian spoke in hushed tones. "Enjoy the coffee, wait for a little more light." They sipped at the coffee contentedly, pleased to be in the cozy, bright kitchen beside a warm stove. As the morning sky brightened, and they finished the last swigs of coffee, Julian proposed softly, "We'll get us each a deer. Maybe not today, but before the season's over. Or, we'll divide the venison we manage to kill."

"Let's try for bucks."

"Beggars can't be choosers."

"Let's be hunters first." Julian rose to his feet, "Then, when we don't get bucks, we'll be beggars." Julian placed the empty cups in a dishpan. "Let's go."

They arrived at the deer blind, 5:45 a.m. Julian took the pivot position in clear view of the entire meadow. Onorio sat to his right and Manuel to the left. They cleared the pine-needled floor where they sat, removing twigs and leaves that could crackle or snap at the wrong time. Julian bolted a bullet into the Springfield's chamber and turned the cut-off to the "up" safety position. Manuel and Onorio levered bullets into the chambers of their .30-30s and cocked the hammers into the safety position at mid-point. Julius sniffed the air and whispered, "Tad of a breeze. From the north. They won't smell us here. Deer from the south, they'll smell us a mile away."

They waited. The sunlight trickled over the easterly slopes. The obscure activities of the quiet, deep dawn resonated—unfolding leaves crackled, and skittering deer mice scratched in the underbrush. No chaotic chirping of birds—the summer birds gone, migration birds didn't rest here, and resident birds yet slept, except a few magpies cackling sporadically. There were no finely filigreed spider webs strung across the forks of branches. Earlier in October, a frost had killed the insects and the spiders disappeared.

"Hunting's a waiting game," Julian thought, "patience a greater virtue than bravado. Would deer come? Baited'em five months. They ate the crab apples and greens pitched into the meadow. Hunting season make them skittish? Sense our presence? Skedaddle before we get a good bead on them? Or, if does come? With their young'uns, what then?"

The sun slid slightly higher and poured into the meadow, illuminating Swannie's memorial mound into clear view. Julian continued reflecting: "Onorio, Manuel, good friends. Hard to have friends among men. Each man for himself. Not Onorio, Manuel. They know to keep their distance, or come in close. Something happen to me, they'd take care of Dahlia, Eddy."

A handsome buck inched to the meadow's edge. Julian, Onorio, Manuel froze—*nada* sneeze, *nada* wheeze. The buck stood behind a cluster of scrub oaks, his faint silhouette blended in the brush. Nose twitching nervously, he lowered his gaze to the rotting crabapples and deftly slipped through the scrub oaks into the meadow, nostrils twitching busily in search of predators. Gracefully, the eight-point buck sidled to the apples, posing in full profile.

Cautiously, carefully, Julian raised the Springfield to his shoulder and drew a bead. "This is a heavy responsibility," his thoughts flicked rapidly, "one shot, one single, solitary bullet to kill the buck and put meat on the table. Hit the head, heart, spine. Buck falls, otherwise, he flees, wounded, weak, selects his place to die."

Julian slipped the cut-off to the "down" position and squeezed the trigger, click! Bad bullet—the twelfth. Once a bullet's fired, it's spent, unless it's a dud. No way of knowing till the firing's done. The buck sprang sideways.

Klack! Ka-lack! Julian ejected the dud, bolted another bullet into the chamber and pressed the trigger—the resounding boom of the bullet, the recoil's sure crunch against his shoulder, a wispy cloud of smoke, sulfuric odor of burnt gun powder—blood spurted from the side of the buck. He vanished into the brush.

Julian bolted another bullet into the chamber, slid the cut-off to "up," and sprang from the blind. The others sprinted behind. They tracked the splotches of blood on leaves and broken twigs where the buck had leapt through the bushes; from time to time, they spotted fresh tracks. Following a trail of broken branches, splotches of blood, and occasional hoof prints, they traced the buck's rapid retreat, fleeing further from the meadow and higher up the sharply rising slope, leaping over gullies, bounding over crevices and thick underbrush.

Puffing mightily, the men finally ascended the crest of the hill, the shooting meadow far below. They peered down the ravine along a path of broken bushes and scuff marks on the flaky sandstone. They slid down the precipitous bank and spotted the buck on his side, wedged against the bare roots of a piñon tree growing among scrub oaks. With the tip of the rifle barrel, Julian nudged the buck's nose, tongue dangling out the mouth.

"He's dead. Got him with a rib shot. Bled a lot."

Julian laid his rifle on the leaf-covered bank, jerked his knife from the scabbard, and cut the buck's throat. Blood dribbled from the throat. Quickly, he whittled the hairy musk glands from the hocks of the buck's hind legs. Onorio and Manuel safety-cocked their rifles and laid them on the ground. "B'fore we gut him," Julian requested. "Check my rifle."

Onorio verified it was safety-locked.

"Good." Julian directed the gutting. "Roll him over to where I can etch the throat." Onorio took the hind legs, Manuel the front, and they shinnied the buck onto his back and pulled the legs apart into a wide wishbone. Julian etched an incision along the bottom of the buck's throat, jabbed into the windpipe, and slit down to the rib cage. Hot, fetid odors welled out the buck's cavity. Julian turned aside. The odor evaporated while he wiped bloody palms and fingers over his denim pant legs.

At the rib cage, Julian lightly lifted the skin, striving to prevent a tear to the thin membrane lining of the vital organs. Julian's hunting knife was not a surgeon's scalpel, nor were his coal-digging hands facile enough to finesse a precision incision. The lining tore at various places. He sliced over the stomach to the buck's pelvis. Onorio handed Julian a knife with a saw blade. He sawed at the bone connecting the hips. This was particularly delicate surgery. Beneath the bone sat the buck's urinary bladder and colon full of bile and excrement, which if ruptured would spill onto the meat and contaminate it.

Once sawing through the pelvis bone, Julian switched from the saw blade to his own knife, etching beneath the colon with the knife's tip and nipping the membrane attached to the buck's spinal column. Onorio and Manuel pulled the buck's hind legs further apart and made ample space for Julian to reach beneath the colon and membrane attached to the spinal column. Cut-pull, cut-pull, cut-pull, Julian nipped along the spinal column, reached beneath the sac, nipping and pulling away a little more of the membrane.

He spilled the intestines onto the leaf-covered bank and asked who wanted them. "Makes good *menudo*," Manuel remarked, "but too greasy for Clara." Onorio didn't want them either. "Good to make sausage, but too much work. Spoils fast."

"Crows, coyotes ain't that proud." Julian laughed as he rolled the intestines down the bank far from the deer carcass. Onorio and Manuel lay on their backs relaxing. During the arduous chase up the mountain, and the intense concentration of the gutting, adrenaline had coursed through them and they felt Herculean in strength. Now, the adrenaline had subsided and they were exhausted. They clasped their hands behind their heads, shut their eyes, and rested for a while. . . .

Smack! A snowball hit Manuel on the leg.

"Hey!"

Julian rolled another snowball and tossed it toward Onorio.

"I'll be!" Onorio and Manuel scooted down the sharp incline where Julian was munching on a snowball taken from a *tinaja*, a deep, hollowed-out rift in the course of a dry stream. The dried streambed received little sunlight and retained snow over several summers.

"It's last winter's snow," Manuel exclaimed excitedly as he gathered snow into a ball and tossed it at a tree trunk. Except where they had scraped, the snow lay undisturbed, frosted with a thin, grainy crust of ice and sprinkled with twigs, pine needles, scrub oak leaves, and shreds of acorns embedded in the grainy crust.

"*¡Pues, como?*" (What? How?) Manuel exclaimed as he dug deeper into the snow. "There's something here, some canvas." Manuel leaned forward on his knees and clawed deeper into the snow to a rolled canvas, the kind used for brattice in mines as temporary partitions to control ventilation and prevent explosions.

Julian and Onorio huddled near. Manuel peeled open one end of the rolled canvas.

"*¡Dios mio!*" (My Lord!) Manuel exclaimed, arching his back and reeling from the canvas, pointing. Onorio and Julian glimpsed at the unfurled canvas. Protruding from the end of the canvas were the thick rubber soles of shoeboots commonly worn by miners. Manuel leaned forward again, as if in prayer, and continued to shove snow from the shoeboots, muttering, "Could be a man in there."

No responses.

Manuel persisted to dig and speculate. "Ai, Dios . . . a dead man in the boots . . . socks . . . cuffs on the pants."

No responses.

"Looks like he was wrapped in the canvas. . . . Shoved down the tinaja—head-first. . . . Covered in snow."

No responses.

"Bugs didn't get to him. Been here a while—buried in the snow." For the first time, Manuel noticed the others were speechless. "*Ven aca*, look." He waved them down on their knees.

Face flushed, Julian dropped to one knee and examined the shoeboots Manuel had uncovered, thinking he recognized the shoeboots to be Jimmy's, the very shoeboots Dahlia had given Swannie. Julian's stomach lurched and a spasm surged into his chest. He believed the body was Swannie's but suppressed the urge to utter his name. Instead, Julian muttered, "Well preserved. Never thought I'd see another dead man tucked in a trench." An involuntary crinkle rippled through Julian's stomach as he wrapped the canvas around the shoeboots and covered them with snow.

"Heck of fix," Julian muttered.

"Heh?"

"Heck! Heck of a fix! Here we gotta a dead man on our hands, and the deer—"

"Keep cool!" Onorio interrupted impatiently.

"Keep cool! How?" Manuel blurted. "Here we are in the hills—twenty-five miles of rugged country between us and Dr. Monty."

"Dr. Monty?"

"We gotta take the body to him! Let him examine it."

"Maybe we should call Boots."

"*Tambien*, yes, him, too!"

"Let's get moving," Onorio cajoled, "we'll haul the deer down. Come back for the body."

"Shouldn't we take the body first?" Julian asked.

"If'n we didn't have a deer—but it'll spoil," Manuel agreed with Onorio. "Hate to say it, but the body's been there a while. A little longer won't hurt. Let's make sure it's covered." Manuel and Onorio kicked stones and dirt over the snow while Julian rolled the deer's intestines away from the body further down the ravine.

They climbed to the gutted deer and tied its legs to a stout tote-branch. "You fellers carry for a piece. We'll rotate. I'll take the lead for now." Julian picked up the rifles. Onorio and Manuel hefted the branch to their shoulders and followed Julian down the ravine. Carrying the deer with legs tied to a tree branch may have worked for Eastern pioneers toting white tail deer, but it didn't work for the Western men and their mule deer. They floundered down the ravine.

Toting the buck was cumbersome. The head was much heavier than the tail. When the head and rack weren't bobbing sideways, they were dragging in the brush, often tangling in the bristly bushes. The tote-branch bore down painfully on Onorio and Manuel's shoulders, causing them to stop frequently, set the buck on the ground, and switch shoulders. At a place where the trail suddenly sloped, the buck slid on the branch and bumped Onorio's back. He tripped and tumbled down the slope. Manuel tumbled close behind. They rolled until the deer whirled over them and pinned them to the ground.

"This won't work." Julian turned when he heard the commotion.

"Tell me about it!" Onorio snapped from beneath the deer.

"Slow but sure, we're getting nowhere!" Manuel was also irked but managed a meek laugh as he rolled the deer off his legs.

"Fellers, there is another way. Straight up the ravine to the ridge, then drop down into Waldron Canyon. From there, we follow the old railbed that was built to haul coal to Colfax. It's a lot further but a sight easier."

"Didn't know about the railbed," Manuel exclaimed as they considered Julian's alternative plan.

"Runs to the end of Waldron Canyon. Somebody had big dreams to mine coal from the Chicorico seam."

"Other side of the mountain?"

"Yep. Owned by the Maxwell Land Grant Company. One day, the mine would'a met the Chicorico mine under the mountain."

"What killed the dream?"

"Dunno. Big dreams, they were. Colfax was gonna be a junction for two railroads to haul coal. The Santa Fé was to haul coal north and west, and the El Paso and Northeastern Railway would'a hauled coal plumb to Texas."

"Colfax nothing but a ghost town, now."

"*Andiamo!*" (Hurry up, let's go!) Onorio interrupted the bull session. "Big dreams won't get us over the mountain!"

"Let's go! When we make the ridge, I'll go ahead for a horse at Bob Marchetti's spread."

Onorio and Manuel grabbed the tote-branch at each end, Julian at the middle. They dragged the buck straight up the slope, step-by-step, two-feet by two-feet, dragging in a rhythm, heave-and-drag, heave-and-drag, stop to rest. Heave-and-drag. . . .

The going was slow on the slippery slope. They had trailed the deer high into the foothills where the sedimentary bedrock had yielded to the rising mountains of the Sangre de Cristo range and formed sheer bedrock slopes thinly veneered with soil and vegetation. The tilted bedrock was once the shoreline of a sea and shellfish fossils speckled the flaky sandstone. Vegetation grew sparsely. Much like scaling a sheer cliff, the hunters had to dig their shoeboots into nicks they etched on the flaky, sandstone surface and wedge their arches on scrawny tufts of grass and skinny trunks of scrub oak.

Forty-five grueling minutes later, they reached the top. Julian clambered down the ravine for the rifles, returned to the ridge, and disappeared among the brush toward the railbed. Onorio and Manuel doggedly followed Julian's trail, dragging the buck down the lee side of the canyon. An hour later, they heard the clippity-clop of hoof beats. Julian arrived on a pinto.

"That's some pony."

"Count Cimarron, Bob calls him."

"Ride him like a cowboy."

"Wannabe. If'n I had my druthers, I'd be ranching." Julian kicked his leg over the cantle of the Mother Hubbard saddle and hopped to the ground. "Bob's waiting at the railbed, giving a lift."

"Say anything about the body?"

"Nope. We'll tell Boots first." Julian gripped the bit and circled Count Cimarron to the trail. The pony stood at attention without twitching or shaking. He knew exactly what to do and waited patiently. Onorio and Manuel cut loose the tote-branch and hefted the buck over the saddle and cinched its legs around the pony's girth. They headed to the railbed.

At the railbed, Bob Marchetti greeted them as they neared his truck and helped load the buck. After transferring the buck to the pickup, Julian offered to walk Count home. "Whyn't I walk Count Cimarron," Julian offered. "Cool him off. We won't be long."

"Okay by me," Bob consented. "Don't need to walk. Ride him snail's pace."

Onorio and Manuel placed the guns and hunting gear in the back of the truck and rode with Bob along the railbed to the Marchetti ranch. Julian waited for the dust from the wake of Bob's pickup to settle. Then, he rode Count Cimarron at a slow gait. Shortly, Julian and Count Cimarron arrived at the ranch house where the men were resting on the porch.

"We may have call to come back," Julian mentioned. "Or, did you fellers already tell Bob?"

"No, we were discussing the elk. They're bugling in the Vermijo."

"No time for that now." Julian gazed directly at Bob. "We have some pretty serious business back up in the hills."

"Serious. Mind tellin'?"

"If'n we can borrow your pickup to haul the buck to Chicorico, and when we come back, we'll fill you in."

"Sounds bad."

"Can't say much now, but you got my word. We'll fill you in when back."

"You boys got another deer up there?"

"Wished it was that simple."

"Mind tellin' what's going on?"

"When we come back."

Bob sensed something was amiss. "Go ahead, take the truck."

"We'll gas her up. Thanks *amigo*."

"Sure, any time." Bob tipped his hat. They drove away.

TWENTY-THREE   CORPUS DELICTI

AT CHICORICO DUTIES WERE DIVIDED. Onorio and Manuel tended to the deer. They hurriedly skinned the hide and sawed off the head. Once reserving bragging rights for themselves, they bargained with Tim Ruker to keep the carcass in the Company store's meat locker in exchange for the deer's head and antlers to be mounted in the clubhouse saloon. Julian visited Dr. Monty to use his telephone to call Boots. He trusted Dr. Monty to keep a secret, which was difficult because there were five telephones in Chicorico and eavesdropping was common on the party line linking Bowers's office at the mine, the clubhouse, the Company store, the principal's office at the school, and Dr. Monty's place.

"We'd better call Boots." Dr. Monty raised the telephone to his ear. "Nobody on the party line." He cranked the telephone and gave the operator Boots's number in Raton. Boots was in his office and agreed to come.

When done with the deer, Onorio and Manuel joined Julian at the doctor's office to wait for Boots. They repeated the tale how they'd found the body wedged in a tinaja and buried in the snow.

Dr. Monty massaged his furrowed forehead. "Folks have been known to bury their dead in the hills. They usually pile rocks over the grave. Or, circle the grave with stones. Covered with snow, you say?"

Again, Julian's stomach lurched, dreading what he presumed to be a fact. Swannie lay in a frozen, unmarked grave in a shady nook in a northerly crag on the side of the mountain. "Not a grave. Most likely hidden, tucked headfirst in the tinaja, plenty far in the hills. Most folks couldn't carry their dead that far."

"Let's wait till you see it yourself," Manuel suggested.

Dr. Monty took the hint. The men didn't want to talk about the body. He asked about the hunting trip. "Seems you boys had some luck, today."

"Might say so," Julian muttered.

The others didn't expand on Julian's curt answer.

"That's mighty fine. Big one, was it?"

"Eight-points."

Julian's taciturn reply signaled Dr. Monty. They weren't in the mood to boast about the handsome buck they'd felled nor the deer blind Julian had rigged to bait the deer. "Boys, I've got paperwork. Make yourself comfortable. Call me when Boots comes callin'."

They sat in the waiting room thumbing through old magazines until Manuel drew their attention to an advertisement in the December 7, 1929, *Saturday Evening Post*: "Say fellers, look'a here." He opened the magazine fully and read from the ad: "'Who's the Boss?'" Manuel pointed to a group photograph of working men. "That's him, smoking the pipe. There's more to th' ad." He read aloud again, "'Men at the top are apt to be pipe-smokers. Pipe smoking is a calm and deliberate habit. A pipe is back of most big ideas.'" Manuel set the magazine on his lap and exclaimed, "By golly! I'm gonna buy me a pipe!"

Relieved to be distracted from their somber task, both Julian and Onorio chuckled.

"An', look'a here. Look'a these ads." Manuel turned to another page. Both left and right pages contained ads for long johns. "Take a good, hard look at'em. What d'ya see?"

Julian and Onorio studied the ads carefully and shrugged. "Men wearing long johns."

"Look again. Them are high quality long johns, Carter's Union Suits on the left, an' them on the right page is cheapos, 'Monkey Wards' long johns."

"Manuel are your screws loose?"

"No, my heads on tight!" Manuel twisted his hand over the top of his head as though screwing on a bottle lid. "The fellers in the top quality long johns is smoking pipes!"

"I'll be durn," Julian sputtered.

"An' they don't call'em long johns—they're Carter's Union Suits! The fellers in the cheapo Monkey Wards long johns, well, they ain't smoking nothing. Jist lounging 'round in long johns. Don't that beat all?"

"Lemme see that!" Onorio grabbed the magazine and studied the two ads carefully.

"See if'n you find any more ads about pipes," Julian requested.

While the three searched other copies of the *Saturday Evening Post* and *Life* magazines, Boots arrived and didn't waste time deputizing Dr. Monty and the others to retrieve the body. "Ride with me, Doc," Boots requested. "See you boys at Marchetti's."

"I'll bring my pickup, too," Julian volunteered. "Need it for the ride back."

They waited for Julian to return with his pickup and formed a caravan. "I'll take the lead," Manuel volunteered, "in Bob's truck. Onorio, you go with Julian."

Boots and Onorio nodded, knowing the road was dusty enough to choke the hardiest miner, and Bob's truck had no windows. A precursor to the Mack truck behemoth, Bob's truck was a high-standing, husky 1927 Mac Model AB with a chain drive, brass radiators and headlights, and a red cab with a folding windshield.

At Marchetti's, Boots requested the use of Count Cimarron. Bob assented. His curiosity spiked, he insisted on tagging along. Boots deputized him, swearing him to secrecy. He was to follow on Count Cimarron, disappointing Julian who had hoped to ride the pinto to take his mind off the grim mission. Julian accompanied Bob to the barn.

Bob laid a saddle blanket on the pony's back and cinched the Mother Hubbard saddle while Julian adjusted the bit and stroked Count's mane. Bob sensed Julian's disappointment. "Quit your brooding. I ride him all the time. I'll take the pickup. You ride Count, wait for us at the junction."

Walking Count from the barn, Julian perked up, mounting Count and waving with one arm. "See ya at the junction." He sat straight in the saddle, trotting Count Cimarron briskly from the ranch yard, until they were out of sight of the men and pickups. Julian's gloom slipped away as he fell into an easy rhythm with Count Cimarron's smooth, confident gait. They rounded a small bluff. Peering back, Julian couldn't see the others following in the pickups. The air was nippy and dry, and the sun so bright the piñon and spruce stood in clear relief among the sandstone rimrocks.

Nobody in sight, he leaned forward in a flurry of whooping and shouting, his arms and legs flapping as he bobbed on the feisty steed. Clouds of brown dust swirled behind the pony and matted the dry grasses and cactuses lining the railbed. With ears pricked up, tail perched high, Count Cimarron settled into a steady stride and the patter of his hooves echoed off the sandstone rimrocks—whoopie-ti-yi-yo.

At the meeting point, Julian dismounted and waited for the others. After a while, the men arrived and Boots asked for advice. "Reckon we'll need much up there?"

"Shovel."

"Pick, maybe."

"Some rope, too."

Boots tied the tools and rope to the straps of the Mother Hubbard saddle. Onorio took the lead. Julian trailed behind with Count Cimarron. They made good time hiking the first part of the trail that gradually ascended the lee side of the canyon, hiking at an easy pace until the trail swelled radically to the ridge. Overhead, they spotted four red-tailed hawks gliding in wide circles. The circling hawks prompted the men to pick up the pace, stopping only to catch their wind. At the ridge, they panicked believing the hawks had detected the buried body and urged in their own languages: *"¡Andale!"*— "Vamoose!"—*"Andiamo!"* The hawks hovered, catching the wind in their wings, banking side to side, fluttering their wings and flicking their tails, eyes on the ground.

"Don't jump the gun," Julian cautioned as quietly as possible. "They're biding time for the deer guts, most likely." Julian dismounted and joined the men, rapidly traversing the ridge. "Can't take Count down the ravine, too steep. We'll poke around." He walked Count along the ridge to a rivulet where running rainwater had eroded a path. He led Count down the narrow path. The horse followed, fetlocks clasped with each probing step. The others scurried down the ridge to the snowy gravesite sheltered in the tinaja. Just as Julian and Count rejoined the others, five fat crows fluttered frantically into the sky.

"Now, watch." Julian pointed to the hawks. "They'll swoop down and have a feast." As predicted, the hawks banked a wing and dived in a slight, swift angle until they neared the ground where they opened their wings and glided onto the pile of remaining intestines.

Manuel showed Boots, Bob, and Dr. Monty the site of the snow-covered body.

"You boys messed up the grave site!" Boots was rankled. "No telling what evidence you destroyed."

Julian, Manuel, and Onorio grimaced, darting guilty glances among each other. They had tried to rebury the canvas-covered body so scavengers wouldn't detect the body and devour it.

"Ease up!" Dr. Monty objected. "Boys kept the scavengers away."

Boots brusquely shrugged his shoulders, dropped to his knees and found a shiny object in the dirt, kicked-up when the men covered the grave. He picked up a bullet shell, blew the dirt from it, and examined the cap. "Appears to be a .45-caliber." He handed it to Dr. Monty.

"Lemme see." Julian examined the shell and passed it to the others.

"You boys done right," Boots eked out a modest apology, "kicking up that shell." Boots untied the spade from the saddle and started shoveling snow from the tinaja. "I'm shoveling real slow so's not to tear the canvas. You boys dig with your hands close to it. Shove the snow away. Careful now, you hear?"

They whipped off their jackets, hooked them onto the saddle horn, and rolled up their sleeves. They knelt and started digging around the canvas-covered body with the same focused intensity as gutting the deer, but there was no joy among them. They harbored morbid thoughts of their own mortality, carefully removing the snow from the canvas. Though they could not see the body, the dead man in the canvas was a doleful reminder of the fragility of their own lives. Handling the canvassed-wrapped body as they would like to be treated once dead, they excavated the snow delicately . . . deliberately . . . deferentially.

The body had been wrapped in a canvas like a cocoon, lowered into the tinaja headfirst, and covered with snow. Rain and wind had exposed the tip of the canvas. With some effort, Boots and Bob pulled the rigid, canvas cocoon from the tinaja and laid it on the ground. Slowly, they stood back, retreating from the gloomy husk of a dead man wrapped in a funereal robe of coarse cotton canvas at their feet. All stared at the frozen canvas cocoon. None touched it.

Flickers of trench warfare—Julian couldn't help think of being back in the trenches—and its aftermath. After a battle they'd won, it was for the living to identify and then cover the bodies of dead soldiers before they were hauled away in a horse-drawn wagon—the death lorries.

"Could be anybody," Boots sputtered hoarsely. "Even Swannie."

A sharp spasm tugged at Julian's insides. "You sure?" Julian knelt next to Boots, reaching toward the top of the canvas.

"Don't touch anything! Let's get an autopsy."

"Can't I look at his face?"

"Leave it be." Onorio lightly rested a hand on Julian's shoulder.

"*Sí, amigo,*" Manuel added softly, "you may not like what you see."

"Sometimes, ignorance is bliss." Dr. Monty placated Julian, who hesitantly backed away.

"Boys," Boots impatiently ordered, "let's get a move on. Not too much daylight left." Boots looped a rope around the canvas. "Manuel, whyn't you and Onorio lift the body. Bob, stand other side Count, hold the body once we got it on the saddle. Julian, rein in the pony. Blindfold him so's he won't spook."

"Won't." Bob nodded to Julian. "Jist show Count where to stand."

Julian gripped Count Cimarron's bit and stroked his mane while the men hefted the body over the Mother Hubbard saddle. The frozen body looked like a rigid, rolled carpet tottering on the saddle. Onorio and Bob balanced the canvas while Boots and Manuel lifted the stirrups and tied them to both ends of the canvas. Count Cimarron stood perfectly calm, a real cowpony gracefully performing his job.

"Boys, scour the area. Don't be afraid to kick up rocks. See anything looks suspicious, call me."

Boots double-checked the slipknots holding the stirrups to the canvas while the others fanned out in all directions. . . . They found nothing unusual or irregular. Too much rain, snow, and wind had glazed the ground after the body was buried in its snowy grave and visible signs of former gravediggers were not evident.

Back at the trucks, Onorio, Manuel, and Boots struggled to lift the canvas cocoon from Count to Boots's pickup. Julian wiped Count's saddle dry. "See you there." Julian hopped onto Count and hied him down the railbed back to Bob's spread. While galloping Count away, Julian raised his left hand and waved back to the others, like flinging flowers backwards. . . .

At Dr. Monty's office, Boots called the district attorney, Fred Loshbahl, who advised Boots to send the body to the state pathologist in Santa Fé for an autopsy without unwrapping the canvas. Again, a spasm surged through Julian. He reeled, grasped the back of a chair, and sat down. He mumbled, barely audible, "Sure like to know something about the body. We found a murdered man."

"Don't jump to conclusions. May not be Swannie." Boots tried to presume professional objectivity but spoke without conviction. "Whoever it is, he sure as hell didn't wrap himself in a canvas and bury himself headfirst in the snow to die—that's for sure."

"Somebody probably hauled his body up the same deer trail we took this morning," Manuel inferred.

"Now, boys, we don't know squat."

"Sure as hell's misery!" Dr. Monty blurted. "Somebody murdered the man."

"An' only one man owns a .45-caliber pistol in Colfax County," Julian added.

"Look'a here, boys. Doesn't do any good to be spreading lies and rumors about men killing men. Yer thinkin' Swannie's in the canvas. We don't know, and won't for a while. What we have here is the corpus delicti."

"Beg pardon?"

Dr. Monty replied curtly. "Boots is referring to the body of the crime."

"Doc's right, 'cept to say we have the body of *a* crime, most likely. That's why I'm sending the body to the state pathologist. He'll determine the cause of death. Might've been natural causes."

"Natural causes!" Dr. Monty scoffed sarcastically at Boots. "You don't believe that."

"What I think don't matter. I'm taking the body to the Raton mortuary. They'll pack it in ice and prepare it for shipping to Santa Fé. The state pathologist will conduct an autopsy and verify the body's identification with medical records. If'n it is Swannie, Army medical records will tell. And, the pathologist will determine how the man in that body died."

"Karl Linderman owns a .45-caliber."

"Julian! Don't get all-fired up! I'm sheriff. I investigate. That goes for all you boys. You done good as deputies. Let it rest, and keep it quiet."

Rumors ran rampant. This was not the first time a body had been discovered in Chicorico country. The Comanche and the Kiowa once ranged the region and buried their dead in the hills and prairies as did Spanish explorers and Santa Fé Trail traders. Coal camp folks buried their dead in the hills when they couldn't come up with the cash for a funeral in a Raton cemetery. This was the first time in recent memory a body raised the specter of murder. Julian and Dahlia were saddened yet relieved. An autopsy would provide closure. They waited anxiously for the pathologist's report.

Linderman was antsy. Like a cornered rattlesnake, he recoiled at trivial comments and minor annoyances. Twice he came to work so drunk he was dangerous to himself and others. Bowers sent him home to sober up. Linderman took that as a cue to report to work at leisure, persisting to binge on moonshine.

Bowers confronted Linderman, who offered no reasons for the drunken sprees. Instead, he coiled and prattled at Bowers. "Boots is slower than the seven year itch. Waiting for the pathologist report to finish his investigation. He's jist the sheriff. I'm top security officer in this coal camp. That body was found on Company property. I'm gonna conduct my own investigation. Any man refuses to cooperate in any way, shape, or form will be fired. Ain't that right, Homer?"

"Oh, yeah, oh, sure." Bowers humored Linderman, hoping to silence him.

Linderman continued to prattle. "Every man has to come up and speak and tell the truth. Jist awful, Swannie being a Company man, and all. You'll see to it they're fired on the spot, if needs be, won't you?"

"Sure, sure." Bowers nodded halfheartedly.

The next Monday morning, Linderman posted a bulletin at the lamphouse where the miners checked out lamps and battery packs before entering the mine. For a few hours, Linderman stood by the poster and drew attention to it. Eventually, he tired, but the word spread. The poster ordered the miners to meet with Linderman to account for their whereabouts at the time of Swannie's disappearance.

Reluctantly, the miners appeared in Linderman's office when they were off-duty. They couldn't afford to lose work time. The short, intimidating interviews were conducted individually. Linderman checked off each man as he appeared and demanded an alibi. When provided, Linderman harassed the men with innuendoes, implying they lied. Yet, he couldn't bully confessions out of innocent men.

Interviews with Manuel, Onorio, and Julian were less intimidating.

"Imagine you don't approve of my inquest."

"It's not an inquest," Manuel blandly replied. "An inquest is an official hearing by a court of law."

"It's official. I'm chief of security."

"Boots is the sheriff. He's official. Yer holding an inquisition, claiming somebody here in Chicorico is guilty."

"Well, hell, Manuel. Somebody is."

"How do you know?"

"Somebody killed Swannie."

"Who?" Manuel asked quizzedly. "Whose body did we find? Nobody knows." Manuel paused briefly before asking suspiciously, "Or, do you?"

Ignoring Manuel's accusatory tone, Linderman asserted, "Julian did it. He had a grudge against Swannie."

"¡Ai, Pedro la hace y Juan la paga!"

"Talking Mexican to hide something?"

"No, I said, 'Pedro does the crime, and Juan is blamed.' There you go, accusing a good man of murder. You don't have proof."

"What do you know about Julian's whereabouts when Swannie disappeared?"

"Ask him."

"You know jig-a-boos. They're damn good liars. They can bullshit their way out'a hell."

"*Un loco rematado*," (Crazy as a bedbug.) Manuel muttered to himself. "You have already decided Julian killed Swannie. Nobody knows Swannie's dead."

"I should'a knowed you'd take his side." Linderman rose from his desk and concluded the interview. "Yer pals with the jig-a-boo."

"Humph! I'm proud to be Julian's friend."

As Manuel huffed out the office, Linderman shouted, "So I insulted a greazer, too!"

Manuel ran into Onorio who was on the way to see Linderman. "Be careful. He's after Julian and crazy as a gooney bird. He's decided Julian killed Swannie."

"Warn Julian."

Manuel nodded agreement. Onorio entered Linderman's office.

"Onorio, whaddaya know?" Linderman stood from his desk, greeted Onorio as a long lost friend, and offered a seat before sitting.

"I know what you know." Onorio didn't sit. "Someone said Swannie came to Chicorico in his pickup, that he had a gas can and an axe, that he found the still and made a fire. That's hearsay; nobody saw him."

"Mrs. Heard saw him. So did Rucker. From the Company store."

"Nobody saw him at the still."

"I say he burned it. Crazy as a loon."

"Did you see him? There's hearsay about gunshots at the fire. Nobody knows."

"You got an alibi?"

"Working, ask Bowers. He keeps the books."

"I'll check that out." Linderman leaned back in his chair, stretched out his legs and crossed his boots. "Everybody's got an alibi. Julian's only man hasn't come forward. You figure he killed Swannie out'a revenge?"

"Revenge? For what?"

"Pissed at Swannie—wrecking his hooch."

"Nope! Chokecherry wine's not worth it."

"Maybe Julian kilt him by accident?"

"No. Accidents don't add to murder. Yer loco. Julian's a good man."

"For a jig-a-boo, you mean to say."

"He's a good man."

"I don't trust him. He hasn't been to see me."

"He will."

Onorio hastened out the office, sought out Julian, and told him about Linderman's accusation. Manuel had already told him. Julian hadn't planned to dignify the inquisition with an interview, but Onorio's report forced his hand. He strode into Linderman's office without knocking. Linderman was sitting with his legs propped on the desk. He dropped one leg to the floor.

"Wanna see me?" Julian stepped to the edge of the desk and remained standing.

"Well, Julian, I talked to lot'a men about Swannie's murder, and they don't know much. Yer gonna say less. You can't trust these men around here. I want you to know you can trust me. Both of us is doughboys. An' a Negro like you, well, these men're liable to lie and say—you did it—to save their skins. The best thing you can do is tell me everything you know. If'n you was involved in some way, well, maybe I can help you."

"Yer not authorized to conduct an investigation. I don't have to tell you anything."

"Well, supposin' I need your help. Maybe we can get to the bottom of this together, you and me. Some of these men, I wanna tell you, they never said outright, but they hinted that maybe you was the one that did it."

"Cut the bull."

"Remember when we was playing poker that one night before Swannie got kilt? You was one of the boys saying to knock a little sense into Swannie. Don't you remember that?"

"I remember blowing off steam, is all."

"You blew mighty hard and griped a lot 'cause he smashed your chokecherry wine. You said somebody ought to knock a little sense into him."

"Well, yeah, I said that 'cause it's true. Swannie had no call to bother my home brew. Wasn't selling it. Folks jist ain't desperate to drink chokecherry wine. Besides, they can get plenty of moonshine."

"Yer acting like you was friends, but face the facts. You had a grudge against him. I believe you went up there, killed him, and hid his body. Maybe it was an accident?"

Julian's temper boiled beneath a calm demeanor. He wanted to punch Linderman but decided against it. "I'm a God-fearing man. I'd never kill another man."

"What'd you do in France, if'n that wasn't killin'?" Linderman planted both feet on the floor.

"I might have killed a German in self-defense. I don't know. We was in them trenches, and I shot."

"Yer a coward, a disgrace to your country! You should'a been out there to kill! They was out there to kill you."

"They was under orders to shoot."

"To kill!"

"To wound—to impede the attack. Wounded are a bigger drag than dead soldiers."

"Bull crap—the gab of cowards!"

Julian was dangerously near an explosion. To punch Linderman in the gums. Make them bleed. Disjoint Linderman's vile mouth. But, Linderman carried the .45 and sought excuses to use it.

"I shot lot'a times—at chargin' Germans. Maybe hit some. Kilt some, I can't say. An' can't say I did."

"You got an alibi?"

"What's yours?"

"I'm conductin' this investigation. Don't have to tell you nothing, but Bowers'll vouch for me."

"Sure, he would. Yer thick as glue."

"Yer cock-eyed."

"Probably killed Swannie for burnin' your still."

"Yer loco."

"There's not a man in camp—excepting you and Bowers—can get his hands on copper tubing and copper pots to make a still, like the one burnt up in the hills."

"Yer talkin' through your hat."

"Copper tubing and pots is used in the tipple to distill water. Before washing the coal. You fellers probably bought extra when you ordered for the Company."

"You are loco!"

"None of us has much cash, jist scrip, to pay for copper riggings and mash." Julian maintained a poker face. "You and Bowers, you could use a Company invoice to buy the copper. And, you got cash to buy mash." Julian leaned into Linderman's face and spoke softly. "B'sides all of that, neither you fellers is worth a hoot at poker, but you always got cash for bettin'—the cash you make selling the moonshine."

Linderman sneered. A blush rose from his neck and suffused his face. He chortled nervously. "You could bullshit your way out'a hell! You sure made a jackass out'a me. Here we're talking about me, when I asked you for an alibi—an' you ain't got one!"

"Nobody needs to know. Where I was is my business. I got rights."

"You got the right to keep your trap shut. A guilty feller usually does. You don't have an alibi, then I'm gonna assume you murdered Swannie."

"Slow down here, Linderman. I'm jist saying I don't need to tell you. This isn't a court. You don't have authority."

"I certainly do have authority!" Linderman yelled pompously. "I am the chief security officer for the Chicorico Coal Company. This is my jurisdiction, and by goll, I have the authority to run an investigation." Linderman's voice blurted into a tremulous vibrato. "You don't wanna give an alibi! I'm gonna make sure Boots knows! You don't have an alibi! That'll cast a lot of suspicion on you, especially since—"

"Since what?"

"You said you was gonna knock sense into Swannie."

Julian lunged, slamming his fist on the desk. "Hang it all! Jist blowing steam!" Pain pierced his knuckles. Prickled up his wrist. His rage swelled. Punch it out with Linderman, mano a mano. The pain stopped him short. He massaged the wrist and flexed his fingers, soothing the pain and considering Linderman's penchant to shoot after provoking excuses to kill. Julian backed away deliberately, all the while massaging his wrist.

"Seems to me, I could tell Boots 'bout your still. How you and Bowers have means to get copper tubing and pots. I saw the still long before Swannie ever set foot in Chicorico. An' I ain't the only man knew about it. Like me, they kept their mouths shut. We all figured it was yours and Bowers. Kept us in cash, the way you fellers play poker."

"That's cockamamie."

"You was making a killing. How else could you keep losing at poker and drinkin' like fish?"

"Won't hold water."

"Wasn't me found the spent .45 shell near that body. Boots did. And, he knows yer only man owns a .45. In all of Colfax County. Doesn't look good for you, seems to me."

TWENTY-FOUR   TOURS DE FORCE

SUNDAY AFTERNOON JULIAN MEANDERED to the outhouse. He closed the door, unhitched his bib overalls, pulled them and his undershorts down around his ankles, and sat. He was browsing through a Montgomery Ward catalogue when the door opened and a .45-caliber pistol jammed against his forehead. "Let's go! Tell your Missus yer goin' to the tipple."

"What the Devil!" Julian caught whiffs of whiskey on Linderman's breath and felt the pistol's cold, rectangular barrel pressed to his forehead.

"Shut your trap!" Linderman hissed, a wild-eye, reptilian look covered his face. "Blow your brains out."

Julian stood awkwardly and pulled on his undershorts and overalls, fastening the straps while the cold barrel pressed hard against his forehead. He walked into the sun. The tip of the barrel had impressed a circle on his forehead. Linderman and Bowers scooted behind, the blunt pistol barrel pressed into his back.

"Dahlia! Be at the tipple. When Onorio comes, tell him I won't be playing boccie."

Bowers threw his arm around Julian's shoulders, like pals walking to school. Linderman followed behind, heading west toward the tipple.

Dahlia sensed something was amiss. Julian rarely shouted at her, and he rarely shouted her first name. Onorio never came for

Julian to play boccie. Just the opposite. On Sunday afternoon, Julian's routine was to pass by Manuel's house and the two of them walked to Onorio's for boccie.

"Eddy, come," she ordered as she dashed through the backyard to the Montaño's where Manuel awaited Julian. "Something is wrong, Manuel." Dahlia told about the peculiar appearance of Linderman and Bowers and Julian's even more peculiar pronouncement.

Manuel invited her into the kitchen where his wife Clara was preparing Sunday dinner. "Stay with Clara. Eddy, too." Already, Eddy was shooting marbles with Arturo. Manuel trotted to Onorio's. They jogged along the railway till they spied Julian atop the tall, seventy foot tipple, the scruffy log scaffolding built over the tracks to cull and load coal into trains.

Julian edged backwards to the tipple's brink, backing away from Linderman, who brandished his .45 pistol at Julian's stomach. Bowers held an open lasso. Manuel and Onorio felt like intruders in a theater during the last act, the actors engrossed in the climax of a Greek tragedy. They were strutting and fretting fitfully on the stage, riveted to a chain-of-events catapulting them to this deadly moment.

This was no play. There would be no curtain fall, call, or actor's bow. Inch by inch, Julian backed away from Bowers and Linderman. They pressed forward, desperation enveloping Julian.

Linderman hissed, "Sign the paper—for Chris'sake!"

"No." Julian shook his head as he swiveled his torso and backed closer to the tipple's brink.

"Stop!" Manuel shouted.

"Watch out!" Onorio yelled to prevent Julian from falling.

Julian twisted sideways and glanced downward toward his friends. Bowers slipped the lasso around Julian's neck. Linderman planted a boot on Julian's backside and shoved.

Julian felt himself falling in a backflip, legs and feet pointing to the sun. The doughboy in him took control. He turned cold, separating emotions from will. This wasn't happening to him. He was a nearby witness. Couldn't feel anything—like when he took the bullet. In the cheek. In the pitch of battle. In France. He witnessed. Watched himself bleed, holding the sagging skin of his cheek and jaw.

He saw himself arching from the backflip. The rope around his neck draped along his chest and tangled around the left leg, which he unraveled while spinning out of the backflip. His knees pressed his face, legs straightened, and his heavy shoeboots thrust him down toward the ground. He grasped the rope directly above his head, wunk!

The taut rope reached its end. He gripped it tightly. Palms slid down the rope. He gripped tighter. Palms stopped sliding—excruciating pain. No longer a nearby witness to his pain. The rope suspended him in mid-air like a condemned man who managed to free his hands and grasp the rope above his head, swinging from the gallows without a broken neck. He bobbed at the end of the rope. His many years as a pick-and-shovel coal miner paid off, his arms strong and grip firm. He kicked both legs and swung swiftly, struggling to catch his foot on a beam. Pain pierced his palms—pulsating proof he had cheated death.

Stunned by the lightning speed of Julian's trapeze tricks, Onorio and Manuel stood tantalized, like deer trapped in the headlights of an oncoming car. "Hold on!" they shouted. "We'll cut you loose!" They clambered up the tipple steps to the deck, spotted Linderman and Bowers ducking into the office, and heard the door slam and the loud click of its lock. Onorio and Manuel dashed to the tipple's edge where the rope was knotted and wedged firmly between two planks.

"Won't do to cut the rope!"

"Let's pull him in!"

They shimmied down the tipple's corner pillars to a mid-tier beam. Onorio grasped a pillar with his left arm, reached out with the right, and clutched the swinging rope. He tugged the rope and pulled Julian closer to the tipple. Manuel clambered to the tier below where Julian's legs dangled, stretched over the side, snatched Julian's shins, and guided him to the beam. Julian lowered onto the beam, took footing, and instantly shoved the lasso from his neck. It flopped and fell, empty-headed and defeated.

Manuel grasped Julian's waist and edged him to the corner pillar.

"Lemme go!"

Julian jerked away, hugged the corner pillar and wiggled down hurriedly, like a bear backing down a tree, except he was without bear claws and his palms were blistered raw. Five feet from the ground, Julian opened his arms and fell backwards onto the ground. . . .

The repugnant sting of ammonia salts penetrated Julian's nostrils and sinuses. He no longer lay on the ground at the foot of the tipple. He lay on Dr. Monty's leather-bound examination table. He turned his head daintily, like a curving candle flame when a draft shifts its course ever so slightly. Awkwardly, he lifted his stiff hands, which felt thickly bandaged, and stared at two very crimson, swollen, and blistered palms.

"Don't worry. Red's not blood," Dr. Monty assured Julian. "Washed your hands, then drenched them in iodine before you come to."

Julian lowered his hands gently, asking, "How'd I get here?"

"Devil kicked you off the tipple," Onorio quipped.

"An Angel caught you," Manuel joked. "Carried you here."

"They're full of malarkey." Dr. Monty stopped the joking. "They saved you. Manuel ran the tracks to get me—like an antelope. After I checked for broken bones, we brought you back in the Buick. Manuel and Onorio hefted you in the backseat."

"Any broken bones?"

"None. You were out cold—after you pitched free from the tipple."

Julian groggily glimpsed at Onorio and Manuel, barely aware they had pulled him of the tipple. "Did'ja get'em?"

"They skedaddled."

"Scrammed before we could—"

"Whoa, hold up boys. Julian's the patient. How you feeling?"

"Shoulders hurt."

"Didn't tear any ligaments. You'd know it."

"Can't feel a thing in my hands."

"Bad rope burns. They'll heal, after a while. Can't use'em for a bit. Keep'em clean." Dr. Monty paused to change the topic. "Boys tell me Linderman and Bowers shoved you off the tipple. What gives?"

"Short or long tale?"

"In-between."

"Linderman was drunk when he came by my house."

"Drinks all the time, anymore."

"Had Bowers with him. They took me by gunpoint to the tipple. At Bowers' office, he wanted me to sign a paper that I did it."

"Did what?"

"Killed Swannie."

"Where'd he get that foolish notion?"

"Not foolish, loco," Manuel injected. "When Linderman conducted his illegal investigation—"

"Investigation? He's just a guard."

"Didn't stop him."

"That unbelievable! I thought the time was past when working men were treated like thugs. He had no legal authority to conduct an investigation—more of an inquisition, I assume."

"You assume right, and that's what I told Linderman." Manuel described Linderman's interrogation of the miners.

"This causes a big problem—guilt by gossip."

"How's that?"

"Linderman knows what he's doing—defaming Julian by spreading vicious rumors about a colored man, knowing some folks are quick to believe the rumors. For some folks, Julian's guilty before he has a chance to defend himself. Down south, Julian would already be lynched, or the Ku Klux Klan would be planning a lynching."

"Boots won't allow that," Manuel surmised, "he's against vigilantes."

"But, Boots has to enforce the laws. Now that Linderman has spread his gossip. Julian doesn't have a chance, like a baby in a rattlesnake pit."

"Julian has to come up with an alibi." Manuel sighed.

"Shouldn't be hard to do."

"He doesn't have one."

"Linderman has no call to conduct an investigation," Julian defended himself.

"That's true. He's not the sheriff," Dr. Monty reasoned, "but, don't take Karl lightly. Think about Sacco and Vanzetti. They were working men. Didn't take much to convict them. Tried and hanged, they were, and they weren't Negroes. Certainly, you have an alibi?"

Before answering, Julian turned his head away from the three men and stared at the light beaming through the window. "Doc, you gotta know, I'm a God-fearing man. I wouldn't kill a soul, even to save my own neck."

"I believe you, Julian."

"Me, too," Onorio and Manuel injected concurrently.

"But," Dr. Monty warned, "others don't know you like we do."

Julian froze his gaze on the flecks of dust sparkling in the sunlight beaming through the windows. "Doc, I was with Swannie jist before he lit the fire."

Nobody spoke for a while. Steam hissed from the chrome canisters where Dr. Monty sterilized syringes and other medical instruments. . . . Julian broke the impasse. "See, even you fellers don't know what to make of the truth. That's why I wouldn't tell Linderman. He's trying to pin Swannie's murder on me. He wants me to confess to something I didn't do."

"But, you just said that you were with Swannie—just before he got killed—or whatever he did."

Manuel jumped to Julian's defense. "Nobody knows what happened to Swannie. He may be alive. Run off somewheres. Might be buried in the hills."

"Might be in the morgue in Santa Fé." Bewildered, Onorio shook his head. "Did that fall make you crazy?"

"Don't you boys remember? We were playing poker, right after Swannie wrecked my wine cellar."

"For the chokecherry wine." Dr. Monty chuckled.

"I didn't think it was funny. After we had taken him in and all. Dahlia treated him like a brother. And, all we got in return is ruined chokecherry wine. I was fightin' mad."

"Yeah, but he did that to everybody in Chicorico."

"Other camps, too."

"You fellers don't think I'd kill a man over spilled chokecherry wine. You have to believe me. I wasn't working the morning Swannie come to Chicorico. Dahlia told me he was in town and heading to the still. I knew he was asking for trouble, taking on Bowers and Linderman."

"Now you are talking loco." Dr. Monty was skeptical. "How do you figure?"

"'Cause that still had to be theirs. They're only ones can get copper kettles and tubing needed for distilling mash. Copper's used in the tipple, too. Believe me, Papa told me all about it, when I was a kid back home in West Virginia. There was a still in every hollow. Them ol' boys got the copper tubing and pots through the Company. Anyway, I followed Swannie up to the still. I found him pouring gasoline over the mess he'd axed to bits. I tried to reason with him, but he kept asking with a quiver in his voice: 'Are you washed in the blood of the lamb?' His eyes rolled, wild and agitated. He was swayed by a divine ecstasy, under the control of a powerful spirit. There was no talkin' to him. I high-tailed it fast. About half way home, I heard the fire popping and saw smoke billowing above the trees."

"That's all you saw?"

"Didn't hear any gunshots, either, like some folks said."

"He saw plenty," Onorio asserted. "Julian's pointing the finger at Linderman and Bowers. I believe him. When we found that body, Boots found a .45 shell. Linderman's the only man owns a .45."

"That could'a been planted there by somebody else. Or, Karl might've been target practicing in the same area."

"Ough! Linderman used Swannie for a target."

"Boys, keep a cool head. Any day now, we'll get the autopsy. That'll tell us a lot about how Swannie got killed. Maybe it's not him."

"Doc's right. Habeas corpus," Julian recited Boots' precaution, "where's the body? We found a body. Who's to say it's Swannie?"

"Linderman seems to think it's Swannie. Tried to force a confession out'a you. He and Bowers tried to kill you. Hard to be cool. Julian, if yer telling the truth—and I'm inclined to believe you—then somebody else must have killed poor Swannie. Somebody who had plenty to lose in that still. Then again, maybe that isn't Swannie you boys found."

"We ought to tell Boots," Manuel suggested.

"Tell him what? That Julian believes his bosses killed Swannie, and then tried to kill him, with you boys as witnesses. A good lawyer would say you boys held a grudge against the bosses."

"Doc's right again," Julian grimly admitted. "I'm lucky anybody believes me."

"I do. We saw Linderman and Bowers push you off the tipple. We had our feet on the ground. Wasn't no nightmare. We'll back you with Boots, won't we Manuel?"

"You bet."

"And, then what? Get fired? Blacklisted? Family evicted, or no telling what?"

Their frenzy fizzled like warm champagne in an uncorked bottle. Momentarily, the telephone rang. Reverend Miller called to inquire about whether the doctor had received the state autopsy report on Swannie. "No, not yet. . . . Any day, I expect," Dr. Monty replied cautiously. His telephone was on a party line with all the other Company offices. "I'd like to come visit you. . . . I'd rather not say. . . . Yes, this afternoon. . . . Be there directly."

"Twice today, the Buick's been put to good use," Doctor Monty bragged as he drove the men out of Chicorico."

Washed, polished, and ready to go at moment's notice, Dr. Monty's 1925, cobalt-blue Buick was the flashiest automobile in Chicorico, powered by a six-cylinder motor that turned wooden-spoke wheels and was equipped with an encased rear mounted spare tire, scruff plates on the running boards, and automatic windshield wipers. Dr. Monty had convinced Van Cise to purchase the Buick to respond quickly to medical emergencies, although he walked to make house calls and most mothers preferred to deliver children at home. Mainly, the Buick was used on weekends for shopping and church services.

At Reverend Miller's, the men sat in the same parlor where Swannie had conferred more than a year ago about the Widow Perkovich. Dr. Monty asked Julian to repeat the tale. . . . Reverend Miller listened attentively, shaking his head in disbelief as Julian described the events at the tipple. When Julian finished, Reverend Miller spoke angrily: "Not the first time Linderman and Bowers proved themselves fools. Julian, I believe you! As God is my witness, I'm seeing to it you get a fair shake. You stay here in my house. You'll have sanctuary here. I'll speak to Boots. Nobody's going to fool with you. Not Boots! Not Linderman! Anybody who comes through that door looking for you will have to stomp or shoot me out'a the way."

Reverend Miller turned to Manuel and Onorio. "You boys tend to Dahlia, and little Eddy. I'll see Boots in the morning. And, Matt," Reverend Miller addressed the doctor informally, "let me know about the autopsy."

TWENTY-FIVE   EVICTION

WHEN MANUEL AND ONORIO arrived in Chicorico, they found Dahlia and Eddy with Clara along with Mary and Anna. Frantically, the women ran out to meet them. Anxiously, the men hopped from the car. Chaos ensued. Everybody spoke simultaneously, spieling versions of the day's events. They spoke rapidly and excitedly and nobody could understand anybody. Finally, Manuel yelled above the hubbub, getting everybody's attention and giving Dahlia the opportunity to ask, "Where's Julian?"

"He's okay now, Dahlia," Manuel reassured her. He looked about apprehensively and then spoke in a hushed tone. "Let's go inside—where we can talk freely."

"Yes, come inside." Clara turned to enter the house. "We all have much to say."

Once in the house, everyone agreed Dahlia should first hear about Julian. Onorio and Manuel took turns briefing the women on Julian's whereabouts, health, and the incident at the tipple.

"That explains everything." Dahlia abruptly ended the briefing to describe her ordeal. She spoke with aggravated reserve.

A while after Dahlia had gone to Manuel's house seeking help, little Eddy and Arturo came running into the house, yelling that Linderman and Bowers were outside. Linderman banged on the front door. Clara latched the screen door and spoke through the screen.

"What do you want?"

"I'm talking to Mrs. Heard."

"Talk." Dahlia stood beside Clara, holding Eddy's hand.

"Your family's in big trouble. Your man signed a confession he killed Swannie."

Dahlia and Clara glared, first at Linderman and then Bowers, while Linderman unfolded a typewritten page. "Says here, it was an accident. He jist wanted to talk sense into Swannie, what with all the friends Swannie had in Chicorico, and all."

Dahlia and Clara still glared.

"I tried to talk him out of it, and—"

"Out of what?"

"Killing himself. Said he'd disgraced his family. Last we saw him, he jumped off the tipple. To hang hisself. Don't know where he went."

"My man's no killer! And, he certainly wouldn't hang himself!"

"No use to argue." Bowers sniveled. "Being's he confessed to Swannie's murder, and run off, I got no choice but to fire him. We're moving you out, Mrs. Heard. Can't have a killer and his family living in the camp. Karl's seeing Boots in the morning. Turning in Julian. You'll have to move your possessions, pronto."

"Whatever for?"

"Eviction!" Linderman testily jeered. "Reckon a gal like you understands!—Eviction!"

Linderman and Bowers strode off the front porch and walked toward the Heard's house. Linderman turned and yelled, "You don't move your junk, I will!"

Dahlia knew what he meant. Linderman would destroy everything they owned just as he had led the charge back in 1914 against the Ludlow striker's colony and set fire to their tents. When the fire subsided, he led the Colorado militia in the raid, looting and demolishing the remains of the striker's property.

Dahlia scurried to the house while Clara fetched Mary Chicarelli. Eddy fetched Anna Perkovich. She brought her older boys. Eddy stayed behind with Arturo, Angela, and the younger Perkovich children.

"We'll haul the big things out." Linderman condescended, standing in the front door passageway. "You little ladies will have to do the rest." He added sarcastically, "Being's your men ain't here in your hour of need."

"Don't need your help!" Dahlia lunged at Linderman.

He deflected her, stepped aside, and screamed, "Mrs. Perkovich! What'cha doing?"

"You can no see? Pushin' dolly."

"That dolly's Company property!" Linderman was rankled. "Don't you—"

"Back away, Karl. Yer brow beating women!" Bowers tugged Linderman's sleeve. "We'll watch. Make sure Company property don't get stolen."

They rested beneath a cottonwood tree in the front yard. The women hauled the Heard's possessions to the Montaño's while Linderman bayed snide remarks, like a hound dog badgering a treed bear cub. "Coal bin ain't yours."—"Make sure you move the hens, too. Or, I will."

Dahlia could imagine Linderman twisting the necks of every one of their hens.

"And, we'll eat'em."

The women emptied the cupboard into powder boxes and carried them to Mary's. Her house had the most storage space, and after Swannie's rampage, Onorio's wine cellar had plenty of room. They placed the soap, laundry, and ironing supplies in washtubs and carried them away. Similarly, they toted filled pots, pans, and buckets. Then, they wrapped Dahlia's small collection of china, glassware, and flatware in towels, sheets, and blankets before toting them in washtubs. Bowers grabbed two kitchen chairs and commenced to carry them.

"Put them down!" Dahlia shouted, a scalding tinge in her voice. "We don't want your help!"

Bowers offered to help more than once. Dahlia scoffed at his offers while she and the other women continued to systematically pack and haul the Heard's possessions. Late in the afternoon after herding the chickens to Mary's coop, Dahlia told Bowers and Linderman: "We're done, except the piano and other heavy items. Our men will carry them out."

"Julian shows here, I'm takin' him to Boots." Linderman rested his right hand on the handle of his pistol.

"Manuel and Onorio can carry it."

"By themselves?"

"Neighbor men will help, too."

"Don't get too comfortable at Manuel's," Linderman warned. "Or, Onorio's. I'll evict both of them for harboring a criminal's family."

Bowers didn't look at the women while he nodded in agreement with Linderman.

"*¡Los hombres estan boñigas!*" After calling Bowers and Linderman piles of cow dung in Spanish, Clara didn't bother to translate for them.

"Come to the house, we have work to do." Mary grinned as she invited the women to her place. She spoke Italian, understood Spanish, and knew the meaning of Clara's contemptuous curse. On the way home, the women giggled as Clara expanded their repertoire of pithy, Spanish phrases descriptive of Bowers and Linderman. Anna recited several in Serbian, and Mary followed with expletives in Italian.

Linderman chided loudly, hoping the women heard above their laughter, "We'll make one last inspection!"

Inside, the two Company men found an impeccably clean, empty house without the common litter of discarded knickknacks and broken objects abandoned when people move to other places. Windows and ledges had been dusted and the floors recently scrubbed, the kitchen glowed with a new application of yeso. As Dahlia mentioned, all that remained of the Heard's possessions were heavy objects: sofa, dressers, beds, mattresses, springs, and the Chickering piano standing along the wall in the living room.

"Let's move it out," Linderman suggested as he gripped a handle behind the piano's soundboard. Bowers gripped the handle at the other end of the piano. Together they strained to wheel it to the front door where they had to lift it over the door's foot frame. "She's chuck full of bricks," Bowers grunted. "Maybe we should let the men move it."

"I'll fix her." Linderman popped out the front door to the backyard and returned with Julian's axe.

"Where'd you get it?"

"B'side the coal shed. Little ladies missed it."

Linderman crashed the axe onto the piano top and chinked a tiny slit across the grain of polished oak. He hacked onto the tiny slit and nicked a deep fissure across the grain. He slammed the fissure with the axe's blunt end and crumpled the piano top. With the rabidity of a ravaging Vandal bent on the pillage of civilization, he chopped around the piano's cast-iron frame structure and demolished its wood and metal-mesh innards.

Frenzied and out of control, Linderman relentlessly crashed the axe into the piano. He smashed its exquisitely polished hardwood and glittering ivory keyboard into smithereens. He splattered aside the splintered ruins into mounting piles and little resemblance remained of the courtly old piano other than the cast-iron frame and soundboard, five square feet of layered softwood, heavily glued and pressed.

Linderman shoved the pulverized soundboard out the door and tossed it into the canyon grasses in the front yard. He returned for more piano debris. As he gathered tangled steel strings, felt-tip hammers, hitch pins, and piles of broken ivory keys, he noticed Bowers frowning in total dismay.

"Don't stand there, like a coon dog, tongue a-hanging. Lend a hand!"

Bowers scowled without lending a hand.

Linderman struggled to slide the awkward cast-iron frame through the living room doorway. From the porch, he hurled the piano's frame onto the canyon grasses.

Twang!

The frame resonated like a tuning fork, bounced, and tumbled onto a cottonwood. Upright and stripped naked, the piano's skeleton wobbled against the tree. Linderman kicked it to the ground.

TWENTY-SIX   COMMON VERMIN

Monday morning, red-eyed Linderman handed Boots a confession for the murder of Ray "Swannie" Swanson that appeared to be signed "Julian Heard."

Boots carefully scrutinized the document. "Julian's signature?"

"Saw him sign it myself."

"How'd you get it?"

"Gave it to me."

"Jist like that?"

"There's more to it. We go way back. I was his bootcamp D.I. He didn't have an alibi as to his whereabouts. When Swannie was killed. I was worried."

"Swannie killed?"

"Yeah, everybody said—"

"Everybody talks too much. We're waiting the pathologist's report." Boots tossed the document to the desk. "It's illegal. The document confesses to the murder of a man that might be alive."

"Everybody's sayin' Julian killed the man—that there body the boys found."

"Yer haywire. Swannie could be alive."

"I'm goin' by what Julian told me. And, everybody else."

"Everybody sure gabs, don't they?"

"Listen here. Yesterday, Julian called me and Homer. We was passin' his house. Said he had something heavy on his conscience.

Needed to get it off his chest. Then, he told us. He wanted to confess and needed us to help type it."

"Type it! What for?"

"Maybe he cain't write. A shaky hand. Hell, I don't know."

"He could'a come here, told me."

"He didn't. He trusts me. We took him to Homer's office to type the confession. Homer typed exactly what Julian said. He signed it with us as witnesses."

"Julian can write. Hands don't shake. Where'd you sign as witnesses?"

"Didn't know we had to sign. Anyways, he kilt the man by accident. Only miner without an alibi."

"How'ja know?"

"Asked them. Conducted my own investigation."

"Durn your heinie! I'm sheriff. I conduct investigations! I don't take lightly to vigilantes."

"Don't blow a gasket." Linderman waggled the document. "Confession says it was an accident. That he had gone to speak with Swannie. They argued. Julian shoved. Swannie fell down and hit his head. Julian insisted he don't know nothing about the way Swannie was buried in canvas, 'cept what he learned when he helped you boys tote Swannie's body down from the hills."

"You know so much about Julian. Where is he now?"

"Last I saw or heard he was gonna hang hisself. He run out'a the office to the edge of the tipple, tied a rope to the tipple and 'round his neck. Me and Homer, we run out to stop him, when Onorio shouts from below. Next thing we saw, he jumped."

"He jumped! And, you didn't help?"

"Manuel and Onorio was helping him. We didn't want them to know about Julian's confession. We skeddadled."

"Why would he give you a confession? Yer not the law."

"I'm his friend. Negroes don't have many white men they can trust. B'sides, I'm in charge of security for the Company."

"Yer not the Sheriff!" Boots glowered, grabbing at the document. "Give it over. I'll take it to Fred Loshbahl. He'll ask questions."

"Do it myself." Linderman rumpled the paper into his pocket and left.

Boots was irritated, his neck muscles tense. He twisted his head back and forth several times while massaging the neck muscles, and the soreness dissipated, but he remained irritated, hands trembling slightly. He sat at his neatly arranged desk, cracked his knuckles, and then meshed the fingers of both hands as though praying. He squeezed them tightly. When his hands stopped shaking, he uncapped a fountain pen and started to jot notes about Linderman's surprise visit with Julian's ostensible confession. The pen was empty. He cursed under his breath, "Bad enough I can't spell worth a hoot—but no damned ink."

Anxious to jot notes of the event still fresh in his mind, he rifled through the cluttered bottom drawer of the desk where he kept supplies until he found an inkbottle. He siphoned ink into the pen, and returned to his jottings, recording the date, day, and time of Linderman's arrival. While he recorded the event's details, a dry ink splotch on the ink blot-pad the size of a dime distracted him. He cursed to himself again, "How'd that get there?" He picked at it nervously, digging his fingernails into the ink-blotter's soft surface.

The telephone rang. Glad to be interrupted, Boots recapped the pen, laid it aside, and picked up the telephone. Loshbahl wanted to see him in the afternoon. "Good, I have some business for you, too," Boots informed the district attorney and hung up.

Boots sat back in the chair and muttered loud enough as if the walls could hear, "Kids might think a sheriff's job is exciting, but more an' half the time, I set in this office and fiddle-fart around." He couldn't relax. Before long, he was pacing about the austere office, nosing around looking for dirty spots on the walls. None. He inspected the rifles he kept locked in a gun case. They were clean and ready for use. He inspected the jail cells. They had sat empty for more than a week and were ready for occupancy. Except for occasional drifters looking for a bed, he couldn't remember previous occupants, which made his job easier. He rather liked empty cells.

Everything in order, he called the telephone operator and asked her to refer any calls to the Sweet Shop where he'd be on business, he told her, although she knew he was skipping out for a cup of coffee. Before he could leave, Reverend Miller arrived. Boots offered him a cup of coffee at the Sweet Shop. He declined, explained his visit was in confidence, and proceeded to tell about the fight at the tipple without revealing Julian's whereabouts.

Focused on the nuances of Reverend Miller's words, Boots listened intently until Reverend Miller finished. Then, Boots responded acerbically, "Pardon my French, Reverend, Karl's a pain in the horse's heinie! Gets under my craw! Takes the law into his hands! I'm the sheriff of Colfax County. I answer to Fred Loshbahl. He answers to higher ups. That's how the law works."

"Karl's in charge of security for the Company."

"That's what he ought to do. Protect Company property from vandals. Leave criminal investigations to me."

"So you know Karl interrogated the Chicorico miners." Reverend Miller's quiet presence simmered down Boots, somewhat.

"The pot's calling the pan black. He tried to kill Julian, and I can't figure out why—all this palaver about how Julian doesn't have an alibi for the time Swannie disappeared. And Julian's so-called signed confession for accidentally killing a man that may be alive. I knew it was fake, signature forged. All we really have is the body of a man buried upside down in a hole in the hills."

"Julian does have an alibi." Reverend Miller gave Julian's alibi.

"Can't verify that alibi. Jist his word."

"His word is good as gold. Any number of men could have killed Swannie, if anybody did."

"Swannie made a bundle of enemies." Boots nodded in agreement. "Every bootlegger and speakeasy owner in the county hated him."

"All the more reason Julian's innocent."

"Is Julian safe?"

"Yes."

"Good. Don't let Karl find him. I'm askin' Fred to call Santa Fé, put a rush on the pathologist's report. That'll help."

That afternoon, Boots called on Fred Loshbahl whose office was on the second floor of the International State Bank. Loshbahl, a tall thin, slightly stooped man—face stern as ever—invited Boots to sit. Boots drew up a chair and reported what he had heard about the fight at the tipple, asking, "Do you think Santa Fé would speed up the autopsy?"

Loshbahl's deeply set eyes glinted from beneath his startling black eyebrows. "That's why I called. It's here." Loshbahl arose from his chair and bent toward Boots, his thick hair almost brushing Boots's face as he peered into his eyes. If Boots hadn't known Loshbahl so well, he might have been intimidated. Yet, Boots knew Loshbahl's intent was to stand close and speak confidentially.

"Boots, what I have to say, and what's in this report, shouldn't leave this room until I'm ready to act on it. Here, take a look at it."

Boots quickly scanned the report, dropping to the line that identified the body. He jerked his head. "What?"

"Yep, body was James Osgood." Loshbahl, known for his assidious love of facts, was enjoying himself. "Long and short of it, Heard's clear—despite that alleged confession—at least until Swannie's body shows up."

"I'll be durn. I knew him, a hot-headed, ornery boy, but not bad."

"I hear tell there was bad blood between Bowers and Osgood, something about a Christmas gala. Osgood probably soiled his own nest by telling revenuer Swanson about alcohol sold at the gala. This supposedly caused Osgood's dismissal, then he disappeared. Now, we know what happened to him."

"I knew about the fracas at the gala and Osgood's dismissal. Never connected him to the body. Like everybody else, I thought he left to Colorado looking for work."

"When you delivered the body down from the hills, word spread fast. His family inquired. They didn't think to report his disappearance till they heard about the body, but they had been inquiring about him in Colorado. Nowadays a man moves on looking for work. He never troubles to write anyone. No news is good news. His family was of the same mind till they heard about the body."

"Did he leave a wife, kids?"

"Nope, not even a girlfriend."

"Sure it's him?"

"The pathologist examined the medical records of both Osgood and Swanson. Records matched Osgood to a T."

"We found a .45 caliber shell near his buried body."

"The report says he was shot, but the pathologist couldn't confirm the caliber."

"Karl Linderman's the only man in the county with a .45. He tangled with Osgood."

"Won't work, all circumstantial. That shell isn't like a smoking gun with fingerprints and registration papers to match."

Disappointed, Boots stood from his chair and prepared to leave. The telephone rang. "Loshbahl, here. Oh, yeah, sure." Loshbahl lowered the receiver. "It's Matthew from Chicorico. He's looking for you." Loshbahl handed the telephone to Boots, who motioned "no" and indicated Loshbahl should speak with Dr. Monty. Loshbahl listened attentively, jotting notes as Dr. Monty told of events in Chicorico.

"Yes, yes, that's what Boots tells me. The two miners saw the whole thing. . . . Who witnessed the eviction? . . . That's all, the women? . . . What's this about a piano? . . . So, it was demolished. Who saw Linderman and Bowers do it? . . . You mean to say nobody saw them? . . . Why not? . . . Huh? People are afraid to speak against Company men? So, if anybody saw them demolish the piano, they wouldn't talk? . . . Even the women didn't see them demolish the piano, you say? . . . Well, we may have something. Thanks for the call. This puts a new spin on the case." Loshbahl hung the receiver and flashed a rare smile at Boots. "Since yer up, drop down to the Sweet Shop. Get us some black coffee. Tell Gus to fill up two of them clear glass mugs he uses for root beer. On my tab."

"Hot, diggedly-dog," Boots cheered up. He shuffled out the office and down the steps of the International State Bank building. Out on Second Street, he skipped by the display windows of the various department stores, doting over his attire in the reflections of the large glass panels. His shirttail hanging, he tucked it while crossing Second Street to the Sweet Shop owned and operated by Kostas "Gus" Markos from Greece.

Gus came to the Ludlow coal camp in 1912 with other Greek immigrants and decided mining was not for him after witnessing the Ludlow Massacre and its aftermath. He tried his hand at making and selling goat cheese. In 1917, he opened a café in Raton offering homemade candy and a full fare of meals, including goat cheeses. Not only was the café a success, it quickly became a popular spot for the businessmen of Raton to get a good cup of coffee and gossip, too.

Boots had a sweet tooth and relished the thought of picking up a piece of candy or two, although he couldn't afford much of anything after paying for his custom-made boots and flashy outfits. Directly inside, three glass counters displayed a tempting potpourri of homemade candy. A fourth was cluttered with knick-knacks, trinkets, bookends, and other Greek and New Mexico curios. Boots browsed the candy counters, his mouth salivating over the wide assortment of hard, semi-soft, and soft candies, some sugared, some with nuts, some braided with frosted flowers or scrolls.

"Here." A stout, durable man wearing a white apron offered Boots a chocolate stick.

"No, thanks, Gus. Fred sent me over for two mugs o' coffee. On his tab."

"Good, good. Take two sticks, on-a house for the law."

"Can't take bribes." He had counted on Gus's generosity.

"Bribe you and Fred, ho!"

Boots gladly pocketed the chocolate sticks in his shirt and walked to the marble soda fountain where town workers were sitting on the high, round counter stools sipping sodas and coffee. Already, Gus had poured coffee into clear glass mugs. "Bring back mugs."

"Always do."

"I'll hold the door for you."

"Thank-ee, Gus."

Holding his arms like a boxer posing for a photograph, Boots carried the mugs in front of his chest as he walked back to Loshbahl's office. He didn't pause to fancy his image in the department store windows but did acknowledge greetings with a polite smile and nod. At the International State Bank building, a passerby opened the door for Boots to enter, and Loshbahl's office door was propped open with a shoe. In the office, Boots attempted to make small talk with Loshbahl while explaining the free sticks of chocolate.

Loshbahl cut him short, rattling his prosecutorial swords: "Cut the gab. We're gonna prosecute Linderman for what he purportedly did to Heard."

"Nothing purported about it."

"What's the proof?"

"Eyewitnesses."

"The two miners?"

"Yep."

"So we prosecute a white man for beating on a Negro? With an Italian and Mexican for witnesses?"

"That's pretty much it."

"That's not enough. May not cut muster with a Colfax county jury. Linderman's white, a former officer, veteran of three campaigns, a Company man, and votes Republican."

"What's that got to do with the price of rice in China?"

"Folks don't cotton to prosecution of their own. Besides, Van Cise wants to keep a lid on it. He wants an ordinary trial. No blow up—like Ludlow."

"That was long time ago. Things change."

"Not that much. And Wobblies have a long memory. They're looking for a case to revive their cause. What better place than Ludlow's backyard? You know? Ludlow's only twenty-five miles north in Colorado?"

"I know where it is." Boots, sullen, usually garrulous, thumbed his coffee mug quietly, a metallic glare on his face.

Fred tried to mollify him. "Politics. Don't like'em any more than you."

"You can't ask me to enforce the law when—"

"It's your job!"

"Why? If'n yer not gonna prosecute."

"Company's important to everybody."

"Company's not above the law."

"Law? Look around! Whole country's in a depression. A big blow up would set everybody back—the mines, businesses here in town."

"Don't matter. Men run the Company. They're not above the law."

"It's not the Company we'll prosecute. That's what Van Cise hopes to prevent. We prosecute the individuals responsible for breaking the law."

"Are you in his pocket?"

Loshbahl scowled. "I won't honor that with a reply."

"'Cause you sold out, too. Like the lawyers!"

"You got it wrong."

"Wrong? Not prosecuting for murder is wrong! Working man shoots his son-in-law for beating his daughter. He gets justice at the end of a rope! Company man murders a man an' tries to hang a second man—he gets mercy. Wrong is right, right is wrong."

"Enough said!" Loshbahl scowled but this didn't intimidate Boots as it would others. "We prosecute a case we can win. Keep politics out of it."

Frustrated, Boots laid his fingers over the rim of the mug allowing the heat of the coffee to evaporate through his fingers. The office air dry and stale, Loshbahl cracked open a window, allowing a cool draft to drift into the room. Outside, drivers geared down their cars to stop at the intersection of Second and Cook. Others gunned their engines, dropped their cars into low gear, and crossed the four-way stop. "Hear them cars outside," Boots said more than asked. "They're filled with folks who respect us. They respect us 'cause they believe we're honest. We enforce the law. We make sure that rich man, poor man—all men are treated fairly. Them working folks in the coal camps. They're no different. They immigrated to this country to escape places where the rich lorded over the poor— where the laws were written by the rich, for the rich."

"Face it! Law and politics mingle in this case." Loshbahl's tone was defensive.

"What's politics got to do with it?"

"Could lose real jobs. Go hard on the Company, it shuts down. Those working men you're defending, they'd be in soup lines— without jobs, roof over their heads."

"So Bowers and Linderman get away with attempted murder to save the Company? Sounds like blackmail to me."

"Not quite. Linderman's on loan from Baldwin-Felts. Strictly speaking, he's not a Company man. Van Cise won't use Company lawyers to defend him."

"Puh! Wiggle room in a compromise!"

"Judas priest! Still don't get it! We can win this one against a bad hombre. I'll pin three charges on him. One should stick, an old prosecutor's trick. Jury's prone to forgive one or two of the charges, but not all three."

Boots listened blankly, keeping his counsel, thinking, "Loshbahl's bargaining with the Devil, a fool's compromise. So am I—far's folks can tell. We're in it together—me and Loshbahl—the law of the land snared in a fool's compromise. I hate this work. Ought'a be a real rancher. Make use of my boot collection."

Loshbahl detected Boots's frustration. "No need to stonewall me. Won't work. Don't you know? Linderman's responsible for killing Louie Tikas, the union organizer at Ludlow. Shot him in the back. Linderman led the charge against the striking miners in the tent colony. Miners weren't there. They were hiding in the hills. The Militia killed women and children, mainly. Now's our chance to nab him."

"Don't have him, yet."

"Arrest both Bowers and Linderman, for the time being. Talk to Bowers about turning state witness."

"What do I tell folks at Chicorico?"

"Nothing! They can come to the trial. They'll see justice in action."

"Chicanery more like it!"

"Damn it, Boots! I didn't make the world! Nothing's perfect!"

Boots stood to leave, thanking Loshbahl for the coffee and chocolate, although he didn't mean it.

"Thank Gus for the chocolate." Another rare Loshbahl smile. "Be a good man, return the mugs."

Tuesday morning, David "Boots" Najar telephoned Dr. Monty. "Your party line galls me. I'm comin' over. Stay put." Shortly, Boots arrived. He taped a sign to the door, "Doctor out all morning," and waited for Dr. Monty to finish treating a child. As soon as the child and mother left, Boots searched the entire office for other people. Satisfied he was alone with the doctor, he locked the doors and drew the shades.

"No need to shade the office."

"There's ears and eyes everywhere here in Chicorico." Boots wasn't sure if he had shaded the office out of necessity or the jitters. "Between you, me, and the fence post, the state pathologist's report arrived. Body the boys found wasn't Swannie."

"Wh-at? Don't tell me?" Dr. Monty removed his glasses, pinched the bridge of his nose, and then massaged the furrows on his brow as though they would flatten.

"Military records showed it wasn't Swannie. Turns out it was Osgood, James Osgood. You know him?"

"Wasn't that the Company kid, weighed the coal?" Dr. Monty winced in recognition, replacing his glasses. "Fired along about Christmas back then?"

"Yep. Never showed among his family. After he was fired. They thought he'd gone without telling'em. Looking for work. When the boys found the unidentified body in the hills, Osgood's folks asked us to check, see if the body was Osgood's. State pathologists checked on Swannie and Osgood. Dental records showed it was Osgood."

"You sure?"

"I'll be hanged and hog-tied, if'n I ain't. Says so in the report."

"Who killed him? Buried him in the hills?"

"Search me." Boots shook his head slowly.

"All along, we thought the body was Swannie, but, then where's Swannie? Is he alive? Buried in the hills?"

"Search me."

"That's not good enough. Yer the sheriff. You ought to know something."

"Lord only knows. Burned and buried in his own fire? Buried in the hills, like Osgood. Or, long gone—good eatin' for the buzzards and coyotes. May be alive, down in Mexico, living the good life, knowing him."

"Knowing you—you'd go to Mexico."

"Whatever folks say about Swannie," Boots mustered a grudging compliment, "he was good. Still may be."

"Going public with the news?"

"Not yet. Loshbahl wants it hush-hush for a while, but Julian's scot-free. No connection to Osgood." Once again, Boots inspected the doctor's office searching for eavesdroppers. He cupped his lips and whispered. "Need your help to make some arrests. Loshbahl's going after Linderman and—"

"And, Bowers?"

"Shh, not so loud. Bowers maybe, Linderman yes—aggravated assault, pure and simple—couple other charges, too."

"Who'll run the mine?"

"Guess Van Cise will use Bill Pratt, Company man from the main office."

"The men will like him much better than Bowers."

"Jist temporary. He should be driving into camp about now. Soon's I make the arrest, he takes over. He agreed to switch automobiles at the mine so we can haul the vermin in the back seat of his sedan."

While Dr. Monty found his jacket, Boots raised the office shades and spotted Pratt outside idling his car. After locking the office, Dr. Monty and Boots strolled to Pratt's parked car. "Follow us." Boots cranked up his Chevy while Dr. Monty hopped in. Boots headed west by the row of elementary schoolhouses. Children were at recess playing kick-the-can, hide-and-seek, and other hunt-and-tag games in the absence of playground equipment. Across the way, the coke ovens were vacated.

Once on the main road, the two-car caravan proceeded between Chicorico Creek on the north and the railway on the south. The road rose gradually at the Company store and continued to rise by the clubhouse and the successive rows of Company houses. Toward the west end of the canyon, the creek angled south and the road dropped crossing the tracks to the base of the tipple. Boots stopped near the tipple. Waiting for Pratt to arrive, Boots explained to Dr. Monty: "Let's haul'em in the back seat. I'll be up front with a gun in their faces. They'll be handcuffed by you. When we're back, you take the wheel."

Worried, Dr. Monty slowly opened the door. "Hope you don't need the gun."

"Me, too."

Boots and Dr. Monty shuffled up the steps of the tipple while a motorcar pulled a train of loaded coal cars out of the mine toward the scales. Overhead, gondola buckets were making their rounds dropping slack onto growing mounds. The cleaned coal rattled down the tipple's tin chutes. Outside of Bowers's office, Boots turned to the doctor and silently signaled him to move behind, while Boots drew his pistol and entered Bowers's office without knocking. Linderman and Bowers were at ease drinking coffee.

"Homer, Karl, yer under arrest."

"Huh?" Linderman curled his upper lip and eyed Boots intently. Bowers whined apprehensively. "We didn't do anything."

"What's the charges?" Linderman glowered.

"Aggravated assault against Julian, and then some."

Linderman lunged for his .45 pistol.

"Put the pistol on the desk!" Boots pointed with his .38 Smith & Wesson. "Take off the gun belt, too. Lay it on the desk. Won't need either, where yer going. Now, turn around, I'm cuffing the both of you." Boots motioned with the barrel of his pistol. They turned their backs reluctantly.

Dr. Monty stepped out from behind Boots and cuffed both men.

"You can't arrest me here!" Linderman blathered. "I'm chief security guard."

"Nobody's above the law."

"Yer treating us like common criminals."

"Common vermin's more like it." Boots shoved the barrel of his pistol into Linderman's back and ordered the two men to walk out of the office.

Outside the office, Bowers spotted Bill Pratt approaching. Bowers turned utterly frantic. His face darkened and shriveled, and the wrinkles on both temples looked like crow prints trampling down the side of his face. "Karl made me do it," Bowers sniveled. "I didn't want to hurt Julian—jist scare him."

"Shut up!" Linderman truculently admonished Bowers. "Boots don't have nuthin' on us."

"I'm fed up! You've been a bully since you came here."

"Runt!"

"Bully!"

"Runt."

"Best you boys get along. You'll be bunking together, least till the trial."

TWENTY-SEVEN NOTHING BUT THE TRUTH

FOLKS IN CHICORICO BUZZED with hopes and doubts. Hopes that Linderman and Bowers would be tried and found guilty for the death of James Osgood. And doubts Company men would be successfully prosecuted and found guilty by a jury of peers. Bill Pratt assumed mining operations. Linderman and Bowers shared a cell giving them plenty of time to concoct their versions of the events leading to the tipple and aftermath. When Boots mentioned Loshbahl's offer to Bowers, he consented agreeably to turn state witness, immune from prosecution, and was jailed in a separate cell. Mike Wright, Raton native son and recent graduate of the University Colorado Law School, was the court-appointed attorney to defend Linderman.

During the trial's opening day, most hopes dimmed; most doubts doubled. Linderman and Bowers would not be tried for Osgood's death. Instead, lesser charges were made against Linderman. After the jury was selected, charges were issued:

Karl Linderman, in an attempt to kill Julian Heard, shoved him off the tipple at gunpoint;

Karl Linderman evicted the Heard family from their Chicorico Company house without legitimate authority;

Karl Linderman demolished the Heard family piano with an axe.

Presiding Judge Tyler Stringfellow ended the first day with instructions to the jury to avoid discussion of any part of the trial with anyone, including other jury members, until trial's end, when he'd instruct them to deliberate on the merits of the allegations.

The jury was sequestered in rooms in the Swastika Hotel, which they considered a treat with linens changed daily, a radio in each room, and full course meals in the dining hall. If desired, individual room service tendered by bellhops was available for soft drinks and sandwiches. No moonshine was sold in the Hotel Swastika's Iron Horse Lounge during the trial.

Boots mingled with coal camp folks at the Sweet Shop where they assembled immediately after the trial. While he socialized affably, he assessed their mood, keeping true to his code as sheriff by refusing to discuss any part of his investigation, findings, or the trial. "You'll hear it in court," was his calm yet firm reply.

Early on the trial's second day, Judge Stringfellow repeated admonitions. No shouting, name-calling, or uncivil behavior would be tolerated. He reminded everyone that an armed state patrolman, the sergeant-at-arms, would evict unruly individuals for the trial's duration. "A decorum of civility is necessary," Judge Stringfellow insisted sonorously, "for the jury to objectively weigh all the facts presented to determine the truth or falsehood of each allegation beyond a reasonable doubt. Cool heads must deliberate if justice is to prevail." Thus, witnesses and the defendant were sworn-in and allowed to explain their unique perceptions of the facts.

"Homer Bowers, do you swear to tell the truth, the whole truth, and nothing but the truth, so help you God?"

"I do."

"Proceed."

"First thing everybody should know. Karl Linderman is a bully. He was always bullying me around, and there was nothing I could do about him. None of the men liked him, either. He was on loan from the Baldwin-Felts Security Agency, and we were stuck with him. I tell you this 'cause he'll probably say he was my sidekick. That I told him what to do, and he did it. That's not true."

"Mr. Bowers, please state the facts about the day on question. Try to avoid editorial comments."

"I apologize for the diatribe. Jist had to get it out. Well, that Sunday morning, Linderman came to my house and told me Julian wanted to see us. We went to Julian's house and found him in the backyard. He asked our help to type a confession. We went to my office where there's a typewriter. Julian told me what to type—that he accidentally killed Swannie.

"On the afternoon of Swannie's disappearance, Julian said he went to the still to stop Swannie before he made a fool of himself again, like he did at Mrs. Van Cise's Christmas gala. Julian and Swannie argued. Julian shoved and knocked him down. Swannie's head hit a rock. It killed him. Then, Julian run off.

"I asked him, 'Was the body you boys found—was that Swannie?' He said he didn't know. After he argued with Swannie and knocked him down, Julian said he never moved the body. Like I said, he lit out after Swannie died—before the fire.

"To tell the truth, I don't remember seeing Julian sign the confession, but I do remember Julian saying he was going to hang himself on the tipple—that he couldn't live with the disgrace he'd brought his family and friends. He slung a lasso around his neck and backed out the office. Karl whipped out his .45 and threatened to shoot Julian in the legs to stop him.

"Julian kept a-backin' toward the edge of the tipple. I tried to talk him out'a hanging himself. But, no, not Karl. He upped and yelled: 'Hell! Give'em what he wants!'

"Right 'bout then, whilst Julian was on the tipple's edge, Onorio and Manuel called from below. Julian turned to see who was yelling. That's when Karl booted Julian off the tipple. I took a'holt the slack end of the rope and wedged it between some planks. Good thing Julian grabbed the rope as he was fallin'."

"Mr. Bowers, please tell us again. How did the lasso get around Mr. Heard's neck?"

"Well, like I said, he slung it over his head."

"Mr. Bowers, there's one more detail I don't understand. You say Mr. Heard placed the lasso over his neck, and you wedged the other end of the rope between planks, just as he fell from the edge of the tipple?"

"Yes."

"Then, how did it come to be tied to a tipple plank so that Mr. Heard could swing on the rope?"

"It wasn't tied to the plank. Lucky for Julian, I took a'holt the slack end that was knotted 'fore the rope tightened. I managed to wedge the knotted end between the crack of two planks. Lucky for Julian."

"Thank you."

"*Mannàggia!*" In a vehement outburst, Onorio jumped to his feet and bellowed, "He's full'a baloney! Lies! Lies! Baloney!"

Manuel attempted to wrestle Onorio down into his seat. He was still bellowing, "Lies! All lies! Baloney!"

Judge Stringfellow barked above the noise of the tussle, "Evict this man!"

The sargeant-at-arms shoved Manuel aside, grabbed Onorio's arm, and ordered him out at the point of a gun. Onorio's face brightened, then paled as he suddenly realized he was being evicted from court at gunpoint.

"Your honor," a disconcerted Loshbahl said, "Mr. Chicarelli is a key witness."

"Well, he's out'a of my court! He can wait outside! Or, in jail, for all I care, until you call him in. And, he'd better keep his temper."

"Easy goes it, so we can have our say," Manuel whispered to Onorio, while the sargeant-at-arms escorted Onorio from the courtroom.

"Anybody else have objections, keep'em to yourself," Judge Stringfellow scolded in a deep, booming voice. "Modern day courts are not gladiator battles—where slaves and enemies were pitted against the best lions and warriors of the state—where unruly fans cheered and booed the gladiators! Humph! Don't you know? The word 'fan' comes from the word 'fanatic,' and I won't tolerate fanatics in my courtroom!"

By the time the judge finished his admonitions, Onorio had settled in a booth at the Sweet Shop and was told to stay there until called by Loshbahl. Inside the courtroom, everybody sat subserviently, eyes downcast, except Bowers and Linderman who enjoyed the chaos and frenzy, knowing Onorio's outburst strengthened their case. Ordered restored, Julian was called to the witness stand.

"Julian Heard, do you swear to tell the truth, the whole truth, and nothing but the truth, so help you God?"

"I do."

"Proceed."

"Your honor, I speak in Onorio's defense. He's angry because Bowers is lying through his teeth, and—"

"Humph!" Judge Stringfellow interrupted and testily bellowed, "How would you know? Do you have a corner on the truth?"

"No, sir," Julian responded deferentially. "But I can tell when a man's lying."

"Well, well, Mr. Heard. Give us the benefit of your wisdom."

"Onorio was angry 'cause he wants to believes in the justice of an American court trial. An' he can't abide liars."

"Humph! What *are* you thinking?" Stringfellow was affronted. "That I'm Pontius Pilate? That I'll wash my hands of this banal affair? Allow a mob to try a man?"

"No, sir. Jist that Onorio and Manuel, they were there. Me, too. I saw what I saw."

"And, you're not objective, precisely because you were there, wrangling with those boys."

"I was there 'cause they forced me to be."

"Mr. Loshbahl! Silence your witness. Instruct him to stick to the facts. Or, you'll take his deposition in private, and he can while away the time with that other miner."

"Your Honor," Julian started to say. "Mr. Bowers doesn't believe in the oath he has taken, going by—"

"Non sequitur!" Wright objected. "Non sequitur!"

"I agree!" Loshbahl added.

Both lawyers approached the judge. Loshbahl promptly attempted to explain Julian's audacity. "Your Honor, Mr. Heard isn't an educated man. He doesn't understand evidentiary procedures."

"Or, etiquette. See to it you control your witness." Judge Stringfellow rolled his eyes. "Or, I'll gag him."

"Now, Mr. Heard," Loshbahl spoke condescendingly, "refrain from extraneous allegations. You have impugned Mr. Bowers' character with your allegations about his integrity. Just answer the questions put to you. I can handle any deceptions during cross-examination. A word to the wise is sufficient. So now please, tell us your version of events on that Sunday without superfluous bandstanding."

Julian slipped into his poker face and waited for awhile to reply until the judge squirmed at the bench and Loshbahl shuffled his feet nervously. "Out with it, man!" Julian rested his sore hands on the railing of the witness box.

"That Sunday noon I was sitting in the outhouse. The door opened. Linderman stuck his gun barrel on my forehead. Said he'd— blow my brains out—if'n I didn't come with him to the tipple. I came out. Bowers was there, an' tole me to tell Dahlia I was gonna help'em at the tipple. He slung his arm around me like we was pals. Linderman stuck his .45 in my back. I shouted to the missus I was going with Bowers and Linderman to the tipple. To tell Manuel and Onorio I wouldn't be bowling boccie.

"In Bowers' office at the tipple, Linderman told me to sign a typed confession—Bowers had already typed it—that I accidentally killed Swannie. He said it was for my own good. Accidental death is not as serious as first-degree murder, he said, especially for a Negro. I refused to sign the confession. Then, Linderman got nasty, started cursing and swearing, claiming that I kilt Swannie and wouldn't owe up to it. Linderman pointed his gun at me. Bowers said I'd better sign. Or, Linderman would shoot me.

"I started backing away. They backed me out of the office. Bowers had a rope tied in a lasso. Karl kept insistin' I sign the confession whilst he pointed the gun at me. I figured I'd back away to the tipple edge and jump over, maybe grab a pillar on the way down. Then, I heard Manuel or Onorio hollering. I turned to see and felt Linderman's boot on my behind, and Bowers' rope around my neck. I fell."

"You fell accidentally?"

"No! I fell with Linderman's help. He shoved me on the behind! With the heel and sole of his boot."

"Mr. Heard, did you tell Mr. Bowers and Mr. Linderman you were going to hang yourself?"

"No."

"Well, then, why did you put the lasso over your neck?"

"I didn't. Homer did."

"That's his word against yours."

"My word is bond."

"Karl Linderman, do you swear to tell the truth, the whole truth, and nothing but the truth, so help you God?"

· "Yes sir."

"Proceed."

"I'm a soldier with a long, honorable record of service to my country. I earned that record by taking orders and carrying them out. Fought in the Philippines, Mexico, the Great War, and ended my tour of duty as a drill instructor in boot camp. Julian Heard was one of the doughboys I trained, like lot'a boys from these parts, even the two lawyers here, Mr. Loshbahl and Mr. Wright. But, I treated all the boys the same, even though Negroes don't make good fighters, most of'em. Julian proved to be a credit to his race. I respected him as a soldier. I consider him a friend and hope he feels the same."

"Irrelevant," Judge Stringfellow declared, "please keep your personal feelings about Mr. Heard to yourself."

"Your Honor?"

Judge Stringfellow recognized defending lawyer Wright. "You may speak."

"I instructed Mr. Linderman to make his feelings known toward Mr. Heard. He wanted everybody to know that he felt no ill-will toward the Negro gentleman."

"Well and good, but let's get on with Mr. Linderman's testimony." The judge turned to his attention toward Linderman sitting in the witness box. "You may continue Mr. Linderman, but try not to ramble with your testimony."

"Beg your pardon. I'll get down to brass tacks. On the day in question, Homer and I happened to be walking by Julian's house. He called us from the tracks and said to me: 'You and me go way back. I trust you and need your help.' He suggested we go to Mr. Bowers office at the tipple where we could speak privately. I remember he tole his missus he was gonna give us some help at the tipple. At the office, he asked Homer to type a confession that he had killed Swannie."

"Mr. Bowers was to confess?"

"No, Julian wanted to confess."

"Proceed."

"I asked him what happened at the still, and when he explained it was an accident, I told him to make sure he says that in the confession. If'n you kill a man—'specially if'n a Negro kills a white man—best it not be on purpose. Or, you'll hang for sure. Homer typed the confession jist like Julian wanted it, and Julian signed it. Then, Julian said he couldn't live with hisself no longer—that he had disgraced his family. Said he was going to jump over the tipple.

"He backed out'a the office. I said I'd shoot him in the legs to stop him. Homer grabbed a rope to lasso Julian to stop him from jumping. Next thing I see he was on the tipple's edge. Manuel or Onorio must'a been passing by and shouted. Julian turned to see who was a-shoutin', slipped, and fell over. Good thing Bowers throwed the rope to him."

"Mr. Linderman, did you say that Mr. Bowers threw the lasso to Mr. Heard just as he was falling off the tipple."

"Comin' to think of it, I can't recall. Either Homer throwed the lasso to him, or Julian put it over his neck. Everythin' happened so fast, can't really say—to tell the truth."

"Manuel Montaño, do you swear to tell the truth, the whole truth, and nothing but the truth, so help you God?"

"I do."

"Proceed."

"Julian's wife Dahlia came to my home. She was frightened. She said Julian had gone to the tipple, under duress, with Bowers and Linderman. I ran to get Onorio. We ran to the tipple. I saw Julian standing on the edge of the tipple with his back to us with Linderman pointing his pistol at Julian's belly. I heard Linderman shouting: 'Sign the paper, fer Chris'sake!' (May God forgive me—for cursing in His name.) Then, I shouted and heard Onorio shouting, too, 'Don't jump!' When Julian turned to look at us, Linderman booted Julian off the tipple. Bowers threw the lasso over Julian's head when he started to fall."

"Thank you, Mr. Montaño, for keeping your opinions to yourself." Judge Stringfellow beamed as he praised, "It's good to have a witness that sticks to the facts."

There was a short lapse in the proceedings while the sergeant-at-arms told Boots to fetch Onorio Chicarelli who was waiting in the Sweet Shop as ordered.

"Onorio Chicarelli, do you swear to tell the truth, the whole truth, and nothing but the truth, so help you God?"

"I do."

"Proceed."

"Hold on there," Judge Stringfellow interrupted. "Just state the facts. You should have heard your partner there, Mr. Montaño. He reported the facts without raising Cain."

"I couldn't."

"Couldn't what?"

"I couldn't hear him. You kicked me out."

"Humph! Well, get on with it. Stick to the facts."

"Manuel come to my place. He said we better go quick to the tipple. Julian was in trouble with Linderman and Bowers. We ran to the tipple and saw Linderman pointing a gun at Julian and ordering him to sign a paper. Bowers held a lasso. When Julian got too close to the edge, I yell—'Don't jump!'—to warn him. He turn to look at us. Linderman kicked him off the tipple. Bowers throw the rope around Julian's neck when he fall off. Then, Bowers and Linderman backed away on the tipple. We ran up to the top of the tipple and saw them go into Bowers' office."

"Are those the bare facts?" Loshbahl asked.

"Yes, they are, but they don'a tell the whole story."

"Enough said."

"Sergeant-at-Arms, escort Mr. Chicarelli out the courtroom." The judge called for the next witness.

"Homer Bowers, you are still under oath."

"Of course."

"Did Mr. Linderman engage in the eviction of the Heard family from their house?"

"You bet he did. More than jist engage. He evicted that poor family without my consent. Like I said, Karl's a bully. He said Julian had signed the confession when I wasn't looking and that we couldn't harbor a criminal. 'You should evict the family from the house,' Karl told me. I didn't believe him about the signed confession, and I told him so. Well, Karl ups and takes it on himself to tell Mrs. Heard to vacate the house. I went along to make sure he didn't hurt Mrs. Heard."

"Karl Linderman, you are still under oath."

"Yes, sir."

"Did you engage in the eviction of the Heard family from their Chicorico house?"

"Why, I think Homer's saddle is slipping, telling tall tales and all. I'd never, well, like I said, I'm a soldier. I took my orders from Homer Bowers. I don't have the authority to evict anybody. He ordered me to evict Mrs. Heard. I tried to reason with him, what with Julian being a doughboy, and old friend of mine. I believed he didn't kill that poor drunk on purpose. He jist made a mistake, a freak accident. Homer wouldn't hear of it. 'Murder is murder,' he said. 'And, if'n you want to keep your job as chief of security, do as yer told.' I did as I was ordered. Homer could get me fired and blacklisted. I'd be out a job in the Depression. Nobody wants an old soldier. Your honor, to tell the truth, I didn't want to evict Mrs. Heard, but I had no choice. It was me or them."

At the end of the day, the judge admonished the jury to remain silent about the trial until it ended and they received his instructions on how to deliberate. Acknowledging Chicorico folks were angered by the judge's treatment of Onorio and Julian, and Bowers's transparent complicity to guard Linderman's derrière, Boots slipped Bowers and Linderman out of the courtroom through the hallway leading to the back of the courthouse to his pickup and promptly returned them to jail. Foregoing a visit to the Sweet Shop where he anticipated a thorough reaming from coal camp folks, he locked the jailhouse and was on his way to his pickup to drive home for supper when Reverend Miller greeted him amicably but did not mince words.

"You know Homer Bowers is lying."

"Now, Reverend, I can't read minds."

"Com'on, Boots. He's covering for himself, and for Karl, too."

"Maybe. Maybe not. What's the proof?"

"Onorio, Julian, Manuel—they're honorable men. They wouldn't concoct a false story."

"Reverend, yer barking up the wrong tree. Talk to Fred. I enforce the law. He prosecutes criminals."

"Think that'll do any good?"

"Doubt it. Fred's not gonna change his strategy. He aims to nail Linderman by using Bowers."

"How's that?"

"By using the sneaky fox to catch the ravenous wolf."

Reverend Miller released a long, slow sigh and tapped Boots's shoulder, muttering as he walked away, "I don't envy you, Boots."

At 9:00 a.m. Judge Stringfellow started promptly by explaining the trial was almost over with several more witnesses to be heard, which would be followed by closing statements by lawyers Wright and Loshbahl.

"Dahlia Heard, do you swear to tell the truth, nothing but the truth, so help you God?"

"I do."

"Proceed."

"Mr. Bowers and Mr. Linderman found me at Clara's house. Mr. Bowers said Julian had confessed to the murder of Swannie. I didn't believe him and told him so. Swannie was a part of our family. Mr. Bowers said because Julian had confessed to the murder of Swannie, I would have to move all our belongings from the house."

"So! It was Mr. Bowers who evicted you?"

"Yes."

"Objection. Prosecution putting words in the mouth of the witness."

"Objection sustained. Jury will ignore that comment, and it will be struck from the court record. Please proceed, Mrs. Heard."

"Well, when I asked Mr. Bowers what he meant, Mr. Linderman rudely shouted, 'Eviction!' And he called me a 'gal.' Then, Mr. Linderman ordered me to move our belongings from the house. Or, he'd do it. And, I didn't trust him.

"My neighbors and friends, Clara Montaño, Mary Chicarelli, and Anna Perkovich offered to help. We moved almost every piece by ourselves while Mr. Linderman and Mr. Bowers wrangled with us to make sure we didn't steal any Company property. Mr. Bowers did offer to help. I declined. We couldn't move the piano and other heavy items. I told the two gentlemen that Julian, Manuel, and Onorio would move it directly. That's the last time I saw my beautiful piano in one piece."

"Homer Bowers, you are still under oath."

"Of course."

"Did Karl Linderman demolish the Heard piano with an axe?"

"I don't know anything about a demolished piano. Karl and I supervised the ladies when they moved the Heard's belongings. We offered to help move the piano. Mrs. Heard told me that Manuel and Onorio would move the piano. So we didn't help where we weren't wanted. We inspected the house, saw the piano, and left. The piano was in good shape, last I saw. An', Mrs. Heard kept an impeccably clean house to her credit."

Dahlia gasped audibly and started to utter a protest when Loshbahl stopped her. "You'll get a chance to respond, Mrs. Heard. No good purpose will come by getting you evicted from this courtroom."

"Karl Linderman, you are still under oath."

"Yes, sir."

"Did you demolish the Heard piano with an axe?"

"By golly, my legs is being tied, putting me at a disadvantage. No, I did no such thing! Good soldiers don't demolish property on purpose. My order was to evict Julian's family. I ordered Mrs. Heard to take their belongings and get out. She did with the help of the other ladies. She tole us Manuel and Onorio would move the piano. I took her on her word. Mission accomplished. My job was done. I don't know nuthin' about any piano getting demolished. Some of those foreigners in Chicorico, they might have a grudge against Negroes. Maybe they did it."

"Dahlia Heard, you are still under oath."

"I understand."

"Did you see Karl Linderman demolish your piano with an axe."

"No."

Judge Stringfellow praised the two lawyers. "Good! Good! Testimony was presented civilly in record time. I'll ask each lawyer to keep closing remarks short so the jury can commence deliberation while still fresh. Lawyer for the defense goes first."

Mike Wright opened his closing remarks with a calm, relaxed demeanor. "I remind you, Commanding Officer Karl Linderman has a sterling record as a U.S. Army officer having fought in the Philippines, Mexico, and France. He stands accused of hurting a good friend and destroying his friend's piano. This is the same man who trained Mr. Heard and many other boys to fight the Germans in the Great War; this is the same man who tried to help his friend Mr. Heard in a time of need. Does this good soldier sound like somebody who would betray a good friend and harm him?

"Mr. Linderman does admit to one unpleasant act. He evicted the Heards—on orders from his superior officer, Mr. Homer Bowers—or, face the consequences. No idle threat! He would lose his job in these times of high unemployment and soup lines. He committed the unfortunate act as a loyal soldier under orders of Mr. Homer Bowers. But, his accuser, Mr. Bowers hides behind immunity to blame Karl for the eviction, even though Mrs. Heard testified that it was Mr. Bowers who initially evicted her. And, Mrs. Heard's piano? Destroyed at the hands of some coward, but who? Unfortunately, nobody saw the culprits.

"What I ask you to do—the jury of honorable and honest men— is to consider Mr. Linderman's sterile record as a gentleman and a patriot and consider the facts of the case. Remember you must be absolutely sure about the facts. I believe the facts presented here do not support conviction on the charges. Rather, we have different versions of all the events with the words of Mr. Linderman, an honorable patriot, pitted against the words of foreign miners." Wright gazed earnestly at the jury. "We should set this honorable man free." He backed away and sat next to Linderman at the defense table.

"Mr. Loshbahl, you may proceed with your closing remarks."

Fred Loshbahl opened his closing remarks with a stern, serious demeanor. "The defense would have you believe Commanding Officer Karl Linderman is an honorable man, innocent of wrong-doing. True, he has an impressive military record. I was one of the doughboys he trained. He was an excellent drill instructor. He taught us to stay alive by killing the enemy. Before the enemy killed us. 'Good soldiers,' he taught us, 'sometimes have to harm and kill other men in defense of their country.' He went on to say,

'Your Christian upbringing taught you it was wrong to kill a man. So you got to trick yourself—tell yourself it never happened. It was just a nightmare. That way, you can sleep at night.'

"Now, the battles are over. Nevertheless, Mr. Linderman is playing tricks with his mind, making claims that he did nothing wrong. He denies his culpability and hides behind the cloak of duty. 'Just taking orders,' he claims. But, Mr. Linderman also knows the Army's code of conduct. It allows for higher principles, that is, a soldier may protest an order that is clearly unethical— such as the order to evict the Heards from their home when in fact, Mr. Heard had not been found guilty of any crime in a court of law.

"Furthermore, Mr. Linderman is an expert on denial, a type of psychology he taught us doughboys—just follow orders like a good soldier, and deny it happened. He thinks he's still a soldier, and he's playing tricks with his mind. He denies his culpability.

"I do not challenge Mr. Linderman's patriotism. He was a good soldier. We are considering the here and now. The facts of this case support a conviction on the charges. Mr. Bowers testified Karl Linderman did shove Mr. Heard off the tipple. Mr. Montaño and Mr. Chicarelli were eyewitnesses who verified that fact and corroborated Mr. Bowers' testimony. Mr. Linderman served our country very well. To that, we are grateful. He also pushed a man off the tipple at gunpoint. He's guilty of aggravated assault."

Judge Stringfellow instructed the jury to determine the truth or falsehood of the charges against Karl Linderman beyond a reasonable doubt. "Start deliberations now, but needs be," Stringfellow suggested, "sleep on your deliberations until tomorrow. I'll check with the foreman first thing in the morning." The jury rallied in a small room adjacent to the courtroom, and court was recessed. Everybody left, including the jury who desired another evening in the Hotel Swastika where they could revel in hotel food and sleep in comfortable beds with clean sheets at taxpayers' expense.

Boots Najar and Fred Loshbahl met in confidence at the district attorney's office. Loshbahl was animated, flush with anticipated victory. "How about that Mexican miner, Montaño. He's got class. He stuck to the facts, and Stringfellow praised him. Don't think that didn't influence the jury. And, what about the way Montaño clinched his testimony against Linderman, when he repeated Karl's words, 'Sign the paper, fer Chris' sakes!' Ha! Then, Montaño apologized to the Lord for breaking His commandment about taking the Lord's name in vain. Jury ate that up, too."

Boots blurted boisterously, "Montaño wasn't putting on the dog!" When Loshbahl frowned, Boots lowered his voice, still speaking convincingly. "Montaño was speaking from his conscience. He believes in the Ten Commandments."

"Hmm." Loshbahl smirked pensively, still frowning at Boots' sudden outburst. "Believe in them or not, it was a stroke of genius to show the jury he was a God-fearing man."

"Fred, I tell you. He's no bag of wind. He wasn't puffing."

"You say he wasn't puffing. I'd say he was self-righteous."

His right leg crossed, Boots had been sitting back in a dark oak chair. Abruptly, he planted both feet on the floor, sat straight, and rested his fists on his knees. "Don't make fun of the man. He was telling the truth, which is more than we can say about Bowers and Linderman."

"Boots, simmer down. You got me wrong. I wasn't making sport of Montaño. Merely admiring the way he invoked the Lord."

"Don't wanna simmer down—not with all them liars swearing on the Bible an' mocking the truth. How about 'thou shalt not bear false witness against your neighbor?'"

"What about it?"

"Bowers and Linderman throttled that commandment! Pack of liars, them two."

"Maybe. But, we'll nail Linderman."

"Still don't like it. All Linderman gets is a feather lashing."

Loshbahl laughed nervously as he complimented Boots, "That's a turn of phrase. You ought to be a lawyer."

Not to be dissuaded, Boots maintained his stern demeanor. "Well, we're gonna have another problem on our hands. Coal camps folks are asking—where's the justice?"

"Justice? That's a mighty high expectation—a grandiose philosophic abstraction—an ideal philosophers invented to describe how life should be. In fact, life doesn't work that way, as far as I can tell. More like Mother Nature where dumb luck and power prevail."

"Loshbahl, that ain't you talkin'."

Loshbal leaned back in his seat, held his head in his hands, and closed his eyes, pensively muttering, "Now it is. . . . In law school days, I thought of myself . . . as a crusader for justice." Loshbahl's evident optimism dimmed as he reminisced. "But, I discovered after plenty of knocks . . . the law doesn't work that way. Since then, I have observed—truth gets pulverized by liars. There's no defense against a good liar."

"*Good* liars?"

"Skillful liars, is my drift. There are fellows can lie to their mothers."

"Coal camp folks know that. But, they expected a trial against Linderman and Bowers. To account for Osgood's murder. Instead, they got a trial against Linderman with Bowers as the main witness."

"Don't they understand? I have to use the snively fox to catch the rapacious wolf."

"Only thing they understand is that Osgood's dead. Swannie's missing, or dead. Julian was almost killed, and his family evicted without cause—not to downplay the destruction of the piano."

"That's a whole lot we can't do much about," Loshbahl replied wearily, his optimism depleted. "The truth is—Linderman's evil. We're lucky to get him. Back in 1914, he saw to it—innocent children, women, and miners were killed at Ludlow. Exonerated by a military tribunal, he spent the Great War teaching doughboys how to kill Germans without compunction—a professional killer."

"Bowers is no better."

"Yeah, actually, he is—though not much. He's greedy, niggardly, and duplicitous, but he's no killer. And, he's our tool to get Linderman. Of course, he lied to cover his hide. And, he covered for Linderman on the destruction of that piano. But, we'll get the greater of evils through the lesser of them."

"Ugh," Boots uttered a deep, glottal grunt because he could find no other way to express his disgust. "Coal camp folks, they won't see the justice in that. They suffered a lot under Bowers. He'll still be around after Linderman's gone."

"Exactly. He'll have to live with his conscience."

"Don't think he gives a care."

"He'll have to live with all them angry miners and their families. He's nothing without them. He'll be lucky to sleep at night."

"Folks might do something violent against Bowers—break the law—and call it justice."

"More like revenge, I'd say." Loshbahl was getting agitated.

"Call it what you want. We'll have to prosecute them."

"Boots." Loshbahl crossed his arms in dismay. "Dammit, the law's not perfect. It's made by men, and I can't fix it. All I have is facts to go by."

Boots sat quietly, thoughtfully, fists resting on his knees for a while and finally concluded, "Onorio Chicarelli was right. The facts don't tell the whole story."

Loshbahl uncrossed his arms and looked at his pocket watch, muttering, "Getting late. Let's call it a day."

Early on the last day of the trial, the judge called the jury back into the courtroom. They had reached their verdicts:

"Of the charge, Karl Linderman, in an attempt to kill Julian Heard, shoved him off the tipple at gunpoint—guilty in the first degree."

"Of the charge, Karl Linderman evicted the Heard family from their Chicorico Company house without legitimate authority—not guilty."

"Of the charge, Karl Linderman demolished the Heard family piano with an axe—not guilty."

Karl Linderman was sentenced to five years in the maximum-security ward of the New Mexico State Penitentiary, Santa Fé.

TWENTY-EIGHT   UNION

EUPHORIA ERUPTED. They whipped Linderman, the Ludlow bully. Biblical overtones—one stone downed Goliath, sweet victory, *dulce est.* Bowers demoted to bookkeeper and Bill Pratt put in charge of the mine. Battle won, allies shook hands and slapped backs: Anna Perkovich, Shorty García, Bruno Bergamo from Dawson, Joe Sonchar from Sugarite, Tom Rodman from Swastika, Jesus García from Van Houten, and many others. Folks had watched and waited and no longer feared to speak of many things, of cabbages and kings and unions, too.

"We have feast for Julian and Dahlia." Anna Perkovich spread the word as folks dispersed from the courtroom. "Come my house, five o'clock tomorrow. We celebrate." That evening she asked her brother George to roast a pig in the old way on a spit over the hot coals of juniper and scrub oak. George drove to a Maxwell farm, bought a young pig, brought it home, and slaughtered it for roasting in the morning.

The next day George tended to the roasting pig while Anna's sons made the rounds gathering jugs and bottles of wine that sprouted in Swannie's absence. Folks sent word they were coming with wine or food for the feast—stews, soups, meats, baked beans, milk for children. By 3:00 p.m. George delivered the roasted pig on a colossal platter and placed it in the center of Anna's table. Clara and Mary bustled in the kitchen arranging the panoply of food prepared by other women. Then, they hurried home to freshen up for the festivities. George circulated the neighbors for extra glasses and dishes while Anna's boys helped arrange furniture for the celebration.

Manuel and Onorio escorted the Heards to the celebration. Julian insisted on taking a bottle of chokecherry wine brewed after Swannie's disappearance. Anna's guest list included anybody who appreciated the magnitude of the victory—a Company man had been convicted in a court of law by a jury of peers for an offense against a miner. Most of the Chicorico baseball team and some from Dawson came to honor their stalwart umpire who had settled yet another score. Reverend Miller and Emma drove from Raton, bringing Mildred with them. Chicorico folks—many who had not been able to attend Judo's funeral—came with dishes and drinks with belated condolences. Others, who had cursed Swannie for destroying their wine cellars and were known to say he had it coming, they, too, brought food and drink.

Anna's house bristled with victory, wall-to-wall folks in the house's four rooms, spilling out onto the back and front porches. No mink coats nor tailor-made suits, but everybody was dressed in Sunday attire. They gathered "like old a'times," Anna thought. They toasted. Ate. Drank. Sang. They talked of union.

"Fellers, remember Don MacGregor?" Manuel shouted to Julian and Onorio over the cacophony of the jubilant crowd. "Ludlow! News reporter for the Denver *Express*."

"Got fired for it!" MacGregor boasted. "Best damn thing ever happened! Fired me up! I'm a Wobblie now. I make news—not jist report it. Here to talk union. Let's go down to Onorio's wine cellar."

"No need." Onorio grinned. "We can talk here."

They found empty chairs. MacGregor was animated about the prospects. "Let's organize a union. Overthrow the Company. Working men have nothing in common with them rich maggots. We'll crush them. We can do it by sticking together."

"Whoa, hold your horses. Yer a communist."

"No, I ain't. Communism don't work. Look'a Russia. Run by dictators. I'm for anarchy, more like it. Don't let that bother you."

"Pah! What's this talk—anarchy?"

"No bosses. Everybody's the boss."

"Every man for hisself! That's all it is."

"We got too much of that. We gotta work together."

"You will—without the big shots."

"Yer touched, like Swannie. Can't have families without fathers, churches without priests. Somebody gotta rule the roost."

"Boys, boys, time's ripe for you to rule the roost. You whipped the Company. You can do it again. Kick'em to hell and back. Organize, don't weep, 'member Joe Hill?"

"We don'a cry!" Onorio snorted. "We don'a want revolution. We wan'a fair wages. Safe mines. Good schools."

"Yer too radical for us," Manuel offered. "Such names you use, Wobblie, anarchy—"

Julian injected, "As I understand, anarchist don't want any kind of government. Well, I fought in a war to make the world safe for democracy. We gotta make democracy work—government of the people, by the people, and for the people. That's the kind of government I want. We gotta have rules."

"Yer plumb loco," MacGregor retorted. "Big shots want democracy, my butt! Like the Devil quoting Scripture! Like them Southern plantation bosses wanted democracy before the Civil War. They were for freedom—freedom to run their plantations on the sweat of their slaves. Company men are no different. They want democracy, like them plantation bosses. They're all for their own freedom—keep you slaves in jobs that kill you. Look what happened to Judo Perkovich."

Talk lulled. Manuel struggled to console MacGregor. "Your heart's in the right place, but your head isn't. Your methods are too radical; loco some would say."

MacGregor slowly shook his head in disbelief, perplexed by the men's reluctance. He stood to leave. Manuel rose, placed a hand on his shoulder, and let him down gently. "You did good at Ludlow. You wrote reports in the *Express* about why miners strike. Sometimes their hand is forced. You did good to join the Wobblies. You and I have talked much about a union. You have helped."

"It's a doggone shame, Manuel. You boys gotta take the bull by the horns—now! Folks'll follow you; they're not afraid anymore, but that won't last."

"Don't get me wrong," Manuel added. "You have helped us see that we must act now. We can't wait. We might go for a Company union. Or, the United Mine Workers. Either way, we won't wait long for it to work. We don't want a revolution to change the world. We want a real union that works for us, that's all."

MacGregor scanned their faces. Julian, Onorio, and Manuel were resolute. Disappointed, he shook their hands and left the celebration. . . .

Within the week after the celebration, Bill Pratt called Manuel aside at the tipple. "I like you. Hope you didn't fall for MacGregor's spiel about the Wobblies."

"How'd you know?"

"It's Chicorico. Ears are everywhere. Everybody talks."

"Too much."

"How about a Company union? The Rockefeller Plan. Instituted after the blow up at Ludlow. Based on cooperation—between operators and miners."

"We want a real union that works."

"We'll make it work. We can form it right now."

"Company union, like Ludlow?"

"Well, yes, like Ludlow *now*. And, other CF&I camps up in Colorado."

That evening Manuel spoke with Julian and Onorio, describing Pratt's proposal of forming a Company union based on the Rockefeller Plan. "Pratt's smart. He knows we got backing for a union."

"He's scared, too," Onorio observed. "Afraid of the Wobblies."

"He's smart to be scared," Julian reacted. "Maybe, he'll make a Company union work."

"Ho!" Onorio chortled. "Like he's Houdini. Pratt may want it to work. Big shots don't care."

"I say we give it a try," Julian proposed, "on a trial basis." Julian glanced at Manuel. He nodded assent, followed by Onorio. "See if'n it works."

"If'n it doesn't?"

"I'll be the first to propose a real union with Manuel as our leader."

In the weeks to come, more supporters appeared to offer congratulations. Ed Doyle and Frank Hayes from the District 15 offices of the United Mine Workers of America in Denver visited overnight. They came to talk union and insisted on meeting in Onorio's wine cellar. Not for concealment, this time. They didn't have to hide. They liked Onorio's choice wine.

"We jist set up a Company union," Manuel reported, sloshing the wine in his glass.

"Company union, like Ludlow?" Hayes asked.

"More like Chicorico," Julian responded.

"Trial basis," Onorio added.

"Boys, I hope it works for you. Yer just as necessary as the capital invested in the mine. You should have some say about working and living conditions."

"Fact is," Doyle added, "most Company unions are masked paternalism intended to slam the door on unions with teeth."

"You've got something precious that won't last too long," Hayes warned. "You've got men willing to talk to you about a union. They're willing to back you." He paused, sipping wine, and waited for the men to consider his comments. They didn't respond. He continued, "Bill Pratt is one helluva a lot better to work with than Homer Bowers."

"He proposed the Company union."

"You scared the Devil out'a him, talking to Don MacGregor. And, keep yer eye on Bowers. He's a weasel."

The caucus ended. Hayes and Doyle weren't as disappointed as MacGregor. Spurned, no. Deferred, yes. "Here, keep this handy." Hayes handed a business card to Manuel. "If Company union doesn't work, call on me. We'll help you make a good union."

TWENTY-NINE   POWERFUL PURGATIVES

THREE WEEKS AFTER LINDERMAN was shipped to prison, Boots made a special trip to Chicorico. He pulled up to the Heard house. Julian, Manuel, and Onorio were clearing away the demolished piano. Before stepping out of his Chevy, he waited for the trailing dust to settle, although there wasn't much.

"Howdy boys." Bodacious and talkative, Boots swaggered to Julian's wire fence and leaned on it. "Nice day to be working."

"No time to bull."

"Sure taking your time movin' that trash. Here it is, the middle of March—"

The three men grunted curses and ignored Boots while they hauled piano rubble to the garbage barrels—euphoria of victory abated.

"Leastwise, you appear to be finishin'."

They persisted with the snub, grunting curses below their breaths.

"What's eatin' you boys?"

Julian dropped the rubble he carried and hollered, "Gutierrez won't haul this mess. Not in the Company contract."

"Pah! Can't haul much with his old mule and buckboard."

"He doesn't haul iceboxes and furniture, either," Manuel grumbled.

"Don't see either in that mess."

Julian glowered. "Boots, what you should see is three generations of my family axed to smithereens by Linderman."

"Jury found him 'not guilty' of axing the piano. Nobody saw
him do it."

"Bowers did."

"Not accordin' to Bowers."

"He's a liar."

"Liar or no, only way to prosecute Karl was to use Bowers."
Boots wasn't expecting this acerbic reception and it seemed paltry
to explain Loshbahl's decision to plea bargain with Bowers. He
watched as the men continued to clear the debris.

Finally, Manuel asked: "Whose side you on, Boots?"

"Law says you gotta prove guilt beyond a reasonable doubt."

Onorio sneered. "Linderman didn't do it, who did?"

"Boy howdy, I don't know."

"You know," Manuel injected sarcastically. "You don't have
the *huevos* to go after Bowers."

"Can't. We gave our word. He was a witness for the state."

"And, he's an honorable man?" Julian scoffed.

"The law has limits. See it all the time, but it's better than vigilantes, like Linderman." Boots was upset by the cool reception.
"See here, boys, I didn't come to split-hairs about the law. I bring
good news. James Osgood's folks sent you boys two hundred dollars for finding his body. They sent a check made out to Fred
Loshbahl intended for 'the good men who found James Osgood.'
Fred cashed it—here, it's in twenty dollar bills." Boots retrieved a
stuffed business-size envelope from his hip pocket and prepared to
hand it to one of the men.

They ignored Boots and continued hauling away the debris.

"Suit yourself." Miffed by the snub, Boots tucked the envelope
into the gate. "Don't let the wind blow it away." Boots turned and
walked to his pickup, mumbling, "Ungrateful hoots. Good wages
for a day's work, I'd say."

Within the hour the men finished removing the debris and
stacking it in a pile to be hauled away to the Raton dump at a later
date. They relaxed in the shade of the front porch. Julian passed
fresh chewing tobacco. They bit plugs, sloshed them around the
gums, and spat onto the canyon grasses beside the porch.

"Fine day for a chew."

"Tastes like licorice."

"Looks like tar."

"Molasses, most likely."

"Some fellers like it heavy-cured."

"I like it light in color, a'most tan. Not too sweet."

"I'm thinking of a pipe myself."

"Like the high-muck-a-mucks."

A good time for a chew on a mellow March afternoon with only the low hum of the tipple's din, no trains running, children in school or home napping.

"Thank heavens, we're done," Julian declared. "Thanks fellers for the help."

"*Prego, prego,*" (You're welcome.) Onorio said.

"Sí," Manuel agreed. "Plenty of time to get you in the house between workdays."

"Won't be the same without the piano."

"*Ai, primero sopitas de miel y luego de hiel,*" Manuel recited a down-home *dicho*, first comes the honey, then the bile.

Julian and Onorio seemed to understand the dicho and continued chewing and spitting the tobacco without commenting.

"Let's look at the money." Manuel opened the envelope. "*¡Ai, que suavé!* Two hundred dollars."

"Don't want it," Julian objected sullenly.

"*¿Porque no?*" (Why not?) Manuel snipped.

"Julian, I agree with Manuel. None of us is rich. Might be paper, but it's good hard cash. This is good luck."

"Good luck that comes from bad luck. Adds up to blood money."

"Huh? It's a reward—a green one! Blood's red."

"Generous one, too."

"Well, don't let me stop you fellers. Take it all."

"*¡Ai, que Julian!*" Manuel nodded his head in disapproval. "Sometimes I can't figure you out. Yer a practical man. What's this talk about blood money?"

"We got it 'cause another man died, and the Lord called us to find his body. We don't deserve it. Part of the Lord's plan."

Onorio conjectured, "Maybe the Lord planned for us to get the reward?"

"And, jist maybe," Manuel added, "the Lord was telling us something about how the Company treats loyal workers. Company didn't give the reward. Osgood's folks did."

"Maybe this, maybe that," Julian scoffed. "Maybe we ought'a give the money to Osgood's church."

Onorio shook his head in disbelief and muttered, "Your head must'a come unscrewed."

Manuel counted out one hundred dollars and handed it to Onorio. "Naw, you hold it, Manuel. Don't spend it." Onorio turned to Julian and promised, "We won't spend it till you get your head screwed on straight. What say, Manuel?"

"You got my word."

After Dr. Monty gave Julian the okay, Pratt offered to put Julian to work every day of the week to make up for back time. He declined on grounds it deprived others time to work. He returned to his normal rotation shift of working two or three days a week, depending on demand. Returning to his regular work routine did not help much. On Saturday evenings, Julian did not attend poker games, and on Sunday mornings, he attended Sunday services grudgingly with Dahlia and Eddy. At church, he would not sing. On Sunday afternoons, he declined Onorio and Manuel's invitation to boccie and horseshoes. Rather, he prowled the hills until late in the afternoon and returned home, tired and taciturn.

Dahlia could no longer tolerate Julian's inordinate dips into morosity. She had tried many things to soothe his rage—preparing favorite dishes, warming water for baths after work, and making excuses for him to Manuel and Onorio. Off-days, he still groused about the house until Dahlia ran out of patience and sent him out. That's when he started hiking the hills during the week when he wasn't working.

The off-day hikes were not enough to quell his discontent. He needed much more to purge the fiery anger festering every time he thought of Swannie's disappearance, Osgood's obvious murder, and Linderman's subsequent trial. He dwelled on each man's fate: Osgood, full of piss and vinegar, didn't deserve to be murdered. Swannie, ornery and befuddled, where is he? Rotting somewhere in the hills? Did Linderman get to him, too? And, Linderman? He whiles the time away in prison without having to work for a living. He'll get out in a few years meaner than ever. Bowers pretends to fink on Linderman to cover his own misdeeds, and he goes back to work like he was innocent—a slap on the wrist."

Julian's mood matched the drab March weather, cold nights, overcast days, no snow or rain, bare cottonwoods, and brown canyon grasses. Even the piñon and spruce seemed to be mired in the last dour throes of winter remission. A frigid blanket of cold air hovered over Chicorico Canyon, trapping gaseous fumes and smoke released from the coke ovens, slack piles, coal trains, home cookstoves, and heaters. The smog sank to the ground and seeped into the tipple buildings, homes, schoolhouses, Company store, and even the smoky clubhouse. At midday, train and automobile lights were turned on; traffic practically came to a standstill, with low visibility for the remainder of the day.

The dark, thick, stubborn thermal inversion lasted long enough for folks to joke about sopping smog soup and bottling the fermenting fumes. Eventually, a Chinook wind swooped down from the Sangre de Cristo Mountains, stirred the air, and dissipated the smog. The lingering gloom slipped away and surrendered to the clean air. The sun seeped through the thin, gray cloud cover.

"Papa! Papa!" Eddy burst into the kitchen where Julian sat sulking over cooling coffee at the kitchen table. "Make me a kite. Look'a Arturo! His Pa made him one!"

Julian peeped out the kitchen window where he saw Arturo flying a kite with Manuel's assistance. He watched the kite gradually ascend, bobbing and dipping as it caught updrafts, its tail weaving in the breeze. "Okay, get some fishin' line, downstairs. Be quick now."

Delighted, Eddy dashed downstairs. Julian found Dahlia sewing in the living room. "Honey, where do you keep the Christmas paper?"

"Not the gift wrapping." Dahlia frowned. Each Christmas after gifts were unwrapped, Dahlia folded and stored the wrapping paper for the next year.

"Jist that soft stuff. Please, honey."

"Oh, the tissue paper," Dahlia relented. In months, she hadn't seen Julian happier. "Bottom drawer of the dresser. Beneath the printed wrapping."

Julian found various colors of green, red, and blue tissue beneath the heavier gift wrapping paper. He unfolded the ironed sheets of tissue and selected the green. He laid it in the center of the table and shaped it into a diamond. Eddy burst back into the kitchen with a ball of fishing line rolled over a stick.

"Perfect." Julian patted Eddy's shoulder. Julian found his jacket. "Come on, let's get us some sticks."

Eddy slipped on his jacket and followed Julian out of the house and over the railway and road. They clambered down the bank of Chicorico Creek. Along the dry bank, they searched among last year's pussy willows for light, supple stalks. "Here's one Papa."

"Naw, too dry."

"This one?"

"Too big."

"Never find any good ones."

"Look for ones aren't too dry. Bend them. If'n they give without cracking, they're okay. For size? About the size of your middle finger." Julian closed his fist, projected his middle finger, and blushed at flipping the obscene finger of contempt. Busy measuring the width of the pussy willows with his middle finger, Eddy appeared oblivious to the obscene gesture.

"They keep breaking," Eddy complained. "Too skinny."

"Try your thumb," Julian advised in relief. "It's rounder. Better to measure things."

The rule of thumb worked well. Finally, they found two supple stalks. More for his protection than Eddy's, Julian offered a bit of fatherly advice as they strolled back to the kitchen. "When yer helping your Ma measure, best to use the ruler or tape. She doesn't like measuring with fingers—middle finger or thumb."

"Why not?"

"Not as accurate." Julian chortled to himself and tried to keep a straight face by jamming his tongue into his scarred cheek. His cheek bulged and appeared to be swollen by an impacted tooth.

Eddy noticed the swelling gum.

Julian removed his tongue from cheek, still striving to fake a serious tone. "Now promise me. You won't measure with your fingers. Ma doesn't like my rule of thumb, er, middle finger."

"Sure, Pa, don't worry. I won't flip Ma the finger." Eddy broke out in laughter and Julian joined as they happily clambered onto the back porch and into the kitchen.

"Get Ma's flour."

Eddy fetched the flour from the cupboard. Julian took a dipper of warm water from the cookstove boiler. "About a cup of flour. Pour it in the dipper."

Eddy measured a cup of flour, pouring it into the dipper of warm water. "Hey, we're making paste! Yum, it tastes good." Eddy licked his fingers.

"You bet! Get a spoon. Mush up the paste. Beat the lumps out'a it."

Eddy stirred the flour and water, dipping his finger in it to test for consistency. "Yum-m-m, really, really tastes good."

Julian was lopping off the tips of the stalks and notching them. He paused long enough to warn Eddy. "Another rule of thumb—eating pasty glue plugs a man shut. You'll need a mighty mean purgative."

"Huh?"

"A purgative, a physics. You know, them nasty N.R. laxative pills for constipation—the ones that gag ya."

"Ugh." The thought of the bitter tasting "Nature's Remedy" pills far outweighed the sweet taste of the paste. "Yu-uck. I'll beat the lumps out!" He whirled the spoon vigorously without further tasting.

While Eddy stirred out the lumps in the paste, Julian tied the supple stalks into a cross. Then, he wound string over the notched tips of the stalks and formed a diamond shape with crossed stalks and string. He dipped short pieces of string in the glue, laid the green tissue paper over the diamond shape, adjusted the paper and the stalks for a good fit, and tied the paper to the tips of the stalks. "Blow on the tips. Dry'em." Eddy blew on them. Lightly, Julian flipped the kite on its back and repeated the process, gluing the paper to the diamond shape.

Julian rummaged through Dahlia's rag box. She overheard him grumbling as he culled through the rags and shouted from the living room where she sat sewing: "On a chair in the kitchen." With scissors in hand, Dahlia set down her sewing and entered the kitchen.

"Jimmy's silk tie? Where's the rags?"

"Use the tie."

"It's a pity." Julian caressed the tie's bright, shiny brown silk cloth overlaid with progressively larger round eyes painted on it. The corneas of the painted eyes alternated in soft yellow and olive green and were set off by white rims, each with a brown pupil.

"The last of them—not much use anymore." Dahlia wistfully sighed. "Jimmy's gone. Swannie, too." She took the tie, trimmed away the lining, snipped it into short bits, and tied short bows along a string.

"Where'd you learn to make a tail?"

"I was a child once," Dahlia teased playfully.

"Pretty smart one, at that." Julian brushed her cheek.

Eddy grinned from ear to ear.

"Haven't seen you this happy in a while." Dahlia was elated by Julian's cheery mood. "Here." Dahlia handed Julian the tail and kissed his cheek. "I've got sewing to do." She returned to the living room.

Julian tied the tail to one end of the kite. "Next a harness." Julian flipped the kite and tied short strings on each of the tips. He joined the strings and held the kite aloft. "Jist like a sail." He set the kite on the table, tied the ball of string to the harness, and attached the tail. "Now, for the launching!"

They scurried out the back door to the meadow in back of the houses where Manuel and Arturo were flying their kite. Julian barked out orders, "You man the kite! I'll run behind with her! About four feet! You dash ahead letting line all the while. I'll hold her by the frame, an' toss her in the sky, whilst we're running!"

Eddy ran ahead. Julian scuffled and tossed the kite into the sky—plop! It fell.

"Pump her a little when I throw her."

Eddy blitzed forward, releasing the string. Julian trailed behind, allowing the kite to catch the air. He pitched it skyward. It veered, careened up, down, around, ascending hesitantly. Julian took the ball of string from Eddy and pumped on the string, leaning the kite into the wind. He stumbled but didn't fall and the kite stayed afloat on a draft rising higher and higher into the gray sky until its colors faded from view. The line reached its end. Julian steadied the kite and handed the line to Eddy who allowed the kite to drift dangerously close to Arturo's.

"Pump her gently," Julian advised. "Let the wind carry her."

Eddy pumped his line and pulled away from Arturo's kite before they intertwined. The two kites hovered in the wind, lazily dipping their tips and twisting their tails, indistinct specks in the cloud cover. . . .

Eddy's kite convulsed. A squall pitched the kite into a downdraft. Arturo's kite followed. Both kites plunged. "Pull her in!—Pull her in!" Julian and Manuel assisted the boys raveling lines and hastily tugging and reeling at a desperate attempt to keep the kites from nose-diving into the ground—the fragile, flimsy kites spinning, plunging.

Diligently . . . assiduously . . . attentively, fathers and sons stabilized the descent of the kites and gradually brought them gently to the ground. They fidgeted with their lines and kites and launched again. Hesitantly, the wind lifted the light kites and wobbly tails until they reached their apex and floated freely, guided by a string and a boy, bobbing and weaving in the wind like hawks hanging in the sky.

That afternoon as Julian stood on the meadow and gazed at the kites lolling above, he indulged in daydreaming and imagined the kites to be hawks. "But kites ain't hawks, hovering and hunting and sweeping from peaks to trees, over hills, and across prairies. Kites are hooked to a string. We hold them down. Hawks are free to fly." His thoughts floated freely. "Even hawks are bound to the earth. They depend on it. There is no such thing as pure freedom, only the superstition we can fly like hawks in our airplanes, which are more like kites harnessed to the earth. Still gotta admire airplanes and their pilots. And, say what about Charles Lindberg, and the Spirit of St. Louis? Making that non-stop odyssey across the Atlantic in July 1927. They, too, could not fly freely like hawks, yet they flew."

THIRTY   TIT-FOR-TAT

THE NEXT SUNDAY AFTERNOON Julian joined Onorio and Manuel pitching horseshoes. As they pitched, Julian persisted to grunt and snort in low, guttural undertones. Not long after a few rounds of pitching shoes, Onorio lost his temper and flared. "Yer out'a kilter! Long time you wouldn't play with us. Now you grumble like an old man."

"E-asy, Onorio." Manuel tried to pacify him. "Julian's had a rough go."

"Who hasn't?" Onorio retorted angrily, turning on Julian. "Friend, yer killing yourself." Onorio threw down his horseshoes. They clattered together and wobbled on the lane. Pitching stopped. Manuel gathered his horseshoes.

"*Tanto le pican al burro hasta que por fin respinga.*" Provoked once too often, the donkey will kick, Manuel complained. "I feel like a jackass. I'm going home for dinner."

"Yer no jackass." Julian smirked and then entreated meekly, "Need your help."

"Help yourself." Onorio collected his scattered horseshoes.

"No need to fight among ourselves," Manuel pleaded with Onorio. "Let's hear him out . . . in the cellar."

They gathered horseshoes and walked to the cellar. Onorio switched on the light in the dank room and poured wine. They sat on the earthen benches, holding their glasses of wine. Onorio raised an arm and slapped his leg. "We're listening. Talk."

Julian did not suddenly burst into a confessional, spewing his frustrations. Manuel and Onorio waited patiently for him to weigh his words carefully.

"There's gotta be more to it. More'an puttin' Linderman in jail."

"He's there. Yer here," Onorio snipped.

"Five years or less, he'll be out," Julian retorted.

"Not afraid of him anymore."

"Bowers running around, free as a deer."

"More like a skunk!" Onorio jested. Manuel laughed.

"Skunk! Deer! He's still free. What about Swannie? And, Osgood?"

"They're better off."

"Better off dead? A dead man don't hear birds sing . . . smell lilacs in the spring." Julian slipped down into his gloom, muttering resignedly, "When yer alive, there's always hope things'll get better—not for Osgood, or Swannie, most likely."

"Lots of good came from the trial," Manuel observed optimistically, attempting to lift Julian's spirits.

"Support for a union." Onorio stood to refill his glass.

The others followed, filled their glasses, and sat on the cool earthen benches.

"Hey, Manuel, how you like my wine?"

Manuel took a tiny sip. "*Muy sabroso*, very fine."

"No vinegar taste?"

"No."

"Eh, Julian, what 'bout you? How you like my wine?"

Julian sipped lightly. "Agree with Manuel. It's fine."

"No vinegar taste?"

"Yer wine's better than your boccie game. And that ain't all that bad."

"Eh, Julian, where'd you get the vinegar? Not'a from my wine."

"Ha!" Manuel chortled at Onorio's old country humor. "Yah, Julian, yer sure full of vinegar, considerin' all we won at the trial."

"I'll allow, joke's on me." Julian let up slightly. "Company union, all we got."

"Hey, amigo, we're on a roll, and it ain't craps." Manuel was animated. "Things couldn't be better. Company union doesn't work, we'll form a real union. We got support. An' we got rid of the *el toro cimarron*, the wild bull. We got even with Linderman."

"What good's getting even?"

"Amigo." Manuel took on a diplomatic tone. "What more do you want? We got Linderman. He's in jail. What more revenge could you ask?"

"A lot more! They tried to kill me. Scared Dahlia and Eddy near to death, and, and . . ." Julian's voice dropped to a bitter murmur. "They destroyed our piano—ruined my family. It ain't so much I wanna get even with Linderman. I wanna make it even for my family."

"Your family?"

"Ain't whole—don't have the piano. A part of our family is missing. Bad enough we lost Jimmy and Swannie. Now, no piano, no music, no joy. Evenings, we sang around the piano. All of us, we looked forward to evenings together. Days, folks come over, mostly kids, for lessons. We always had music in the house. Dahlia made a little cash with it, too."

"Julian, I didn't think that . . ." Manuel's voice trailed off trying to offer consolation.

"Sorry 'bout the vinegar joke, Julian." Onorio was genuinely contrite. "But, we can't bring back the old piano. It's a wrecked pile of junk."

"Don't have to. Gutierrez wouldn't take it. I still got it."

"You want a new piano?"

"That'd help."

Conversation lulled. Manuel refilled his glass. Offered to refill the other's. Julian declined. While refilling Onorio glass, Manuel suggested, "Let's pitch in and buy one."

"Take lots a cash. Scrip's worthless."

"How much?"

"Eight hundred dollars."

"*¡Hijo, mano!*" Manuel burst out. "That's a bundle!"

Equally surprised, Onorio asked, "Hoy boy, where'd you get the price?"

"Out'a book at the library in Raton. Dahlia got us a card. And, the little lady librarian, Mildred—"

Manuel interrupted, asking, "The one sweet on Swannie?"

"Yep. She helped Dahlia find the address. I had Dahlia write the American Piano Company in Boston. They took over the Chickering Company. They sent me a catalog and are mighty interested in selling pianos. It's the Depression, even for the rich, I reckon. Told me they would send one free of charge."

"Nothin's free?"

"That what I thought. They must be loco. I didn't believe it. Thought they'd made a mistake. I figured they didn't know they was writing to a working stiff—a Colored one to boot. Not many working men own a Chickering piano. They must'a been fooled by Dahlia's smooth handwriting and good English, I reckon. Read their letter two, three times. Said the same thing each time: if'n I liked the piano, I could keep it. Jist send the cash. Or, if'n I wanted, I could write, and they'd take it away, no charge to me. They'd even take my pile of junk and deduct a hundred dollars from the cost. Seven hundred still needed."

"That's still lots of money," Manuel exclaimed, and then determinedly affirmed, "We'll get it, somehow."

"Yeah!" Onorio pitched in eagerly. "We already have two hundred in Andrew Jacksons—Osgood's reward."

"No, that's your money. Don't expect you fellers to buy me a piano."

"We won't! You'll win it! At poker!"

"Yah, high stakes poker! At the clubhouse!" Onorio raised his glass. "When the stakes get high, we'll back you."

"You bet! Yer better than Bowers—"

"And, them other Company men."

"Take a while," Julian noted, a glint in his eye.

They raised their glasses and clinked them together. Manuel proclaimed, "We got more time than money!"

The next Saturday night at the clubhouse, Manuel divided the two hundred dollar reward. "Comes to sixty-five dollars each." Manuel counted out the money. "I broke one of the twenties. There's five dollars left."

"You fellers divide it," Julian offered.

"Hold it in reserve," Onorio suggested.

Manuel shoved his sixty-five dollars in the right pocket, the extra five in the left. "It's almost eight. Let's see who shows."

By 9:00 p.m., Bowers hadn't shown his face. Osgood's replacement, Roy Barthol, and several other Company men and miners Shorty García and George Yaksich showed up to play. When Bowers didn't show, the men agreed to start the game. The Company men and miners were not inclined toward high stakes poker. They knew their limits. Onorio, Manuel, and especially Julian could easily beat them. The poker game broke early.

The following Sunday Julian attended church services and sang along with Dahlia and Eddy. Reverend Miller and Emma were pleased to see and hear him sing with gusto. After dinner, he joined Onorio and Manuel at boccie. He complained wistfully, "Gonna take a while to raise the cash."

"Things'll pick up," Manuel speculated skeptically. "Be patient."

"Don't have forever."

"Need Bowers to show," Onorio fretted. "He's got the cash that counts."

"Paah! *¡Cada cubeta huele a lo que tiene dentro!*" (Every bucket smells of its contents!) Manuel castigated. "He smells of fear—afraid to come. Face the music."

"He better change his tune." Onorio doubled his fist and punched the open palm. "If he knows what's good for him."

"Like him or not, without Bowers, it'll take a long time to raise the money," Julian admitted wearily. "We've got to set aside our rancor toward the man. Entice him to play. Be like lassoing a snake."

That evening after supper, Manuel visited Onorio with an idea to entice Bowers to the poker table. That sat on the back porch. Manuel offered Onorio chewing tobacco. Onorio declined. "Thinking of quitting myself," Manuel commented as he bit off a cud. "Thinking of a pipe."

"A pipe?"

"Yeah, like I showed you in Doc's *Saturday Evening Post* an' *Life Magazine*—sitting in a smoking parlor in a fancy hotel, smoking a pipe and reading a newspaper."

"He-e-ey, those are for big-shots."

"*¿Que va!* I'm as good as any of them big-shots."

"Don't make you a big-shot to smoke a pipe."

"Don't wanna be."

"Give me a cheroot any day."

"Them little cigars that're cut square at both ends?"

"You bet."

"*¡Ach, cunques del café!*" (Ugh, they taste like coffee grounds!) Manuel grunted.

"Least you can taste it. Fancy pipes—they jist burn away the tobacco, stink up the room."

They sat on the back porch bantering over their tobacco of preference for a short while until Manuel spoke of the reason he had come to see Onorio. . . .

The next Wednesday, Bowers was sitting at his desk when Onorio and Manuel walked in. Startled and pleased since most miners avoided him, Bowers shoved his chair back, stood quickly, and rushed to meet them at the door with the same conspicuous cordiality he used with other miners.

He shook their hands and felt his fleshy palm crumple in the firm handgrips of the two miners.

"Boys not working?"

"Wednesday. We're off."

"Oh, ye-a-ah," Bowers quipped, faking nonchalance. "Memory's going. Julian's working though. I sure hope he catches up. Bill told him to work all he wants."

"That's why we're here." Manuel tactfully focused the informal discussion. "We know you want to help Julian."

"My plea-sure," Bowers fawned obsequiously. "I stand ready to assist Julian any way I can. He's a loyal employee and a good worker."

"Good, good. Say mind if we sit down?"

"Make yourself to home." Bowers was pleased. They rarely sat when they entered his office. "Care for some coffee?"

"I'll try some of your swill."

"Onorio?"

"Sure, sure."

Bowers did not question their cordiality, although he was unaccustomed to it. Rather, he hastened to accommodate the men.

He turned to a small, potbelly stove that heated the office. "Say, Manuel, mind toting a couple a logs from outside?"

"Big shot of the Chicorico mine?" Onorio strained to be affable. "Burns wood in the monkey stove?"

"It's the juniper. Smells like perfume."

"*Es verdad.*" (It's true.) Manuel chuckled, returning with two small logs. He shoved one into the potbelly stove and laid the other to the side. "Do like the perfume of juniper."

"Be a minute or two for the coffee to perk. Set it up this morning."

"Now that Linderman's gone, who drinks coffee with you?"

"Hardly nobody."

"Should'a told us."

"Well, sure."

"Coffee get bitter?"

"Waste a lot. But, sure am glad things are back to normal. Glad Karl's not here. He used to scare me."

"Yeah, he was a bully. Pushed everybody 'round. Say, still have his .45?"

"Boots confiscated it."

"His Studebaker?"

"Everything. All Karl's property been impounded. He'll get it back when he's out." Bowers stood up. "Jist a sec', coffee might be ready." He filled two mugs along with his, handing the mugs to the men. "More like rotgut," he joked apologetically while Onorio and Manuel sat in front of his desk, bending over their coffee and blowing over its heat vapors, giving them temporary obscurity.

Manuel took a swig. "Ahh, not bad—a bit strong." He set his mug on the desk. "Still wanna help Julian?"

Bowers's voice and jaw quivered simultaneously. "Yeah, sure, how can I help?"

"Need lots of cash."

"For what?"

"High stakes poker."

"But, I don't see—?"

"Think about it real hard."

"Yeah, hard cash for poker," Onorio injected.

Bowers didn't take long to ponder. "No si-ree. You boys are too good for me."

"You don't want to play high stakes poker?"

"Not to lose."

"You got to. Onorio and I want you to play for high stakes with Julian."

"Don't seem fair. He'd run me dry in no time."

"What'a you know 'bout being fair?"

Bower didn't answer the question. Manuel continued to prod. "That's why yer gonna need lot'a cash."

"Why would I do that?"

"To help Julian."

"So you can sleep easy." Onorio's wick of patience was burning low.

"I sleep easy now."

"You shouldn't. You sided with Linderman at the tipple. And, the eviction."

"Weren't for me, Karl wouldn't be in jail."

"Weren't for you, Julian would have his piano."

"Say boys," Bowers whined in a high-pitched, falsetto voice. "Karl bullied me. What could I do?"

"*Sono tutte scuse!*" (Excuses, excuses!) Onorio growled, his short wick fizzled. "In the old a'country, they say: 'cut a sausage in half, both sides full of baloney.' Now, look! I slice you in half: both sides full of baloney."

Bowers didn't understand Onorio's old country wit and canted his head sideways.

"No more baloney! Get cash. Play poker with Julian. Make sure you lose."

"That's baloney."

"He needs seven hundred dollars to buy a new piano."

"Cripes. That's lots of green backs."

Onorio thumbed his coffee mug, then stood. He gazed out the office's tiny window with a vague look in his eyes, working out what he wanted to say next and allowing his temper to cool. Still gazing out the window, Onorio asked evenly, "How much a man worth?" He continued gazing out the window, pausing for a long time for Bowers to register the gravity of the question. "Take Osgood. He's dead and buried. . . . Soon his skin and bones will rot to a pound of dust."

"At the most." Manuel sighed.

"How much you get for a pound of dust?"

Bowers sensed he'd better respond. "Pooh, can't give it away."

"A live man, how much?"

Bowers stared gloomily at Onorio, who was still gazing out the tiny window that allowed a little light to trickle into the office. After a while, Onorio sat down and pressed his point. "Take Judo Perkovich. Poor man gets killed. Company pays for a pine box."

"Not the coffin, we didn't. Jist the pine vault."

"How much that cost?"

"Five dollars, probably."

"Judo's life was worth five dollars to the Company?"

"Hey! Company gave his widow a permanent job."

"Worthless—paid in scrip."

"It's still a job."

"Okay," Manuel injected, "for the sake of argument, how much will the Widow Perkovich make a year?"

"Hmmm." Bowers fidgeted his stiletto moustache. "Let see, maybe one hundred dollars. But, she gets more—a roof over her head, food on the table, a doctor."

"She probably doesn't make that much, but we'll allow it." Manuel carried Bowers's figures to a logical conclusion. "She works for twenty years, she'll make two thousand dollars. Judo's life is worth two thousand and five dollars?"

"Where'd you get the extra five?"

"The pine box."

"She can't complain. That's twenty years with a roof over her head and food on the table for her family."

"Who takes care of her when she's old, can't work?"

"Welfare. Her boys. I don't know. Nobody owes her a living."

"You owe Julian a piano."

"Why me? Nobody saw Karl demolish the piano."

"You did."

Like a caged chipmunk without hope for escape, Bowers merely cowered without showing signs of contrition for his complicity. Manuel pressed the proposal. "Your life worth more than the cost of the piano—seven hundred dollars?"

"Can't put a price on a man's life." Bowers dropped his eyes and crow prints wrinkled along his temples for what felt like a long time to him. "Are you boys threatening me?"

No response. Manuel and Onorio sipped at their coffee.

"Sounds like it to me." Bowers squirmed nervously, still fingering his stiletto mustache.

Drinking slowly, Onorio and Manuel eyed Bowers over the rims of their mugs. They drank the last of the coffee, set the empty mugs in front of Bowers and left. . . . Three minutes later, Manuel popped his head back into the office door. Bowers still slumped gloomily at his desk, eyes glued on the two empty mugs. Manuel winked. "Our secret. Don't tell Julian. Thanks for the coffee."

Saturday evening rolled around much more quickly than Bowers had wished. With Roy Barthol, he showed at the clubhouse at 9:00 p.m., an hour later than usual. Hardly acknowledging the new Company man, Manuel and Onorio greeted Bowers with pretentious cordiality as though he were a former fraternity brother whom they didn't like but hadn't seen in a long time. Bowers nodded apprehensively. Onorio and Manuel found chairs for Barthol and Bowers and they joined the playing circle.

While Julian shuffled the cards, Manuel opened the game. "Say, fellers, we've come on some extra cash."

"Good luck," Onorio injected. "Osgood's folks put up a reward when he didn't show at home. They gave it to us for finding his body."

"Like I was saying, extra cash," Manuel continued. "Let's up the ante and stakes a bit."

"How many bits?" Barthol cautiously asked.

"Yeah," Shorty added, "I'm no Rockefeller."

"Dealer's call." Manuel deferred to Julian.

Julian finished shuffling the cards and handed them to Shorty to cut. Julian dealt clockwise to Barthol, Manuel, Bowers, Onorio, Shorty. "Ante's five."

"Dollars?"

"Yep."

"Pretty rich for me." Shorty winched as he anted. "Hope I can stay the game."

"What's wild?" Barthol grumbled as he anted.

"No wild cards. All accordin' to Hoyle. Seven card stud, jacks or better opens."

Julian dealt the first two cards face-down and peeked at his cards, a pair of sixes.

Bowers peeked at his pair of aces, but didn't propose to open, thinking, "Ain't that the luck. Best possible hand in the first draw, but, but, Manuel and Onorio, they're a'watching."

"Any openers?" Julian asked.

"Hit me," Barthol opened, holding a pair of jacks, face-down.

"Barthol, jacks or better," Julian announced and dealt, calling each card as it appeared face-up. "Barthol, ten of diamonds; Manuel two of diamonds; Homer, ace high; Onorio, eight of diamonds; Shorty, two of spades." Julian turned a six for himself, thinking, "Hmm, three sixes. Two down, one up. Beats everything showing, even Homer's ace. Not likely he's got two aces down." Julian called the round: "Ace high, Bowers' bid."

"Five dollars."

"Five dollars!" Barthol protested.

"It's only money." Bowers scowled.

"Okay, okay."

"Too rich for my blood." Shorty folded. The others anted five dollars.

Julian dealt and called the cards: "Bowers seven, Onorio five, and me nine. Barthol, eight and Manuel four." Julian paused and studied the cards on the table, announcing: "No pairs showing. Nor possible straights or flushes. Ace still high. Bowers?"

"Five dollars."

"Onorio's in. . . . I'm in. . . . Barthol?"

"You boys are high rollers, ain't you?"

"Shut up!" Bowers truculently admonished Barthol. "It's only money. You can't take it with you."

"I'll see ya, once more anyways," Barthol grumbled. He held a good hand, a pair of jacks face-down. He didn't know, nor did anybody else, that Bowers held a pair of aces face-down—and an ace face-up—the highest three-of-a-kind possible. Julian held a low three-of-a-kind, a pair of sixes face-down, and a six face-up.

"I'm in." Manuel slid five dollars into the pot.

"Two more cards up," Julian announced as he dealt. "Bowers still ace high."

"Five dollars."

All but Barthol added five to the pot. Disgusted, Barthol whined as he threw in his two jacks, "cri-men-ee!"

"Folding with a pair of jacks?" Julian raised his eyebrows.

"Hell, I ain't rich."

"You work for the Company. You got cash."

"Gotta make it last. Next hand, maybe."

Julian dealt and announced, "Bowers' still high."

Bowers couldn't believe his awkward situation, thinking, "Damn, damn. Here I have one of the highest hands possible, and the highest stakes possible, but I'm done for. Should'a never allowed Linderman to wreck the piano. Damn, damn, damn." Bowers glimpsed at Onorio and Manuel. They gazed placidly at him, their faces revealing nothing. "They're stonewalling me. They don't care what I'm holding." Bowers remembered their recent visit with him to discuss the price of a man's life. "Wasn't a philosophic, academic discussion. They were askin' how much I value my life. Crap, they got me." Tiny beads of sweat prickled at his temples. Brashly, Bowers blurted: "Ten dollars!"

"Manuel folds, Onorio folds," Julian announced. "Leaves me and you."

"Better quit while yer ahead." Bowers pointed at his ace-high.

"I'll see your ten." Julian met the bet. "Last two are down." Julian dealt two cards face down to Bowers, and then dealt his own cards face down. "Paltry hand," Julian thought, "even with three sixes. Yet, Bowers can't beat me with a pair of aces, unless he has three of them."

Bowers examined his cards. He still held two aces face down, and one ace face up. He glimpsed at Julian's deadpan face and couldn't read it, pondering, "He's got to have at least three sixes. Julian bluffs, but never at these high stakes." Not wanting to win, Bowers groaned.

"Ace still high," Julian softly announced. "Your call."

"Ten dollars." Bowers smugly shoved two five-dollar bills into the pot.

"Too rich for me."

Manuel surprised Julian. "I'll back you."

"Me, too," Onorio announced, "with what's left of the reward money."

"What's in the pot?" Bowers asked.

"If Julian's in," Manuel said as he counted, "one hundred forty."

Shorty and Barthol rasped, "Whe-e-e-e-w."

Julian eyed Bowers, who wasn't very good at keeping a deadpan face. He fidgeted and squirmed, wiping the sweat beads from his temples. Julian glimpsed at Onorio. He nodded. Julian glimpsed at Manuel.

"*¡De veras, el hombre es loco!*" Manuel smirked as he spoke in Spanish, implying Bowers was crazy for certain.

"I'll see your ten." Warily, Julian slid two five-dollar bills into the pot. "What you got?"

"You first."

"Three of a kind." Julian laid out his hand, three-of-a-kind in sixes.

"Gaw! You called my bluff! Never thought you'd have three-of-a-kind." Bowers picked up a face-down ace and pitched it on the table.

Low wheezes, whistles, gasps from the others.

Bowers carried the charade curtly. Faking a pair of aces rather than three-of-a-kind, he deftly folded the third ace into his other cards and shoved them into the discard pile, all the time blathering, "Drat the luck. Three of a kind beats a pair—even aces. Drat the luck."

Julian, pleased but skeptical, said, "Never known you to bluff."

Low sniggers and tongue clickings from the others.

"Pair of aces is high," Bowers prattled. "But, I could'a had three aces—and you'd be dead in the water." For an instant, Bowers eyes met Julian's, then Bowers nervously darted glances at all the other players, blustering, "First time for everything. Only money. Easy come, easy go." He chortled nervously.

"You done it, amico," Onorio slapped Julian's shoulder.

"Sí, amigo, you did it—fair and square." Manuel hurriedly gathered all the discards and shuffled them together.

Knowing Bowers's stingy reputation, Barthol was stumped. He rubbed his hair in disbelief, muttering, "Bowers betting all that money on two aces?"

"Yer all loco." Shorty smirked, shrugged his shoulders, and remarked, "Hell, it don't matter. Julian's gotta buy drinks."

Delighted, Julian called, "A round for everybody!" He sat back in his chair counting the pot.

"I'll put the cards away. Get the drinks." Manuel walked into the main section of the clubhouse, returned the cards to a drawer under the bar counter, and spoke to the bartender. Then, he returned carrying a tray with six shot glasses, each filled to the brim with moonshine. To prevent spilling, he placed the tray in the middle of the table, and gingerly handed a glass to each of the men.

"Here's to Julian." Shorty lifted his glass.

"Hear! Hear!" They clinked glasses and cheered.

Bowers offered a toast: "May Lady Luck always be your companion, but never Miss Fortune."

"Bravo!"

"Hear! Hear!"

"Yer a sport," Bathol praised Bowers, adding, "Round of whiskey best part of the game."

"Everybody wins something."

"Nobody goes home mad."

"'Specially Julian. He's a pretty happy man, leastwise." Barthol snorted. "He's gonna sleep good tonight."

"Like a baby."

"Me, too," Bowers added.

"Huh!" Shorty exclaimed. "You ought'a have nightmares. You lost a bundle."

"Jist money."

"Since when?" Shorty was dubious. "You always been so . . . so . . . niggardly."

"Ho!" Onorio scoffed disdainfully.

Bowers squirmed in his seat. Shorty's comment had cut coarsely into Bowers's superficial magnanimity.

"I'm no fool!" Bowers blurted pompously. "I'll win that money back! Next week, wait an' see!" He glimpsed at Julian through the side of his eyes. "Unless yer afraid to lose it."

"See you next week.